speak

Fanny Smiths

contents

CHAPTER 1

Scarlet pushed her legs up against the wooden side of her pen, doing her best to stretch. With a small groan, she gave up and bent knees; sending pain throughout her body. The 3 by 4 animal pin she was locked in gave her 5'5 body barely any space to move. Straw littered the ground, as a bed, a place to go to the bathroom, a place to sit; it made her body itch. It didn't help that her feet and wrist were chained, and after wearing them for so long her wrist were raw and bloody. The straw just made it worse. She was sore, bloody, dirty and hungry. Sighing, she pushed some greasy strands of hair from her face.

"Scar, psst, scar- are you okay?"

Sitting up, Scarlet lifted her hands. She paused, and listened, before giving two solid knocks on the wooden wall.

"Good, so am I."

Scarlet gave a small smile, leaning her head on the wall. One the other side, in one of the other 34 pins, was her best friend Renee. She had been in the woods with Scarlet on the faithful day that she was kidnapped. They had taken Renee, only because she had fought for Scarlet's freedom.

Kidnapping wasn't rare, it was quite normal. They were traded through the Slave Trade, along with other beings who didn't pay back a debt, sold themselves or were forced into it. There was much bad in the world just as there was good. Good people ended up doing deals with bad people- and they paid for it in the end. Scarlet's mother, her single mother who raised her on her own, always told her not to use her powers- ever. But being the 18 year old rebellious girl she was, she did. Her mother, so good, told her not to use her powers. She, herself, did and because of it was taken from her wholesome world into the dark Slave Trade market.

With a small huff of air, she looked up to the ceiling of the wooden train cart.

"Yeah, I'm right with ya Scar. This sucks."

It was moments such as this, where she was locked away and alone; that she could speak. Renee was only a piece of wood away- yet because she wasn't able to sign, mouth words or even write a note, she had no way of communicating with her friend.

~~~

Stumbling out of the train car, Scarlet's bare feet shuffled along with everyone else who was in her chain-group. The sun blared down from the sky, blinding her. Her whole body was sore, and her legs shook from being unused and bent. She had been locked away in her pin for... she didn't even know. She had lost track of the days. She knew it had to be at least a few weeks.

The Handlers screamed at everyone, as the moved from the dirt area outside the car to a blocked off area behind a plain, wooden stage. There were other chain-together groups, and people mumbled softly to each other.

"I just heard some others talking, they're saying we're in Voirol!"

Renee's breath was hot against Scarlet's ear, and she turned to face her.

'How do you know?'

Renee shook her head, a held a hand out. That meant she didn't understand what Scarlet had mouthed to her. Which wasn't uncommon, and being Scarlet's hands were bonded together; she had no other option. Reaching out Scarlet spelt out each letter, one by one, on Renee's palm using her fingers.

'T-h-a-t's a 5 w-e-e-k t-r-i-p f-r-o-m T-o-b-u-s.'
~~~

"It also means we're basically on the other side of the world... We're never going back."

Renee casted her eyes away, as she swallowed back a lump in her throat. Scarlet looked to her friend chained beside her, but did nothing to comfort her. It was her fault they were chained, thousands of miles from their home land and about to be sold off as slaves for the rest of their lives.

"Alright, come along you rats- move it!"

One of the slave Handlers came over to Scarlet's group, picking up the end of the chain. He pulled on it, and the guy attached at the very front stumbled forward, nearly falling. Counting, Scarlet saw she was fourth in line, and Renee was fifth. There was only seven to each group, so she figured they were on the end of the group.

They were led from behind the stage, and out to face the crowd. Though Scarlet wanted to freeze on sight at all the people standing at the auction, she was forced to keep moving. She had a hard time getting up the stairs, her feet fumbling. When she did, she stopped behind the guy chained in front of her. When the last few people of their group reached the stage, the Handler screamed at them to face the crowd; raising his whip with a threat.

Scarlet turned to the crowd and felt her stomach drop. She was between wanting to cry, and be sick to her stomach. The feeling didn't die as she watched the first three people in front of her auctioned off. The first and last guy went to the same man, who seemed to be a farmer of some sort. The girl between them went to a male also, though Scarlet had high doubts that the poor child would not be working in the fields. She was much too pretty for that.

When it came her turn, some random Handler unhooked her ankle chains from the chain line, and pushed her forward into the Auctioneer's arms. She was quick to pull her body away, and tugged on the sack-dress that hung off her frame.

"Now, this here folks, may look like some scrawny, stupid, girl- but let me tell you there is more to her then meets the eyes. This here is a Blessed human! She may not speak, but her gift makes up for all words that can be said. Now, Blessed human, show the crowd what powers you possess!"

Scarlet stood frozen, unable to move as her stomach did flips inside of her.

"Girl- Obey him!"

From the corner of her eye, Scarlet could see one of the head Handlers marching from the corner of the stage. He wasn't the head Handler from the train, so she figured he must be a local. When he reached her, her forcefully grabbed her chin- causing Scarlet to release a gasp. His hard blue eyes met her, as his grip grew tighter.

"Do as he says. Now."

Releasing her, she swallowed and slowly nodded her head. His hand hit the full left side of her face, and was so forceful, she fell to the stage. A few in the crowd laugh, others got silent, most started to whisper.

"When a superior talks to you, you are to answer promptly and properly!"

Scarlet shook her head and attempted to sign; but another smack to her face forced back down to the stage.

"Wrong answer-"

"Wait- please, let me explain, no stop!"

"Answer me!"

When Scarlet didn't, he hit her again.

"She can't speak-"

"Answer me!"

He hit her again, her mouth letting out breaths-of cries.

"I can interpret for her, I-"

Renee was cut off a smack to her face from another Handler, only he had a wooden reed on hand and it cut her cheek. The Handler, having lost his temper, sheathed a sword from its place on his waist.

"I shall teach you to be so distrustful!"

"No!"

No one paid mind to Renee as she cried out for her friend, but the whole crowd gasped at Scarlet. The Handler had lifted his sword, with the intention to cut off some sort of body part from Scarlet. But as he was mid-swing, the sword was ripped from his hands and he was pushed back and lifted off the stage.

The whole crowd went silent as Scarlet held her hands up in front of her face. Her left, held the Handler in the air, and her right held the sword where it had stopped in mid swing.

Dropping her left and flinging her right, the Handler landed on the stage and the sword went for the crowd. No one was hurt, though a few did duck and scream in fright.

"Well, folks, there you go! Is this stupid mute Blessed or what?! Can I get 200?"

"200!"

"300!"

"2,000 gold!"

The crowd let out a gasp.

"5,000!"

Another gasped came from the crowd. Meanwhile Scarlet stood back up, her left eye swollen shut and her whole body throbbing. She listened with a plain face as her price went up to 10,000 gold, 15,000 gold. And when it seemed like she was about to be sold for 17,500 gold; a clear, demanding voice calmly stated '1 million gold'. Everyone in the crowd gasped and looked around for the owner of the voice. The crowd then parted as five men walked through the crowd. They were all finely dressed, and had their eyes covered by sunglasses.

"My, oh my! Is anyone willing to up that bid? No? Going once... Twice... Sold- to our mighty King! Congratulations your majesty, though just as warning she's not that bright. She doesn't speak!"

The crowd laughed lightly as the joke, but when the man in the middle of the group- of whom Scarlet guessed to be the king, didn't laugh everyone was quick to be silent once more.

"A-hm, right then, onto the next! We got us here a real, natural beauty folks!"

As the Auctioneer went off on how wonderful of a woman Renee was, Scarlet was moved down from the stage. She was taken straight to their King, and was released of her chains by his order. Before she could show him some sign of respect and of thanks; he called out-

"50,000 gold for the girl!"

"...Going once...twice... sold- once more to our mighty King!"

This time around, the auctioneer kept his jokes to himself as Renee was led over to the small group and he went on to the next trade. As Scarlet, Renee was freed from her chain, hugging her friend after giving the King a bow of respect and thanks.

"I have all I came for, let's go."

He led them, two men to both of his sides formed an arrow shape as Renee and Scarlet walked in the middle of it. They were lead to one of those fancy black limo that were limos yet still short enough to be a car. The King climbed into the front passenger seat, one guard took to the driver's seat as the last two were sat in the back with Scarlet and Renee. They drove though the town, passing different homes and building that were mushed together side-by-side. The car was then taken up a winding road before pulling in between opening gates. Both girls looked out of the window, awe struck. A small 'wow' even escaped Renee's lips, and Scarlet nodded her head slightly agreeing with her friend. The road and surrounding grounds were beautiful- to say the least. It was all colorful and perfectly manicured, down to the blades of grass and the grave road.

When the car stopped, they were in front of a huge- no, it was not a huge home, it was a mansion. Spanning two stories fully across, it even looked to have a third and fourth floor in the middle. A servant was right at the passenger door, opening it for the King. A few others waited a few off, and he turned their gaze to them.

"Make sure the two girls in the back are properly taken care of. They are mine now."

And he was gone. Poof, like magic, Scarlet and Renee were alone. A servant opened their door and the four men who escorted them there left after the King. A small, young girl came up, giving a nod.

"Hello, please follow me."

~~~

The large wooden door slammed shut behind Scarlet like a bomb to her heart. Turning to face it, she turned back to the room. It was bare, and cold. Obviously meant to be a dungeon of some sort from ages before, the only light came through the small barred window on the locked door.

Running up to the door, Scarlet hit her hands on it a few times, sliding against it as her head begun to spin. Closing her one good eye, she focused on her breathing as she slipped into the darkness.

~~~

When she opened her eyes again, Scarlet was no longer in the dark, damp room- but lying on a bed, in an all white room. Looking around, she noticed that fact that she was hooked up to different machines, and had an IV in hand and a catheter below. With eyebrows drawn down, she looked around the room. It looked to be a mixture between an extremely nice hospital room and an extremely nice nurse's room. Along one full wall and half of another; were cabinets, shelves, tons of counter space and a good sized sink. The door stopped it, and on the other side of it was a small love seat, with two separate arm chairs and a low coffee table in the middle of it all.

Scarlet let out a small gasp, her eyebrows rising as she saw Renee, on a small twin sized bed that seemed to fold down out of the wall. She was sound asleep, her chest slowly rising and falling. She wore a comfortable looking uniform of black skin-tight pants and a button down collared shirt. On top of it all, she was clean and her face held a slight pink hue to it.

Scarlet looked around her bed, and found nothing she could throw to wake her friend up. But what she did notice was that her body was fully clean, her curly brown hair was clean, and she wore a soft, long hospital dress. She also noticed that the left side of her face seemed to be healing nicely, with her eye opening fully.

I must have been out for at least a few days- the wound was bad.

Along with her healing face, she noticed her wrists were properly wrapped. A quick peak under covers revealed the same for her ankles.

Turning her eyes back to Renee, she too had wraps on her wrists and ankles.

When Scarlet came to the conclusion she had nothing she could throw at her friend, she resorted to plan b- snapping and clapping. After a few snaps and no result, Scarlet only needed to clap twice before her friend sat up in a daze.

"Huh-what-wha- Scar? Scarlet! You're awake!"

Scarlet nodded her head, as she stood. Heading to the door, she pressed a button on a small pad next to it, before moving next to her friend. With her hands free, Scarlet was free to sign and talk with her friend.

'What happened to me?'

"You passed out, the little beat down that Hander gave you was worst then it looked. You've been out for a few days, but nothing major has happened."

'What happened with you? You look lovely.'

"Aw, thanks, the King showed me to my new room- which is amazing, and told me get cleaned up. There's a closet filled with different clothes that could last me a year and the bathroom is granite! Then, when I was called for a meeting with him, he told me what my duty as his slave would be- to interpret for you!"

'What?'

"Yeah, he paid easily 45,000 more gold for me then he could of- just to speak for you! Literally!"

Scarlet nodded her head, and before she could ask another question, the door opened. A woman dressed in matching navy blue scrubs strolled in with a smile on her face. It was clear she was nurse. With a clipboard in hand, she came over to Scarlet, smiling.

"Alas it's so good to you up miss; you had quite the knock to the face."

Hanging the clipboard on the wall behind her bed, the nurse grabbed a fresh pair of gloves from a box- which also hung off the wall.

"Let's take a look and see how you're healing- and miss Renee you're next after her."

"Yes ma'am Dr. Cartson."

Ah, so she is a doctor, not a nurse. Scarlet thought to herself.

"Now miss Scarlet, this may hurt just a bit, but even it's too much for you just tell me. I'll get you fixed up with some nice pain killers."

The gentle pressure on her on face made Scarlet twitch, but it was nothing horribly painful. The only bad part was when the doctor lifted her eye lid to look inside.

"Alas your face seems to be healing perfectly miss. Now let's take a look at those wrist and ankles and give them some fresh bandages."

Looking down to her now bare wrist, they were pink and covered in ugly brown scabs. The doctor put some funky smelling salve on them rewrapping them afterwards. She repeated the process on her ankles and Renee.

"Now girl, you should only need the bandage for maybe another week at the most. I'll come and visit to make sure all is well with them. Alas we wouldn't want the King to have another fit, now would we?"

Scarlet looked to Renee, her eyebrows haven fallen again.

'What does she mean?'

Dr. Cartson watched as Scarlet's hands fluttered about, before turning to her gaze to Renee.

"What was she saying?"

"She was wondering what you mean by that."

Dr. Cartson peeled off her gloves as she nodded her head as she tossed them in the trash. She strolled back over to the bed.

"Oh, well miss, when our mighty King discovered that Renee and you have been taken to the dungeon of all places-he had a huge fit! He blew up though, when it was discovered you had passed out from you injures. We thought he was going to destroy the castle- again! Ahaha, but alas, all was well once you came into my care."

Scarlet's handles flew around again, and Dr. Cartson understood none of it.

"Scar is wondering why the King got so mad, we are only slaves."

"Because, miss, once you come under the hand of our King- you are treated with the best. The King wants his whole land taken care of and that includes the servants of his home. You two shouldn't have been taken to the dungeon, you should have been brought straight to me to be seen to. But, alas, a mistake took place and was paid for."

"Scarlet asked 'paid for?'"

"Oh yes, the little female servant it was she who took you to the cells, and thus she was the one to pay?"

"Um, Scar, slow down- okay, 'how was it paid, did she get hurt, is she okay, surly the King was kind on such a young girl.' Whoa, Scar, relax."

It was clear as day on Scarlet's face that she was very distraught of the young girl getting some cruel punishment. She was only a child, maybe 16 at the oldest.

"Oh no, alas, the King treats each case rightly as it should be. She committed a capital punishment by disobeying a direct order from the King. So she was forced to pay for her deed."

Scarlet begun to ask what the punishment was as Dr. Cartson turned towards one of the cabinets. Instead of relaying the message on, Renee brought a finger across her throat. With a silent gasp, one of Scarlet's hands covered her mouth and the other her throat.

The rumble of Scarlet's stomach caused Dr. Cartson to turn from where she was working.

"Alas, I bet you're hungry, I'll have lunch sent down right after I give you some pain relief."

As she strolled over, she pushed a small metal table. Stopping next to the bed, the doctor brushed away her blonde bangs from her forehead.

Clearly she's human; she does not have the colorings of any other creature.

Lifting the needle up to the light, the doctor pushed back her bangs once more before bending back down. Opening a small side tube on her IV, the doctor stuck the needle in and pushed the pale blue liquid into Scarlet's body.

"There we go."

She pulled the needle out, re capping it, and placing it on the table. Moving it away again, she was quick to clean the mess up. Grabbing the clipboard from the wall, she opened the door that was opposite of Scarlet's bed.

"Lunch shall be in soon. Good day misses."

CHAPTER 2

Lunch was brought to them both on sliver platters, and at the sight of all the different foods- Scarlet wanted to cry. Every bite was an explosion of flavor and melted her to the most inward core of her body. Along with the pain medicine, Scarlet felt like she was in a dream.

'So what happened after they found us?'

"Well, was still awake, and the cut on my face was already scabbing up. So I didn't need much help, but you. You were bad, and like Dr. Cartson said- the King had a fit. We were both taken care of, though you were done first. When I was done getting my face fixed- see there's barely a scar, the King called me to him. I was nervous, the say the least. In that meeting is where he told me where I'd be serving him and that I would be given a proper room. Let me just say, too, that the room is more than proper. I could easily fit my old bedroom, living room and bathroom into the whole thing. That's how big it feels."

'Wow, sounds nice. Do you know what my fate is?'

"No, sorry Scar, but whatever it is, it must be big. I mean, you're Blessed, he's not just going to throw you to kitchen."

'True.'

By the look on her friend's face, Renee knew Scarlet was more than worried about her position within her new lord's house hold. Reaching out, Renee wrapped a hand around Scarlet's good one- as in, the one without the IV.

"Scar, relax, it's going to be fine. I promise. Now let's finish up lunch."

~~~

After what was left of their lunch was taken away, the two girls were left to talk. Thanks to Renee Scarlet was able to chomp down on a piece of peppermint gum- her only addiction. They were checked on a few more times by Dr. Cartson, but other than her visits were left alone. It was quite boring, despite the fact that the two were the best of friends. They sought entertainment through Scarlet's powers.

Closing her eyes, Scarlet pushed her flat hands out, circling them opposite directions of each other as they reached their full extend.
~~~

Flipping her palms to be up, she slowly lifted them. Giggling, Renee gave a small clap as she begun to float up from her chair.

"You're doing great Scar; you got us both up this time!"

Giving a small smile, Scarlet lowered her hands, only placing them down she felt the bed against her back once more. Opening her eyes, Renee was rocking in place with a wide grin directed towards her friend.

'I'm going to go to sleep now.'

"Okay, let me dim the lights. If you need me, I'll be on this bed, right here."

With the lights off, Scarlet's eye lids fluttered close.

~~~

"Now, Scarlet, remember get the berries and return home. Make sure you and Renee stay together and, most importantly, no using your power!"

'Yes mother, I know.'

Closing the door to their kitchen, Scarlet started off towards Renee's home two house to the right of her own. Knocking on the back door, Renee's mother opened it. Her hands were full, with a child on one hip and a kettle in her other hand, she smiled.
~~~

"Hello Scarlet."

Scarlet waved and greeted Mrs. Ragon with a huge smile.

"Renee is coming right now."

As she said it, Renee pushed past her mother and embraced her friend in a hug.

"We will be mom, come on Scar- let's go!"

Grabbing the hand that didn't hold Scarlet's wicker basket, she pulled her off. Turning, Scarlet gave Mrs. Ragon a wave of good bye.

"Bye girls!"

As the girl entered the forest and the path became uneven, each held up their skirts to free their reining legs from the burden. As a law in their home nation of Tobus, ruled by the High werewolf Lord Rolle; all females were to only wear dresses and men pants. Being a well sized nation of simple wealth from the mining, most people dressed modest. Scarlet and Renee were no exception. Their dresses were plain, and dull in color. The sleeves were fitted down their arms and their wide collared necklines were high. A simple sash as the hips gave the loose slip-dresses shape along their body lines. By most other countries it was considered old-fashion, dull, or unstylish. For the girls, it was life. It was what they were born and taught.

Slowing down, the released their dresses as they came upon the clusters of berry bushes. Releasing hands, the girls begun to fill their baskets up. They worked silently for a few minutes, until a berry hit Scarlet right on her temple. Looking to Renee, she was busy plucking at the berries. Narrowing her eyes, Scarlet went back to her bush. Before long, another berry hit, only this time Scarlet moved fast enough just to see her friend bending back down.

Picking up a few berries from her basket, Scarlet tossed them across the small clearing. They hit Renee's head making small 'splat' sounds. Turning, Scarlet couldn't help but let out a silent laugh.

"Hey!"

Grabbing a handful of berries, Renee tossed them at Scarlet. Before they could hit her, she stopped them midair and tossed them back to Renee. They hit her face, leaving little red stains behind.

"Oh- that's so not fair!"

That was the start of their berry war. The two girls got so into it, they didn't hear the small group of feet slowly moving towards them or feel the pairs of eyes watching them. Just as Scarlet pulled all the berries from one bushes, aiming them at her friend; large hands popped out from the brush behind her and pulled her in. The berries went flying, and Renee stumbled forward after her friend.

"Scarlet!"

Picking up her skirt, she ran through the brush that Scarlet was just pulled into. Seeing no one, she paused for a second.

"Scarlet!"

Scarlet, having been pulled into some huge, dirty man's arms- fought her capture. He had covered her mouth with his hand, to stop her from making any noise. As if she could. The man and his three thugs pulled Scarlet along the forest, as she heard Renee calling out for her.

"We need to hurry-"

"-Get away from the girl-"

"-This one will fetch some pretty coins!"

It was another common moment in her life that she wished she could speak. Then it hit her though, she wasn't able to speak- but her kidnappers were. Closing her eyes, and hoping she didn't catch any strange disease, she opened her mouth. Pushing her teeth out she bit down hard on his finger- the metallic flavor of blood filling her mouth before she was pushed to the ground. The man cried out,

"OW! The bitch bit me!"

"Oh man up!"

"HEY!"

Running up to them, Renee pushed herself at the man that Scarlet had bitten moments before. It was just enough force to push the man to the side and forced Renee to the ground.

"Quick- grab 'em both!"

~~~

Scarlet's eyes fluttered open, and scanned around. After a few seconds, she saw that she wasn't in the woods on that faithful day, but in the white room, of the King of Voirol's castle.

How strange, to be serving under a King whose name I don't even know

She stretched out on the bed, her body the least sore it had been in, what felt like forever. Relaxing her body, she took a deep breath. She was enjoying the time she had the moment, being her fate working for the King was unknown.

Where ever it is Scarlet, it will most likely be something high, or grand, or maybe even both. I am Blessed, and that is what must have caught his attention. I wonder what his name is- or if he's a vampire maybe he is a werewolf- or possibly a human. I should have paid more attention during my school days.

Scarlet laid for a while, thinking to herself; as she did often. With no one around, she allowed her mind to wonder freely.
~~~

I wonder what he's like; Renee said the castle is grand from what she's seen. No corner was left untouch everywhere you look is grandeur. When will I meet my savor, my new Lord, my owner- the king?

Scarlet only stopped thinking to herself, when the door opened. Dr. Cartson walked in, head to toe in red scrubs and her blonde hair back in its normal bun. She was humming lightly as she slowly dimmed the lights back up.

"Alas, good morning miss Scarlet! Glad to see you up before me, did you sleep well?"

Scarlet nodded, knowing if she tried anything else it would go beyond what Dr. Cartson knew.

"Wonderful, it's just wonderful. Well, miss I got some great news today. After talking with the King, he has said that you can be moved to your room today! When you're settled in, the King is even ready to meet you! Isn't that wonderful?"

Scarlet gave a small smile and nodded her head despite the fact that her whole body turned ice cold and heavy as stone. She felt nowhere prepared to meet the King, but knew that it would have to happen at some point. She just didn't think it'd be so soon.

On her little fold down bed, Renee moved about, making a few small noises. Rubbing her eyes, she slowly sat up.

"Good morning miss Renee, did you sleep well?"

"Wha-um, yeah, yeah I did. What time is it?"

"Just a tad past nine."

"Oh wow- so early!"

Scarlet gave Renee a look, and Renee replied with a lazy eye roll.

"Well miss, if it was up to me I'd let you sleep in, but alas, it's the King's order and I'm not to disobey that."

"Right, of course- whew."

Renee stretched her body out as she stood, shaking her hair loose before pulling back into a low ponytail. She had gone to her room the night before to change, but the outfit was literally the same minus colors. She had replied to Scarlet's doubtful face with 'King's orders'. Apparently her whole wardrobe was of the fitted pants and button down collar shirts with varying sleeves.

"Besides, today is a good day. The King has released miss Scarlet with the okay from me. After breakfast a few hand maids will be coming here to help her change. She has a meeting with the King- one you will be at too, so you'll have to get a tad more fancied up."

Renee nodded, and watched as Dr. Cartson removed Scarlet's blankets.

"I'm going to get that catheter out, but in order to do so; you're going to have to use the bathroom right after wards. Okay?"

Scarlet nodded, as she was laid back down. Dr. Cartson then put in stirrups on the edge of her bed, making sure they were secure before having Scarlet rest her legs in them. She then proceed to remove the catheter. Renee turned away, unable to watch Dr. Cartson pump water into the tube. She only turned around when she deemed the deed done.

"Now miss, if you don't take these pills- then it's going to hurt to go to the bathroom. You should only need them for a day or two. But if you feel like you need them longer, feel free to ask. Now I'm going to get that IV out and unhook you and hopefully you need to go soon."

As Dr. Cartson worked on Scarlet, Renee kept her busy.

"So, did it hurt?"

Dr. Cartson watched Scarlet's response, as she removed the sticky-pads from her chest.

"Miss Renee, what did she say- it seemed very animated."

"She said it wasn't as bad as dying, but it wasn't like floating- or flying in the air."

Dr. Cartson laughed, as she helped Scarlet sit back up. The last thing she removed was the IV, placing a small gaze on her arm and tying it tightly with a piece of cloth. She only paused, when Scarlet started to talk to Renee.

"She has to use the bathroom."

"Oh good, can you help her, and I'll start cleaning up here?"

"Sure, come on Scar; let's get you into that bathroom."

When they came out of the bathroom, Dr. Cartson had finished cleaning up and the treys with breakfast had been delivered. Refusing to get back into her bed, Scarlet took a seat on the small loveseat. There she and Renee ate breakfast there, until the maids that Dr. Cartson warned about arrived. Two or three would have been a few, instead they got nine. Two attended to Renee, and the other seven to Scarlet. Each woman had her job and did only that job. It was dizzying.

When it was all over, Scarlet found her plain gown replaced with long, simple pale purple A-line. She wore brown slippers exactly her size and a small leather corset on her chest. Her hair was twisted up and behind her head, in an elaborate bun.

Turning to face Renee, Scarlet smiled. Her hair was fixed nearly identical to her own, and the only thing changed on her outfit was she was wearing flats and had on some strange over-coat. Its straight-cross neckline was so low it rested right under her breast. It was buttoned all the way down to her hips, where beneath it the skirt flared out to the ground. Renee smiled to her friend, walking over to her and grabbing her hands. The hand maids left them with a curtsied, leaving them alone for a few minutes before set guards were to summon them.

"Oh Scar, you look amazing."

'Thank you, you too.'

"You think you're ready for this?"

'Yeah, I don't have a choice.'

Renee gave a small smile and squeezed her hands.

"It'll be fine; the King isn't as horrible as you may believe. I promise."

Scarlet nodded her head, letting out a sigh as she did.

"Good."

A knock at the door stopped Renee from saying else, as it told them it was time.

"Come on, you'll be fine."

Stepping into the hall was like stepping into another world. Unlike the very white, plain room, the hall was covered in dark wood and rich colorings. Everywhere Scarlet looked, was like seeing a new piece of art.

There were four guards waiting, all dressed in suites. Despite the fact that there were no windows in the hall, and the lights weren't all the bright, all four men wore sunglasses. They were all large in height but only two were large in size. With silent nods to each other, the two girls were centered between the four, and led down the hall.

~~~

Scarlet lost count of how many twist and turns they took, but after what felt like an endless walk, they stopped. The two large doors they faced were the same dark wood found though out the castle. There were no guards protecting it, so Scarlet did wonder for a few seconds if they had come to the right door. But when the main guard knocked on the door, and opened it on command, she knew they were in the correct spot.

"Do you have them?"

"Yes sir."

"Send them in."

"Right away."

Opening the door fully, the guard stepped aside to allow the girl entrance. Scarlet gave a nod of thanks, and Renee verbally thanked
~~~

them. Stepping inside, it was clear that they were entering an office. One wall had floor to ceiling book shelves and the opposite wall had a large fire place with windows so large they could past for doors. Along the wall opposite of the door, was a large desk, with two chairs in front and one behind. The one behind was large, leather and very grand. The man sitting in it was even more so.

He had black hair slicked back on his head, the ends curling at his neckline. His pale skin had the smallest red and purple hue around his eyes. His was finely dressed in a simple button down shirt and Scarlet could guess suit pants. And when she saw the shade of his eyes- the unmistakable pale blue- near white color, she knew at once what creature the King was. Vampire.

Pausing beside the two large leather chairs, both girls bowed to the King. Scarlet signed a formal greeting, as Renee did the verbal.

"My King it is an honor to see you once more, and Scarlet says 'my lord'."

"You may rise, and have a seat."

They did as they were told, Scarlet silently struggling to keep her butt from slipping off. Her soft dress did not mix well with the leather chair.

"Scarlet Solomon, you have been sold and bought into my kingdom. As someone who is to take citizenship of Voirol, you are to hereby pledge your alliance to Voirol and its King. Do you agree?"

Scarlet nodded, looking to Renee and then back to the King. He stood, and picked up a large book that sat on the corner of the desk.

"In my hands I hold the key to the people of Voirol- the Rules of the Old. The principles our land was based upon and still rules to this day. Please stand before me and place your hands- hmm, never mind. Repeat after me... I, Scarlet Solomon, here by solemnly swear in the witness of the high King and other witnesses to pledge my full self to the country of Voirol from this day forth. I pledge to place the duty of doing what is best for the country on top of my own deeds. From this day forth, I give up any citizenship of any other country and any other alliances. I shall live by Rules of the Old, and be judge by them accordantly. From this day forth, I am a Voirian."

As Scarlet signed out what the King said, Renee 'translated' for her. When Scarlet finished she placed both of her hands on the book and bowed her forehead to the edge of the cover. It was her way of showing the King that she truly meant the pledge she took.

"Very well, now that, that is done, we can move onto business. Please sit."

The King placed the book back on his desk, moving back to his seat as Scarlet sat back down.

"Scarlet Solomon and Renee Ragon, from this day forth you are no longer slaves. You are to be servants of my household, and of our country. Renee, you know what your duty is- to translate for Scarlet. Scarlet, your duty from this day forth until I say otherwise- is to be a teacher."

Scarlet couldn't hold back the shocked look that shadowed her face.

He wants me to be a teacher... How a mute Blessed girl who is called 'stupid' supposed to be a teacher. Surly he is joking; he most likely wants me out in the battle field, serving my power fully.

'I'm sorry, I don't understand. A teacher?'

"She is asking why a teacher."

"Because I want to learn the language of sign, and I know of no one better to teach then a mute. You can both see and hear me, something a deaf or blind person cannot."

" 'Why would you want to do that my lord? Surly there is no one you know who cannot speak as, I.' "

"True, but it is never too late or too hard for a King to learn something new; to expand his horizons and knowledge."

" 'Oh, I see.' "

"Our lessons shall be every day from noon to two; we shall break for a lunch, and shall start tomorrow."

" 'Yes sire.' "

"Do you have any questions for me before you are shown to your room?"

" 'Only one sire, I was wondering if I could learn the name of my new king.' "

"My official title is King Cainwen Dufur, you may call me 'sire' 'my king' or 'my lord'."

" "Yes sire. Thank you.' "

"You are dismissed. The guards outside shall show you to your rooms."

The two girls rose, curtsied and then left the room.

CHAPTER 3

C ain strolled over to the window in the large study room, crossing his arms as he stopped, he looked down below to the town. The train stopped on the edge of town, the stage resting right next to it. He watched as a few workers set up the dividers behind the stage- the place where the new slaves would be held until it was their turned to be auctioned off. Most came out, scrawny and dirty, some scared. But they always had that same look in their eye, freedom. It was so close yet so far, like when provoking a small child with toy just high enough that they can reach up to touch it, but just far enough up that they couldn't.

His right hand, closest friend, and cousin; Klaus strolled up next to him.

"I've been told, or so the Traders are claiming that they have a Blessed human in this group."

At the word 'blessed' one of Cain's eyebrows rose. Blessed humans were rare, and hard to come by. Someone would be paying a hefty golden price for the human. Yet at the same time, Cain felt pity for the Blessed. Despite the name, it was more of a curse. Blessed humans had wondrous powers, but great power can quickly corrupt even the purest man.

"I think I may just take the trip down there to see this Blessed human for myself."

"And pray tell dear cousin, what happens when they have no Blessed human? It could easily be a lie as it could be the truth."

Klaus clasped a hand on Cain's shoulder, shaking him.

"You must learn relax dear cousin. Whether they give the truth or a lie, the rumor will give the Trade some excitement. Look now, the train has barely stopped, the stage is barely built, but already people are squishing in to see the Trade."

Cain pulled his shoulder from his cousin's hand, turning as he did.

"Despicable, the whole lots of them all are!"

Taking a seat next to the empty fire place, Cain picked up a few papers from the table, his eyes scanning over them.

"Oh, you don't mean that! Here, open the windows, the fresh air will do you good. The winter was hard on you!"

Cain ignored Klaus, keeping his eyes down. The truth was the winter had not been hard on him- but the girl had. The girl who spelt of Jasmine and peppermint, the one he had spotted while at the shopping market during his time in Tobus. He had stormed from the High Lord's meeting, having gotten into a small squall with the High Lord. Taking his car, he drove, stopping randomly at the market.

After spotting the girl, he had returned and things with the High Lord were settled. They all left on good terms, with papers signs and chest puffed out like real-men.

Cain had spent the rest of that day, and the next, in search of the girl. When she never showed up, he was forced to return back towards his own home land. Since then, the girl had haunted his dreams, sleeping and awake. It seemed no matter where he turned or what he thought- she was there to haunt him.

"So, are these papers confirming that the land in Drale is ours?"

Cain shuffled through the papers once more, trying to push the thoughts of the girl from his thoughts.

"Yes, the secret delivery team brought them this morning. Next the small cabin on the land will be fixed up and used as our headquarters there."

"Good, Muis needs to learn his threats won't go unanswered. His head's too big for his title."

"He is stupid-"

"Wait."

Cain held up a hand, and Klaus stopped speaking almost at once. Despite their blood ties, and long standing friendship, Cain was still King. Klaus was to respect that.

Standing up, Cain dropped the papers back down on the coffee table, and lifted his nose to the air. Taking a sniff, he moved over to the open window, pushing past Klaus. He didn't turn from the window, instead looking down to the stage where the auction was to set to start at any moment.

"Do you smell that?"

Behind him, Klaus lifted his nose to the air, taking a sniff. His nose wrinkled at the sour smell of unwashed bodies. He highly doubted that was what Cain was referring to.

"No, what is it?"

"Jasmine."

Looking down to the stage, the first chain-group of slaves were being brought up. Focusing on two girls standing next to each other, Cain leaned on the seal. Something about the short brown hair that hung limply around the girl to the right seemed familiar. Moving his eyes to the girl to the left, he froze as she turned to face the girl behind her.

"Cain?"

Pushing off the seal, Cain spun on his heels.

"I'm going down there."

"What- why?"

"To buy what's mine. Isos, Enaro, Peron, Vern and Klaus, let's go."

Without questioning his cousin any more, Klaus followed after Cain the four body guard falling into steps behind him.

~~~

As Cain stepped out his car, he realized that Klaus had been right. People were squished up next to each other, their bodies forming human walls between him and the stage.

"When a superior talks to you, you are to answer promptly and properly!"

Cain turned his head at the scream, noticing that a girl laid on the stage with fear in her gaze at the Head Handler.

"Wrong answer-"
~~~

"Wait- please, let me explain, no stop!"

"Answer me!"

Cain watched as the man hit the girl again, and he found his hands clenching into fist. Taking a breath he looked beyond the dirty smells, and found the one he was looking for. Jasmine, looking to the girl, he knew at once it was her. It really was her.

"She can't speak-"

Behind her, the girl Cain remembered as smelling of peaches spoke out. The Head Handler ignore her, keeping his gaze down on the jasmine-girl- his girl, Jasmine.

"Answer me!"

He hit her again, he hit Jasmine and Cain watched as her mouth let out breaths-of cries. He felt his anger rising, but also knew he needed to keep his cool. His enemies had just as many spies in his land; he was sure, as he had in theirs. He couldn't risk letting the whole world see he was so protective over some human girl. Because he was, he was ready to destroy the whole world, as long as it meant his Jasmine was safe.

"I can interpret for her, I-"

A smack to her face with a reed cut off and silenced the peach girl. The Handler was clearly getting annoyed with the girl, and was ready to act. Jasmine's eyes held pure fear as the Handler ripped his sword from his belt.

"I shall teach you to be so distrustful!"

"No!"

The peach girl screamed out, but not even Cain could keep his eyes on her. Jasmine raised her hands, and in that moment everything froze. Using her hand, and some power, she pushed him up and away... all without ever touching him. He stood frozen, as his sword hung mere inches from her chest. The crowd around him went silent. Opening her eyes, Jasmine looked to the lead Handler. She dropped him to the ground, lowering her left hand. Her right flung the sword to into the crowd, and people scattered to avoid it.

"Well, folks, there you go! Is this stupid mute Blessed or what?! Can I get 200?"

"200!"

"300!"

"2,000 gold!"

The crowd let out a gasp, though Cain felt no threat.

"5,000!"

He waited for the right moment to move; watching Jasmine rise, the left side of her face was sickening. Looking at it made Cain's blood boil and he could feel his pupils dilating. Relaxing his hands, he cracked his neck.

"One million gold for the girl."

The whole crowd gasped, went silent and begun to mumble among themselves.

"My, oh my! Is anyone willing to up that bid? No? Going once... Twice... Sold- to our mighty King! Congratulations your majesty, though just as warning she's not that bright. She doesn't speak!"

The crowd laughed lightly as the joke, but soon stopped and parted a way to let him through. Cain didn't move from his spot, and watched as they brought Jasmine to him. As she walking towards them, he leaned over to Klaus.

"Go to the castle and get the funds straightened and be warned; I'm getting the next one along with her."

Klaus nodded, before backing away and moving down the street.

"A-hm, right then, onto the next! We got us here a real, natural beauty folks!"

She paused in front of him, her eyes casted down.

"Release her of the chains, now."

She was released at once, keeping her head down. He snuck a glance to her, though his ears were with the auction.

"50,000 gold for the girl!"

"...Going once...twice... sold- once more to our mighty King!"

The auctioneer chose to keep any joke about the peach girl to himself, a wise choice in the long run. They moved peach girl from the stage and down to him. When she arrived, he had them free her from her chains as well. Then they left, he had what he needed.

~~~

Arriving back at his home- of which some called a mansion, other a castle; he was prepared to see that the girls were cared for himself. Looking up, he could see Klaus and Claudia standing in one of the windows. Their faces were grim, and he knew at once they needed his presence. Looking to the small, group of three staff members, he gave them a small frown. He pointed to his car, looking each one in the eyes.

"Make sure the two girls in the back are properly taken care of. They are mine now."

The three nodded, and he was off.
~~~

Climbing the stairs by two, Cain quickly strolled to Klaus's office. Opening the door, Klaus had taken a seat in at his desk, as Claudia rested one hand on the back of the chair to stable her bent over body. Her free hand pointed something on a paper the two looked at.

"What is it?"

The both looked up, straightening themselves. Claudia folded her hands over each other, and strolled to the side of the desk.

"There's news from eastern border, three days ago it was talk that Muis was going to put out a draft out. The rumors of war are still floating around and no one thought anything of it. Until Muis start-ed talking to his High Court, these came in just now, look."

Cain strolled over and looked at the papers on the desk. It seemed to be letters, but red ink circle random words. It was clear it was a secret message within the letter itself.

"How did we get this?"

"One of the spies snuck it, copied and sent the real on its way."

Cain nodded, as he slipped the papers back to Klaus.

"Write and tell them to keep their eyes open and ears clear."

"I will. So, moving onto more important matters, how did your little buy go today?"

Claudia looked from her brother, to Cain.

"You went to the Slave Trade today? Why? You haven't expressed any needs for new servants."

"I told him of the rumors of there being a Blessed human there, and surprise, surprise there was."

"There was?"

"Yes and our dear cousin here paid one million gold for her."

"One million- gold!?"

"Yes, I did, and I paid fifty thousand for the girl after her."

Klaus let out a whistle, shaking his head.

"Please don't tell me the mighty king of Voirol is falling for the rumors."

"No I'm not, and the business I have with those two young women is none of your concern. Keep me updated on Muis; I'll be around."

Cain then turned and stormed out of the office. Claudia moved to sit across from her brother, sighing and tossing her legs over the chair. She begun to pick lent off of her pants.

"So what happened at the auction, how are you sure this woman is Blessed?"

"Because she used her power, she stopped a sword, floating it in the air, push away a man who is easily over 300 pounds of pure muscle and then floated him in the air."

Claudia swung her head to look at her brother, her blonde hair falling over her shoulder.

"So?"

"She never touched them."

Her blue eyes got wide, as she swung her legs down, sitting up.

"So do you think Cain bought her for her power?"

"I'm not sure. He was acting strange right before we went there."

The two siblings couldn't talk any more on the subject, as a loud scream pushed through the air like a hard slap.

~~~

Cain rushed into the dungeon, pushing the door so hard it broke into pieces. As he had been approaching, he had heard a voice calling out 'Scarlet, can you hear me, Scarlet' the voice was gone when he marched in. The main guard standing duty quickly stood up, grabbing his helmet to keep it from falling.

"Where are they?"
~~~

"Far cells to the left sire!"

"Get them out- NOW!"

Cain could feel his fangs rip out with his snarl, as his anger reached an all-time high. The guard, a fellow vampire himself but not of any high rank, shrunk back before scurrying off down the hall. Cain followed, pausing as the guard opened the first door. Pushing the guard aside, Cain leaned into the door way and was met with the peach girl. She stood frozen, not moving.

"I'm sorry about this, please come out."

Moving aside, the peach girl slowly shuffled out. She had her eyes casted down.

"Thank you, my lord."

"May I have your title?"

"Renee Rogan of Tobus, my lord."

Cain nodded his head, happy to finally have a name for peach girl. Turning to the guard he pointed to the door that held his Jasmine.

"Open it and free her!"

The guard did as he was told, but as the door open, a body fell out. Using his beyond-human reflexes, Cain caught Jasmine in his arms.

Holding her in his arms, he could feel her gentle hartbeat telling him she was still alive.

"Get doctor Cartson, now!"

The guard nodded, and rushed off.

"Scarlet!"

Cain looked from... Scarlet, to Renee, where stood behind him with wide eyes.

"Her name is Scarlet?"

"Yes, yes, Scarlet Solomon- is alive, is she-"

"She's alive but needs medical attention. I sent for my doctor. She'll be tended too, and so shall you."

Standing, his eyes didn't move from the small cut on her face. It had clotted but left blood lines down her face. She nodded her head, and casted her eyes down.

~~~

"So, I wrapped the wounds on her wrist, and ankles; her face is pretty bad, but it should be better within the week. And for you, miss Renee, just put this cream on a few more times and your cut will be gone in no time. If you're lucky, you'll have no scar."
~~~

Renee looked from the mirror, to Cain, to Scarlet, laying in her bed, and then the doctor.

"I will thank you."

Cain wasn't looking at her, or Scarlet though. His gaze was to the door, where a tall, thin man stood.

"Renee, this is Vern, one of my closest body guards. He will show you to your room and you can get cleaned up there. Vern make sure get to get Claudia to stock Renee with a few outfits until we can buy her, her own."

Vern nodded, and led Renee away. Cain released Dr. Cartson to go get something, for something. When he was alone, he moved over to the bed where Scarlet laid. He ran a finger down the right side of her face, his whole body seeming to buzz to life.

Scarlet, much better fitting name than Jasmine, even though you are delicate like a Jasmine.

When he pulled his finger away, his body stopped buzzing though his finger went numb. He looked at it, as he moved away from her, just as Dr. Cartson came in.

~~~

"...I shall live by Rules of the Old, and be judge by them accordantly. From this day forth, I am a Voirian."
~~~

"I shall live by Rules of the Old, and be judge by them accordantly. From this day forth, I am a Voirian."

"You may remove your hands and sit down.

"I hope, the clothe fit you well."

"They do, thank you sire."

Renee ran her hands down her pants, looking uncomfortable.

"I'm glad they do, it shall be your uniform while you serve under me."

"Yes, sire."

"Now, I'm sure you're wondering what your job is to be while in my household. To ease your mind, it's a simple task really, something you claimed you could do."

"Sire?"

"You are to translate what Scarlet says."

"What- I'm mean, sorry, excuse me?"

"Yes, you have said she cannot speak, is that right?"

"Well, yes. I mean, I've never known her to speak and we've been best friends for the longest time. She was born mute, sire. If she ever spoke, it'd be to me."

"Of course, so that is why I need you. I cannot understand her methods of talking, but you can."

"Well she's the only one I know that no one else really does this, signing language."

"And that is what I want to learn."

"Not to be rude, sire, but are you planning on using her powers?"

"Possibly, a king is only as great as his people. A war can only be won with weapons hidden away."

"So you're going to hide Scarlet away?"

"Yes but no. She, and you, shall stay here, under the impression as my teacher and I the student, so you shall be hidden, but in plain sight. I trust you shall not tell the details of this little meeting to her?"

"Oh- of course, sire, but...I may be over stepping my place, so forgive me, how do you plan to hide us when you bought us at a public auction?"

Cain leaned his elbow on his desk, cracking his knuckles.

"You'd be amazed at what a good rumor can do."

~~~
~~~

And that was how King Cainwen Dufur killed off Scarlet Solomon. The people at the auction had seen her beaten, and the guard had seen her passed out in a dead-like state. Soon the gossip was that the Blessed human died from her injures, and was given a private Burning.

He had been overlooking the local paper, which wrote a small article on her, when he had gotten the news that she was well enough to finally be summoned to him. That's exactly what he did.

~~~

Lifting his head to the approaching footsteps, Cain waited for the knock. When Vern peeked his head in, he simply asked if he had them. When Vern replied with a 'yes', he had them sent in. Through the crack door, he didn't get any scents minus Vern's which was slightly unpleasant being he smelt faintly of blood- as almost all vampires do. Unlike human blood, which can be quite mouthwatering, vampire blood was bitter and clotty. It was a natural defense to help keep others off of you.

When the doors fully swung open, and Cain caught his first glance of Scarlet since she had been put under Dr. Garston's care, it took everything in him to not leap up and latch onto her there. Not only was she healthier looking, but the gown he had chosen was the perfect color to offset her coffee hair and eyes. It gave her white skin
~~~

a sort of glow, one that no words could ever explain. As they took a seat on his command, the doors behind him closed and they were left to their affairs.

As he brought up her 'duty' to him, she did not try to hide the shock on her face. Her hands moved around, in a beautiful manner, as she spoke in the only way she knew how to. Moving his gaze slightly from her, he looked to Renee, waiting for her to interpret.

"She is asking why a teacher."

"Because I want to learn the language of sign, and I know of no one better to teach then a mute. You can both see and hear me, something a deaf or blind person cannot."

" 'Why would you want to do that my lord? Surly there is no one you know who cannot speak as, I.' "

"True, but it is never too late or too hard for a King to learn something new; to expand his horizons and knowledge."

" 'Oh, I see.' "

"Our lessons shall be every day from noon to two; we shall break for a lunch, and shall start tomorrow."

" 'Yes sire.' "

"Do you have any questions for me before you are shown to your room?"

" 'Only one sire, I was wondering if I could learn the name of my new king.' "

"My official title is King Cainwen Dufur, you may call me 'sire' 'my king' or 'my lord'."

" "Yes sire. Thank you.' "

"You are dismissed. The guards outside shall show you to your rooms."

The two girls rose, curtsied and then left the room. He watched them leave, the doors cutting off the wonderful smell that seemed to wave off of Scarlet in large amounts. He knew at their next meeting, he'd have to explain more of his plan to her. To tell her of her faked death, and the fact that he did indeed plan to use her powers. There hadn't been a Blessed human since his toddler years, which happened to be a few thousand or so. Blessed only came when the world needed them, and if he was right- then it was not just his kingdom that needed her, but himself as well.

CHAPTER 4

The double doors opened, and Scarlet's mouth fell. With wide eyes, she slowly entered 'her' room. Pausing just far enough in, Renee and the guard Vern squeezed in behind her. Turning on her heels, she faced the two.

'Is all this for me? Is it all mine?'

The guard, Vern, slide his pale green eyes to Renee. Renee looked from Scarlet to him.

"She's asking if it's all for her- if it's all hers."

Vern turned his gaze back to Scarlet, giving a small nod.

"Yes, this is your sleeping quarters. The near right door is a sitting room, which has a door that leads out to the hall; the small door to the far right by the windows is your closet, fully stocked; those two small double doors on the left lead to your bathroom, also fully stocked; behind those curtains there are French doors that lead out to your private balcony, though I am to advise you to not jump down from it- the flowers beneath it have horrible thorns. Anything you need, you only need to ask. The king will do his best to meet whatever you ask."

"'Okay, thank you.'"

Vern gave another head nod, slipping an ear-length strand of auburn hair behind his ear.

"Of course, now if you excuse me, I will leave you for the night. Dinner shall be served in three hours, but if you need anything before that, you can pull that rope in the corner and a maid will be here at once."

Scarlet gave him the sign of thanks, and he left the room; closing the doors behind him.

'Wow, this room is wow.'

"I know, just wait till you get to know the rest of the castle."

'The Castle? Wow, will I be getting a tour or something?'

"I'm sure the king will allow me the right to show you around this week, it's not like you're expected to stay cooped up in this room for the rest of time."

'We are still his slaves though, if he wanted-'

"Now, now Scar, the king has clearly stated- though by law we belong to him; we are not slaves. We're servants to him."

Scarlet gave a shrug, her wide eyes still taking in her room.

"Well, I'll leave you to... take in your room. Explore a bit, even though it's just a bedroom, you'd be surprised at what the king stocks for his workers."

Scarlet nodded, and waved goodbye to her friend as she closed the doors behind her. Turning slowly, she faced her room once more. Compared to the dark halls, and the wooden office, her room looked as if it was the misfit of the family. Pale grey walls with black accents covered her four walls. The yellow curtains were light in color yet blocked out the light perfectly. Between the two doors to the right, was a large black wooden four poster bed. The comforter was a pale yellow while the pillows were a mixture between white and yellow. There was a small foot stool on the end of her bed, the color of black matched her bed and night stands. Beside the windows were two plush chairs, with a small table between them. The floors were wooden, but a large, thick pale yellow carpet covered up most of the darken wood. There was a well sized desk pushed at an angle in the left corner of the room, opposite of the windows.

Moving from her room, she entered her sitting room. From what she was always told; sitting rooms were very formal and somewhat small. Though the room was formal, with a matching chaise lounge, two couches, one love seat and two chairs; along with the different sized tables, it made a complete living room set. The room itself though, was large enough to be the size of her old kitchen and living room in her mother's home. The far right wall and one that connected to it were covered in large windows that started at her knee level and went up to nearly the ceiling- which was easily 25 feet if not more. The color scheme from her bedroom went on into her sitting room. The only differences being her furniture was different tones of pale greys and white while her walls were a solid yellow. From the left side door to the far wall of windows, the wall was covered in a large book shelve- packed with books. Though Scarlet had never been much of a reader, she was willing to reconsider it with all the books she now had her fingertips. Moving to get a closer look, she ran her fingers across a row of spines, a small smile creeping on her face as she retracted her hand. In Tobus only the most rich had books to keep. Schools shared them, and free libraries were rare. Scarlet only knew how to read and write because she had no choice but to learn it. As she had been taught through the years, she taught her mother as well.

Her mother. A small ping of pain shot through her, and she was quick to spin on her heels.

No need to think of her. This is my home now. My freedom is gone; I lost it the day I didn't listen to her. The king bought me and I took the oath, this is my home.

Going back into her bedroom, she moved around the bed, and headed to her closet door. With a soft click, she pushed it open, and flicked on the steam-powered ceiling lamps. With the sudden flash of light, she was taken aback even more. Levels upon levels of hanging clothes met her with a blaze. The right side of the 'first' level was wardrobes, filled with minor things such as under clothes or socks or stockings. The left side was shoes, all types of shoes in all styles, in all the colors you could imagine. Above them, for four high levels, were just clothes upon clothes. For a moment she wondered how she was to reach the high levels of clothes, but when her eyes spotted a small track, she was able to find a rolling ladder.

Letting out breaths that would count for her 'laugh', she moved to the ladder. Grabbing it, she pushed it along before hopping on the moving object. When she hit the end of the track, she was stopped with a jolt- and found herself flying forward into a stack of shoes. The shoes came crumbling around her, one even landing on her head. Pulling the shoe from her head, she set to placing each pair back onto their shelve.

Coming out of her closet, she ran her hand along the curtains before pulling at them and hooking each one on its own little hook. When all twelve curtains were pulled aside, Scarlet stepped back to admire the view.

It was breath taking. Though she was only on the first floor, she had a perfect view of the grounds behind the castle. The grounds were perfectly kept, with brown pebbled mixed gravel paths surrounded by different types of lush plants, it was beautiful. Lanterns metal posts were stuck along the paths, though nothing hung off of them. Scarlet could only guess that they were add manually each night- or maybe only on certain occasions or days.

Looking around her room, she decided she loved it with the curtains opened. The light made the room seem larger and even grander. Plus, she loved the view. Surviving her room, she realized there was one place she had yet to see- the bathroom.

In her small two story home in Tobus, the bathroom she had shared with her mother consisted of a large metal tub with a water spouse; a small wooden bowl for a sink, and a simple toilet. The tub was raised off the ground by a foot or so, so that you could stick warm coals under the tub to warm the water. Coal was too expensive for her mother and her to afford, so they used wood to warm their house. The wood didn't really work, so they typically took quick, cold baths. A small hose connected the side of the tub to the wall, where the water would drain out. The wooden sink hung on the wall beside the tub. It would be plugged by a plug, and pulled out from the wall to rest over the tub. From there you would have to pump water into it, and then let it run out into the tub. Their toilet worked in the same manner only it had its own small water pump, and the hose that connected it went underground into a small sewage tank that Scarlet's mother paid a good price to get cleaned out twice a year.

Pushing the two small doors in, she leaned on them for a second long, as she took in the room. There were windows along one side of the room, giving light through curtains that blocked out her room but allowed light. The left wall was all mirrors. The white granite countertop ran with the mirror, a soul sink with brass features sat in the middle. Along each side were different makeups, perfumes and other random tidbits that Scarlet could only guess belonged in a bathroom. Across from the sing, resting just slightly off center from the room was a claw-foot tub that seemed to be made of some sort of marble or smooth white stone. Scarlet had never seen such grand materials before, so she could only guess what they were. The features on it were brass too, the tub even having a shower head, something Scarlet considered real fancy. A curtain rod kept up a plain white fabric curtain, though it was opened at the moment. To the right of the tub, near the edge of one of the two large windows, was a free-standing brass towel rack. In the far off left corner, behind a dressing screen, there was a single toilet. But it was nothing to compare to the one in her old home. This one was much nicer, and much more advance then her own.

Standing in the middle of the room, she rolled her lips into her mouth. Looking around, she eyed the tub, mostly at the faucets. The one for cold, but mostly the one for hot.

Well, Vern did say I have a few hours until dinner. Whose know who I'll be dinning with- it could be the king himself! I don't want to smell like... medical... A small bath wouldn't kill me.

Starting the water, she plugged the tub when the water was so hot it felt like he skin might melt off. Standing she grabbed a bottle of bath salts; she knew these from the time she aided her mother on her job as a house-nurse. Pouring a small amount into the tub, she also added in a few drops of jasmine oil and a small round ball of fizzle soap. As the tub filled, she went to the closet, and picked out a simple, red gown to wear to dinner. It seemed, as Renee, she had a certain amount of options of clothes to wear. While for Renee it was pants and a shirt, for Scarlet it was some sort of gown- though she did have a few pairs of pants and shirts.

Entering back into the bathroom, the large tub was barely half way full. Placing her fresh dress aside, she easily slipped out of her corset, shoes and dress. She wrapped a towel around her naked body, and pulled out every single hair pin; allowing her hair to hang. Moving to the tub, she sat on the rim, running her fingers around in it before turning the faucets off. She then removed the wraps from her ankles and wrist. Slipping out of the towel, she grabbed a bottle of hair/

body soap, placing it on the small metal shelve that hung off the side of the tub. Finally, she fell into the water, with a huge gasp. It was so hot, it was wonderful. Her wrist stung and ankles stung slightly, but beside that it was as if her whole body had been wrapped in a warm, wonderful smelling blanket. Releasing it, she fell into the water more, until only her face floated. Closing her eyes, she took in the sweet smells of her additives, her body relaxing, and the pain slipping away.

~~~

Leaning on the rim of the tub, Scarlet tucked the edge of her towel under her armpit. Tipping her head to the side she began to dry her hair with a separate towel, rubbing her dripping locks in it. Flipping her head forward, she wrapped the towel around her head. As she brought her head back up, there was a knock at her bedroom door. Popping her head out of the bathroom, she saw Dr. Cartson popping her head in.

"Miss Scarlet, is it alright if I come in?"

Scarlet tightened the towel around her body and nodded her head. She would need to ask for a set of bells- it was something her mother had thought up. Dr. Cartson came in, closing the door behind her.

"I'm just here to check on your wounds and clean them- though you seemed to have taken care of that- you enjoyed the bathroom already, I see."
~~~

Scarlet gave a shy smile as her face slightly colored. Moving aside, she allowed Dr. Cartson entry to the bathroom. Stopping as Scarlet closed the door; the doctor seemed to just realize that Scarlet was wrapped in only the towels.

"Oh my, alas, I was caught up in my own thoughts. You are in barely anything- I can come back later."

Scarlet held a hand out, stopping the doctor as she shook her head.

"Oh my, well, why don't you go get change and I'll get the gaze and what not. If I am correct, you should have some right here in this cabinet..."

Dr. Cartson begun to open up the cabinets under the counter, as Scarlet slipped behind the dressing screen. Slipping off the towels, she hung them on another towel rack, and slipped on her underwear. Next came a chest-shaping corset that really only held her breast up, but nothing more. Next came the short under slip, a piece of clothing that some girls even slept in. Or Scarlet was told, despite her semi-fair looks, men tended to fall away from a mute girl.

"Whenever you're ready dear!"

Stepping out from the screen, in only her underclothes, Dr. Cartson paid no attention- if she even noticed Scarlet wearing near-nothing. Directing her, Scarlet took a seat on the small stool that had been pulled out from where it had rested under the countertop. Scarlet sat, and Dr. Cartson went to work. When she finished wrapping Scarlet's wounds, she dismissed her to get dressed. She put everything back in its place, and Scarlet finished the process of getting her outfit on.

"Alas dear, I do believe that this is the last time those wounds need to be wrapped. The scabs seem to be on well enough, though if you ever want my-oh my, Miss Scarlet, alas I must say that dress is lovely on you."

Scarlet tugged at the sleeves on the dress, hiding the white gauze, as she stepped out from behind the dressing screen. She gave Dr. Cartson a small smile of thanks, knowing the woman wouldn't understand anything more.

"Now, what are you going to do with your hair?"

Scarlet shrugged her shoulders, as ran a hand through her damp locks. She really hadn't thought about how she would wear her hair, in all realities the dress she chose was the first one she saw that seemed appropriate for dinner.

"Well alas, I have no daughters of my own, but if you sit back down I'm sure we can figure something out."

Dr. Cartson gave her a small smile, and Scarlet returned it as she sat down.

~~~

Scarlet paced around her room, pulling a fabric curler from her hair as she did. Her small heels made a muffling noise, and the small train of her dress drug behind her. She held the fabric curlers in her hand, as she took out the last few. Pausing at the small dressing table, she dumped the curlers onto it. Running her fingers across her scalp, she pushed her hair in all sort of directions. As she released her fingers, she gently shook her head, and looked at herself in the mirror. Her cheeks were slightly flushed from her nervous pacing, and her bottom lip was a tad red from her biting it. At any moment she was to be summoned for dinner, and the whole thought of it made her head spin. She had never been to a royal dinner before- or even a semiformal one! Her whole life consisted of the small cottage home she had shared with her single mother. They had never been rich enough, or known anyone enough, to be invited to such a grand event.

Only the highest of the high in Tobus dined like a king would. Scarlet and her mother were nowhere close to high on the social standard. It was rumored, that the reason Scarlet had been born mute, was because she was a bastard child. The rumor claimed that Ms. Solomon had been the secret whore of one of High Lord Rolle's sons. She
~~~

became pregnant and instead of killing the child right off, Scarlet was cursed. What many people did not know was that Scarlet was more than just a mute, she was Blessed. Thus growing up she knew she was not related to the High Lord- despite the fact that her mother never revealed her birth father. Scarlet still struggled a bit when growing up, unable to speak her mind. She was grateful to Rene because she did have a voice, and wasn't afraid to threaten even the largest of bullies.

A knock at her sitting room door pulled he from her thoughts. She walked from her bedroom, and opened the door. Vern was there, waiting for her, as was Rene. Stepping out, she closed her door behind her.

"Wow-oh-wow Scar, you look great."

Scarlet smiled and thanked her friend. She wanted to say the same to her, but couldn't. Rene was in the outfit that was becoming her signature look; a collared button down shirt with skin tight pants and boots. Scarlet was starting to believe that, that combination outfit was to be worn at all times by her friend. Though, this one was a tad more fancier then her earlier outfit. The shirt was long sleeved, and fitted to her thin arms like fresh leather. The shirt was tucked into her waist high pants, which in returned were shoved into her knee high boots.

Scarlet started to respond to her friend, but stopped when Rene held her hands.

"Don't, I know my outfit is nearly identical, but it's what I as given. Seems like you- miss teacher friend of mine, will be wearing dresses for your uniform."

Scarlet gave a small smile, and nodded her head. No way was she about to spill the facts of her huge closet. The three then started their way down the hall, Scarlet allowed Vern and Rene to lead- being the two knew the huge home better than she did.

Through yet another maze of hallways, she was lead through one rather large door. It opened into a huge dining room, easily three times her new bedroom. It was an inner room, and thus windowless. But the forest green walls were not left bare, portraits of different people, different groups, were perfectly placed among the room. The ceilings above her were painted in the most delicate ways and in such details that she couldn't even make them out from so far below them. There was one large chandler hanging in the middle of the ceiling, with two smaller ones towards the ends of the room. The table itself was some sort of fine wood, and could easily seat thirty people if someone chose to.

Tonight though, the room was nearly empty. Minus Scarlet's small group, and what Scarlet figured were other servants of the king, there was one woman. Her ivory skin was flawless, and her red hair was sleeked back so that it hung straight down her back. Small, thing sliver wires were twisted about each other and rested on her head, Scarlet knew almost at once what it was- a crown. They were in the room with a royal. The queen smiled at them, her teeth being only a few shades whiter than her skin.

"Good evening and welcome. My name is Queen Dolra, and I shall be your host this evening."

Rene and Scarlet bowed their heads as they bent forward. Vern gave a simple head nod.

"Please rise, and take a seat. I am sure you are hungry."

The two girls stepped forward, and took the seats to the left of the head of the table. Queen Dolra, instead of sitting at the head, sat to the right. She smoothed out her blue gown, before looking up at the two girls.

"You must forgive my husband's absent. He wanted to join us tonight, but business called him away."

"We are honored to have you here at least, my lady."

The queen smiled once more, and nodded off to one of the side servants. With a short nod for a reply, the servant left and the others followed swiftly after. Not even a minute passed before they started to return, sliver platters, bowls and pitchers of all sizes within their grasps. The food was laid out along the table where the three women sat, and each was left to fill her plate to her pleasure. They were silent as they did this, the only noise being the clatter of the sliver.

"Your highness, if it's not out of my place to ask, I was wondering if you gave such a grand meal to all of your new servants." Renee had taken the leap, and broken the silence. The queen places a small, but very rare piece of meat on her plate before looking up to her.

"No, but you two are not any normal servants. My husband tells me that Scarlet is a Blessed human, and that despite her lack of vocals, she still finds a way to communicate. He believes that by learning this strange signed language that it would benefit Voirol as a whole. Our military already uses a similar process, though it is nowhere near as extravagant as Scarlet's." She took a small bite of the bleeding meat, not even blinking an eye as her wine glass was filled with a thick red liquid too dark to be wine.

"Oh, I see, thank you for clearing that thought up."

"Of course, now, if you two don't mind I would like to learn more about you. I am told you two hail from Tobus, is that correct?"

"Yes ma'am."

"Tobus doesn't produce many slaves for the Trade, how did you two get mixed up in it? I'm a assuming you two were captured together so you must be quite close." The queen took a sip from her glass, her eyes gleaming. They would have been a beautiful shade of green, but the whiting cast over on them bleached them out to where just a hint of pale green was visible. Renee looked to Scarlet, and with a deep intake, she nodded her head. Renee turned back to the queen.

"That's right, your highness, Scarlet is my best friend in the whole world and I'm hers. We grew up as neighbors, just one house plot separated us and we went to school together. Our mothers had been close friends before our births so I guess you can say the bond that holds us was meant to come, naturally. I don't think I would change it." Renee looked to Scarlet, and with a smile she nodded her head no. Reaching out, Scarlet wrapped her hand in Renee's, giving it a gentle squeeze as they shook them. There was no way in any shape or form that she would change the fictive kin bond they shared. Releasing her friend's hand, Scarlet did a few signs anyone would understand.

'I love you like my sister.'

"She says she loves me like a sister."

"Ah, I see. How marvelous, a bond such as the one you two share gives hope to the world that those types of love and care are still out there. I take it that is the reason you two ended up in the Trade together?"

"Sort of, we went out one afternoon to pick berries in the forest behind our homes and we ended up in a berry war. We thought no one was a round, so Scarlet used her powers, but there were people. A small group of men took Scarlet first, and I chased after them. I couldn't allow them to take her I would never be able to show my face to Ms. Solomon again if I let them take her. We fought, hard, but they over powered us..." Renee looked down to the food she had been sliding around on her plate with her fork, "I didn't even get to see my mother one last time. There's so much I wish I could have told her."

"Your mother, did you not have a father- what about Scarlet. Excuse me for being frank and forward but I wish to know everything about the two girls who captivated my husband enough to spend a million and fifty thousand gold on when his record before had only been three thousand."

Scarlet could hear the slight tint of bitterness that under lied her silvery tone. Either the queen was mad at the king for spending so much on two humans- despite Scarlet's abilities- or she was threatened in some way by the two girls. Perhaps it was a cocktail of the two.

"My father works in the mines in the mountains of Tobus. He's gone for much the year, and I only ever saw him the holidays, maybe a few rare weekends here and there. We lived so far from the mining camp and all his money went to caring for us so he couldn't afford to come out as much as he liked. Needless to say, my parents loved each other, me and my three younger siblings."

The queen nodded, and then looked to Scarlet. "And her?"

"Her mother raised her alone, she, well..." The way Renee hung the sentence left the queen wanting more information on the Blessed human.

"Yes?"

"Ms. Solomon never married, and there were rumors for years that the reason Scarlet was born mute was because she was a bastard child born out of wed lock."

"My mother died many years ago, when I was only a child. My father was a wealthy noble man, and owns a whole fleet of trading ships- spice trade that is- and was always busy. I given it all in life, but was raised by governesses and slaves. So I can relate to a point of the absent parental figure or figurers."

Scarlet's free hand curled in her lap. Queen Dolra had just claimed to have it all growing up but because her mother died and her father was busy making a ton of gold she was left to be raised by elsewhere people. She would have to disagree with the queen on that matter, in Scarlet's mind that would be a near perfect life.

CHAPTER 5

Dolra had been filled with a mixture of anger, spite and pure shock when she learned of Cain's latest slave purchase. Never in their near two thousand years of marriage had he ever gone to such an extent to get two girls- two human girls into their home. In order to give him some sort of credit, the one he paid a million gold for- Scarlet- was a Blessed human and the other, Renee, her voice. Dolra still wasn't fond of the idea. Cain never did anything without a reason and Dolra was a smart woman. There was much her husband did not tell her, but there was also much he need not to tell her.

"I see you killed off your little human, why?" Dolra sat in her husband's office, sitting opposite of him, reading the local paper.

"Why wouldn't I? If Muis discovered that Scarlet had lived and was in my position- hell if any world leader found out, they would all declare war on Voirol just to get her in their own possession." Dolra lowered the paper, looking at her husband. His hands slide a few papers around on his desk but she could not tell if his eyes actually read them.

"Besides the war, and her powers, what would be so horrible to not having her on our side?"

"She is a Blessed human. The only good thing is to have her on our side. I've seen her power- though it was a small show, I've seen it. She will amaze to great levels, and when Muis declares war, we're going to want to have her."

"Cain she is merely a girl, I think you put too much faith in her."

"No-no, she just needs some training. In a week or so, I'm going to have Claudia begin training her to fight."

"So you see her as a weapon, a tool for you to use in your own personal gain?"

"Not for my personal gain, but protection for my people! When she's not training, I plan to learn her language of sign."

"I don't know why you would waste your time. She won't live long, Blessed humans never do."

Dolra casted her eyes back down at her paper nonchalantly. It was true. Blessed humans were lucky to live to 30. Beings always fought over them, the Blessed would run or chose a side. War would break out and in their time of need, the Blessed were killed. A Blessed human is most vulnerable in the stage of using their power. They had to focus all their energy, all their being, into their power. And in the age old saying; if someone could not have something, then no one could.

"That is why I'm going to have Claudia teach her! Claudia is the best fighter I have, and if Scarlet is to live to her full human age, then she'll need to know how to protect herself."

"Why do you seek to protect her?"

Cain let out a growl, slamming his fist on the desk. Dolra jumped just the slightest, not enough to be noticed.

"Do you not hear me? She's a Blessed human. If you wish to remain on the throne of this country you will come to accept her. She will learn to fight. She will live in this home. She is mine and there's no fight there."

~~~

She hadn't expected to have dinner with them, them of all the beings in the world. She was one to dine with only the finest in the lands, yet thanks to the deeds of her husband and with the threat of war with Drale; she found herself dinning with the two humans; alone. Her dear husband along with his right hands found themselves entangled
~~~

with new information from the eastern border. Dolra never found herself hating Muis than more during the dinner with the two slaves. None the less, she planned to find out all she could on these two girls and perhaps find out what Cain saw in them- minus the gift of the Blessed human.

So she dressed in one of her less extravagant gowns and found herself staring down at the two humans for nearly two hours. It amazed her; how the non-blessed one, Renee had been willing to give her own freedom- her own life- in order to protect the Blesses human. Scarlet own Renee her life, to which she knew it would never be repaid. She felt it the moment Renee begun to speak about their kidnapping.

Dolra could read beings... feel them. As a vampire she was already an extraordinary being, and with that perk some would consider a Blessing. Dolra didn't. Blessings were for humans, vampires were Gifted; she was Gifted. Not really, no. Gifts within the vampire species was common, and seen as normal. The powers, the maximum ability the powers held, were nothing close to a Blessed human. No one really knew why, only because the only known Blessed humans were all dead... minus Scarlet. She was hard to read. Without her voice, Dolra could only read her body movements- and even that was task being she used her body in modification speech. What little Dolra could get from the girl, was nothing but innocents. She was nervous, and truly loved her friend as she said. She seemed to have done nothing wrong in which to get the cursed title of Blessed.

Dolra found herself coming to hate the girl.

~~~

"So, how was your meeting?" Dolra looked at her husband through her armoire's mirror, running her gold-handled hairbrush through her thick, fiery locks.

"It was a meeting, boring and stressful. How was dinner?"

"It was a dinner, boring and stressful." She looked at her husband, as she copied his words. He ran a hand through his black hair, stopping mid stoke when he felt her gaze.

"I'm sure it wasn't that horrible."

"It was, I dread those two little pets."

"They aren't pets." Cain strolled over to his wife, resting a slightly tight grip on her shoulder, "They're people. People- who are going to help us get through the war." Dolra's blood went slightly cold- despite her body's natural cool temperature. She slowly sat her hairbrush down, and turned to look at her husband.

"So, it is confirmed, there is to be a war?"
~~~

"Yes, no, we're preparing for the worst. Klaus has the Generals preparing their men, we're going to slowly call in the reserves and Claudia is getting her best fighters together to train them all." Dolra found her gaze turning back to the mirror, where she stared at herself.

"Do not fret, my dear," Cain leaned down and kissed her hair, "When the war comes, Scarlet shall be prepared and protected. We shan't lose it."

CHAPTER 6

Allowing the corset of her dress to fall to the ground, Scarlet stepped out of the dress, allowing it to pile up on the ground before bending down and picking it up. The fabric, still so soft despite being worn, would wrinkle if she left it there. She couldn't bring herself to just leave the gown there, so she laid it across the back of her desk chair, unsure of anywhere else to put it.

Strolling to her closet, she dug around a few random drawers before finding a suitable night gown. Slipping it on, the cream silk fabric brushed her skin like butterfly wings. She had never worn such a frock before. When she was with her mother, they wore plain, simple clothing made from some of the most affordable fabrics available, unfortunately they wound up paying cost elsewhere- mostly in the softness of the material.

The thought of her mother made Scarlet's stomach roll. She had been trying to forget about her old life, and told herself repeatedly that her mother was better off without her. But it still hurt. She highly doubted the pain would ever truly go away- how could it? How could one fully forget the one person in the world they treasured over life itself? The pain may go numb through the years, but it would never go away. That thought hurt the most.

Pulling back the covers of her bed, Scarlet climbed in. Turning off her bed-side lamp, she laid back into the bed- it too was like nothing she could have ever dreamed of being in. She stared into the blackness of the night, feeling a sudden, uneasiness creeping around her. The air had gone stale, and the mashed noises of the outside world stopped. As if they could sense the evil that was coming upon her. Scarlet blinked but didn't dare close her eyes, though her black room could trick her mind into believing that they were closed. It was as if she could see it, the dark hands slithering out from beneath the darkest part under her bed, and slowly they moved up the walls, curling as they reached the ceiling. Then, in a swift, smooth motion the clawed black hands came crashing down upon her.

Jolting, Scarlet's eyes opened. Slowly sitting up, she adjusted herself as her covers fell, and looked around. The dream had felt so real, the weight of the dark hands and their sharp claw marks digging into her skin, yet when she looked down upon her arms they were free from any sign of abuse. She rested her free hand on her heaving chest, using the other to prop herself up. Crawling to the edge of her bed, she dimly lit her bed side gas lamp in order to read the small clock.

2:35

It was still early into the night she realized, and if she could back to sleep within the next half hour then she might be able to get in a much needed few more hours of rest before her seven am wake up. Turning the lamp off, she laid back down and scooted around under the sheets in order to get comfy. She had specific orders from the King to be at the library for their first lesson at noon, but Renee had asked her to join her for breakfast and an after-breakfast stroll through the castle to help her get her footing more. Apparently, her dear friend had been using all her free time from Scarlet and her duty to the king to explore their new home. Scarlet had accepted, of course. She couldn't count on others to guide her throughout the castle for the rest of her time here. Most tended to already see her as a weak, stupid being because her lack of voice and so she often times found herself trying to work a little bit harder in order to not just show the world that she could do things but do them to their possible best.

Scarlet is not alone in the battle, though there are no other Blessed humans, there are beings who are different and stand out from their own kind- be it vampires, werewolves, goblins, or witches. Because of these quirks or curses, they too have to show the world that despite being different they can do much anything any anyone else.

Scarlet wasn't quite sure when she fell asleep, but she found herself being a woken from a knock at her door. She barely had time to sit up, before she heard it swing open and a person entered. Renee closed her bedroom door before strolling over to the bed.

"Well good morning, princess."

'What time is it? Why are you here so early?'

"Early? Scar it's almost nine! I waited for you to join me at breakfast for an hour!" At the sound of 'nine' Scarlet tumbled to the edge of her bed to check her clock. Though she wanted to believe her friend, Renee was known to be one to pull a joke or prank every now and then on her best friend. With a slight gasp, Scarlet saw with her own eyes that it was indeed near nine. As she stumbled from her bed, she wondered how she had been able to sleep for so long. Normally she was one to rise with the sun and fall at the rise of the moon.

Rushing into her open closet, Scarlet stumbled back a step. There were so many gowns, so many options and being she was still shaking the sleep from her body, it was all over whelming.

"Whoa, Scar... your closet, is amazing." Renee had followed after her friend, standing in the doorway. She was taken aback by the size of the room and wardrobe for her friend. While she had to wonder if the king just had all these gowns laying around for no reason, she was also slightly jealous of her friend. Renee had both a room and closet half the size of her friend and was given the basic. "Where did you get all these gowns- did the King just have them on reserve or something?" Scarlet looked over to her friend and shrugged. She honestly hadn't thought about it, but now that she was; Renee was right.

'I don't know, I don't even know what to wear, help me?'

"Sure, let's see," Renee hopped onto the ladder and it moved a few feet as he weight met it. She scanned the second row of dresses, moving toward the more casual ones- though that was a word to be put lightly towards the gowns. Even the more plain and modest ones were gorgeous to look at. After picking through a few, Renee pulled out soft petal-pink gown and held it out to her friend. "How about this one?" Scarlet nodded, grabbing the gown from her friend. She honestly didn't care what dress Renee would have chosen, she would have agreed to an old sack. Scarlet was one who preferred to keep on a timed schedule and was often shaken slightly when plans changed on a whim. Having over slept, shook Scarlet more than it should have, but none the less she knew it would all be okay. Renee wasn't mad at her and as she came out of her bathroom, fiddling with quarter-length sleeves, she was surprised to see both her friend and Vern standing at the door between her bedroom and sitting room. She slowly walked over to them, looking between the two for someone to give some sort of explanation.

"Good morning miss Scarlet." Scarlet smiled at Vern and gave a head nod in return. "Miss Renee stopped me earlier and told me of how you missed our breakfast meeting." Scarlet's cheeks flushed slightly. She barely knew Vern and wasn't pleased on how her friend told him of their morning plans. She didn't want him to get the wrong impression- she was not one to run late. "She asked me to bring up a tray of breakfast for you, which is currently in the sitting room." Scarlet gave a small smile, lifted her right hand to her chin. Bring it down, she brought it down in the direction of Vern.

"Hand to chin and then out towards a certain person or group is how she says 'thank you.'"

"Ah, I see, well, you are welcomed. I hope you have a fair day, good day." Scarlet waved to Vern, taking his spot in the door way as he left out of her sitting room to the hall. Looking to Renee, Scarlet pushed her slightly.

"Hey- what was that for?!"

'He's going to think I'm lazy or don't stay on schedule- why did you have to tell him?'

"Well it's not like I can exactly waltz into the Kitchen and demand a tray of food. Besides that, Vern is... nice. Even for a big-bad vampire guard, we've spoke a good amount when you were out. The King refused to leave you unguarded, and more times than not Vern was there. We started to talk and, I don't know, I guess we could be seen as friends or something along that line. I mean, Scar, this is our home now. We might as well try to make the best of it right?" Scarlet, who had since taken a seat and begun to eat at the growling of her stomach, nodded. "And beside the King, what better ally to have then one of his most trusted guards?" Taking a bit of her roll, Scarlet glanced away as she nodded again. Renee was right, while Scarlet was still wrapping her mind around her new living arrangements she hadn't even thought about befriending those beings around her. What was to stop her? It was not as if she sought to escape the King or her current home. Though it was not the most ideal situation, Renee really had only been trying to make the best of things. Scarlet should have been praising her friend rather than scolding her like a mindless child.

~~~

"So, do you think you're starting to understand the layout of the castle?" Scarlet nodded her head, as she and Renee walked through another long hall, linked and intertwined at their elbows. They had taken the few hours they had between Scarlet's late breakfast and
~~~

their first lesson at noon to tour their new home. Though Scarlet couldn't move through the halls freely on her own yet without the fear of getting aimlessly lost, she did understand the role of each level.

Though they weren't allowed to go down through most of it, Renee started in the basement. That was where the holding cells, the infirmary she was first held in, and a large training room were situated. The first floor above that was split into two halves with the left side the most formal out of the two; with a large ball room, and two quite impressive meeting rooms, a war room, and the grand dining room, Scarlet doubted she would ever spend time on that side of the home's main floor. There was also, of course, the kitchen where all the meals were cooked and next to that the laundry station; both of which Scarlet believed she had a better chance of finding herself in. The right wing of the first floor was where she and Renee resided, along with several other empty guest rooms. Scarlet saw Renee's room for the first time- it was a hall way down and two doors across from her own- and found herself wanting to curl back. Renee's room was much more plainer than her own, nor did her closet or sitting room match up to Scarlet's. The color placements throughout were near the same in every way, only hers were in cool greens and blues rather than yellow and grey. It was a pretty room, but the view was bland being it only over looked a portion of the front yard. If their unequal rooms bother Renee, Scarlet could not tell, but she knew her friend had seen her face twist before forcing itself into a smile.

The second floor was more for the King, Queen and a few others that Scarlet wasn't quite sure how they fit in but none the less did. Along with the King and Queen's private rooms, spaces and offices; that was all along the left side of the floor while on the right there was a large library, and a theater room. The third floor was the only floor they didn't have time to visit, but what Renee knew about it was that one half was used as an attic for storage while the other half was retrofitted and many servants of who the King had bought slept there. Scarlet wish she could wonder why the King hadn't placed her or Renee in the attic, but it was hard to. Though she grew up in a rather poor setting, she still had a brain within her head. Yes, the King claimed she would be his teacher, but he clearly kept her alive and separate from others for a reason. He may have saved her and "freed" her, but he was still a King and she a Blessed human. Anyone who had some part of a mind could figure out he hand plans for her and her powers, what those plans were was a true mystery.

~~~

Returning to the library, the two girls entered through the double doors together. As just an hour before, Scarlet found herself taken aback. The small wall worth of books in her sitting room was nothing more than a mere speck when compared to the King's library. The ceilings of the room could have easily been double that of her room and was filled top to bottom by bookcases all filled with books- some
~~~

even over flowing in some places. The book cases went up so far that there was a rather heart pounding maze of metal catwalks hanging throughout room, some of them even donning ladders. Throughout the main floor of the room were a few chairs, couches, a chess table here, a card table there; the library seemed to also serve as an entertainment area.

Scarlet could only assume that her lesson with the King, however it was to play out, would happen at one of the few tables set through the room. For a moment she thought mayhap she could choose- she would love to sit by the large fireplace but at the same time she wished to settle by the large windows that over looked the grounds. She stopped herself at that, scolding herself for allowing her mind to get the best of her. He was the King; of course he would sit where he pleased.

"Did you ever think you'd see so many books in one place in your life?" Scarlet, who had found herself staring at the ceiling as she got lost in her thoughts, turned back to her friend and shook her head.

'No, and to think we can read them!'

"Yeah... it's crazy." Renee moved over to the nearest bookcase, and begun to move through the titles, making out loud mental notes about each one. They had arrived early, and the King still not having arrived, she saw no reason why she should have to be bored until he did. Scarlet, on the other hand, went over to the chess table. Bending down, she examined it but dared not touch any of the pieces. She had seen and heard about the game of chess, but it was something one who had both brains and funds did to pass time. Scarlet never considered herself to be much smarter than the average creature, and never had the funds to take time to learn the game and buy a set of her own. In fact as she leaned over it, taking in each detail of each piece, she realized this was the first time she had the chance to be so close to one in real life.

It looked confusing, how was one to understand each piece? Clearly they must have all have had their own function but how did that portray into the use of the squares on the board- why would one need the board at all? Scarlet found herself with questions she would have never imaged she would ever have- but the one that haunted her the most was why she was questioning the board. She had never shown such an interest in books or chess before arriving in Voirol, so why was she having them now? Were these the thoughts the privileged had daily? She hadn't realized that without aiding her mother and focusing all her thoughts into helping her that she was now left with nothing to really do. Other than miss her mother and slowly accept her new home, role and hope that whatever the King truly wanted with her would not be a fate so horrid she would rather wish for death.

As that last thought passed through her mind, she casted her eyes away from the board, rising back up as she did. Moving away from the chess table, she found herself wondering over to the window. Resting her hands on the side panels of one, she closed her eyes as the sun basked over her in a warming glow. She wished to forget about her powers, and where she was at, even if only for a few moments.

She didn't hear the door to the library open, but at the sound of a throat being cleared and a book falling to the ground just mere seconds after it, she opened her eyes and turned around. Seeing that the King stood in front of the closing library door, she bowed to him first before walking over to him. Glancing over to Renee, Scarlet caught her as she rose from picking up the book she had dropped. Clearly the King had startled her, and the slight pale pink coloring her cheeks confirmed that she was embarrassed by it.

"Good afternoon Scarlet." Scarlet gave a single head nod to the King in a return greeting as she stopped a few feet front him. Without Renee next to her translate, it was futile for Scarlet to attempt anything but a wave or nod to the King for a greeting- and a wave was just not proper to greet anyone who sat in a status above one's own.

"Your Majesty." Renee stopped next to her friend, slightly out of breath as she bowed to him. Renee was not one who enjoyed surprises and did her best to avoid them. Scarlet knew that was something she would never admit to the King, no one but only those closest to

Renee knew secrets such as that. "Renee, I find the day so far has been fair for you?"

"It has, thank you." As she said that the King held out a hand towards one of the table. "Shall we sit before continuing?"

"As you wish, pray tell what table suits you." The King looked from Renee, to Scarlet, to her own surprise. "Being that Scarlet is the teacher, and I the mere student, I believe it would be best for her to choose." He waved his hand slightly towards her, before pulling it back. It was then Scarlet noticed the small folder resting in the nook of his left arm. Her heart pounded; there was no denying that, as she pointed her hand out towards the table near the window. As she did, she looked to both Renee and the King, looking for approval. Renee's face remained blank, but the King gave her a small smirk. "The table by the window it is." He led them, both girls falling two steps behind him. They also allowed him to choose his seat first, leaving Scarlet and Renee to choose the two seats across from him. As they scooted into the table, he opened his folder, pulling out a small pile of papers followed by a pen and ink container.

"I was told you two were exploring my home today; please tell me how it went." Scarlet, who had since casted her eyes down as she waited for the King to take, felt her face being to flush as her eyes grew wide. "It was lovely, sire, Scarlet is still learning the layout of the home so I thought I might give the courtesy of showing some of the rooms. And explaining the home to her."

"So all went well?"

"Very much so, sire."

"That is always good to hear; now before we begin out first lesson I must speak to you both on other matters first." Both girls remained silent, though Scarlet's heart was still pounding. The King, taking their silence as a motion to go on, did, "What I'm going to say will be blunt but there is no other way to say it. I will not repeat knowledge that we all know. Scarlet, I killed you." Scarlet wasn't startled by this news, just slightly confused. What did he mean he killed her?

Seeing the confusion on both of their faces, the King pulled out a newspaper from his folder, and slid it across the table to the two girls. Leaning over the table, both watched the paper get closer to them. The paper was already open and folded to a page that was random for them, but the main article of the page told them that it was indeed not a random page.

Blessed Human Dies Hours After Purchase To His Highness, King Cainwen Dufur.

It was late afternoon yesterday, during this week passed Slave Trade. It had started out as any other Trade, with the exception that the crowds below the stage the near spilled out beyond the street. Word had caught wind that this week's Trade would be a once in a life time event. The Trade claimed to have a Bless human, the rumor was so strong that it even brought out his highness King Cainwen Dufur. The human they claimed was Blessed was fifth in the first line up for trade, I myself was there in the fourth row in the hopes to catch a viewing of the Blessed. First glance the young woman resembled a baby mouse, small, timid and not one bit wimble- yet quite daunting eyes, some might claim beauty. The Handlers on the stage went through a small fit to get her to display her power, being the creature frozen; it was only as her life was nearly ended by a sword that her powers finally emerged. Around me, the murmurs that claimed lies and hoax were silenced as the creature lifted both the Handler and his sword into the air without a single touch to them. Then the murmurs of shock, fear and even admiration quietly filled the air, like a light wispy fog in the morn. Freeing the Handler, he fell to the stage as his sword went flying into the crowd- right towards me. Creatures, including myself, scattered about in an attempt to avoid getting hit by the deadly weapon. Fate was kind, and no lives were lost as the sword found itself to the dry, packed dirt ground with a small cloud. The bidding started after that, but soon ended. When his Royal Highness King Cainwen Dufur called out 'one million gold', the Blessed human was his- as was the girl after him. Both were terribly beaten up, the Blessed human more so then the other and both were whisked away. Both were barely free of their chains. The town of Scow woke up after that, and soon it seemed that all of Voirol knew about the Blessed human- whose only known name is to be Scarlett. Sadly, I am the one who was informed in the early hours of this morn just mere moments before the press was set to print this paper by a very trusted informative, that the Blessed human Scarlett died last night. Her wounds were too great and help came too late, so she succumbed to them in the late hours of the night. I have also been informed by my informative that the Blessed human Scarlett was given a very private Burning and her ashes buried. It is always a sad event when a young person passes on, but the wound seems to hurt even more so when the young person has a gift so amazing as to be Blessed, only to be lost to the world. We shall never know what greatness Fate held for the Blessed human, nor do we know anything more of her than her name, Scarlett. Her story, along with being the first title of bear Blessed human in thousands of years, dies with her.

Scarlet looked up from the paper, to Renee. 'They spelt my name wrong.' Renee just nodded, a somber mood having washed over them. "I am sorry I had to do that, but there was no other choice Scarlet." Both girls looked back to the King, as he took the newspaper back. "You two are not aware of this, but the world is not as stable as we would prefer it to be. If anyone of the other rulers- what am I saying? The other rules of the other lands would have heard about Scarlet, if they didn't know about her already. History speaks of the past Blessed humans, and I'm sure you both know the stories- of the pain and havoc, the wars and families torn. I will not allow history to be repeated, so I had to kill you off. Scarlet, from this moment on, you're dead. Only the trusted creatures of this castle know of you and that's how it's going to be kept."

"So Scarlet's never going to be allowed to leave the castle? To keep her caged as if she was a prized pet?" Renee, somewhat shocked by the King's blunt statement, lost all sense of manners. The King, noting her distress, dismissed it. "No, that would be cruel. You both are free to go into Scow, but with the proper preparation and fake identification. Outside my home's boundary Scarlet is not Scarlet. She can't be. Now being we are on the subject of proper preparation, I have set it up for you both to train in the arts of self-defense and light combat with Claudia, the head trainer of my army. It will take place in the basement nearly daily, after we have completed our studies but before dinner. It is good for any creature to know at least the basics of saving one's life. Is it not?" The King, having been resting the newspaper in his lap, put it back into the folder and removed it from the table. "Yes, of course sire, but I have one question for you." He looked to Renee, his risen eyebrows telling her to go on. "You said that you wish to not repeat history, is that correct?"

"Yes it is."

"Then why are you preparing us for a war?"

CHAPTER 7

Renee was bold. Not just for a human, not just for a human speaking to a four thousand year old vampire, but for a human speaking to a thousand year old, royal vampire. For that, Cain had respect for her boldness. Most would never even think to be so daring to him, yet, Renee barely blinked an eye.

He knew it wasn't the right time yet, they were not to know of the tension between Voirol and Drale that was near to breaking their bond. Should they find out the truth, then all hope would be lost. Scarlet was as delicate as a jasmine flower and thus needed to be treated as such. Perhaps her best friend did not see it as clearly, for she spoke boldly with little fear to show. But he was still the King and she a mere human.

"I find myself somewhat enlightened by the thought that should there ever be a war, you believe me to be one to send two helpless humans out into it. No, Renee, I am not preparing you for war but rather life. You serve under my laws, your daily work is commanded by me, and you live in my home. I am without a fault one of the highest power heads in our known world; just living in my country automatically puts one at risk for the loss of life. I prefer that all those who live under my name to know at least some sort of basic self-defense, even my mill farmers to the Far East, who know nothing other than caring for the land and themselves, are knowledgeable in this life saving skill." He realized at that moment the harsh tone his voice carried, and the two very different looks on each girl. Scarlet's pale skin had gone just a shade lighter as her cheeks flared with colors, while Renee's face was deadly neutral, giving away no clues. With a small sigh his eyes casted down before returning to their faces. "I understand, with your background coming from Tobus, why you would see my actions as hostile." His tone was much smoother, and should it work as it almost always did then the two girls would soon sense a soothing calming affect claim them.

"I understand the power of status and how that destined your fate, and because that was so you were treated as such. You see fights-self-defense or otherwise- as something for only one who wishes to spill the blood of many." Of course, without one of the three speaking, they all knew this to be true for most soldiers. "It's a horrible way of thinking and reflects poorly on not just Lord Rolle but all of the men of his family prior to him. A good citizen is a well-rounded citizen, and the same goes for a leader- which is one of the reasons why we are here today. Now, are there any more questions?" Cain watched Renee lean back slightly in her chair, unofficially stepping down from the battle. Beside her, and from the corner of his eye Cain saw, Scarlet roll her lips once as the color that had slowly returned to her face left it once more. When she nodded her head, he looked at her with a risen eyebrow. Taking a small inhale, she looked to her friend, before looking at Cain. Her hands begun to fly around in the air, so quickly that they stopped moving only mere seconds after starting and fell back into her lap.

"She ask for a bell and a notebook." Cain found his head tipping slightly, he could understand the meaning for the notebook- but why the bell? Keeping his eyes on her, he addressed her rather than Renee. "Why do you need a bell?"

Seeing that Cain had spoken to her rather than her friend sparked something in her eyes. Cain couldn't name what it was quite yet, he didn't know her well enough yet to understand the language of her eyes, something told him it was a feeling that was rarely ever shown. She brought her hands back up, moving them slower than the first, and though he didn't understand one thing spoken through her hands her eyes never left his.

"The bell would be for when she is alone in her room or bathroom. It would be a signal to outsiders on whether or not they will be allowed to enter into her bedroom. It would make communication easier, sire." Cain fought a smirk that dared- sought to, fought to surface. Renee had found her manners once more, for her voice spoke with the sticky texture of honey.

When Cain had first met Renee, he fell under the impression that she was simple girl with a simple mind that would not be hard to mold. It was only just now, a few days later that the truth was slowly seeping through to him. Renee was a predator. With that thought blistering his brain, he wondered how far she would go, to what extent could he push this human? Despite her lowly upbringing, she would make a great ally, but also a deadly enemy. He was glad to have her as the former rather than the latter.

"I shall see to this, and you shall have a hand bell delivered to your room this by afternoon. Are there any more questions, or request, before we start the lesson?" When he got nothing from either girl, he clasped his hands together, "Very well, allow us to begin."

~~~

"I have never been a teacher before, my lord... but I shall do my best to teach you... My language, though it looks complicated... is not as evil as it looks at first glance... Many of the words Renee is saying... I do not even speak...There is just not a need." Both Scarlet and Renee spoke in a slow pace- Scarlet's hands tried to take care to make each
~~~

word obvious for Cain while Renee processed what she was saying into words. Cain watched them both, his eyes sliding from Scarlet to Renee every few seconds in a sense of checking. "I would first like to teach you the alphabet... because if you know how to spell words, though it is harder than the actual signs... then you can speak my language." Picking up his stylus, Cain dipped it into the ink and begun to take notes. He intended to learn this language and when old age was to succumb him in an eon or so and should his memory fail, he would be able to look back on these notes, and remember.

The letters started off easy enough, 'A' was the four fingers folded over the palm while the thumb rested to the side, 'B' had the four fingers risen straight while the thumb rested on the palm. It was around 'Q' where he found himself beginning to lose his sense. The lettering became not only more elaborate but much more difficult to sketch out. He suddenly felt like he was a young child once again, sitting in the same library only he once sat at the tables learning from a tutor rather than a small woman. He could fondly remember then, to his school year struggles and how he would sit for hours hunched over his work. He wanted to be prefect, to be the best, to be nothing less than what was expected of him.

~~~

"No, you crossed your pointer and middle finger, and rest your thumb on your ring finger not your palm. If you just put your two
~~~

fingers next to each other while resting your thumb on your ring finger you're actually signing U rather than R." As Renee translated, Cain watched Scarlet with careful eyes. He had since moved on from his notes to actually trying out the letters and while he sought no issues with creating the letters- remembering which letter was which was what truly causing him ill will towards the language. He was in the middle of attempting to sign R once more, when a solid knock sent the library doors swinging open. Being pushed from behind, a rather large food cart entered into the room, stopping a few feet in. Stepping out from behind the cart, a petite silver haired woman dressed in white bowed to Cain.

"Good after my lord, I come with lunch." Rising back up, Ariana gave a small smile. "To start you off there is a morning-picked leafy green salad with the dressing on the side, the main course is an arrange of light tea sandwiches on fresh bread and to finish off- the drink of your choice." She stood, despite her small human frame, tall with her head proud. She took the deepest pride in even the most simple of meals or drinks. Not that she had no reason not to. Her family had been serving under Cain for nearly a millennium as their chefs and were one of the very few, extremely trusted humans serving under him. They had proven themselves and earned the trust and title bestowed upon them. "Shall I serve it to you now or do you wish to wait?"

"Thank you Ariana, I think that choice is up to the teacher- Scarlet?" Cain looked to Scarlet and her eyes grew wide once more- something he was starting to realize she did without full thought. He could see the question in her eyes, and the nerves as she glanced over to Renee. Closing her hand in a fashion that set her fingers over her thumb, looking like she was attempting a poor shadow puppet, she brought that to mouth. With a nod, Renee turned her gaze from her friend back to Cain. "A break would be good, let us enjoy lunch." Cain had to wonder how Renee was able to get a full sentence from just one simple motion, but then he remembered one of the first things Scarlet had taught him- her sign language was blunt, and thus Renee had to interpret the Morse code like language into their complex words.

As Cain focused on his inward thoughts, Ariana set forth quickly, uncovering all her food and making a plate for each of the three at the table. While the old chief needed not to ask the King what he preferred, she did not know what to get the two girls. That was when Cain learned that while Scarlet loved a nice slice of ham, Renee refused to eat any meat that wasn't white and so she had turkey. As she made up the plate for Renee, Scarlet tapped her friend's shoulder to get her attention. Her hands fluttered around, and the one thing Cain was able to understand was when Scarlet pointed to Ariana. Renee nodded her head once more, and looked away from her friend. "Excuse me, um...Chef?" Ariana turned at the sound of her title, her wrinkled face folding as she smiled. "Oh do forgive me, I am Ariana. I'm sorry for not introducing myself sooner. I should have when you were both in the kitchen this morning but one of my under chefs nearly burned my bread, and, and I'm getting off topic. I'm sorry."

"It's okay, I'm Renee." Renee and Scarlet both smiled at the chief as she placed Renee's plate on the table. "Thank you, I was just, well Scarlet here wondering if you were perhaps the chief who made our previous meals?" Ariana gave a small smile at the mention of her art and lifted her chest just slightly. "I am- I'm both the head chief to the kitchen and the personal chef to our good King. Have been since the day I turned 17, and I'll be going on 40 years next year"

"Wow, well, Scarlet wanted to thank you, and that your food is wonderful. It's some of the best she's ever had and I have to agree with her." Ariana's chest fell slightly, as a wave of humility rushed over her at the kind words of the two girls. "Thank you for that, you are both mighty welcome." Ariana then went back to putting Scarlet's plate together, putting just a bit more care as she did. Once everyone was served, drinks and all, Ariana gave another bow and left the room; the small group starting to eat their meal.

The room was silent for a few minutes, the sound of chewing and silverware hitting the plates being the only sounds echoing in the air. The two humans were tense, Cain could tell. They attempted to give the appearance that they were relaxed, but he could tell. It was something that neither empowered him nor offended him. While some beings fed off of others fearing them, and others sought anger that they might be seen higher, he did neither. He had found in over the past four thousand and five hundred years- give or take a few decades- that beings would never be fully relaxed around him. He was a vampire, he was a king, and he had wisdom. The three, when put together in a cocktail, demanded that one never fully put their guard down. But he wanted them to at least trust with him enough to not look as if someone had pulled their muscle to their capacity.

"I am curious," As Cain sat his glass down, the two girls looked to him, "being I myself never spent more than a week there, what was it like to live in Tobus. What was the daily life of an average citizen like?" he took a bite of his sandwich, leaning back in his chair. It was an honest question. It was easy for him to travel, and when doing so to not just receive the best of the best but be kept from the worst of the worst. In doing so, he was accepting that he was somewhat deceived into- or they tried to get one to- believe that indeed the land was great in beauty, well-behaved citizens and prosper. Cain never understood how one would be willing to allow themselves to be so blinded- unless they were extremely lacking any brain.

"I... I don't speak for Scarlet when I say this, but I liked my old life. It was plain and simple, and I know many people outside of Tobus view that as boring; I can't. I rarely saw my father, who is a miner; his work forced him to leave my mother, myself and my three younger siblings for most of the year. I missed him and what he made might not have given us much but it gave us enough. We weren't out on the streets, living in alleyways with nothing to eat. My family was, and is, getting by- which is the goal in life." Cain nodded his head, once more impressed with Renee. "What about you Scarlet, do you agree with Renee?" Scarlet looked from Cain, to Renee and then back to Cain slowly nodding her head as she did. Cain dropped his eyes down as he played with the corner of his napkin for a second before looking back up. There was something about Renee's answer that did not settle right with him. Her voice was much too monotone at the answer, and despite only knowing her for a week and half's time, he knew her voice to never be that flat.

"Hm, interesting, I cannot say I agree with you both. I do not believe that the goal of life is to just 'get by'. One should seek out a goal, and with that goal in mind work hard to get to it. Life is meant to be enjoyed; it should be a tangy mixture of hard work and pleasure. To just make it enough to get by is not just wasting away life but slapping it in the face. Do neither of you face anger towards your High Lord? Surly you both know that the coal that comes from Tobus fuels areas throughout the whole world- and the jewels are some of the finest and most sought after. How do you hold no anger, even now?"

"My lord," Renee's voice held an edge to it that encouraged Cain to sit up, "should the words you just be spoken have come from my mouth when I lived under the High Lord Rolle I would be viewed as an enemy of the Court. I would be arrested, put in jail and then on trial where I would most likely be found guilty. Surly you know that any enemy of the Courts of Tobus, once found guilty of their crimes, is put to death. So no, it is not hard to reset the harbor of hate against the selfish pompous rulers when even the thought of it could get you killed." Cain grabbed his wine glass, swirling the red liquid as he brought it closer to his lips. "Then aren't you glad you're not in Tobus?" Renee's jaw set before she took a slightly forceful bite of salad. He had gotten under her shell, and seen a real piece of her. "I must agree with your real thoughts, though. The Court of Tobus is set up like a triangle and it's a sobering thought to see so many so poorly off. I could never be one to allow my people to suffer so, but, as a wise man once told me, not every ruler shall be a great one-" Cain cut himself off midsentence as he watched Scarlet's hands fly around in a furry- the slight flush of her face giving off her emotion. Instead of relaying her message, Renee gasped and soon her own hands were signing. Cain could only guess a few words here and there, but whatever it was the two were clearly upset with each other. "May I ask what you two are discussing?" The two girls froze at the sound of his voice, and both turn to look at him; dropping their hands to their laps as they did. Neither spoke, but when Scarlet elbowed her Renee glared at her, before letting out a sigh.

"Scarlet wishes to know why, because you claim to be such a loving ruler, you would be willing to kill a teenage girl just because she misplaced two slaves."

"Though it is not a law put in place by myself, it is law that if a direct order by the ruling hand is disobeyed that the offender or offenders be put to death- as payment for breaking the law and for dishonoring themselves. The woman who put you in the cells rather than have you taken to Dr. Cartson was already on a watch from prior events and being you nearly died from your injuries, I believe death to have been the right punishment even without the law. Now, I know in your eyes I am most likely a monster- a murder of an innocent human. That is part of your hypocritical brain-washing education from Tobus. Don't kill, love all, be good but if you even think an ill thought against us we'll see to your death through a rigged trial. I, unlike the ruler of Tobus, live to my teachings and laws of my land. The law of the land is, if you outwardly disobey the ruling hand, then you are to be put to death; so how could I allow her to live? In doing so would make me a hypocrite to my own law and untrustworthy in the eyes of my people. I do what is best for everyone. I always have and I always will." Throughout his whole speech, the flush in Scarlet's cheeks died away as his calm voice spoke only reasons of truth. Tobus, as many countries and lands, was a deeply unbalanced kingdom. In a somewhat retrospect of the moment, Cain should have realized that, even with their most recent agreements, should war strike and should Tobus choice to join- it would not be on his favor. Voirol and Tobus were neither allies nor enemies, but when the time came for battles he doubted they would chose to come together.

~~~

"Vern, have my car readied. I want to leave in ten- and please tell me someone has made it to the market to get that bell. It's almost three." Vern nodded once at Cain, before leaving Klaus's office. Cain, having just entered the office was greeted by the back of his cousin's strawberry blond hair. Hunched over at one of his book cases, he pulled a book out before standing. "Hello cousin, where are you off to? Tell me, how was your first lesson?" Klaus made a motion for Cain to take a seat by the window, to which he did. Taking the seat opposite of him, Klaus rested his book on the arm of the chair.

"If you must know my every where about, I'm going to make a quick trip over to Theo's. She sent me a message while I was in my lesson."

"And how was that lesson?"

"It was fascinating. It looks complicated, and in Scarlet's words 'blunt' but it's so simple it's almost hard to comprehend. I took notes, and I plan to keep taking them because this language requires real
~~~

work." At that Klaus let out a hearty laugh, tipping his head back from Cain. "Oh my- may the world forbid that the great and powerful King Cainwen actually have to put work in learning something!" Cain waited for his cousin to finish his laughing fit, his face showing no emotion minus a raised eyebrow. "Okay-okay, I'm done."

"Are you sure?"

"Yes."

"Good, I was afraid I would have to kill you before getting you opinion." At the last half of Cain's small statement, Klaus tipped his head. "Opinion, on what matter my dear cousin?"

"I'm not quite sure; I question why Theo summons me. She is not one to just-" Cain stopped talking at the request of Klaus's risen palm. "Dear cousin, Theo is absolutely one to invite you to her shop for tea. Now if it was coming from Pals, yes I would question it. Perhaps our friend just misses you?"

Cain scratched his chin, glancing out of the window as he spoke, "Do you think it has to do with Scarlet?" The smile on Klaus's face dropped. It had been over a week since the paper with the fake story had been released to the public, which led Klaus to bring up a very valid point, "If it did, why would she wait over a week from the public release of Scarlet's death to invite over to talk about it?" Cain shook his head at his cousin.

"I don't know, that is why I came to see you first. Knowing Theo, she doesn't do anything in life without reason. She probably doesn't believe the story- hell I wouldn't be surprised if she smelt the lie from five miles."

"So if that is the case, what will you do?"

"I don't know, I could continue to lie to her and deny that Scarlet lives, or I could confess the truth to her." Klaus leaned his elbows on his knees, bringing himself to Cain as he fell back in his chair. "The question, the real question dear cousin, is not what you should do, but whether you trust her enough-." Klaus was cut off by Cain's absent mindlessly out-loud thinking, "We've known the Deaeque sisters for over two hundred years..."

"What do you think Theo would do with Scarlet? What would she want with her?"

"To poke and prod her like a test subject, try to study her like one her microorganisms she looks at under a microscope. She'd want to try to understand her, why is she- what inside her makes her different, what makes her Blessed?"

"I could see Theo saying those things, but Cain; she's a scientist- one of our best. She questions everything in the world and seeks to answer every question."

"Are you telling me that I should trust Theo and Pals?"

"Why mention Pals?" Cain looked at Klaus, waiting for him to answer his own question. The two sisters were closer than Cain was with his own wife, so until sworn to secrecy- which they both would be- it would only be assumed that Theo would tell Pals. "Wait, never mind. Forget I asked. But to answer your question, no, I'm not telling to do or do not trust them. You said it; we've known them for over two hundred years, you trust them... but do you trust them enough to have the truth?"

CHAPTER 8

Pulling off to the side of the street, Cain set his car to park before turning it off. The steam powered engine hissed and whistled as it begun to cool off, and as he climbed out of his car; Cain examined the surrounding area. The street was somewhat busy with afternoon bustle, but none of the beings walking around paid him any attention. Not that he minded. Closing and locking the door to his car, Cain slipped the key into his pants pocket as he strolled up the sidewalk. Stopping in front of a plain brown and frosted glass panel door, he gave it two knocks before a buzz told him it was unlocked. Stepping inside, Cain's eyes went straight up, ignoring the small living space in front of him. He scanned what he could of the open second floor, but saw nothing from where he stood. "Theo, you up there?" He closed the door, and started towards the spiraling metal staircase. "I'm up here." Theo's modulated voice rang out and slightly echoed against the vaulted ceilings. Stepping onto the lab floor, Cain searched among the cluttered tables until he spotted the top of unnaturally vibrate red hair. Theodora stood at the end of a rather long table that was covered in a number of glass tubes, beakers, flask and burners. In one gloved hand she held a long glass stirring, placing that into the flask in her other, the sound of glass hitting glass filled the air. "Don't move a muscle." As she stressed out each word to Cain, she pulled the stirring out and replaced it with a thermometer. Once she got the proper temperature, she pulled the thermometer out and rushed over to another table. Tipping the flask over, the slightly blue liquid spilled out into a funnel and was filtered into a small test tube. "I'm almost finished." Knowing better than to disrupt her current work in progress, Cain remained where he had stopped at the end of the stairs. Leaning a hand on the railing, he studied the werewolf at work.

Setting the empty flask down, She used a set of forceps to pick up a single grain from a petri dish and then proceeded to drop it into the test tube. As the grain and liquid mix a small wisp of smoke begins to rise into the air. At the sight, Theo slightly frowned but it was from concentration rather than disappointment. Grabbing the tube with a small metal holder, Theo then rushes off to a third table where a small sphere sat in a stand. Tipping the test tube, the now green liquid emptied into the sphere. Grabbing two small metal rods, Theo placed them into the sphere and closed the opening. With a small stratifying click, Theo pulled the rods out, rose back up and smiled.

Pulling her goggles up to her forehead with one hand, Theo grabbed the sphere with the other. "Catch." She threw the orange-size sphere at Cain and, after he released the rail, he caught it with ease.

Once he had it in his hand, he held it up and examined it. On the outside it was a patchwork of metal and weighed no more than a pound. Bouncing it up into the air a few times, he then looked to Theo as he took a few steps towards her, "What is it?" She was turning down a flame burner, a small smile forming on her plum painted lips. "A prototype." Cain looked down at the sphere once more, as his eye brows came down, "A prototype of what?" Looking back up, he was taken back at the gas mask in her hand. "You'll see." Placing the mask over her face, Cain had intended to ask more questions but was taken back at the sound of a sudden chime before being overwhelmed by a dense grey smoke. The smoke was thick, throat choking and filled the air with one of the foulest smells Cain had ever encountered. Falling to his knees, Cain can only focus on coughing as his senses were overwhelmed. He wasn't sure how much time passed, it may have only been a few moments yet it felt like hours. The thick cloud filled his lungs and clouded his mind- slowly shutting it down. He fought the overwhelming urge to pass out.

The sphere, still in his hand, was then ripped from it and slowly the air around him begun to clear. He sucked at the clearing air, his lungs desperate for real air. As his lungs took in the clear air, the urge to go to sleep begun to pass and he found himself slowly working his eyes to open. Blinking hard, his vision was blurred around the edges but he was not yet blind. As his eyes scanned around from where he had fallen, he noticed the glass panels to the far wall had been open, allowing the smoke to leave the lab and the fresh air to come in; above him the ceiling shook slightly as they worked at full power to help clear the air. A foot away from him, Theo stood with the sphere in her hand and she slowly removed the mask from her face. Placing the mask on the table nearest to her, she then held a hand out to Cain. He took it and she pulled him up with ease, patting him on the back once as he regained the ability to take a full normal breath. "What-what is that?" Theo smiled at Cain as he pointed to the sphere in her hand. Holding it up in a fingerless gloved hand, she tossed it once. "While it is a prototype, I like to consider it at pay back."

"But what is it?"

"A smoke bomb- but not just a normal smoke bomb, this one is modified. I found a chemical formula that I believed would affect not just humans, witches, and werewolves but also vampires. It was am extremely difficult task with your biological structure differing as greatly as it does from all other beings but it wasn't impossible! I just needed to test it, which is why I had you come over. Now that I know the formula to be a success, I plan to adapt it to be able to be used in the field- I'm talking five, ten, maybe even fifteen miles radius."

She tossed it up once more, a proud smile gracing her lips. "It will knock humans, and witches out cold while driving werewolves and vampires to near death-like states."

Though he wanted to be upset with his friend, Cain was deeply impressed and was reminded once more why he had befriended the werewolf Theodora Deaeque. "I could have you killed Theo, on acts of treason. Is that why you brought me here, in an attempt to kill?" Theo gave him weary eyes as she placed the smoke bomb beside her gas mask. He crossed his arms in an attempt to make it appear that he was serious with her. "But you won't and no- yes- slightly. Clearly not, had I chosen to kill you I would have done so many years ago, I merely needed to test the bomb and you happened to be here. I brought you here though, for tea. We haven't spoken in a few weeks and I'm curious to know how the royal family fairs." She made a motion for him to go down stairs, which he did with her on his heels.

Theo motioned to the small living area of the open floor, and Cain went over to take a seat. As he did, she went over into the small kitchen, hanging her goggles on a wall hook. As she set to work getting the tea prepared, she glanced over to Cain. "So, how have things been lately, any news with Drale?" As one of his top scientist, Cain had kept Theo within his small loop on the subject for nearly the past five months. Such things as her wide-range smoke bomb would be crucial to have in war times but were not made over night. "I cannot be sure, but it is looking as if Muis is moving towards war." With a somber hum, Theo nodded her head and pulled the screaming kettle from the flame on the stove. "I'll have to get working on increasing the radius of Little Grey won't I?" At the somewhat confused face of Cain, she goes on, "It's what I'm calling my new smoke bomb. I was stuck between Little Grey and Little Buddy; Little Grey ended up winning." Cain nodded his head, and watched as Theo carried over a small tea tray. "But I know you didn't ask me over here to speak about the Drale matter, now did you Theo?"

Sitting down the tray on the coffee table, she looked up with slightly glowing golden eyes, and took a seat across from Cain. Looking back down at the table, where Cain had reached out to, she watched him pick up the newspaper that had been lying on the table. Despite being a werewolf, a cat like smile curled on her lips as Cain held the paper in his hands and read the headline out loud. "Blessed Human Dies Hours After Purchase To His Highness, King Cainwen Dufur... Tell me Theo, did you ever believe the papers?"

"I wish," Theo poured a cup of tea for herself before pouring the wonderful red life Cain depended on from a separate bottle, "that I could say that I did, but I know you all too well sire. Muis, as you just informed me, seems to be moving towards war, and you are not one to give up on any being so easily." She took a sip of her tea, "I'm just curious to know if you were going to tell me or attempt to wash this horrid lie over me. That was why I hit you will Little Grey today- I don't like being lied to and I hate being fed a bad one at that- I mean, at least put some effort into it! Honestly- who came up with this cover?" Cain laughed, unable to do anything else. "I am now ashamed to admit that I did."

"Could you not at least come up with something more than just succumbing to wounds as a cause for death? You could have come to me." Her glowing eyes flickered with a small ping of pain. Inwardly, Cain sighed to himself. The flash had lasted no more than a half a second, but it had been there. "In the moment of the time, you did not enter my mind, I will not lie. I acted as a King first and that was to get her killed. Muis already wants me dead; I don't need to tempt any other rulers."

"As I can understand, do you plan to share the truth with Pals?" Cain lifted an eyebrow at Theo, and took another sip from his cup. "Are you telling me that I was unable to fool you yet I could fool your twin sister?"

"Oh no, the brain of my sister is almost nearly as bright as my own, I was just curious to know the time line."

"I believe I may see her sometime this week, she is due to return from her vacation from the seaside in two days- is she not? I am sure Claudia will be anxious to talk to her. She got her trainers together today for their first meeting and Pals was the only one who wasn't there."

"I'm sure Pals will be just as anxious once she gets the update and it's three days, her airship gets in, in the early morning..." Theo took a small sip of her tea and the room settled into a silence that begged to be broken. Suddenly Theo shot up slightly in her seat, unable to contain herself anymore. "So when can I meet her?" The sparkle in Theo's glowing eyes returned once more as she changed the subject back to Scarlet. "At the soonest... I would say a few months' time."

"A few months' time?! Honestly now sire, you cannot expect me to wait that long-" Cain cut her off, "I do. I know you Theo, and you wish to study her like one of your microscope slides." Theo frowned, and took another sip of tea. Cain sat back, and took a sip from his own cup, quietly waiting for her to retaliate.

"I wasn't going to do much." Ah, there it was, "Just a few tubes of blood, a hair strand with a follicle and maybe a few skin flakes- just to compare. She would have only been here a few hours tops..." Glancing up from her cup with a loose innocent head shake, Theo said nothing more. Cain watched her. He knew there would be no way for him to just talk her out of studying Scarlet. He needed to do more, to draw her in and give her a reason, one she could not fight nor would she want to fight, to not study Scarlet. Perhaps a sooner meeting was meant to take place. He could not talk her out of her strong will but Scarlet might be able to charm her out of them. "Would you care to come to dinner tonight? I could have Ariana make your favorite meal." Theo studied Cain, and he waited. "I would love to, but you must know you're not going to talk me out of my study."

"I'm not going to try to."

~~~

"No." Dolra looked at Cain, spinning around to face him from where she sat in their shared sitting room and watched him enter into his bedroom. She stood, and angrily followed after him. "Cain!" Turning mid step, Cain faced Dolra. If her face could emit color, Cain was under the impression it would be redder than Theo's false hair. "What my dear?"

"You know what! You invited Theodora to dinner without even considering my opinion-" With a groan, Cain found himself rolling his eyes as he once did when he was a young vampire, "You like Theo- I did not think you would mind!" Cain turned and started back towards his closet to change. Behind him Dolra frowned and let out a scoff, "My personal preference on her is not the subject- the fact that you once again made a decision without my, your wife's, opinion! We're supposed to be a team Cain- a team!" Cain turned, holding a grey jacket in his hands, and looked at his wife with the most serious
~~~

of faces, "Dolra- it's a dinner, not a meeting to declare war!" Cain slammed the jacket back onto the rack, angrily searching through the rest. "I'm sure even if it was I wouldn't find out about it until the damn gunshots filled the air!"

"What is wrong with you?"

"Me? What's wrong with me? What's wrong with you?! You told me right before you went to Tobus that once you settled matters with the High Lord; we would see each other more, yet I've seen less of you! Then the only time I do see you is either when you come to tell me some official news or to say goodnight. But you had more than enough time to go and buy those two little pets of yours, but not enough to join me for dinner thus leaving me with them, but you can go to Theodora's and invite her to dinner and show up for her...Cain it's..." With a small exhale, his wife closed the space between herself and Cain, reaching for him as she did. "It's not just about all that... I miss you, you haven't come to me for weeks and I miss you... your presence... the feelings I get from your touch." She ran her fingers across his shoulder, trailing them along the back side of his neck before moving them back down. Sighing, Cain ran a hand through his hair before looking to his wife.

"I'm sorry, you're right. You're my wife, we're a team and I haven't been taking your opinion into consideration these past few days,"

The look Dolra gave Cain had him changing his response, "weeks, weeks, and I'm sorry."

"So you'll come to me tonight?" Cain pulled his wife closer as she asked this and planted a light kiss on her forehead "Yes." She closed her eyes, and gave him a small smile as he held her. "Now may I be allowed to get ready?" She opened her eyes, looking with a small slight look of disappointment before nodding her head. Giving him one final smile, she twirled from his arms and out of his closet.

CHAPTER 9

Tipping her head to the side, Scarlet would have let out a hum if her body would allow her. Looking at her refection in the small bathroom mirror, she felt a conflict within herself. One side, the side of her that screamed the loudest, told her to remove the strange, foreign clothes from her body- she was never meant to be a fighter; a second, that was loud but nowhere near the first, told her that this was what the King had order and she lived under the King's laws now- so she would learn to fight by his ruling; lastly, there was a third side, this one was much more quitter than its counter parts but it was the one scared her the most for this one liked the idea- the freedom of her new outfit, learning to fight and becoming something more.

One must chose to always remain calm, no matter what the situation calls for or how dire it may be. For staying calm one will gain both clarity in the mind and mouth- and with that comes inner peace thus creating outward peace. To harbor a fear leads the harboring of anger which thus leads hate and hate can only end in suffering. The High Lord and the Courts wish for the people of Tobus to live in the best, clear state of mind. That is why the following list is constructed clauses made up of things one must avoid at all cost- and the reason for it- and should one fail you might face severe consequences.

For some odd reason or not, the introduction to the Code of Mind and Conduct found itself playing within Scarlet's mind. Pulling her hair up and back into a bun, the raspy male voice of her sixth year teacher continued on within her mind; reading off each of the clauses on the list. Sticking a hair pin in, she stopped Mr. Nite's voice in a ponder to herself. She hadn't thought of school since she finished her final year- her tenth year- nearly two years; and she most defiantly hadn't thought of her sixth year teacher in easily two times that. Reaching for another hair pin, Mr. Nite's voice resumed its reading, and this time Scarlet did nothing to stop it.

Opening the door to the small bathroom she had been told to change in, Scarlet stepped out into the spacious training room and walked over to Renee. Renee, who had changed first, sat on small bench by a large rack of different sized blades that could only be assumed to be one for those of on lookers who wished to watch the practice. As she walked over, Renee eyed her once over before letting out a low whistle. "Wow Scar, I don't think I've ever seen you in such clothing. I've never seen you in pants before... You look... different."

Suddenly, Scarlet felt extremely self-conscious and found her arms wrapping around her stomach. Renee was right- the form fitting one piece with both leather breast plate and leg armor was like nothing Scarlet had ever worn. Not to even mention the fact that the one piece was that of a shirt and pants- the latter being a clothing Scarlet only rarely ever even looked at let alone wore. There is also the fact of how form fitting the clothing really was, while it allowed her more movement then she ever imaged her body being able to have, it layered her body like a second coat of skin. It was in the bathroom that she realized how thin she truly was, and how utterly disgusted she was with it. Her near protruding ribcage and narrow hips were nothing but a reminder of her hard childhood and her time spent in the Trade. Beauty was found within a flat tummy but rounding curves of a real woman's body- something Scarlet knew she would be forever haunted by the lack of.

'You look... nice.' Scarlet gave a small smile to her friend, while she envied her. Dressed near identical to Scarlet, minus the leather amour for a simple leather vest, Renee's outfit hugged the soft, near womanly curves of her body.

Envy, is one of the worst emotions. Mr. Nite's voice filled Scarlet's mind once more as she took a seat next to her friend. Envy skips over anger and leads straight to hate and suffering. It those who we are closest to, it has been shown, are the ones we are most envious of. While you are encouraged to befriend and love those fellows around you- you must be weary of how close one allows themselves to get to others. For should you get too close, these emotions are sure to bud and bloom.

"Thanks Scar." Renee returned her smile. Scarlet had to wonder, if Renee ever shared thoughts as her own. Did she blame Scarlet for what happened, or did she blame herself for ignoring the Code- but it was not just she who had, Scarlet was just as much to blame. They had both ignored the teachings of taught in their later school stages lives and chose to allow their sisterly love to bloom. As a result, they sat alone in the brightly lit training room; waiting to break even more of the Code that had been their livelihood for so many years.

~~~

The double doors to the room suddenly swung open with a startling bang. The first thing the two girls saw, and what forced the doors to open, was a rather large rolled up mat floating in the air. It was soon reviled that the mat was not floating, but being carried by a slightly petite, blonde bob headed woman. Walking over to a far, barren corner, the woman dropped the mat and with a swift kick it unrolled. Placing her hands on her hips as she over looked her handy time, she nodded once before turning. Spotting Scarlet and Renee, her hands
~~~

fell as she rushed over to them. Within a few seconds she was in front of them, looking them both over. Scarlet moved to stand, ready to properly introduce herself but the woman held a hand up stopping her. "No, don't... Let's see... you," she looked at Renee, "Must be Renee and you," she turned to Scarlet, "must be Scarlet. Yes? No? Yes?" Scarlet nodded her head and the woman smiled at her.

She had a dazzling smile, and the normal tell-tale signs of a vampire; pale skin, near white pale blue eyes and a beautiful body. The one thing that threw off her natural beauty, mostly her face, was an ugly slightly jagged, pinkish, scar that ran the length of mid forehead to the near tip of her jaw line; it even dared to go over her eye and eyebrow leaving the latter with a small bald spot. Standing, as she reached a hand out to Scarlet, Scarlet shook it and took a closer look at the vampire. "I'm Claudia, head trainer of the special elite forces- and whole army really." From the few cut outs on the front of her shirt Scarlet noticed a few more pink lines along Claudia's skin. The vampire must be covered head to toe in the battle trophies.

"As you guessed, I'm Renee and that is Scarlet." Releasing Renee's hand, Claudia looked back at Scarlet. Or looked up, she was one of the shortest vampires Scarlet had ever seen and was lucky to be push-ing 5'2 if Scarlet had to guess. "I was so excited and honored when my cousin asked me to train you- I've never worked with anyone so powerful before, there are so many possibilities to- wait, wait. I'm getting a head of myself. I'm sorry. Before I go jumping further into the water, I need to know what skills, what level, have you ever been trained in any form of fighting or self-defense?"

Scarlet quickly nodded her head no, but then begun to move her hands. Claudia watched her, an eyebrow rising slightly as she brought her fisted hand into her open palm. "We were discouraged to learn or parts take in any violent situation in Tobus, but there was one time when I... punched a boy in the face." Claudia shifted her eyes between Scarlet and Renee. "She said all that?"

"Yes."

"And you understood her?"

"Yes." Claudia ran her eyes over Scarlet as Renee replied and nodded. "I understand now why my cousin wishes to learn this language. It's incredible... Why did you punch the boy?" Claudia suddenly turned her attention back to Renee, whose face begun to be overcome with color. "I, um, well in fourth year some stupid boy from school... he, well, he called Scarlet.... He called her a weak bastard child... So I punched him in the face, gave him a bloody nose and broke a finger in the process." A smile light lit Claudia's eyes, as she folded her arms over her chest. "Understandable... understandable. Well, if you treat this training in the same way you do each other, moving beyond your pacifist beliefs won't be too hard. Just imagine that everything you're fighting insulted your best friend and you'll have no ill feelings towards the thought of fighting."

~~~

"You're like a gibbon- do you know what that is?" Scarlet looked from where she stood frozen, Claudia had just thrown a knife at her and had it been real it would have stabbed her straight through her pounding heart. Luckily for Scarlet, it was nothing more than hard rubber and paint. In a response to the question, Scarlet shook her head, gathering enough senses to bend down and pick up the fake knife. "Throw it at me. Aim to kill." Biting her lip, Scarlet weakly threw the knife. It barely made it to the other side of the mat where Claudia stood. She watched in silence as the knife bounced on the mat. "A gibbon is a native, white furred cousin of the apes creature from the jungles found in my homelands down south. Their bodies are long and angular; prefect for moving through their homes in the trees. They're the fastest moving tree-livers. Despite their wonderful, powerful forms; they're extremely gentle and sweet creatures. That is why you're a gibbon." Claudia walked over and picked up the knife. "But, when I get finished with you; you will be the slow, sweet looking but toxin seeping Loris. Just wait. Now, try again, only keep both eyes open and feel the swing from your back. Feel the aim in your shoulder blade and you'll never miss a mark no matter what type of
~~~

knife." Claudia tossed the knife at Scarlet, who fumbled but caught the rubber knife.

It had been decided early on by Claudia that Scarlet, with her thin frame, would focus less on hand-on-hand combat and more on distance. Scarlet did not have muscle or the strength to take on anyone up close; she had a better chance of taking down someone from afar-from both a good blade and her own powers. Renee, in the near same physical state as Scarlet, was about twenty feet away getting a training that neared Scarlet's but focused a bit more on swords rather than knifes. Scarlet paused, watching her friend as she begun to spur at her trainer with a wooden sword. While Claudia was offering support, her main concern was Scarlet and that left Renee with one of the officers Claudia had brought in; though she claimed that in a few days her 'right hand, partner in crime Pals' would have returned to the city from some trip she took. Claudia made it clear to them both that Pals would be their second Claudia in training.

"Okay, okay, that was better!" Claudia scooped up the rubber knife again. "But like I said before, feel it your shoulder, you know what?" Claudia skulked over to her, sliding behind her. "Take the knife," She held it out, and Scarlet took it, "Get into the stance." Scarlet stepped back on her right food, finding balance, she placed the knife in her dominate hand. "Now, bring your shoulder back, and your wrist up-remember the closer your target, the tighter you bring it back. If your target is long range- no wrist bending. Keep it straight and keep the blade from going too much." Scarlet adjusted her grip on the knife, and then felt Claudia's fingers over her own. "No, no, not so tight, little Gibbon. The knife needs to be an extension of your arm, it should slip from your hand like a wet pebble or as if it was coated in butter. Now take aim at the target, from where you stand it's a middle distance. So lift and twist your wrist just slightly, now, on my say" Claudia took two steps back, never taking her eyes off of Scarlet. "Now." Rolling her lips, and holding her breath, Scarlet brought the knife forward and closed her eyes when she felt the handle leave her hand. After a few seconds of no noise she slowly opened her eyes. Claudia had moved to the target, a small smile on her face. While the knife was far from the bulls-eye, the rubber knife just barely cleared the bottom the foam target hanging from the wall. "And it only took twenty seven tries little Gibbon! Again." With that, Claudia grabbed the rubber knife and holding it out brought it back to Scarlet.

By the time their practice had ended a few hours later, leaving on a relaxing yet still intense warm down, Scarlet was prepared for a warm shower, a relaxing dinner and then bed. But as she and Renee left the basement, Claudia and her officer staying behind in the training room, the two girls were greeted by Vern.

"Good evening miss Scarlet, miss Renee. Cain asked me to relay a verbal invite to you both; he asks that you both invite him and Queen

Dolra to dinner tonight." Scarlet looked to Renee. The King was supposed to be at dinner the night before, yet he never showed up. Was tonight to be a repeat? As if sensing the wariness, Vern gave them smile that could blind the sun, "There shall be a special guest who is looking forward to meeting you, miss Scarlet." Scarlet gave a small smile and a response. "Um, we'd be honored to join the King and his guest tonight. What time should we expect to be called on?"

"Dinner is at seven, in the main dining room and it can never hurt to be a few minutes early." Scarlet nodded, giving him a small smile. Their eyes met, and as they did, her morning argument came creeping back into her thoughts. A small blush crept onto her cheeks, and she found herself fumbling a goodbye before rushing away.

Vern's smile fell as he and Renee watched Scarlet rush away. He turned back to Renee, "Is- she okay?" Renee's wide green eyes looked up at him and she smiled. "Yeah, yeah, she's fine; just tired, the training Claudia started with us is; we're not use to it. We'll be fine, we'll adjust..." She nodded her head, unsure of what to say. Vern understood her jumbled up explanation and nodded in return. "Um, I'm going to go, I need to shower before dinner- will I see you there?"

"Oh, no, no. I have plans and it's not really a dinner I'd fit into." Renee bit the inside of her cheek and nodded her head. "Oh, really, okay, if I can ask, why wouldn't you fit in?"

"Despite my outward being, and centuries of servitude to his high-ness; stiff back chaired, seven course meals aren't my forte. Outside of work, I prefer a worn pair of pants, an oil stained shirt and my cycle."

"You drive a motorcycle?"

"I own them, buy them and fix them up and then resale; why do you ride?" Renee's face colored slightly at that. "Oh, no, I um, I've only ever looked at them. It was a luxury in Tobus that my family couldn't afford. I'm going to go now." Biting down harder on her inner cheek, Renee rushed down the hall in the same manner Scarlet had just moments before.

~~~

Safe behind the closed door of her sitting room, Scarlet could finally feel the flames in her cheeks dying away. Opening her eyes, they casted down to a notepad and a bell; waiting on her small coffee table. Gliding, she bent down and picked up the two items. Closing her eyes, she held the bell up and rung it. It wasn't the bell she grew up with, but it sounded just like it. For a few moments, as she enclosed herself into the darkness, she allowed herself to relish in the sweet memories the sound brought. Opening her eyes, the memories were gone almost at once and she was left with nothing but an ache in her chest. Taking another breath, with her newest items in her arms, she went into her bedroom.
~~~

Move along Scarlet. Forget about your life in Tobus. That life is dead.

Placing the items on her desk, Scarlet found her way to one of the chairs by her window. Taking another deep breath, she glanced over at the clock on her nightstand. It was five ten. She weighed her options, debating on whether to take a well-deserved nap or a well-deserved long pre-dinner bath. Standing, she pulled at the side strings of her leather breast plate. Stripping off her second skin, she walked into her bathroom. Turning the faucets on the tube, she plugged it once the water reached the perfect temperature. She mixed in her cocktail of bath items into the water, bath salts, jasmine oil and a round ball of fizzle soap, and climbed in once the tub was full. Sinking into the warm blanket, Scarlet's body relaxed. She could feel the sweat floating from her body, as the bubbly fizzles surrounded her.

Scarlet stayed in the bath until her fingers were swollen and wrinkly. Climbing out, she used to towels to wrap both her body and her hair. In a slight, wet-feet against cold floors, waddle she made her way to her closet. Scarlet begun to pop her lip, making a small and obnoxious noise, as she browsed her closet searching for the right outfit.

What to wear, what to wear? Keep it simple, she pulled out the corner of a beautiful and in her mind somewhat gaudy lime green gown, because most of this isn't you. Pants, beads, silk fabric, and whatever this is. She pulled out something that looked like a blanket, but wanted to be a shawl of some sort with a hole in the middle. It only confused Scarlet and she put it back. *This isn't me... none of this is me- of course it's not. Scarlet you idiot, of course it's not the old you but it's the new you. So, just accept it already. Why can't I accept it?* Biting her bottom lip, she finally settled on a peach gown that wasn't as gaudy as the lime green dress, but it wasn't something she would have worn in Tobus. But as she was coming to accept, she wasn't in Tobus anymore.

Adjusting the fabric of her dress where it bunched under her green belt, Scarlet made her way back to her bathroom. Removing the towel on her head, she picked up her brush and begun to move it through her hair. Brushing it all over to one side, she sat her brush down and begun to twist her hair into an easy but intricate looking braid. Tying off the end with a dark, small, ribbon; she then twisted it up into a bun and stuck in a few hair pins. Satisfied with her work, she took a step back, examining herself in the mirror. The thoughts of the perfect bodies Claudia and Queen Dolra entered her mind and even Renee's body- though not as perfect as that of a vampire it was still something more than what Scarlet had.

Renee slid into Scarlet's room at 6:45 right on the dot. Scarlet was sitting in the chair by the window, flipping through a book of nature photos. Renee strolled over to towards Scarlet, smelling fresh of a shower, her sleeveless, button up, collared blouse's tail blowing out behind her. "Ouh, Scar, I like you in that color. It gives your skin a... glow." Renee sat down across from her, slipping off her boots before folding her legs under herself and smiled. "Whatcha reading?" Scarlet smiled, holding up the book and showed the cover of the book to Renee. She read the cover and then nodded at her, in both approval and impression. "I think you should mark your place, cause dinner is in ten and when Vern said it wouldn't hurt to be early- he meant that we need to be early." Scarlet nodded, standing. Walking over to her desk, she ripped a piece of paper from her notebook and placed it into the pages of the book. As she did that, behind her, Renee unfolded her legs, placing her feet back into her boots. Standing, she strolled over to the door, waiting with her hand on the handle as Scarlet came over. Linking their arms together, the two left the room.

~~~

Just as the two came into the main entry way, a servant, dressed in a plain grey dress, opened the front door. A thick accented 'thank you' came floating through the door way, right before the owner of the voice. Scarlet's step faltered as she froze. The creature that stopped short of the door was like nothing Scarlet had ever seen. She stood tall, not just in the sense of her perfectly straighten back and heels, but that her height without the stiletto boots was easily 6'2; add in the heels and she stood 6'5 or 6'6 easily. She had copper skin, like that of wiring, and hair that was not the natural, washed out red, but
~~~

bright, artificial red that was twisted into dreadlocks. With her hair pulled back into a simple pony tail, it made her facial features seem even sharper. The one item that stood out the most to Scarlet, were the eyes. The color of a fresh gold nugget, they held a natural glow to them- reviling her werewolf blood to the human.

Taking a look around the room, her eyes settled on the two girls as she removed her fingerless gloves; handing them to the servant. Tipping her head to the side, she looked as if she was going to come over to the two frozen humans but before she could a voice calling out behind them stopped her. She looked up and smiled. "Theo, you're early. I thought for once I might actually beat you!" Moving towards the stairs, the werewolf, Theo, bowed as she reached the bottom steps. "Sire, I'm always early- you'll never beat me on that." The King's foot found the last step as his hand found Theo's. It was then the King noticed Scarlet and Renee. Releasing Theo's hand it went to move it to her back, "So tell me now, which one is she?" His hand paused in midair as Theo turned and pointed at Scarlet and Renee. "And how did you figure one of those two is she?" Theo gave the King a look that balanced on the border of 'really?' and question. "Because, that peach gown, that adorable egg-shell top; the colors don't fit the servant colors. They're too bright." The King chuckled, placing his hand on Theo's lower back as he led her over to the girls. The action itself wasn't meant to be any more than a good will jester and the King would have aimed higher if he could reach.

"Theo, may I introduce you to Renee Ragon" Renee bowed as the King waved a hand towards her, but Theo instated on reaching out and shaking her hand "and Scarlet Soloman." Not making the same mistake as her friend, Scarlet held her hand out for Theo. "Scarlet, Renee; this is Theodora Deaeque, one of Voirol's leading scientist and engineers... and one of my closest friends."

"Please, call me Theo. Everyone does and I'll be the first one to tell you that Theodora and Deaeque are both mouthfuls. Well, except for the mute one, clearly you don't speak and I just stuck my foot in my mouth. I'm sorry." Scarlet nodded her head once, giving her introduction in the only way she knew how to. "Scarlet says it's okay, it's a pleasure to meet you, and I agree with her." Theo had watched Scarlet's signing like a child with a new toy. Without saying a word, she reached out for Scarlet's hand. When she grabbed it, pulling her forward an inch, Scarlet both jumped and froze all at once. Bring her small pale hand into her large, dark hand; Theo brought it up to her nose. Still frozen, Scarlet watched with wide eyes as she felt the werewolf's deep intake on her hand. Opening her eyes, Theo examined Scarlet, "So strange, you look no different than any other human, you smell no different than any other human; yet you could destroy the world!" Scarlet felt the blood drain from her face, and blinked rapidly as her head begun to spin.

"Theo!" With the call of her name, Theo was pulled from whatever trance she had been put in and released Scarlet's hand. Taking a few steps back, she held her hands up in a peaceful manner. "I'm sorry, again. I'm not always myself when I get excited; and no words can explain how excited I am to meet you, Scarlet." Scarlet went from all blood loss to her face, to the blood rushing to the top of her skin in a blush. She was sure she would be lost to a faint at any moment. Pointing a finger at Theo, Scarlet then spelt out O-K-A-Y. "You're okay." Scarlet looked at the King, impressed that he had remember the alphabet so quickly. Seeing her face, the King gave a small smile, "I remembered the O and K from our lesson today and figured the rest out. What you said earlier, on the other hand, went straight over my head." Scarlet relaxed.

"You will soon, sire. Scarlet has faith."

"It's barely two minutes pass seven and yet it seems as if dinner has already started without me." The small group turned, and watched as Queen Dolra floated down the stairs; her baby-blue gown hugging her curves and pooling at her feet. Stopping at the bottom of the stairs, she gave a tight smile towards Theo, "Theodora." Theo gave a flat, closed lip smile towards the Queen as she bowed, "Your high-ness."

"It's been a while, Theodora, hasn't it?"

"It has, I trust your highness is faring well?"

"Wonderfully, and yourself?"

"Perfect."

The conversation had nothing to with Scarlet and yet she found herself fighting the urge to recoil back. It was too neat, too tight; without being in the room with the two no more than two minutes both of the humans knew that the vampire queen and the werewolf scientist clearly did not get along. It was also within those few moments that Scarlet realized how much this dinner would surpass the night's prior. She was dreading it.

CHAPTER 10

Casting her eyes down, Scarlet shifted uncomfortably in her seat. The small group of beings had only been in the dining room for no more than ten minutes and yet the itch to go fleeing from the room grew by the moment within her. The words exchanged between Theo and the Queen was brief and each one laced with ice.

Scarlet stuck her fork into the salad in front of her, moving in small, slow motions. She stuck a small piece of a cucumber into her mouth, idly moving around a cherry tomato on her plate as she did. "Scarlet," at the sound of her name her body jerked and the small tomato was knocked from the plate into her lap. She looked up, bringing her free hand down to her lap. She gave the King a small smile, hoping that no one had noticed. "Why don't you tell Theo here a little bit about yourself, she's quite... curious about you." Scarlet's eyes widened a bit as she glanced from the King, to the werewolf, and lastly to Renee.

Renee, who had just stuck a rather large bite of bread into her mouth chewed with chipmunk cheeks for a few seconds. Scarlet was the only one close enough, being the two girls sat on the same side of the table, to see the tears form in Renee's eyes as she forced the food down. She looked towards Scarlet, whose risen eyebrow was asking her if she was okay, and nodded. "What would you like to know? That is, if the King and Queen do not mind sitting through stories they have already heard and information they have already gained."

"No, no, please, this dinner is a chance for Theo to formally know you two. Start from the beginning, and go from there." The King held out a hand towards Renee. As he did the salad plates were removed and replaced with the main course. "Of course, thank you." Renee gave a small nod towards the King, knowing that her thank you being nothing but a formality. "Scarlet was born in the small town of Khan, Tobus which is only a few miles from the Capital of the country. The cottage she born in was the one that her mother raised her in."

"Just mother, did your father work? Perhaps he perished in a mining accident?" Theo's placement of her words were blunt and took Scarlet back slightly. "Her father was someone she never knew, he was never in her life and her mother never spoke of him. Even though her life was hard, between bullies, rumors and having little money... it was still her life."

"And you always wished to change it?!" There was a small sparkle in Theo's eyes, one that hinted more towards an urge to know rather than give out sympathy. "No. Her mother worked her hardest and tried her best to make Scarlet's life the best. She worked her fingers to the bones as a seamstress, often sporting bags under her eye yet she was always there for her. She taught Scarlet everything she knew, allowed her to become her apprentice. So that one day she could provide for herself, so she would have the best life possible and-" Renee cut herself off as Scarlet's eyes fell to the untouched food in front of her. She made a small motion, one mean more for herself than for Renee. It was then, in a small, single blink that soul tear fell from her eye. Taking a deep breath she suddenly realized where she was at, looking up at the silent table. Without excusing herself she pushed her chair back and rushed from the room. The royals and the werewolf all looked to Renee. "I don't understand, why did she just go rushing from the room?"

"Perhaps it was your blunt tone or lack empathy, Theodora. Most preferred to be treated as living beings rather than thing." Renee, who was straight across from Theo, stiffened slightly at the change in her eyes. Long gone was the gleam of knowledge, and in its place was determination. "Or maybe, my queen, she fell under the impression that some of us had lost interest?" Queen Dolra's eyes fell into slits and Renee fought the urge to pull what Scarlet had and rush from the room. "Renee, what did Scarlet say?" The King's voice broke up the forming fight but the glaring gazes were still there. "She said, she would have the best life possible and... she never even got the chance to thank her... Or say 'I love you' one last time." Renee casted her own glassed over eyes down, part of it was for her friend's pain while the other, was from slight guilt.

~~~

For the second time that day, Scarlet found herself leaning against the door to her bedroom in a fluster. She had thought that she was finally coming to accept her new life. Yet, for the first time since her kidnapping, she had allowed herself to truly focus on her mother. There were so many words, so many things, and so many strings left untied with her. She couldn't even image what her mother was going through, what feelings an emotions she must feel. The ache in Scarlet's chest- which had started up in dinner- grew more, though she tried to fight it. She didn't want to cry, didn't want to focus on everything in her life that would never be completed, but the more she fought it the more it hurt. She didn't want fancy gowns or tubs so big she could near swim in it. She sought no riches or wishes for a better life. She had never wanted any of those things, never ask of any of them. All she wanted in her life, and all she wanted now, was her mother.

With a silent sob, Scarlet's knees begun to buckle in until she fell onto them.
~~~

~~~

"Thank you, again Theo, for coming."

"Oh no, sire, the pleasure is all mine. It was an interesting night."

"Yes, it was, have a safe ride home."

"I shall, have a lovely evening sire." The King gave Theo a nod, closing the front door behind her. Renee watched in silence, amazed that she had made it through the dinner in one piece. The King kept insisting her to speak about Scarlet, and a little on herself. It was as if he wanted to prove something, though nothing else pointed to that. When Renee wasn't speaking endlessly, over and over about Scarlet, Theo and Queen Dolra seemed to be two seconds from attacking the other. Renee was slightly jealous over the fact that Scarlet had gotten herself freed from the dinner, but then after would come the feeling of remorse. Scarlet was clearly having a harder time adjusting, no matter what the mute Blessed told her. Renee wished that she could make it easier on her friend, but what was she to do? There was not much power in her hands and what little she did hold; she held to with a grip tighter than death. "Renee," She turned to the King, "Go to the Kitchen, and have Ariana make a plate up. Take it to Scarlet. I'm sure Scarlet is not too hungry, but should she gain the urge for something then she will not be out of luck." She nodded her head
~~~

but as he turned to go up the stairs, her voice stopped him. "Sire." it was now his turn to look at her, "Yes?"

"Did you get what you wanted?" His eyebrows fell and he gave her a small frown. "Excuse me?" Renee took a few steps forward, praying she wasn't making a mistake. "From Scarlet and that werewolf. You were doing something, I could tell."

"Pray tell me what that something would be, Renee." The King, who had taken two steps up the stairs moved back down. "I don't know, I may not have gone to some fancy, high class school or whatever but I'm smart enough to put two and two together. That werewolf is a scientist and you are a King in possession of a Blessed human. One thing Scarlet didn't mention about her mother tonight is that she spent her whole life hiding Scarlet from the world. Protecting her from those who sought to use or abuse her for their own personal reasons."

"Are you implying that I seek to misuse Scarlet?"

"No, I'm implying that without Ms. Solomon I'm Scarlet's only front line defense... and you can bet as sure as hell is hot that I'll die before I let anything happen to her." The King studied Renee, his eyes looking her over once. At her sides she had fisted her hands, in the hopes to hide the fact that they were shaking. "Most wouldn't dare speak to a King in such a tone or tongue... Nor would they indirectly threaten him..." Here it was to come, he would surly kill her. She wish she had the power to control her tongue yet she never could. "You have moxie Renee, never lose it. Now get to the kitchen before everyone eats what is left." She nodded her head. "Of course sire." Both turned to go towards their own destination, "One more thing Renee?" She turned, and nodded, "You need not worry about Theo, Scarlet showed her tonight the one thing the mulish wolf needed to see about her." Renee found her heart race picking up once more. Merely by the fact that she had been right, the werewolf had wanted Scarlet. "And may I ask what that was sire?"

"That she's human." With a quick spin, he was going back up the stairs, leaving Renee alone. Only slightly confused.

~~~

"Scar?" When there was no answer, the door to the bedroom opened, a triangle of light from the sitting room spilling in as it did. "Scar?" Renee repeated herself again, entering into the dark room as she did. "I brought you some food, still warm." Renee moved towards the bed, where the outline of Scarlet's back was gently lit from the inpouring light. She didn't move from where she laid, her slow rising chest telling her that she might be asleep. It was barely eight thirty, but Scarlet had always been one to enjoy her sleep. Setting the food on her night stand, Renee peered over her friend. She was indeed, a sleep. "Oh Scar." Renee brushed a small stray hair from her barely
~~~

visible face. Leaning down she placed a light kiss on her forehead, "I love ya Scar. Sleep tight." Standing back up, Renee backed away and left the room.

It was only when she heard the door to the hallway close, that Scarlet opened her eyes. She sniffled, in an attempt to keep the snot in her nose, but in the end she ended up using the sleeve of her nightgown. She stayed on her side for few seconds before the smell of the food beside her bed forced her stomach to growl. Placing a hand over her stomach, she sat up. A good-size silver platter waited for her. Reaching over she removed the lid, and was met with the wonderful, mouthwatering smells of a small steak with steamed and mashed veggies. Sitting up, Scarlet picked up the fork and begun to eat.

~~~

"Good morning Renee." Renee smiled, as she came to a stop short of the kitchen door. "Hello Vern."

"And how are you this morning?"

"Just fine, and yourself?"

"I'm wonderful. Working on my bikes always puts me in a good mood the next day. How was your dinner last night? I heard a bit of gossip that Scarlet left before the end of the second course."
~~~

"She did, she was tired. The day had been long and all..." Renee glanced away, rubbing the back of her neck. "There's something else." Renee pulled her hand from her neck, and shook her head. "No, not at all." Vern crossed his arms, "Come now Renee, you can trust me, you can talk to me. I do not go running to the King with everything I learn."

"Why does the Queen and Theo hate each other so much?" Renee was startled when Vern uncrossed his arms and closed his eyes in a chest-heaving laugh. "What's so funny?" She felt the bubble of both anger and... hurt... forming. "They do not hate each other, oh no, on the contrary they both like and admire the other very much."

"But last night, they were so... cold." Renee crossed her arms, as Vern returned to his normal state. "They admire from afar, I should have added. They might be very cold and formal, but they are friends in their own strange way." Renee slowly nodded her head, "I see. Well, I'm going to go get some breakfast before waking Scarlet up. If I can't get her out, would you be willing to bring her a meal?"

"Of course."

"Thank you."

It's been two months since my last update for this story, I know. But I've had a lot going on in my personal life. This past summer I took summer courses, my laptop of three years finally started to give up on me and my mom got diagnosed with Cancer. So I've basically taken over her role as house-cleaner, free babysitter/ drop-offer/ picker upper for my nephew when my older sister is working and shopper (I've learned so much about coupons it's not even funny). On top of it, my fall semester just started and I'm taking 5 classes. I'm somewhat stressed, over worked and in over my head. But I swear I'll keep writing. (Thank you average 20 readers. You rock.)

CHAPTER 11

Dolra turned to her side, facing her husband. He turned his head, remaining on his back. She reached a hand out, running a finger over his forehead, "Thank you." Catching her hand, he gave it a gentle kiss. She gave a small smile, satisfied with the fact that she was waking up beside her husband after a wonderful pleasure-filled evening prior. "How could I not? It's my duty as King to please the Queen and believe you are that Queen." Her lazy grin grew across her face, and she looked at Cain dreamingly. She had spent the last few nights with him, and had forgotten what the morning felt like to wake up with someone beside you. "Thank you." Cain kissed her hand once more, before releasing it. "I must get changed, Pals's airship is due to come in at ten and Claudia set up a meeting for the three of us at eleven. So I will be forced to cut my lesson with Scarlet short today." Cain climbed out of the bed, leaving nothing but a breath of cold air as he did. Dolra rolled to her back, and resisted rolling her eyes. She cared for her husband, but she hated that his little pet of a human had started to consume his life. She held King Muis accountable for some of that hatred. If the pompous man wasn't so bent on war, then perhaps Cain would have never gotten the Blessed human in the first place.

Who was she kidding? Of course he would have- Scarlet was a Blessed human. But perhaps so much of what little free time he had, would be less spent on her and more on Dolra. She was a selfish, vain woman. Not that she minded, it should be added. Her attitude, and her noble father, had gotten her the crown to the country and the hand of the King.

Coming out of his bathroom, the room got a fresh wave of Cain's favorite after shave. It was one that made Dolra's toes curl and her back arch. The scent got stronger as he moved closer to her. Leaning over her, he gently pecked her lips and whispered a good bye. She watched him leave her to go be with another girl.

~~~

"My Lady, your car is ready." Dolra, who had been staring mindlessly out of the window, turned. Nodding the guard, she stood from her seat and left the small sitting room. She moved silently, in a manner so graceful that one would believe her to be floating. Stepping out into the mid-morning light, the air rested at a perfect temperature
~~~

with a slight breeze. Her driver greeted her with a nod of his head as she moved down the stairs towards him. "My Lady." He opened her door and she climbed in. The driver said not one word to her as he got into the car, and begun to move away from her home.

Many girls have had the dream of becoming a princess. None ever think of what is to come once the title of Queen is passed on to them. Dolra had never been one of those children. She had sought out the crown for the power, the status. But with the feared title of Queen, also came duties she would much rather ignore or pass over all together. Cain was the bronze, the protector. Dolra was to be the love, the face of the royal family. The thought was always slightly sickening to her. She had never been one to be see love as a strength. Perhaps it was from the lack of love received in her motherless, nanny filled, childhood with a father of whom she rarely saw. From what little she did see of her father along the years, she learned that love was more or less of a bonus for one's life. After all, many had lived their whole lives alone and progressed just fine. She had always believed she would be one of those women. Until one grand party, the gossip of the night was of the red head's ability to catch the eye of the young, and very eligible Prince. When one catches the eye of a royal, it is not something so easily given up. Luckily for her along the way she found herself not only enjoying the Prince- but loving him.

The car came to a soft stop, steam rushing suddenly from the sides of the front hood. Climbing out of the car, Dolra held up a hand to shield the sun from her eyes. "I shan't be long, I have tea at ten thirty with the Society." The driver nodded, and she entered into the fabric store. Stepping into the store made Dolra feel as if she was stepping into the home of an old friend. Her mother had come to this shop, and she insisted her nannies to come here when it came time for her to get a new dress. "Ah, good afternoon my Queen. Welcome back." A small, pale skinned girl stood behind the counter, glancing up from the paper she had been writing on. "You must forgive me, I'm in the middle of taking stock. Please take a few minutes to look around, we just got new stock yesterday." Dolra nodded, and begun to slowly shift through the slightly hazardous isles of stacked fabric. The worker hunched back over, a few strands of black hair falling over her forehead.

Feeling like a young child once more, Dolra ran her hands over a few bulks of fabric. Stopping on a maroon lace, she shimmied a small portion out to get a better look. It was beautiful, a mixture between a table cloth lace and a spider's web. "It's lovely, isn't it?" The werewolf came up beside her, her brown eyes glowing just a slight bit more. "We just got it in." Dolra nodded her head, pulling the bulk out more. "It is, I don't believe I've ever seen such a pattern before... I must have it." Wrapping the lace back up, she tucked the bulk under her arm. Dolra's eyes roamed a few more rows before stopping on a blue that appeared to be a dark, muted teal. Standing on the tip of her toes, she pulled the bulk free from where it was smothered. Tuning to the werewolf, who had been following her heels, she handed the teal fabric to her. Pulling the lack from her arm, she compared the two colors. "What do you think? This maroon lace with this blue for an accent?" The wolf looked at the two colors, narrowing her eyes before looking back up to Dolra "Maybe a small ribbon at the waist, a choker for the neck." Dolra smiled. "Just what I was thinking. Ten yards of the lace and two of the blue." The werewolf nodded, taking the two bulks. "Right away my Queen." Turning on her heels, the werewolf rushed away, Dolra slowly following after. By the time Dolra reached the counter, the werewolf had cut the fabrics. She was folding, and wrapping them in brown paper. "Add it to my tab and have sent to my seamstress." The wolf nodded, tying a thin strand of twine around the package. "Very good. Good day."

"Thank you my Queen, I wish the same to you."

Dolra left the shop, and went out to her waiting car. Climbing in, the door was closed behind her. As the car pulled back out onto the street, her eyes wondered out to the scenery beyond the window. They passed by the air field and it's entrance, where crowds of people had gathered. Some were waiting for airships to come in, some were waiting for them to go. Huddling together to say goodbye to a loved one as they go or great one as they come. She scanned the crowd, as if she was expecting to see her husband's head or even Theodora's wild red mane of dreads. She knew better, Cain was busy getting prepped for the meeting and Theodora was most likely still sleeping. As the turned a corner, she lost sight of the air field and begun to return her mental state of preparing for her weekly tea meeting.

CHAPTER 12

If it was humanly possible for her, a small hum would have been escaping Scarlet's throat. The King had called their lesson quite early, explaining to the two girls that he had a rather important meeting that late morning. Free until her afternoon training, Scarlet wanted to take this chance to explore the grounds of her new home. In the few weeks she had been there, she had yet to go outside beyond her balcony. Turning a corner, she gasped and stumbled back. She had run straight into another being. Catching herself before she could fall on her behind, Scarlet quickly looked up. Her face, already flushing, grew redder as she met glowing, golden eyes. Bringing her hands to her chest, she did her best to mouth the word 'sorry' to Theo. She then pointed to her hair, holding a thumbs up. Perhaps a compliment on her new tawny-braids would help the werewolf not be too angry with her. Theo only frowned, moving past Scarlet.

Her heart begun to race. Theo was angry with her, she had gotten a werewolf mad. She had never done anything of the sorts before, so she wasn't sure what to do or how to fix it. Turning, she watched Theo round a corner, the tail of her dress flicking behind her. Sighing, Scarlet glanced up to the ceiling before starting back on her way.

~~~

Scarlet stepped carefully around the hunched over gardener. With eyes glanced down, she avoided his tools, and was able to see him set a little bundle of slowly budding white flowers into a hole. Sensing her eyes, the gardener held up a new bundle towards her. "They're called Jasmines. Beautiful, aren't they? The King asked for some to be put in- asked for them by name. Here, have a sniff." Leaning forward, Scarlet took a small whiff. The scent was near heavenly. Pulling back, she smiled and gave him a thumbs up.

"Scarlet!" Renee came up the path, walking faster than normal. "Finally! The King has summoned us- well you, but you know. Come on." Not even fully registering what had happen, Scarlet picked up her skirts to run after Renee. Seeing how fast her friend walked when freed from the confinements of a skirt had Scarlet second guessing the idea of pants on a woman. Remembering the past few afternoons, spent training in the second skins with Claudia, her thoughts quickly turned against the idea of pants. She would settle for running in skirts, as she always had.
~~~

Catching her friend as she slowed to enter into the kitchen, Scarlet huffed. Claudia's dream of whipping her into shape was still in the beginning forms. Renee glanced to her friend, the corner of her left mouth lifting in a smirk. "Beat you, again." Scarlet frowned, and slightly swatted at Renee. "I'm sorry, I couldn't help myself!" Renee grabbed Scarlet's hand, leading her through the kitchen. As they exited out into the hall, Scarlet freed her hand.

'What does the King want to talk about?'

Renee shrugged. "I don't know, all I know is I was in the middle of planning the memoir of my life when Enaro, one of the Guards for the King, told me he wanted to see us at once." Scarlet gave Renee a tip of her head. "What?"

'Memoir of your life?'

"Okay, okay, you got me," Renee held up her hands in defeat. "I was in the library, trying to see how many books I could balance on my head when I had a pillow between them." Scarlet's risen eyebrow was all Renee needed to understand the unspoken question. "I got to seven." Scarlet smiled at her friend, her chest moving in a silent laugh. Her chest stopped moving as they slowed, stopping in front of the King's office closed door. Two guards stood in the same spots the last time Scarlet had been here, the day she first met the King. With neither girl saying a word, the guard to their left moved and opened the door.

"Isos?" The King questioned the guard. He bowed, and announced the two humans had arrived. "Send them in, send them in, thank you." Isos moved aside, allowing the two to cross over the threshold. Scarlet watched the door close behind them, "Your highness." Renee's voice had Scarlet spinning back to face the King. Grabbing her skirt, she curtsied. "Scarlet, Renee. Thank you both for coming so soon." Scarlet's eyes scanned the room, and grew wide at the sight of a mirco-braids pulled back into a pony tail. Scarlet took a quick step forward, her hands moving so fast that Renee almost didn't catch it. Alarmed, the King looked to Renee. "Um, she says that if this is about this morning that she didn't mean to bump into Theo. She was so caught up in her own mind, that she just didn't see her. She's sorry." The King looked at Scarlet, puzzled. As Renee translated for her, the werewolf facing the King stood and turned. "Theo?" The King looked absolutely bewildered.

Before anyone could say anything else, the door cracked open for a moment before being thrown open. "Just move- he knows I'm coming. Fate be on my side!" Everyone turned to face the voice. Standing at the threshold, giving the stink eye to Isos, was Theo. She stood there in all her glory, red dreads pulled into a bun. Scarlet felt her head get light, as the blood rushed from her head. If Theo had not changed her hair, then who had she run into this morning?

"Theo, welcome." The King smiled. Theo closed the door and bowed. "Sire, thank you for inviting me. Oh look!" Theo rose, and smiled at the sight of Scarlet, "The mute human and her translator are here! It is lovely to see you after our interesting evening the other night." Scarlet blushed, and the Theo look-a-like cleared her throat. Theo straightened her back, turning to her look-a-like. "Oh look, it's my long lost sister." As the realization settled over her, Scarlet wanted to slap a hand to her forehead. Of course, the only logical explanation to a Theo look-a-like was if they were related!

"Scarlet, Renee, this is Palsea Deaeque. Pals, this is Scarlet Solomon and Renee Ragon." Palsea moved from where she stood, moving closer to the three. Meeting Theo half way, the two hugged. "Pals, welcome back. How was your trip?"

"Thank you, it was fine. I got to relax on the rocky shore, and think about everything that lied await here for me." Theo rolled her eyes. "You can't just say for once, my trip was lovely? Or thanks for asking sister, it was good." A small frown formed on Palsea's sapphire lips. "No, I can't." Taking a step away from her sister, Palsea turned her attention to the two humans. "Hello, I am Palsea. Many of those who I tolerate call me Pals, you may call me Pals." Scarlet nodded and Renee mumbled out a thank you. "Why don't we all take a seat?"

~~~
~~~

There were only two seats across from the King. Both Theo and Pals insisted that the two girls take the seats and they would stand to the side. As the King talked, informing them of Pals joining their trainings four times a week, Scarlet casted a glance to the sisters. The more she looked, the more she realized that the two were not in fact identical. Minus the most obvious sign, being their different hair colors and styles, each one had little features marking her. Theo had a beauty mark just under her right nostril, while Pals had a scar running flat from her temple across her cheek. She had also learned, after the King stepped out for a moment and Pals caught Scarlet staring at her shoes, that Pals never worse heels. Theo refused to be seen without them. Pals claimed it was unpractical. Theo called the dresses Pals always wore unpractical. Pals argued that the two front slits, which went all the way up to her belt, gave her freedom of movement while keeping the appearance of a lady. Theo scoffed, pointing out that her skit was useless and she wore leggings underneath. Pals grabbed her sister's arm, lifting it. She said Theo's sleeveless shirt was useless when she wore sleeves almost meeting her shoulders- with fingerless, leather gloves. Theo called Pals's shoulder armor ugly. Pals rolled her eyes, calling Theo out for acting plain childish. It was when Theo called Pals's color of lip paint ugly that the conversation was lost. Scarlet noticed, watching the twin werewolves, that Pals remained unsteadily calm. She would only raise an eyebrow every now or then. Theo, though, was the complete opposite of her sister. Her body remained leaning against the wall but her face showed her every emotion.

As the two bickered, both demanding the other take something back; Scarlet glanced to Renee.

'Is this what it's like to have a sibling?' Renee gave a small chuckle, crossing her arms over her chest. "Oh yeah, all the time." Sadness filled Renee's eyes, and she casted them away from Scarlet. Sensing her sadness, Scarlet reached a hand out. Unfolding Renee's arms, Scarlet grasped her hand in one of her own. Renee gave a small, grateful smile but didn't turn her eyes back to her friend.

The two sisters finally drew the battle when the King returned and the meeting went on.

"That's just a brief brush of what you two will learn. You'll get a better explanation from Pals this afternoon. Do you have anything to add before I release you?"

"I do actually," Theo stepped forward, though the question was directed at her sister. "When can the lovely Scarlet come to visit me?" The King frowned. "Theo, we've already-"

"Oh but sire, we haven't. You said you would think about it." The King's eyes turned deadly towards the werewolf. Her eyes only sparked in the challenge. "The answer is still No, Theo." Theo gave a large smile, showing off slightly pointed teeth. "Why don't we ask Scarlet? She is free after all." During this whole exchange, the grip Scarlet had on Renee's hand had gotten so tight that her finger tips were going cold. "Ask Scarlet what?" The vampire and werewolf turned to face Renee at the same time, breaking their staring match. "Theo wants to run test on Scarlet it." Renee gasped, not from the news, no she gasped from the pain in her hand as Scarlet's grip somehow got tighter. "Not on her, just her blood and DNA in the form of body hair! You make me sound so evil sire."

"Maybe because you are!" Renee stood, pulling her hand from Scarlet's grip. The King and the twins both turned their attention to her. "How dare you think you can experiment on Scarlet as if she was no better than dirt! She is a living being as you or I!" Theo narrowed her eyes, the sudden sense of fear filling Scarlet's chest. "It's called ethics, but I'm guessing a little human from that joke of a nation Tobus wouldn't know that. Your High Lord is too busy keeping you all stupid and poor! I may be a scientist but I have my morals." Renee scoffed, "yes, your morals that right you to cut open and study Scarlet. Just like her mother feared!"

"That is enough!" The King's cold voice shook everyone to the core. But even his command could not calm the fire roaring within Renee. "And you! You revealed Scarlet to those dogs, after you would promise you would protect her! You're no better than the thugs who kidnapped us!" Theo bared her teeth, flashing sharpened canines. Pals reached for her sister, placing a tight grip on her upper fore arm. The King's face remained calm but the stylus in his hand broke. "Renee, I do believe your service is no longer needed for the day. Scarlet can write anything she needs to express." Renee shook her head, pushing out her chest to give her tiny body height amongst the giants in the room. "No, I won't. I told you with my dying breath-" A loud clash suddenly silenced the office. Everyone looked to the sight of the sound. Two shattered glasses were sprinkled on the ground, Scarlet's skirt brushing them. She apologized for breaking them, licking her lips and looking to Renee to translate. In fact, the King and the werewolves looked to Renee too.

Taking a calming breath, Renee brushed her hair behind her ears. "Scarlet is sorry for breaking the glasses," Relaxing slightly, Scarlet went on. "But we, as in the three of us, were fighting so much. She tried to get our attention but nothing was working." Renee took a quick breath, almost struggling to keep up with her. "If we would allow her, Scarlet would like to speak." Pals pulled Theo back and the King sat back down. Renee lowered back down into her seat, as Scarlet stepped over the glass pieces. "What exactly, do you want with Scarlet? And, please no big words, she is just from Tobus- the country of stupid and poor." Theo's cheeks flushed slightly. As many, she was one who often later regretted what she said in the heat of anger. "I apologize, for what I said. When in battle, I go for what I know will hurt. I hope you will not hold that against me, Scarlet." Theo shook her arm from her sister's grip and stepped forward. "I'm not asking to lay you on a table so that I may cut you open. I seeks some vitals of blood, some strands of hair, skin cells- which is just a scrap of skin from your arm. That is what I would be doing my test on. In return, we could learn so much; about how Blessed come to be. If there's a connection between the lines of your kind."

"She wants to know how you would connect her to the others, the ones before her."

"The last Blessed human came hundreds of years before my time, I will not lie to you. I have not personally studied him, or the ones before him but other scientist have. Scientist in my family and I have access to their research."

"If your ancestors were not able to find out much, what would be different now?" Theo gave a small smile, moving around the chairs towards Scarlet. "Technology. In just my two hundred and twenty years I've seen the world transformed. Our advancements in science have opened doors my ancestors could only dream of! With your help, we could be on our way to a wonderful, new horizon." Bending down to one knee, Theo rested right at her chest level. "Please Scarlet, you could be missing link. The one that makes thousands of years of research worth it." Theo's hands surrounded one of Scarlet's, the darkness enveloping the light. Pulling her hand away, Scarlet responded. "Give her until tomorrow, she will inform the King of her decision before their lesson. May we be excused?"

The King nodded his head. "Yes, have a good afternoon Scarlet." Standing, Scarlet curtsied and moved around Theo. She still rested on her knee. "Renee, stay." Renee, who had begun to rise, returned back down. The door open, and closed. Scarlet was gone. Theo slowly stood, "Sit, Theo." At the King's command she sat. "You two... What can I say? Isos!" The door to the office opened. "Sire?"

"Send for a maid, there was an accident with some glasses." Isos bowed his head, and left the room. "She had to break glasses. You two should be ashamed. I don't care if you two despise each other to the center core, do not allow it to happen again. Whatever Scarlet choses tomorrow is the final word."

"As I would stand by my best friend's choice, no matter my own opinion." Theo casted a glance at Renee, before sitting up straighter. "As would I. She is a Blessed human, but she is still a free human. She has her rights."

"Very good, you both are dismissed. Pals, I still have some matters to discuss with you." The King glanced up to the wall clock. "Claudia will be here soon. She is eager to see you and we can all..." The King looked to Renee, "talk." Renee gave a small head nod, standing.

~~~
~~~

Scarlet kept her skirts tight in her right hand, a folder in her left, as she rushed through the halls. Rounding the last corner, she dropped the fabric and slowed to a walk. Pushing her body into the door, Scarlet entered into the library. Closing the door, she opened the folder. Another thing she had asked for, and had gotten thanks to the kindness of Vern, was some way to find her way around the room of books. Amazingly, within a few hours, Vern had given her a folder filled with pages. The directory listed off the main sections of each book genres, subgenre, what level they were on and where. Flipping through the pages, she settled on history of science section. It was as good as a starting place as anything else.

Strolling along the history section on the second floor, Scarlet ran her fingers over the spines of the books. Any book she thought would help, she pulled and marked its place. So far she had three, two journals written by a Deaeque and the third a basic written over all of the past thousand years of scientific discovery. Sitting herself on the ground, Scarlet begun to look through what she had picked. The three books wielded nothing. They were indeed filled with knowledge, but not the knowledge she sought. Returning the books to their rightful place, she moved on. Scarlet continued to browse the shelves, repeating the process, until she reached the end of the section. A corner. Huffing, Scarlet frowned. She had learned much, but nothing gave her the knowledge of whether trusting the

Deaeque twins should be done. If she should allow herself to be tested on. Glancing down, she noticed a rather beautiful book spine.

Of course all of the books were beautiful to Scarlet. Growing up the only books she saw were tattered and old, so to hold one that didn't feel like it was going to fall apart- it was beautiful. There was something about the one that had caught her eye. It was in no different of size or color than the rest, but it seemed to sing out to her. Reaching out, she curled her fingers around the book. Pulling, only the top half would move. Suddenly there was loud shutter that had Scarlet jumping back from the books. With a gasp, she watched as the bookcase magically slid back just a hair of an inch. Grabbing the railing, Scarlet casted a glance down towards the door. When no one came rushing in, she turned back to the bookshelf. Stepping closer, she held a hand out, gently pushing against the shelf. As it swung in, Scarlet realized that it was only a small section of the shelf that actually moved. It opened to a dark tunnel. For her it was a perfect size, but for anyone larger they would be forced to bend down.

Should she go in, or should she not. Scarlet knew she should not, yet when she spotted a stray lantern on a small table a few feet away; she ran to get it. Twisting the nob for the gas, she ran the spark starter until a flame was lit. Returning to the tunnel, she took a shaky breath and entered in. Holding the lantern out, Scarlet kept herself closed away from the somewhat clean walls. The tunnel soon ended, Scarlet only walking thirty or forty feet in. Instead of being a dead end, or going to some long corridor, it emptied out into a large space. Lifting her only source of light up and around, it bounced off of nothing. Turning, Scarlet searched the left, and then right wall nearest to her. Finding a small switch, she flipped it and stared in wonder. The room was not large, but it was made of stone. The lights along the wall made her lantern useless, so she cut the gas to the flame. Looking around, the room was a library within a library. A full wall of bookcases just higher than her head were filled, and the rest of the room was filled with a small couch, a few chairs, and two coffee tables. Setting the lantern down, Scarlet moved to the bookcase. These books, unlike the ones in the main library, were much less grand looking. They were gruff, and more personally published than professionally. The spines were nameless, and held no claim to who might have written them. Pulling out a smaller black leather book, Scarlet flipped open the cover.

Property of Charles S. Miner

I was told to start this journal by someone very close to me, after all who would expect a blind man to write? This is the only safe haven I have. The only place where I can fully confess and kill the witness with no consequences. With as wild as a life I have lived, it's what I need. Guess that's what I get for being Blessed.

The journal fell out of Scarlet's hand and landed on the ground. Gasping, she fell to her knees and opened the journal once more. She reread the page, her lips quivering. Placing the book on the coffee table, Scarlet grabbed another book. Flipping the brown cover open, she read the ownership; A Copy of the Journal of the Study and Finding of Florence Avery Conducted By Dr. Sweeney-Gardiner R. Deaeque the Third. Scarlet leaned over and landed on her hip; holding the book to her chest. She couldn't believe it. Scarlet's glassed eyes scanned over the books once more. She had found it, she found the information that would give her the knowledge to make the right choice.

~~~

Pulling the bookcase-door open, Scarlet stuck her head out. Seeing that the library was as she had left it, minus the light of the day, Scarlet stepped out. The bookcase behind her closed with solid thud, and she started towards the nearest stairway. She held her lantern in one hand, and Charles's journal in the other. Exiting the library, she started back towards her bedroom. Her heart beat fast, as she was sure her secret would be discovered. She rounded a corner, entering another hall way, counting in her head how many more she had left. "Scar!" She froze, half way down the hall, and turned. "There you are! We get one afternoon off and you go missing!" Renee jogged towards
~~~

Scarlet, slowing as she reached her. "Where were you?" Scarlet held up the journal, opened it quickly and closing it just as fast.

'I was reading, in the library and I fell sleep.'

"Oh, I looked in there. I must have missed you." Scarlet nodded and took a few steps, "You missed dinner, do you want to head to the kitchen together and see if we can get Ariana to warm some food up?" Scarlet shook her head no, motioning that she was going to bed. "Oh, okay. Goodnight." Scarlet nodded her head, and rushed away.

Once in her room, Scarlet hid the journal under her pillow while she changed, and only took it out once she was snuggled under her covers. She could only stare at it, and run her hand over it's cover. After finding the case studies, Scarlet hunched over each one, learning. There were at least three Blessed humans before her; Charles, Florence and Miles. They were like her. They had all been studied on. They learned barely anything about why they were Blessed, but they had learned something. Or so the case studies showed. She had been so engrossed in the journals she lost track of time, and didn't read any more of Charles's journal. Wiping away a stray tear, Scarlet opened the journal.

So what shall I tell you first? What secret to I dare write down, in full trust of you and hope it not be found? I get visions, which is my Blessing. I can chose to see the past, and I can try to tell the future. My parents always believed that I was Blessed from birth, though I don't remember my first vision happening until I was four or five. Some days I miss them, I guess that shall be my first secret to you. A grown man, missing his ma and pa. How can I not? They were too young, and did nothing to deserve the burdens that I weighed. They were killed, many years ago. Sometime, when the sun is high and shines on my face; I can hear their voices. Without any drawings from my Blessing, I can hear my ma humming or my father's boots stomping. Every person has a certain step- did you know that? People who see, they don't notice it. How can they? It takes great focus and energy to listen to how one walks. Why do all that when you can turn and just look with your eyes? My eyes are useless. My second secret, journal, is where I live. I hail from the south, so I hide in the north. The manor is large, with many rooms. It rest on a large plot of land, surrounded- I'm told- by hills on the front and mountains in the back. The owner, a werewolf, lives alone. Her only son is grown and live in the nearby city, but he visits. My only fear, he is a scientist. My third fear, journal, is that I make a mistake. I slip and reveal myself. One mistake could get me killed.

-CSM

Scarlet slowly closed the journal. Unsure of where to hide the journal, she placed it back under her pillow. Turning her light off, she slipped deeper under the covers. She was numb. Reading Charles's journal was an experience. The feelings filling her were new, and strange. Common for most everyone, but never for herself. Because for the first time in her life, Scarlet didn't feel alone.

CHAPTER 13

Scarlet landed on the ground, a pain filled gasp escaping her mouth. "That was one of the worst defenses I've ever seen. Clearly Claudia has taught you barely anything on the matter." As the last words fell from Pals's mouth, a knife went whizzing by her head. It grazed her hair and landed in the padded wall behind her. Her golden eyes moved, her head following as she faced the knife. "I'm sorry I didn't teach her your area of expertise, Pals. I was too busy teaching her how to throw a knife and swing a sword. Not to mention build muscle." Claudia stopped at the edge of the padded rug, her sword still in hand. Renee remained behind her, frozen in the spot where they had been training. Pals pulled the knife from the wall, spinning the blade with quick flicks. "Of course, how rude of me. I'm not sorry though." In a blink of the eye, the knife went flying from Pals's hand. Scarlet watched with wide eyes as the blade came closed to Claudia's face. Claudia did not duck or dash from the knife's course. She stuck a hand out, and without losing breath caught the knife by the handle.

Rising from the ground, Scarlet had to applaud. The vampire and werewolf looked to her, as she signed to them. "That was amazing." The two turned their attention to Renee, who nodded her head towards Scarlet. "That's what she said. She thought it was amazing." Scarlet glanced over, and gave a single nod to her friend. Renee refused to look at her. Scarlet frowned, and looked to Pals. "Thank you. Pals started it though, I merely finished it." Claudia smiled, sticking the knife back into the holster on her waist. "Come on Renee, back to work." Pals shook her head, watching Claudia leave before turning back to Scarlet. "Take your stance." Scarlet rooted her feet into the mat, focusing on the prowling werewolf. "Now, remember, the key areas of weakness on anyone. Neck, shoulder, arms, legs and groin. Ready?" Scarlet barely nodded before the werewolf was launching herself towards her. Gasping, she flung herself to the side, and ducked. Spinning on her heels she latched herself onto the werewolf's back just as she was turning to attack once more. Pals tossed her head back, hitting Scarlet straight in the nose. Her elbows went into Scarlet's ribs, the sudden pain releasing her leg's grips on the werewolf's waist. Scarlet landed on her back, her hands to her face. Her nose was hot, but it was still intact as one piece.

"I wasn't even trying. Get up." Pals looked down at Scarlet, her face natural. "You know you could be a little nicer Pals, it is her first lesson." Claudia, in the middle of battle with Renee, glanced over to the group. She blocked a strike from the human's wooden sword, and then counterattacked. "I'm not nice Claudia." Pals bent down, hovering over Scarlet's face. The werewolf checked the human's nose. "It's your job to build them up, and it's mine to tear them down." Pals stood back up. "Your nose is fine, now get back up. It's your turn to attack me." Scarlet silently groaned to herself.

~~~

Their training for the day ended, and Renee left the room without a second glance towards Scarlet. Scarlet had watched her friend hang up her sword and quickly leave. Scarlet remained on the bench, resting her head in her hands. She couldn't help but feel both anger and sadness. Renee hadn't spoken directly to her since their morning lesson with the King. "There is something wrong. The air between you and your friend buzzes. What has happened?" Claudia took a seat next to Scarlet, sipping water from a glass. Scarlet lifted her head. She wanted to tell Claudia what was wrong, she had no one else to speak to on the matter. Besides, it was no secret to why Renee was mad. But the question of how was she supposed to communicate, was what stopped her.
~~~

Pointing to the door, Scarlet then pointed to herself and locked her pinkies together. Claudia tipped her head, giving a small smile. "I don't know what you're saying but I want to." Scarlet nodded her head, and pointed to Claudia and then across the room to where Pals threw fist at a dummy. She locked her pinkies again. "Me and Pals?" Scarlet nodded and showed her pinkies once again. "We have a connection?" Scarlet motioned 50-50. She pointed to the two again, and then gave herself a high five, laughed at nothing and hugged herself. "We have a relationship? I'm sorry to tell you but Pals has been seeing someone very seriously for many years." Scarlet shook her head no and pointed to the bracelet on Claudia's wrist. She made the motion of exchanging and then held up their wrist. "Exchanging matching bracelets? Like friendship bracelets?" Scarlet bounced and shook her head. "Oh I said it?" Scarlet nodded, locking her pinkies once more. "The locking pinkies mean friendship?" Scarlet nodded, smiling slightly. "Okay so your friendship with Renee..."

Making an O on each hand, Scarlet interlocked them like a chain before breaking them apart. "Your friendship is broken! Oh I got it! I got it!" Claudia smiled at her advancement. Suddenly, she frowned. "Wait, why is your friendship broken?" Scarlet pointed to Pals, standing. "Pals?" She shook her head the vampire, before standing on her toes. Jumping slightly, Scarlet did the best imitation of Theo she could think of. "Oh, you mean Theo! Wow, you got her sway down." Scarlet nodded, sitting back down. She pointed to herself, and then

Pals once more. Claudia nodded, her voice soft and low. "Okay so you and Theo-Oh... You must have said yes to Theo's offer, didn't you?" Looking away, Scarlet nodded, blinking at the forming tears. "And Renee isn't too happy about that is she? My cousin told me about the little spat between her and Theo in his office yesterday." Scarlet nodded her head again.

She wanted to make the best choice possible. Her mother's biggest fear was losing her daughter to a battle over her power or the curiosity of a laboratory. Her biggest fear growing up was that someone would discover her power and take her from her mother. The worst that could happened to her, had. She didn't have to say yes to Theo's offer, but Scarlet was desperate for answers. Growing up, she was never allowed to question why she was born Blessed. The facts were the facts dealt and she was to take them with pride. Yet she had the chance to get more facts, to understand. The science journals showed exactly what Theo had told her. The worst that could happen would to find nothing, but the best could lead them to places of the unknown. It was her life. If anyone would be getting answers towards her Blessing, it would be her. Yet, no matter how mad she was to gain and keep the knowledge of her abilities for herself, Scarlet would never forget the look on Renee's face when she gave the thumbs up to the King. She had only seen that look once before, many years ago when she was child. There was a trial in town, everyone was to attend. Scarlet and her mother were not ones to go against a Town Calling. It had turned out that two lovers had been found together. Unfortunately the older pauper man was married and the wealthy young woman was promised to a rich tycoon. When it came the woman's time to testify, she claimed all innocents. Without the courage to look the man in the eyes, she pointed her hand out to the side and called rape. The man's face, the pure and raw emotions that coursed through it, could be matched to Renee's that morning. The look of utter betrayal. The man was convicted, hung that afternoon. Though Scarlet had not been allowed to view the hanging, she felt as if her own body was currently hanging from a noose.

"If it's in my consent to say, she'll get over it. Being friends, best friends, does not mean you agree with each other. Or all the actions you each choose to do." Claudia casted a glance over to Pals, giving a small smile. "Trust me, I know. Just, give her some time. She'll come around. Until then, would you like to join me for dinner tonight? I'm having a small 'welcome home' dinner for Pals. My cousin, brother, and Theo will all be there. I feel that we have gotten to know each other over the past few days, despite the lack of words. And besides, what will one more mouth be?" Scarlet pointed to the door and shook a finger. Claudia shook her head. "No, Renee doesn't need to be there. You just talked with me without her aid. You're stronger than your realize Scarlet, mentally. We'll get your physically strong soon enough. So will you come?" Scarlet nodded her head, and gave a thumbs up. Claudia smiled. "Wonderful. I'll inform my cousin and you two can ride together." Claudia watched Scarlet's hand, smiling. "O-K; okay! I got that! Okay."

~~~

My fourth fear, is love. I've never been in love, and the thought is terrifying. I had my parents love, and they had mine but it is not the same. I do not know the warm embrace of a lover, or the fire of emotions felt when two become one. I do not think I want to feel it though. It's not fair that all I would get is their touch and voice. They would get all of me and I would only get a piece of them. I know that is a selfish thought, but since I will never fall in love- I don't care. Which leads to my fifth fear, I am a man of many fears journal. I fear being alone. Even on the run, claiming names and jobs that are not truly mine, I remain around all. A very influential vampire mob, a pack of werewolf whose gang ruled the coast of two whole nations. I even spent time among the elfin ruins in Odin. I'm sure they were beautiful. I was alone during that time, and it was bad for the soul. No being is meant to be alone. We were all created to have lives that intertwine with each other. I fear that my Blessing might force me to be alone, and if that happens I do not know what will come of me.

The knock at Scarlet's door startled her, her whole body seizing up where she sat. Closing Charles's journal, she frantically opened up a bottom draw of her desk. Dropping the book in, she tore a few blank papers from her note pad and covered the book with them. Closing
~~~

the draw, she grabbed a stylus with one hand and her bell with the other. Giving the bell a small ring, she dipping the stylus in ink. As the door opened she begun to draw out the alphabet in cursive. "Miss Scarlet?" Looking up from her looping L, Scarlet gave Vern a small smile. "The car is ready, the King is on his way to the Foyer now. She signed 'okay' and thanked him. He nodded once, keeping the door open for her. Putting everything away, she stood and left her room.

She begun to walk down the hall, Vern closing the door and quickly catching up to her. "If I can say," Vern broke the silence that had grown over them, not that Scarlet could do much to change that. "You look quite nice tonight, green suits you." A warm blush grew over her cheeks and she thanked him. Unable to stop herself, she brushed back a strand of her hair and twisted the end around her finger. Rounding the corner, the two entered into the Foyer. The King stood in the center of the room, turning when he heard them near. To Scarlet he was more dashing in his formal suit, complete with a top hat, than when he was dressed in a normal suit. "Good evening Scarlet." Stopping, Scarlet curtsied in greeting. "Shall we go?" He motioned to the door, and Scarlet gave a straight nod. She took the lead, and the King followed behind her; a hand hovering over her shoulder blades. They entered out into the cold night air, Scarlet holding her wrap closer to her shoulders. A black steam car waiting at the bottom of the steps, it's engine rumbling. The driver waited, hand on the back door's handle. Moving ahead of her, the King stopped at the door, holding a hand out. Giving a small nod of thanks to him, Scarlet too it and grabbed her skirts with the other hand. Sitting down, she slid over just as the King climbed in. The driver closed the door, and climbed into the front seat. Scarlet noticed the large glass panel that separated the small cab, giving them both complete and little privacy.

"You're looking lovely this evening, I don't believe you've ever worn green around me before." Scarlet pulled herself away from the window, where she had been glued. Totally captivated by the city. The buildings were all so large, though bleak in the night light. She singled a thank-you to towards the King and turned back out the window; unable to help herself. "This is the first time you've been out of the manor. I cannot believe the thought has only now just dawned on me." Scarlet nodded, looking back at the King. His face was neutral but there was an emotion in his eyes. "Well, if your training continues as it is, you'll be a normal face among the masses here. You need see the city for all it's true beauty, not like tonight. The rain is gloomy." Rolling her lips, Scarlet attempted the most basic signs to get her message across. The King watched her, his pale eyes never wavering. "You like the rain? Really?" Scarlet nodded, making the motion for rain but not sure how to say beauty without confusing him. So she spelt out pretty instead. If you don't know the word, change the sentence. "I do not mean to sound harsh but rain is anything but pretty, Scarlet. It's cold and cruel. It weakens the body." Scarlet frowned slightly and shook her head. A finger went to her ear, and then she swayed her body. "The sound is soothing, that is true. The bad outweighs the pleasant in the end." Scarlet shook her head, knowing they would never agree on the subject. Casting her eyes back to the window, she watched the city pass in thick streaks of color.

The car slowed, and then pulled to the curb. Through the light rain, Scarlet scanned the building. It rose high, at least four floors if not more. But it was also narrow, matching it's surrounding neighbors. The driver climbed out from the car, an umbrella in hand as he walked around it. Gathering her skirts, Scarlet climbed from the car. She remained under the shelter of the umbrella, watching as the umbrella was passed on to the King. Offering an arm out to her, Scarlet took it as they begun to walk forward. The stone steps leading to the front landing were slick and steep. Reaching the landing, Scarlet reached for the brass door knocker. The sound seem to echo through the near silent night. The door opened, light from within spilling out, and Claudia's head popped out from behind. "Good evening! Come in, come in! Welcome." The King motioned for Scarlet to go first. She gladly did, entering into the warmth of the room. The front room was tiny, with the whole space being nearly filled by the spiraling staircase. Behind her, after the King had entered, the front door was closed and locked. "May I take your things?" Coming from what appeared to be a parlor, a lanky man servant appeared. Slipping her coat off, Scarlet handed it to him, and gave him a small nod in thanks. "Come now, everyone is gathered among the second floor den." Leading the way, Claudia appeared to almost float up the stairs in her gown. Scarlet had only ever seen the vampire in pants and boots; to which she was stealthy when in them.

Coming to the second floor, Claudia led them to the first door way. The den, as with the rest of the home, was cozy. A fire burned in the fire place, warming and lighting the small space. A small table lamp, settled between two chairs, was also illuminating. Settled on the two seats were Theo and a vampire Scarlet had never met. Across from them on the stretched out couch was Pals, sitting closely to yet another man Scarlet had never seen. "Everyone, look who just arrived!" Everyone looked, and stood. They all bowed to the King. "Klaus, come here." Claudia grabbed at the vampire, pulling him over towards Scarlet. "Scarlet, this is my brother Klaus, baby brother this is Scarlet." Klaus extended a hand, Scarlet took it smiling. "It's nice to finally have a formal introduction. I'm the head of the intelligence team." Claudia frowned, and swatted her brother's arm. His eyes, matched his sister's yet his slicked back hair was strawberry blonde rather than golden yellow. "No work tonight Klaus. I already told you!" Even in her heels, Klaus towered over his older sister. A bell's ringing filled the air, and the lanky man servant was suddenly besides Scarlet. She inched slightly closer towards the King, the being closest to her. "Dinner is served." Claudia smiled, clapping her hands togeth-er. "Shall we?"

The group was escorted to the main dining room, just down and across from the den. If Scarlet was to be honest with anyone, including herself, she would admit to her nerves. For the past few weeks, ever since they were taken, it had been Renee and her. They had each other to lean upon in daunting new times. Tonight, on the eve of Pals's welcome home dinner, she was alone. Entering into the dining room, her seat was pointed out by the notepad, stylus and inkwell. Sitting, she smiled and thanked Claudia. "You're welcome." The vampire returned the smile, taking one end of the table. The King took the seat straight across from Scarlet. Theo took the seat to her right, and Klaus was beside her. Across from them, sitting next to the King, was Pals and the mysterious werewolf beside her. "Scarlet," Pals caught the human staring at the male. "This is my longtime business partner, and boyfriend Rony Loth. I can assure you he is trust worthy of your secret." Rony smiled, a hint of joy gleaming in his glowing amber colored eyes. "I have to be, otherwise I would have never won over Pals's trust. Or her heart." He wrapped a tan hand around one of her own, their two skin tones melting into a near ombre. Pals glanced down to his touch, her face remaining neutral. Meeting his eyes, she lifted an eyebrow as something flickered in her eyes. "Though I do not consider my personal affair as proper dinner conversation; he is correct." She looked back to Scarlet, entwining her fingers with Rony's.

Giving a small smile, Scarlet grabbed the stylus and dipped into the inkwell. Writing quickly, but making it legible, she then passed the notepad to the King. He read it out loud, "If you trust him, than I shall trust him." The King smiled, handing the notepad back to her. Pals nodded, and Scarlet was sure the werewolf was grateful towards her. "I believe, if you spoke, you'd be the most formal sounding human. You write as a poet would." Theo turned to her table mate. "I like it! Oh, and thank you for agreeing to come and see me. I cannot wait, there are so many-"

"Theo!" Claudia's voice cut the werewolf off, as the lanky servant came in with the first few plates. "There is no speak of business tonight. Tonight is a night of laughter, and merriment as we welcome home your sister. Now, let's enjoy the meal."

~~~~

The next morning, after a breakfast taken in her bedroom, Scarlet dressed for the day. She would have normally taken it with Renee, as the best friends had been doing. Yet with her invite to dinner the night before, Scarlet hadn't the chance to attempt to speak with Renee. Not that she was fully sure that Renee would be willing to speak with her.

She acts as if I'm the one who did something wrong. I've done nothing.
~~~~

Coming up to the library doors for her lesson with the King, Scarlet slowed. At the same time, from a different direction, Renee did the same. The two stopped a few feet from each other, each looking at the other. Scarlet spoke first.

'You and I need to talk. Now.'

"There's nothing to talk about Scarlet. Even if there was, I'm sure you'd love to spill it with your new friends. Yeah, I know about last night." Renee took a step to the side, and Scarlet mirrored her.

'It was just a welcome home dinner. An intimate affair, nothing more. You're treating me as if I've done something wrong.'

Renee scoffed, rolling her eyes. "Because you have Scar! Your mother worked her whole life to protect you and now you're just willing to give it all up? For-for what? The fake friendship of the King and his lackeys or the possibility of gaining a sliver of information?"

'You shouldn't speak about the King in such a way.'

"I'll speak however I damn please. Can't you see they're being nice because you agreed to those test?"

'They're being nice because it's who they are. I'm choosing to do the test because I want answers. Is it so wrong to ask why I am who I am?'

"Yes! You are who you are and you should just accept it."

'No! All my life I've sat back and accepted things how they are. I was told if I did, then everything would be okay. I've never asked questions, I never fought back. Now look where we are! Thousands of miles from our loved ones. I did everything I was told to do and yet my life still turned out bad!'

Renee shook her head. "Scarlet, listen to yourself. You're not you, you're changing. Remember who you are! You're Scarlet Solomon. You were born and raised in Tobus." Scarlet shook her head.

'No, I'm not. Remember that the King said? That Scarlet is dead and if you can't accept me-'

"Then what? You'll go running to the King, or to Claudia? These beings aren't your friends Scarlet. They never have been and they never will be! They only want you for your powers. You're just too stupid and naïve and caught up in yourself to realize it." Scarlet was stunned by her friend's harsh words, and took a small step back. Holding back the forming tears, she swallowed.

'I'm not stupid, you're just jealous!'

Spinning on her heels, no longer thinking about the lesson with the King, Scarlet ran from her friend. She got just a corner down before the tears came. This was not the first fight they had ever had, but it was the most serious. No matter what, though, they had never allowed their anger to control their words. Scarlet might not have been upset with Renee before, but as of now she was.

I'm not stupid.

CHAPTER 14

"What happened? Where is Scarlet?" Cain crossed his arms and glared down to the human sitting in the plush library chair. He had come that morning ready for their lesson, only to find Renee staring out of the window. "I don't know. I told you, we got into a fight and she ran away. I didn't-" Renee huffed, and ran a hand over her face. "I said some mean things, and I wish I hadn't but I did. I didn't mean them though. If I knew where Scarlet was, I would have gone to her and apologized by now." Renee buried her face into her hands. "Well, she can't have gone too far. She's not allowed off the grounds. And Renee," Cain stopped in the doorway of the library. "This is the second warning, control your temper. Being friends is not about always agreeing, but rather respecting each other's differences."

~~~
~~~

Cain slammed the door behind, pausing in the shadow of the building. His eyes scanned the land. There were a few gardeners scattered about the greens and flowers. The figure of three men standing knee deep in the lake gently swished nets through the water. Two women kneeled at the bottom of a statue, shining rags held tight in hand. Cain saw no dainty human, with long hair that swished. Taking a deep breath, something he rarely did, Cain entered out into the sun light. He followed the path, every worker stopped and acknowledged him as he did. Asking each one about Scarlet, he ended up getting pointed down a lesser used path by one of the lake cleaners.

The path was made of pale, miniature pebbles, and lined with looming trees to the right. The lake was to the left, the water stretching out for miles. If it hadn't been a scene that Cain had viewed thousands of times; he would have been mildly impressed. Something caught the corner of his eye, and Cain turned his head back to the path in front of him. A small figure sat hunched over at a small dock on the lake. Her dressed was hiked up, and her bare feet dangled in the water. Nearing, as he came up to the deck, Cain heard small sniffles. "I was told what happened." Scarlet jumped, he hands grabbing the dock to prevent herself from falling into the water. Glancing up, she quickly wiped away the tear stains. "Mind if I join you?" He was already removing his shoes when he asked, and was sitting when she shrugged. "Here, this might help you." He handed her a small journal with a built in stylus and ink well. She thanked him, and placed it off to the side. Rolling up his pant legs, he stuck his feet into the water.

"It's beautiful, isn't it?" Cain broke the silence that had settled over them, cast his eyes out to the water. Scarlet nodded, glancing at the journal sitting between them. Cain took notice, "You can trust me Scarlet, if you want to talk." Taking another glance towards the journal, Cain saw her grab it. She wrote quicker than anyone Cain had ever seen, and in just a few blinks he held the journal. All my life I've been scared. I no longer wish to be scared. You want me to become a fighter, so a fighter is who I'll be. I refuse to speak to her. Looking up, Cain watched Scarlet step back onto the pebble path. He could not help himself but to smile.

~~~

"You must be kidding me- you can't do this." Claudia stormed around Cain's office, walking the path of an invisible eight. "I am King, I do what I please." A swish filled the air, and a knife was plunged into a stack of papers beside Cain. He casted his eyes to the stack, before moving them up. Claudia released the knife, leaning back. "You're wasting a perfectly good day- do you realize how busy I am? I take my afternoons off, afternoons I could use training the horrible excuses of reserved soldiers, to train Scarlet and Renee. For you to just cancel it in the blink of an eye is rude to not only me but Pals!"
~~~

"Do not bring me into your argument." Cain looked past Claudia, to where Pals sat on his couch. She had her eyes casted down into the latest issue of her favorite fashion magazine. "Pals doesn't seemed too bothered by it." The werewolf flipped a page. "Oh, I am greatly annoyed, sire. Missing even one day is a risk I would prefer not to take. But you are the King and I respect your command." She lazily flipped another page. Of all the things Cain admired about Pals, it would have to be her monotone voice and face. She had learned how to fully control them both, thus giving the enemy one less thing to work upon. The only time he ever saw her express any true emotion, was when her arguments with Theo escalated to a boiling point. But even in those moments, she was clearly in control of herself. That was, in Cain's belief, what made her so deadly. "Thank you for the support Pals." Claudia's words were laced with a mixture of sarcasm and actual gratitude. "Of course." Pals dog eared a page, and then flipped to the next.

Cain pulled the knife from his desk, holding it out to Claudia. "They are fighting like children right now, you would not get anything productive done with them." Claudia took her knife back, place it back on it's place on her belt. "So what are you doing to do to fix it?" Cain, who had been dipping his stylus into some ink, paused. "I'm supposed to fix it?" Claudia looked at him as if he claimed the sky was orange. Even Pals looked up from her magazine. Claudia mumbled under her breath, rolling her eyes. "Of course you're supposed to fix it! Looking though, as if you will not, I guess I am forced to step up to the plate." Cain shook his head, but Claudia cut him off before he could even protest. "Pals, I'll need your help. Cain, send dinner down to the training room. These girls shall be friends once more by two and then it's extra practice." Locking the knife in, Claudia left the room. Cain still sat dumbfounded. "Pals?" The werewolf had risen, magazine stuff under her arm. "I'm not just doing this because of our friendship, I'm doing it because I agree with her. Good day sire." Once Pals was gone, Cain shook his head. Picking his stylus up from the ink, he went back to his business.

He was responding to a letter sent from one of his Captains stationed in the trader's base at the bottom of the Blue Mountains. While raids were common, they had become more frequent in occurrence. Normally it would not be a call for alarm, raiders and bandits could always be tamed. There was belief, by multiple trusted sources, that Muis was behind it all. Cain was writing to instruct his captain and his men to take no drastic course, yet. Muis was preparing for a war and so a war Cain would give him.

~~~

"I need you both to take a seat please." Claudia looked at the two humans standing in front of her, "Now." Her hands gripped the desk she leaned against. Renee frowned, and Scarlet paled but they both sat down. Claudia nodded, "Good, Pals, care to take over?" Standing
~~~

straight the Claudia moved to give Pals the space in front of desk that she had been occupying. Moving to the back of the room, she took a seat next to Cain. "Normally I only bother myself to deal with fights of those with my own sister. I have injected myself into yours because our current situation requires us all to work as one team." Pals lifted herself onto Claudia's desk, her spine remaining straight. "So you," she looked to Renee, "are going apologize to Scarlet and Scarlet" she turned her eyes to Scarlet, "will listen." Renee's eyes glanced over to Scarlet, who sat with her arms crossed.

"Scar, look," Renee turned in her chair, resting a foot in it as she did. "I'm sorry, okay? I said a lot rude and mean things. It was wrong, and I know it. I'm sorry. I guess I wasn't adjusting as well as I thought I was. That's no excuse for my behavior over the past few days, I just hope you will forgive me. Please forgive me." Scarlet responded, and Renee nodded her head. "I understand, thank you." Cain stood, moving to the corner of the room where the desk sat. "I take it that all is well between you two once more?" Cain took a stance to the side of Pals. "In some ways yes, in other ways no, but it's okay. We're still a team." Cain nodded, crossing his arms. "That's all we ask of you." The door to the office opened, and everyone turned.

"Hey Claud, have you-cousin." Klaus stood at the threshold, a few papers gripped tightly in his hands. "I was not expecting to see you all here, but never the less you are the people I was looking for." He glanced to Scarlet and Renee. "More or less." Cain meet his cousin, glancing down to the papers in his hands. "What is it?" Klaus held the papers out to his cousin. "These just came over our military's secured telegraph line. It's not good." Cain snatched the papers from his cousin, pulling him into the room as he did. Claudia and Pals both rose and moved towards Cain and Klaus. "What's happened?" Klaus looked to his sister, giving her a frown. He shook his head in a way to tell his sister to speak no more. "Damn it Muis." Cain shoved the papers into Klaus's chest. Claudia ripped the pages from her brother's grip, holding them so that she and Pals could read them. Stopping mid-page, Claudia looked up to her brother. Cain had moved to her desk, her desk phone in his hand. "Klaus, how have we responded?"

"We haven't." The sound of the phone slamming down filled the air. "We have now." Cain stood straight. "There were a few of Muis's men, older and worthless to him in the big picture. Kept in one of the prisons. Down south, near the sea. They're going to be executed by sun down. He dares kills my men, then I shall kill his." Pals lowered the paper in her hand, "Yes but is it enough?"

"It's enough to get the message across. I shall not be the one to swing the sword first, but if he dares swings it at me then we are prepared to defend." Pals did not agree with him, Cain could see it in her eyes. But she dare not speak out against him. He would have commented, but the sudden movement of hands pulled his eyes away from the werewolf. During the whole dispute, Cain had forgotten that Scarlet and Renee were still in the office with them. While he and his group were caught up in their discussion; Renee and Scarlet had started their own. All with their hands. "Can I interrupt you two?" Both of the humans tensed, dropping their hands as they turned to face Cain. "May I asked what you were both speaking about?" Scarlet looked to Renee, as her stare moved between them. "Scarlet, was just reminding me to, um, mind my own business." Cain nodded his head, "That's very kind of your Scarlet, but unfortunately this is your business now too."

"Cousin." Both Klaus and Claudia took a step towards Cain, but he went on despite their protest. "I had hope that there would be more time. That I could continue the charade and keep you both in the blissfulness of being naïve."

"Cousin, do you really believe this is the best time?" Cain held a hand up, both silencing and stopping Klaus in his tracks. Klaus retracted his steps. "Renee you asked me once, weeks ago, why I was preparing you for a war. My answer to you was truthful, I prefer to always be prepared. What I did not tell you, was that Voirol was near war with Drale." The two humans looked at each other. "Was? So you fixed the problem?" Cain shook his head. "No, I've tried to avoid war at all cost but Muis... Today he had a small troop of my men captured. They were on his land, but were there on permission. Raids through the Blue Mountain pass have increased. Instead of warning them and allowing them a chance to fight; his men shot three of the four straight in the back. I shall return the favor by killing some of his own." Scarlet frowned, sinking back in her seat. Cain felt a ping of something deep within him. He didn't like to see her frown, especially at him. "So what does that mean, for Scarlet and I?" Renee stood, yet remain rooted in the spot. "At sunset, Voirol will officially be at war with Drale. The battles will not come swift or sudden. It might take weeks, or months, but Muis is coming. And when he does, Scarlet must be ready."

"You plan to put her on the battle front?"

"I plan to save the world."

~~~

"What are you doing?" Cain entered into his wife's private room, only to enter into a war zone. Clothing, shoes, hats and other accessories were scattered among every piece of furniture and the floor. A few hand maids walked about, folding things. Dolra came out from her closet, a dress draped over her arms. "Hello darling, I'm packing. What else does it look like?" Cain stepped over a pile of boots. "Perhaps a war? What are you packing for that causes this much of a disarray?" Dolra handed the dress in her arms off to one of
~~~

the maids who packed it away in one of the open trunks. "My yearly trip to the coast of Illi, and then the southern island paradise of Janja. I'm also thinking about maybe detouring to Onomi, apparently my cousin Flower has not been well these past weeks." Dolra glanced down, pulling a scarf from the trunk by her feet. She scolded one of the hand maids. "Ah, yes, of course. About that my dear, I don't think you should go on your trip this year. Or to visit your family." Cain rested a hand on her shoulder as she chose between two pairs of boots a maid held up. "What? Why not?" She turned to face him. He glanced around to the maids moving about the room. "Leave us, all of you. Now." Whatever each maid had been doing, they all stopped and shuffled out the door. Once alone, Cain locked the bedroom door. "It's Muis. A troop of his men killed a troop of ours. I plan to return the favor and by sunset..." Dolra, who had been unfolding a new gown from it's paper, lowered it. "We'll be at undeclared war." Cain nodded his head. Dolra frowned, looking down to the gown in her hands. Hoisting it up, the marron lace pooled out. "Look, I just ordered this gown made. Isn't it beautiful?" Bringing it back down she begun to refold it. "You're still packing." She placed the dress in a trunk, pushing on it. "Yes. Darling, I'll be fine. Both Illi and Janja are thousands of miles from Drale, and are protected by the Endless Mountains. Janja is a volcanic island in the middle of the Orange Sea! Then there's Flower, she's the nearest friend I've had for nearly my whole life. I would never forgive myself if something was to happen to her and I was not there." Dolra packed away another gown, glancing up to her husband. Cain frowned, his arms crossed. "It's only a few months, I promise I'll be careful." She made her way through the mess to him, planting a light kiss on his lips. "When does your air ship leave?" Resting a hand on his chest, her smile fell from her face. "Tonight. I'll be in Illi by the end of the week, if the wind allows."

"Where else is your air ship going, for refueling."

"Kuko first, and after we pass the Endless Mountains, Onomi. Then it's Illi." Cain nodded, glancing about the mess. "I wish you a safe trip my dear."

"Thank you darling."

A/N: Okay, so it needs to be noted that the image in this chapter is a crudely drawn map that I drafted up this afternoon. I don't often share photos of the maps I make for stories- and all my made-up world get maps drawn for my own sanity... And to help me write. I wasn't planning on creating a map for this story but I needed to, so I did. If you want to see a some-what large version of it, please PM me and I will send you the link. I know the picture is small on Wattpad and my writing can be messy. (And God save the island of Janja; There was no volcano planned and then it was added on and then I missed spelled freaking ORANGE. .-.)

Keep Reading! <3

CHAPTER 15

Scarlet watched Claudia silently, as she pinned a photo to the foam bullseye. "This is Muis." Claudia put emphasis on each word. Stepping so Scarlet to see, she found herself somewhat humored by the image. On the yellowed image was a rather large, older man. His white hair was pulled back into a ponytail, streaks of black throughout being the only sign left of his younger years. His lips were full, a cocky up-twist upon them but his nose tiny, a pair of tiny round spectacles resting at the tip. It might have been the wrinkles, or the natural slants of his eyes, but he appeared to have no sclera. Two black voids stared into her eyes. Claudia's finger striking the center of his forehead broke Scarlet from the trance. "This is the spot you want to aim. If you aim at him, you aim to kill. There's no excuses." Claudia quickly moved out of the aiming range, "Take a try at it."

Pulling a knife from her belt, Scarlet shook it gently in her hand. Claudia had surprised her that afternoon with her very own knives.

They weren't new, but in an actable shape being they were an old set of Claudia's. For sure they were a step up from the rubber and wooden ones she had been using for the past few weeks. Since the King's revelation about the war nearly three days ago, Claudia and Pals had stepped up the intensity of the human's training. Not that Scarlet minded all that too much. It kept her mind off of the awkward situation with Renee. Scarlet had been willing to forgive Renee, that was the easy part. The hard part was trying to be as close as they were before it all. Scarlet no longer wish to confine in her friend, and thus had no one. She once again felt alone, more alone than she ever had.

Taking a stance, Scarlet licked her lips and took focus on the photo. Pulling her arm back, she released the knife to the photo, missing his forehead and hitting his second-chin. Spinning she moved further back, and repeated the process. She missed once more, hitting a fat cheek. She moved even further back, and threw her last knife. It hit Muis's forehead dead center, the impact creating a satisfying thump. "Good, you're getting better every day. Now get your knifes and do it again. This time, I want a running start. Starting back to front. After that, front to back." Scarlet nodded as she jogged to retrieve her knives.~~~"Scar!" Pausing at the door to the training room, Scarlet looked back just in time to see Renee coming over towards her. "You're going over to Theo's tomorrow right? For the testing and stuff?" Scarlet briefly nodded her head. "I um, I talked to the King this afternoon and he said if we take Vern with us then we could go to the market tomorrow. I was thinking, we could go, you know after. If you want." Scarlet could tell that Renee was biting the inside of her cheek, a nervous habit. Scarlet looked away, before looking back and nodding her head. Renee gave a relief smile. "Thanks. I'll see you in the morning." Nodding goodbye, Scarlet left the training room.

~~~

I had a strange dream last night. I think it was a possible image of the future. Before I really mastered my powers, the best way for me to get an image of what has been or might be was to go to sleep. They're not common anymore, but I can still get them. In this dream I stood outside, towering cliff covered mountains behind me and rolling hills to my front. What should have been beautiful was over shadowed by the looming fear and tenseness in the air. There was a shutter, and suddenly I was surrounded by a battle. A war.

Looking around, I met a pair of black voids that felt as if they were seeing to my inner core. The man gave a wicked glee, as there was an explosion. The ground around me shook and looking back to where the man's eyes had moved, I turned just in time to watch pieces of the mountains cliffs fell. The warriors scattered, one dressed in slightly darker armor standing out to me as he helped an injured woman. She hobbled, having clearly hurt her foot and held a hand to her shoulder. His armor was missing a large piece from the chest plate, and his helmet had been abandoned. Turning back to the man, he had raised
~~~

a bow with an arrow ready to fire. The arrow went flying through the air. I'm not sure who it was meant for, but the man pushed the woman to the ground. He took the hit, falling to the ground. The woman, on only her knees, pulled a knife and sent it towards the man on the horse.

I do not know if it hit him or not. I woke to a cold sweat, my heart racing in my chest. It was the most vivid image I've ever gotten in my dreams. Perhaps it's a sign, towards these test I've begun with Dr. Deaeque. Or perhaps there is a war greater than the one I face. Unless asked about it, I shall tell no one but you journal.

-CSM

Scarlet placed her book marker into the journal, closing it. For being blind, Charles had some of the nicest writing Scarlet had ever seen in her whole life. Setting the journal under a pile of papers in her nightstand draw, she closed it and turned her light off. Settling into the covers, she flipped to her side. Yawning, her eyes gently closed.

~~~

A gentle wind wisped stray pieces of Scarlet's hair. It had been pulled back into a high ponytail, yet she remained in her night gown. She looked at the surround area, confused to where she might be. She scanned the mountains in front of her, and turned to meet large hills that seemed to roll to the horizon. She turned back to the mountains,
~~~

looking for nothing yet everything. The sound of a battle cry coming from behind her, had her turning. If she could have screamed, she would have. Muis ran towards her, sword in the air. She was frozen, her feet rooted from the fear. The distance between then shrunk and as he swung his sword towards her; Scarlet lifted her hands in defense. Closing her eyes, she prepared for the pain.

None ever came. In fact, when she reopened her eyes, she no long stood in the field. She laid on the wooden planks of a dimly lit study. Slowly sitting up, she tensed at the hunched over shadow sitting at the desk. "Who goes there?" The figure turned, and Scarlet scooted back, hitting a couch. Looking normal enough with short, cropped curls and skin darker than the night; the man's eyes were what put fear in Scarlet. Where normally rested the cornea he had nothing but spots that looked as if they had been colored with a grey pencil. His eyes scanned over Scarlet. "Oh, it's just you. Well, please, take a seat." He motioned to the couch that was jammed into her back. Shaking, she barely lifted herself up to the couch. The man turned back to his desk. "I was starting to wonder if you were ever going to show up." Scarlet frowned, realizing that she was in dream. "Well," the man turned back to her, this time a writing quill in hand, "Aren't you going to speak?" The frown grew deeper on Scarlet's face. Pointing to her throat, she made an X. "You can't speak?" She shook her head yes. "Have you ever tried?" Scarlet shook her head once more, getting more annoyed with the man by the second. He twisted his head slightly, "Well have you tried in the last two minutes?" She shook her head no. "Well then try." Scarlet looked at the man like he was crazy. "Now." He mumbled something to himself, glancing away. Taking a deep breath, Scarlet prepared for what was to come.

"How?" Her eyes popped open, her hands flying to her mouth. "I spoke!" A small shrill escaped her lips. "I spoke! But, but, how, how is this even possible?" The man smiled, revealing that both of his upper canines were missing. "How is anything possible Scarlet?"

"How do you know my name? Who are you?" The man crossed his legs, placing his quill on the table. "I'm sorry, I skipped over the introductions. How rude of me. I am Charles Seafra Miner, please to meet you." Scarlet held a waving hand out, "Wait, wait, wait. Charles Seafra Miner, so Charles S. Miner?" Charles nodded his head, giving another smile as he leaned back in his chair. "You're, you're him?" He nodded his head again, "The one and only. Well, I was named after my father but I'm the only Blessed Charles." Scarlet shook her head, glancing around the room. "How is this possible- how can you see me? You're supposed to be blind."

"That's the great thing Scarlet, here the boundaries of mortality hold no rulings. Here we are free of any deformity." Charles stood and came to sit next to Scarlet. "Where is here?" She looked from him to the windowless study once more. "I'm afraid I can't even answer that question. We are nowhere, yet everywhere. It's all a part of our journey."

"Our journey?"

"Yes, Blessed ones, we intertwine. I'm not sure how it really works. But being I was the Blessed human before you, it is my duty to speak to you." Scarlet was confuse. "Your duty? I don't understand." Charles adjusted himself, turning more towards her. "Well, let's see if I can explain it another way. The Blessed before me was Florence Avery. She lived four hundred years before my mortal time. She was deaf yet she could read the mind of any person of her choice. I was taking a walk one afternoon, when a vision of her appeared in my head and then I was transported to the most beautiful place. I say that because it was the first and only time I ever saw in my life. Just like you and I, she informed me of who she was."

"This is still all so confusing. I don't understand any of this. Just tell me how I got, and why, I'm here."

"Well, think about it Scarlet. How are you able to control things with your mind, how could I see the future or Florence read minds? Why is our world filled with creatures that some other worlds believe to only be fables or myths?" His colorless eyes searched her, and he leaned in. "Magic." Scarlet could conclude that his explanation made sense. It was the most logical one. "Okay, but it's still hard to accept." Charles nodded, leaning back into the couch. "I know, I felt the same way when Florence came to me."

"So why am I here? Are you going to tell me something or what?"

"You're here because your Calling Time is upon you."

"My Calling Time?"

"Yes, you see, the world and everything around us; is living. It has us all set down a natural course. Then, as if sensing the coming danger that threatens to destroy it, we come along."

"Wait, are you telling me why I exist? Why I am Blessed?" Charles nodded, as the tears welded up in Scarlet's eyes. "Please go on."

"We were created to protect the natural balance of things, to take on and destroy whatever threatens to ruin it. When it's our time to do so, that is called our Calling Time."

"So I am set to go head on with Muis?"

"I cannot answer that, the future is never fully set. But the war that Muis will create is your Calling Time."

"So what happens afterwards? Do I lose my power? Do I die?"

"No, you were born Blessed and shall remain so until you die. And, honestly you can die at any time Scarlet. We are not created just to serve our purpose and then return to the beyond. We are still granted a full life if we can survive."

"How did you die?"

"Disease. There was a horrible disease spreading through the world during my time. It was called the Blind plague, ironically. It was silent, swift and deadly. It could kill a human child in two days, a grown human man in five. I was living with the mother of Dr. Sweeney-Gardiner K. Deaeque. He was the lead researcher in finding a cure for it. I allowed him to take some of my blood, once he found out I was Blessed. It turns out because of my blindness I lacked a key area if my brain and that effected my overall DNA. And when tested against the plague," The realization washed over Scarlet's face like a wave. "Your blood was the antidote. I learned about the Blind plague in school, they said they found the cure through someone's blood. A Blessed human too, but they never mentioned a name."

Charles nodded. "Yes, I know. I asked Dr. Deaeque to omit my name. If I was to be a hero, I wished to remain a nameless one. They drained my body while my heart still beat," Charles casted his eyes away from Scarlet. "I can still see the tubs draining me. Feel death's noose slowly get tighter upon me. I'll never forget the last words I ever heard. They were from Dr. Deaeque's mother. 'You did good, Charlie, thank you.' She said. 'Thank you for saving the world.' And then nothing." Charles opened his eyes, looking back at Scarlet. She wiped away the few stray tears that had fallen from her face. Suddenly, the mantle clock struck three. They both looked to it. "Oh no, time is almost up." Charles turned back to Scarlet. "Scarlet, before our time together is over, there is one more thing I must share with you. But what I share cannot be ever spoken aloud."

"Why?" Charles shrugged at her. "It's just the rule. It's about us, about Blessed humans. Have you noticed a pattern in them, anything?" Scarlet thought hard, but the sudden rush of time made her thoughts jumble together in her head, so she shook her head no. "The reason you lack a voice, is because you are Blessed. I was blind; Florence was deaf; the Blessed before her, Miles, lack a memory and the first Blessed human, Nora, was crippled. She could not walk. We are chosen to be Blessed and because we are given a gift we must give something back in return. It's not our choice and we have no control over it; it's just how it works."

"Can I ask you a question?" Butterflies filled Scarlet's stomach. "Of course." Charles bent his head to try to make eye contact. "You wrote, in your journal, that you had no one to trust. How did you recover from that?" Charles sat back, nodding his head slightly. "I started the journal. You see, my dearest and nearest friends were dying. They were cousins and were the only family I felt I had throughout most of my life. I was so close to one that if I held any real sexual attraction to any being- it would have been him. The cousin I was closer to lived slightly longer than the other, and upon his death bed I confessed I was losing the last person I fully trusted in the world. So he told me to start a journal... I still remember hearing the last breath he ever took. It was forever haunting."

"So, do you believe I should start a journal?"

"Yes. Because even the people we trust the most, can turn. When you can trust no one, then you can only trust yourself." Suddenly, the ground begun to shake. Scarlet, out of habit, scooted closer to Charles. "What's going on?" Charles scanned the ceiling, as pieces fell from it. "Our time should not be up!" He screamed to no one, but the shaking got worse. He looked back to Scarlet. "I'm sorry Scarlet, our time together is up. It was my great honor to get to be your guide. Remember, to get you must first give. That is the key to any life. To get, you must give!"

"Thank you." Embracing him in a hug, Scarlet closed her eyes as the world around her fell to pieces.

~~~

There was a soft melody playing on the radio, filling the car cabin. Scarlet kept her gaze to the window, not truly looking at anything. "You're nervous." Scarlet turned to Pals, confused. "You have bags under your eyes from a bad night's rest, you put your hair in a bun but it fell apart before I came for you and those shoes." She pointed
~~~

to her green flats. "Do not go with that shade of grey. Your fashion is normally on acceptable terms as is your hair." Scarlet touched her hair self-consciously. "Do not worry, if it wasn't me, no one would notice any real difference. But I take pride in noticing things, and fashion." Pals would glance over, but not fully look at Scarlet. She kept her eyes to the road, which Scarlet was grateful for. Pals was the one driving. "If you do not wish to do this, you don't have to. My little sister can be a bully when she chooses. Despite the ethics she swore to up hold." Scarlet shook her head, and turned back to the window.

Pals pulled to the curb of the street, and turned the car off. Scarlet's eyes were gazing up at the rather tiny building in front of her. "Pals leaned over, looking up. "It might not look like much but this is only Theo's personal lab. It's where she started. The one in her home and the University are much grander in scale, but she likes to remain near her roots." Pals climbed out of the car, mumbling something as she did. Scarlet scrambled to follow after, choking herself as she attempt-ed to climb out of the car while still buckled in. Releasing the latch, she stumbled from the car. She barely made it to the edge of the stone walkway when the door opened. Theo filled the entrance, removing a pair of goggles from her eyes. "Right on time, as per normal. Thank you Pals." Pals moved over, allowing Scarlet to walk to the doorway alone. "Of course, now I'm off, I have another appointment I must be getting to." Theo waved as Pals got back into her car and drove off. Scarlet stood beside her, silent. "What she meant is that she has a date with Rony. Come now," Pushing off of the door frame, Theo pulled Scarlet inside. "We have work to do!" Once more stumbling over her feet, Scarlet was pulled into the building.

"Come, come now." Theo pulled Scarlet up a twisting set of metal stairs, not giving her a chance to even glance at the bottom floor. "This is my lab. It's tiny, but it's where I do some of my most secretive work. My University lab is grand but too public, and to keep all my research in my home is just foolish." Scarlet's eyes roamed over the multiple tables, all filled with a range of different things. "Sit." The werewolf all but pushed her straight into a swirling chair. "Where to start?" Theo picked up a clipboard, mumbling to herself. "Where to start? So many places, so, so many places. Ah!" She sat the clipboard down and picked up a small glass container. Inside it contained a tiny cotton swab. "A swab of some saliva, and then some blood, a nail clipping, a few strands of hair-" The werewolf gasped, "Oh- and, and, a urine sample! How did I miss that?" She quickly flipped a few pages on her clipboard, and scribbled on one. "Okay, back to business. Open your mouth wide."

~~~

The door to Theo's slammed open, Pals stepping over the threshold as it did. Scarlet sat her cup of tea down, resting it in her lap as Pals singled in on Theo. Theo stood, a cookie in her hand. "Palsea! I wasn't expecting you back here until tonight. How was lunch?" Pals closed
~~~

the door, nearing her sister. "It was fine, until this." She stuck out her left hand, and on her finger was one of the largest rings Scarlet had ever seen. Theo smiled, jumping up and down; the cookie in her hand flying into the air. "Eiiee! You said yes! You said yes!" Theo grabbed her sister's hand, examining the ring. "Of course I said yes." Pals pulled her hand back, "Then Rony tells me the wedding is in two weeks. Two weeks. He has been planning the whole thing secretly for months!" Theo squealed once more, "I know! Isn't it great?" Pals took a seat, pouring herself a cup of tea. "I do not know. A wedding is meant to be planned by the bride and yet all I get is my wedding party and the dresses." Theo rolled her eyes. "Oh please Pals. You hate any sort of planning that isn't fashion or war related. I think Ron-a-Rony did great." Pals took a sip of tea, having poured herself a cup. "You are correct there."

"So does this mean you're asking me to be in your party?" Theo grabbed another cookie, placing the whole thing in her mouth. "Yes, you both actually." Theo's body suddenly heaved forward, and pieces of cookie came flying from her mouth. She beat her chest, coughing. Scarlet quickly stood, hitting the table and slipping her tea. Fisting her hand, she gave the best whack she could muster to Theo's back. Swallowing the cookie, Theo stopped coughing and thanked Scarlet. "You want Scarlet in your party? Why?" Pals took another sip of tea. "Because quite frankly I sometimes find myself enjoying her company more than I even enjoy yours or Rony's." Theo protested, but Pals ignored her. She instead turned to Scarlet, who had sat back down. "So Scarlet, will you be in my wedding party?" Scarlet refused, using basic signs to communicate to Pals that she didn't like her picture taken. "Your face shall be cover, Rony and I simply adore masquerades. It's the best party theme. Please be in my wedding." Just as Scarlet was about to agree, feeling extremely grateful towards Pals, someone knocked on the door. Theo stood, two cookies in hand, and opened the door. "I'm here for Scarlet." Theo stepped aside, allowing Renee to enter into the lab. Theo's eyes scanned Renee as she did.

"Hey Scar, you um, ready to go?" Scarlet nodded her head, standing. "Scarlet, you did not answer me. Will you?" Scarlet nodded her head, yes, giving Pals a small smile. "Will you what?" The werewolf and Scarlet looked at Renee. "I am getting married," Pals stood, sitting her tea cup down, "and Scarlet has agreed to be in my wedding party." The shock was clear on Renee's face. "Oh, well, um, congratulations."

"Because of your... history with my sister, I cannot ask the same of you. But I would hope to see you in the crowd, so that you might ease Scarlet's burden of communication." Renee gave a small smile and nodded her head. "Of course, thank you for the invitation." Pals gave a single nod. "Very good, I must get home to contact my parents and then the fabric shop. I have much to do in two weeks. Good day."

Later, after saying her farewells to Theo, Scarlet found herself in the back seat with Renee. Vern sat in the front, driving the two. The whole cab was rather silent. "So you're going to be in Pals' wedding?" Scarlet glanced over to Renee, nodding. "That was, really nice of her." Scarlet nodded her head a little harder, trying to imply the sarcasm she felt. "We're different Scarlet, it's as simple as that. I apologized and I'm going to work on not forcing my view point on you. It's all I can do." Scarlet nodded her head. 'I know, I understand.'

Scarlet was fascinated by both the market place and the amount of money she had to spend there. Though she did not expect much, if anything, from the King for her service to him- he paid her rather handsomely. And the market place. Oh the market place was like nothing she had ever seen in her life. It was large, roaming out into endless blocks of street carts and shops all just for goods. Every place was unique, offering its own stock of items. It amazed Scarlet. Growing up in their town in Tobus, there was one market place for both food and goods. It was small, maybe two blocks at the largest. It was all so overwhelming and Scarlet loved it. She found herself eagerly dashing from each place to the next, star struck. At one point, she even forgot about how upset she was with Renee. Until they entered into a book shop. Sitting upon it's own pedestal was a tan leather journal. Charles's words echoed in Scarlet's mind. When you trust no one, you can only trust yourself. As much as Scarlet loved Renee, and she claimed of attempting to change, she was having a hard time believing she would ever fully trust her again. So Scarlet bought the journal when Renee wasn't looking and hid it among her other bags.

The next shop they went to was a fabric shop, which also tailored custom dresses. There were bulks of fabric stack upon each other; from the floor to the ceiling. Scarlet thought of her mother, and for the first time- she didn't feel any pain. Instead, she heard two familiar voices in the far corner of the shop. Making her way through the aisles, Renee following behind her, Scarlet paused and smiled. "I literally just held up that color!" Pals shook her head, remaining calm in the face of storm Theo. "No, you showed me mint, this is mint-green." Theo threw her hands in the air. "Mint, mint-green, they are literally all the same shades!"

"They are not-oh Scarlet, Renee. Hello. It is wonderful you are here. Scarlet I need you." Pals moved away from her sister, holding a piece of fabric up to Scarlet. "Look? You see? It complements your skin, it compliments Scarlet and it'll compliment Claudia. That horrid, mint isn't your shade and it would wash Scarlet and Claudia both out. Thank you both, I'm leaving now." Pals left, going down the nearest aisle without a glance back to her sister. "Pals? Palsea! Come back! Don't leave me!" Theo went rushing after her sister. Scarlet looked from the werewolf to Renee.

'What just happened?'

Renee shook her head, looking down to the pile of multiple shades of green. "I do not know." Spotting a rather pretty looking green silk,

Scarlet bent down to pick it up. Holding it up, Renee commented on it's beauty and the two went back to shopping.

~~~

Journal Entry Number One

I was told by a dear friend that I should start a journal. I have lost the ability to fully trust anyone ever again. I had only one person left with me. I love the person still, but their views differ from my own on many manners and subjects. When you trust no one, you can only trust yourself. These are words for any Blessed to live by. My name is Scarlet, and I am Blessed. I did not choice my fate, it was thrust upon me. I have no voice, I never have nor ever will. To get, you must first give. If there is anything positive that comes from my Blessing, it has to be the satisfaction of knowing I am as I am because the world needs me. Without me the world as it is known would end forever. I am to save it. I fear, and this is the first of many, that I just might lose my life in the process. Surly it would be worth it, wouldn't it?

-S
~~~

CHAPTER 16

Air hissed through Scarlet's teeth. The sound of the wood upon wood mixed with her pounding heart, clouding her ears. Her vision was tunneled, focus on the attacking vampire in front of her. Blocking an attempt from them, she let out a small gasp as they responded. She found her wrist being bent in the most unnatural way, and released the wood from her hand to save them from breaking. They both watched the sword land just outside of her reach, and Claudia gave a wicked grin. Lifting her wooden sword, she swung it towards Scarlet. Sensing the move, Scarlet ducked, and sent her elbow into Claudia's rib. The vampire grunted, falling back a step. Taking the moment, Scarlet sent a rather nasty right hook into the crook of her jaw. Claudia let out a small cry, before falling to the ground in a heap. A string of curses fell through her lips as Claudia rubbed her jaw. Scooting to her knees, she looked back at Scarlet. Her eyes scanned her, and she nodded. "Good job." Scarlet smiled, falling to her own knees before finally coming to a rest on her side. Her whole chest burned, sweat stung her eyes and she lost feeling in three toes. The fight had lasted no more than five minutes and yet she felt near to death.

A hand fell into Scarlet's eye line, and she took it. Claudia pulled her into the air, Scarlet coming off the ground a few inches before standing straight once more. "You are just blossoming my little Gibbon. I do believe you shall forever carry that title. I was a fool to think of you as a Loris. You were clearly born a Gibbon- my little Gibbon. Now we must be going, Pals is expecting us at 5 for our gown fitting." Giving direction to the other trainers in the room, Renee included, Claudia strutted from the room. Scarlet followed silently, not looking back to meet Renee's gaze. Scarlet couldn't help or stop the feeling of guilt that rested in her. Renee was doing all she could to please her, yet Scarlet felt that by agreeing to be in Pals' wedding that the wedge between them was being forced upon them more. Scarlet's lack of trust, and Renee sensing it, did not help the relationship between the too either.

~~~

Claudia's whole body shuttered and she yelped. From where she stood beside her, Scarlet watched with eyes wide. "Sorry Claud." Pals spoke through a teeth of metal sewing pins, "If you got yourself measured routinely, then I wouldn't be doing this." Pals stuck another
~~~

pin through a small bunch of fabric. "Pals you know I'm not one to rush to the fabric store weekly. If it fits and there are no holes- I'm a happy vampire. Ow!" Pals looked up at Claudia. "Stop moving. You should care, these measurements from a year and half ago are so inaccurate. You've lost easily two inches everywhere." Claudia turned, cursing as she was stuck by a pin. "Well it's not my fault! Loosing Larson meant I lost his family cooking. He may have been a real one, but the men in his family knew how to make good food. Especially their signature blood-wine. I don't know how they did it, keeping it so fresh and tasty while also preventing clotting." Claudia fell away into another world, moving away when Pals told her she could carefully change out of the dress. "The men in his family were also self-absorbed pricks." Claudia said nothing, just left the room. Pals rolled her eyes, slightly shocking Scarlet. It was the most emotion Scarlet had ever seen her express. "This is why I like you," Pals ran her hands over Scarlet's sides, feeling the fabric of the dress. "You don't speak. You're simple, and I enjoy simple. Turn around and place your arms up in the air." Scarlet did as she was told, feeling a gentle tug at her back. "Now down." The fabric grew slightly loose, but was remained tighter than it's previous state. "Out to the sides, both of them." Pals pinned the fabric, and turned Scarlet back around. Her eyes scanned over her body, taking in her full shape. "I don't understand you, Scarlet, what are you trying- never mind. Here, I have a piece of paper somewhere." Scarlet, who had been attempting to ask Pals a question, watched the werewolf throw a number of things into the air or out to the ground before finding a piece of paper and a pencil in a drawer. "Use this."

At your wedding, shall there be dancing?

"Of course." Pals looked up from the paper. "It would not be a party without dancing. Rony loves dancing." Pals reached for a skirt at her legs that was not there, she wore pants that hugged every muscle on her legs, and gave a twirl. "Nothing but the music and your partner. Feet shuffling and skirts swirling. Turn for me Scarlet, as if you were dancing." Scarlet did as she was told, hoping she was doing it correctly. Scarlet had never danced in her life, so she never fully learned. She stopped when her head begun to hurt, and held it in her hands.

"Hm, yes, the skirt is beautiful dancing." Pals came over, picking up the fabric, and swished it around. She looked at Scarlet's bare legs, and gave a small frown. "Tell me Scarlet, and I am just now realizing this- do you own pants?" Scarlet slowly shook her head no. "Well why not?" Scarlet shrugged, unable to give any more of a response. "That must be fixed. I have your measurements now- I shall contact a good friend of mine. Every woman should wear pants." Scarlet quickly shook her head, and attempted to explain why she didn't care for the fashion choice. Pals watched her, not saying a word. "You trust me Scarlet. I know your taste in fashion and will not steer you wrong."

"Who won't wrong what?" Claudia joined them, back once more in her ash grey jumpsuit. She pulled at her corset; adjusting it. "I wish to update Scarlet's wardrobe. She owns not one pair of pants." Claudia hummed. "I must say I agree, were you thinking Riann?" Pals nodded, motioning for Scarlet to go change. "Yes, she won't question who I'm buying the clothes for." The two continued to talk, the door muffling their voices as Scarlet entered into the small bathroom. Scarlet could hear their voices still, going on about Riann, and her work. Undoing the zipper at her side, Scarlet gingerly slid her arms from the fitted sleeves. The dress then fell from her near shapeless hips. She was careful to pick it up, aware of the pins in the back. Placing it off to the side, she slipped back into her own clothes. She buttoned the collar, glancing at herself in the mirror. Pants, she had never fathomed the idea really. Renee wore pants daily, Scarlet hadn't seen her in a dress once since stepping foot in the King's home. She took a step back, examining herself. Perhaps it was the lighting in the bathroom, or the slight color in her face; but Scarlet felt as if something had changed. Exiting the bathroom, Scarlet returned the work-in-progress piece back to Pals. The two looked at her, as she reached for the paper once more.

I cannot wait to see what you create for me. Thank you for your kindness.

Pals and Claudia smiled, as the vampire gathered a few more things. The three then left the large studio and saying her farewells, Scarlet left with Claudia to return to King's home.

It was nearly seven by the time Scarlet found her way back to her room, and yet the sun was still setting. The summer was nearing, spring was coming to it's end. Pulling herself free of her wide leather belt, Scarlet ran her hands over her sides. She realized then that her fingers ran over a smooth surface. Stumbling into her bathroom, Scarlet tore her shirt off. In her mirror she was meet with perfectly smooth skin, there was not one rib visible. She hadn't gained weight, or at least she hadn't thought she did. All of her clothing's still fit, yet her body had filled out. Leaving the bathroom, she slowly moved away from the door.

Standing in the middle of her room, the sun rays casting long on the ground, she attempted to count how long she had been living in Voirol. She had lost track of the days that she was traveling with the Trade, her memories consisting of blurs. Once in the King's home she tried to count the days, at first she did. Yet at some point, and she did not know if it was days or weeks, Scarlet stopped counting. Perhaps, even, stopped caring.

Six months. She had been taken from Tobus nearly six months to the date. Suddenly, she felt as if she wanted- no, needed to cry. Because at the thought of her old life, of her mother; she no longer yearned for it. Moments and thoughts that would have her broken in a fit; were now nothing more than a simple ache in the back of her chest. She frowned, and grabbed a dress to wear for dinner. Changing, she couldn't help but watch herself in her full length mirror as she did. Each movement of her new body fascinated her. Once dress and unsure of what she should do next, Scarlet walked to her desk. Taking a seat, she pulled out her journal.

Journal Entry Number Two

I realized tonight that it's been near six months of the day of my kidnapping. I cannot believe so much change has happened is such a small but of time. Once ago when I would think of... before, it would bring nothing but fitting sorrow to my body. Now, though, I feel as different as I do to most of my memories. Some people believe in Fate, goddess or higher beings that have unlimited control over us. I'm not quite sure what I believe in, but perhaps my life was always set down this path. I'm becoming something I would have never even imaged just a few months ago. My body has changed, my style has change. I have changed. I'm going to start wearing pants. I'm not comfortable in them one bit- a life-hood in dresses will do that to a woman. But I'm going to start wearing them. Renee, Claudia, Pals, and Theo all wear pants. Women in this country wear whatever pleases them. The only being I have yet seen to don a pair of pants is the Queen, but perhaps she prefers her beautiful gowns. Who am I to judge?! I am excited to try pants out.

-S

~~~

The next day, in the hours after her morning lessons with the King and her afternoon training, Scarlet found herself roaming the gardens. The sun warmed the air, its rays warming her skin. She milled by workers, fingers brushing over a flower petal or two. The clear sky had never seemed so blue and Scarlet felt as if she had never heard so many birds. The whole world felt alive. As if it was alive for her only. Hoping off of the pebble path, she slipped her shoes off and walked to the edge of the lake. She sat her shoes, and basket down by the edge before moving closer to it herself. Settling down, Scarlet reached for a roll of bread from the basket. Ripping it up, she tossed a few pieces into the water. Waiting, she watched the pieces get soggy and slowly start to sink. As they did, the pieces were suddenly scooped up by a small duck. Smiling, Scarlet tossed a few more pieces towards it. The two played a game, Scarlet would throw pieces to get the animal to slowly move near her and the duck would get bread. Just when it seemed that the duck would eat straight from her hands, a small chirping filled the air. With slight dismay, Scarlet watched the duck rush off to a set of cattails. Following the creature, bread still in hand,
~~~

she brushed aside a few of the long blades. Peering down, she smiled at the small batch of ducklings crying for their mother.

"You should give them dry grain." Startled Scarlet's body grew stiff and she lost the last bits of crumbs. Turning, she was met with the shadow of the King. His frame blocked the sun, and he held a rather large case in his hands. "I'm sorry. I must have startled you." Scarlet nodded, and started to breath once more. She couldn't remember when she had stop.

It's okay. What's the box?

The King looked down to the case in his hand, "Oh this?" He held it up, giving her a smile. "It's a camera. Look." Bending down to her level, the King placed the case in between them. He unlatched and opened the lid. Scarlet studied the contraption, and at the nudge of the King; picked it up. It wasn't too large, but somewhat heavy in her hands. "This is the main piece, there's a flash but it's rather a pain to work with." She sat it back down in it's case.

I've never really seen a camera before.

"You haven't?" Scarlet shook her head.

No, it was against the Code. And my mother never had the money.

The King frowned slightly, and picked the camera back up. "Well, now you do. I'll even show you how it works." The King hit a latch on the side, and suddenly the front came popping out at Scarlet. "You have to unlatch it first, and then slid in the still. Like this." Reaching into a pocket, she watched him take a small square and stick it into the camera. "This will give me four photos. All I have to do is hold it up, point and click. Now...Smile." Scarlet frowned, and shook her head.

No, no. No photos. Not of me.

There was a slight nudge at Scarlet's knee, and she looked down. Letting out her own laugh, she reached out her hands and picked up the group of baby ducklings. She held the three little creatures in her hands, unable to keep herself from smiling. Holding her hands up, she turned to the King. As she did, the King held up the camera and there was a clear click. Frowning, she sat the restless babies back to the earth. "I'm sorry." The King lowered the camera, a small smile on his face. "I couldn't help myself. Everyone deserves to have at least one photo of themselves." Slowly, the frown on Scarlet's face turned into the tiniest grins. The thought of her face, for one single moment, being frozen in time forever, was thrilling. Growing up she had always been taught that photos of oneself were vain. Vanity rarely ever led to anything good, and so the Code discouraged them.

Scarlet casted a glance at the camera, watching as the King aimed it at the nest. With another click, he lowered it. Sensing her eyes, he looked over to her. "Would you like to take a photo?" Scarlet was going to decline, going to shake her head no, but instead she nodded. Her smile grew. The King stood, and offered her a hand. She took it, her warm fingers wrapping around his cool skin. It almost felt to her as if they were perfectly fitted. Releasing his hand, he held the camera out to her. She took it once more, and held it up- just like he had. "Aim it at whatever you want." She looked through the eye hole, seeing the world through the small round lens. "When you find something, place your pointer finger over the small button on the upper right side." Spinning, she focused on the King, and clicked the button to take the photo. Lowing the camera, Scarlet gave her own laugh. She handed the camera back to the King. "That was unexpected."

We're even now.

The King took the camera, unable to not chuckle himself. Bending down he kept the camera out but closed the case. "Would you care to spend the afternoon with me? I know you have training this afternoon but perhaps you'd like to take a few photos first?" Scarlet nodded her head, and followed after him.

CHAPTER 17

Cain had glanced out a window, as he was walking down a hall. He saw Scarlet slowly strolling through the gardens, the sun bouncing off of her. He paused at the window, his eyes following her. Through the brick and glass; he could smell her. He still smelled faintly of her, of jasmine. There was something in him, something out of his control, which drew him to her. He had been able to sustain whatever it was, so far, with their daily lessons. Some nights they had dinner. They were never alone, of course. Despite their uneasy friendship, Renee was faithfully there for Scarlet. If it wasn't Renee, then she was under the watchful eye of his cousin Claudia. This was the first time, since he pulled her from the cell in his basement, that he had seen Scarlet truly alone.

He had to go to her. To spend some true time with her. So he went to the attic, and dug out a gift that Dolra had given him a few years prior. Photography had never been a true interest to him, but Dolra had still given him the gift. After a point of time where the thing had gone unused, it was moved into the attic. Now, for the first time ever, it was seeing the light of day. He didn't approach her at first, instead he watched her. Even as she fumbled after the mother duck, he could only see her beauty. When he did finally speak to her, she jumped. Instant regret flooded him, and the same feeling returned after he took her photo. He deeply hated seeing her unhappy.

She took his offer to take a photo. He offered her his hand, and she took it. Her hands had smoothed in areas, while hardened in others. The warmth her hand offered seeped through his whole arm. And he didn't wish to let her go. She did, and she also took his camera. She held it up, he silently watched her. She moved it along the horizon, as he explained how to use it to her. He hadn't expected her to turn and take a photo of him, but she moved at the pace of a human. He at least had the time to pose for the photo. She returned his camera, claiming they were even. She would have left. He could see it in her eyes, but when he asked her to stay... she did.

Though he originally had no real place in mind, his feet took him to the small dock. The same one that he once found Scarlet at during the peak of her friendship argument. He hadn't paid attention to dock before, he rarely did to his home anymore, but it was in a rather ideal place. Secluded on a small round bend, always in the perfect amount of shade. The sun seem to glimmer perfectly from their spots on the dock. Setting her basket down, Scarlet lowered herself to take a seat on the dock.

I love this lake. It's pretty.

"It is. I've lived here for thousands of years, I stopped looking after a while." He took a spot near her, and held up the camera. "Here," he held it out to her, "you take it. You see more beauty in the world than I do." She took the camera, looking at it. She shook her head, sitting it back down.

I see no more beauty than any other.

"I don't think that's true." He picked up the camera, aimed it at the tree tops and clicked the button as a flock of birds went through the sky. He lowered it, and set it back on the docks.

Why do you suddenly have faith and interest in me?

He let out a small chuckle, toying with the camera. "I've always had interest in you." She hadn't been facing him, he could only catch a glimpse of her jaw. She moved just slightly at his response and he caught a pink flush on her cheeks. Looking up, their gazes met. They both smiled.

~~~

Returning back to the mansion, the first worker he saw Cain handed off the used film to them. With strict instructions to get it developed
~~~

at once, they rushed off as he headed off to a meeting. He had said his farewell to Scarlet in the gardens, leaving her to go to the basement as he went up to the second floor of his home. Through the maze of hallways he worked his way to the meeting room where the war meeting was waiting to take place. Approaching the door, a guard swiftly stepped forward and open it for him.

Stepping into the room, the door closed behind Cain. Every being sitting at the large oval table stood and bowed. He waved for them to sit, and took his spot at the head of the table. "Good afternoon, thank you all for being here." Cain glanced at the papers already sitting in front of him. "First order of business, what is the current status at the boarder? Anything new General?"

"No sir," General Rey, who sat three seats down to Cain's right, stood up. His hair was nonsexist on his head, and only had a few crowfeet in his sun kissed skin. But his neatly trimmed white beard gave away the werewolf's true age. "Beyond the current attacks, which we've always neutralized, there has been nothing new." His voice was gruffly, set so from too many years of smoking. "I do have men deployed, my best majors leading them." Cain nodded, making a note and General Rey sat back down. Cain took another glance to his list. "Major Deaeque, please share your latest update." Pals stood, her eyes scanning the group. "Sire, I am pleased to announce that our flower is budding much greater than we could have first hoped for." The group of high military leaders looked among each other, clearly lost. Only General Pirtle, Cain's cousin, seemed unaffected by the werewolf's new.

"Pals, please share with your fellow soldiers of our secret weapon." Pals nodded. "Of course sire." Picking up the folder that she had been quietly been guarding with her own life, Pals walked to the front of the room. "Before I go on, I trust you all to remember that you swore an oath on your life to keep these meeting confidential." No one said anything, a few had even stopped breathing; their chest immobile. Giving a single nod, Pals opened her folder and tossed out small stack of papers and photos. "Over the past four months, Major Claudia Pirtle and myself have been secretly training this nation's secret weapon to defeating Muis." General Rey picked up a newspaper clipping, exclaiming out loud. "By the power of Fate- are you telling me the Bless Human lives?" The Command Chief of the Air Ship fleet snatched the newspaper from his neighbor. Frowning when the General snatched it back. "Yes, the Blessed Human indeed is alive. She has been living under this roof, under an alias. She was injured badly, but she is now not only healed but thriving. With training from Major Pirtle and myself, she has become a solider within her own rights."

"So she is prepared to fight, today?" Pals casted her eyes down for a brief moment before looking Chief Dowdy. "Yes, she might not be the strongest or the fasted but her mind is sharp. She can throw and hit the aim near perfect with a knife, her thin frame is perfect for hand to hand and if she must she can swing a sword into the right spots." Cain nodded, and Pals gathered her papers. "The fact that the Blessed Human must be our most well-guarded secret. At least until we strike Muis down." The military leaders all nodded, and Cain thanked Pals.

"Next, Admiral, how is... Captain Kerns, where is Admiral Wiles?" At the sound of her name, the Captain grew stiff and her eyes wide. "Well sire," Captain Kerns stood, her uniform looking far too foreign on her lanky body. "Admiral Wiles refused to come." Cain frown, adjusting himself in the leather seat. "Why?"

"The Admiral believes you are lacking on your duty to the fleets," As she spoke, Captain Kerns' body went from awkward to powerful. "He respectfully sent me in his place so that the men and women wouldn't feel abandoned once more." The anger rose slowly within Cain's chest. To prevent injuring anyone or breaking anything, his hands gripped the chair arms. "If you and Wiles were not so perfect at your job; I'd have you both put on trial for treason and mutiny. To defy any order given by me by law is punishable by death. I have gotten your updates, and have acted accordingly. Now sit down." The Captain sat, her chest remaining puffed out, but her muscles tight. "If Wiles wishes to have my presence there so badly, consider it done. I shall arrive Monday. I expect you and your seamen to be ready."

"Monday? That is almost a week from now? Why can you not arrive sooner?" Cain, who had been making another note, paused. "Because I have a wedding to go to. I shall be there Monday." Captain Kerns scoffed, and leaned on the table. "A wedding? Really sire? We are in a war and you prioritized a wedding higher than visiting the mass of your naval fleet?" Cain finished writing and sat his stylus down. "For this particular wedding? Yes, next matter."

"Oh no, no, no. Who the hell is getting married who's so important that they delay a whole naval fleet's inspection?" the human was suddenly cut off, not by Cain but rather Pals. "Mine. It is my wedding." Cain could sense that the human was fighting the urge to cower back. Instead she kept herself straight but leaned back in the chair. "Honestly Major Deaeque, of all the being. I never thought you to be one to place her own self so selfishly over the wellbeing of this whole nation." Pals went on, her scarily monotone voice laced with anger. "Normally I refuse to make such a fret over a simple ceremony but because my fiancée has been secretly planning this event for two years I shall fret. So excuse me for feeling no pity on the subject of our currently nonsexist war for just a few days in exchange for the happiness of the man I love. I have served this nation, have given everything I can offer, for well over 200 years. And over that time King Cainwen has become a dear friend to us both and I am honored that he would place us both so high. Get over yourself." Gathering her papers, Pals calmly stood. She turned to Cain. "Excuse me sire but I believe my presence is no longer required here. If you require a Major, I shall send Major Pirtle up at once. I have a Blessed Human to teach." Bowing, Pals then left. Captain Kerns watched her, taking a deep breath. Once the door closed, the slam shaking the whole wall, the room was left with a tense silence. "You're one hell of a lucky human, Ericka." Klaus sat back in his chair, bitterly laughing as he dug the crevices of his teeth with his tooth pick. Captain Kerns frowned. Cain rolled his eyes, picking up his stylus and made another note. "Next order of business."

~~~

"I must apologize for yesterday afternoon. I never meant to lose my temper. The full moon is next week, though, and my wolf is much antsier than she's been prior." Cain changed the hand he held the phone receiver, crossing his legs as he leaned against his desk. "I understand, Pals, all is forgiven and well."

"Thank you. Have a wonderful day sire."

"And you, I hope your dress is everything you wish for."

"Thank you."

Hanging up the phone, Cain pushed himself up. He left his office and headed towards the library, sure he would catch Scarlet there on her day off. He had been told by a few maids and guards that she
~~~

often spent time in the large chamber. Though Cain would never admit it to anyone out loud, he was very fond of the human. Even if you were to remove the strange pull he felt to her, he genuinely enjoyed her company. She had been so quite when they first met, like a scared child. Slowly she found herself and begun to trust him. That was when he realized how much he enjoyed her company, despite her lacking voice. Positivity was her strong suite, she could find beauty in the ugliest blade of grass. If she viewed something negatively, she told one so but was not willing to fight upon any subject. There was a grace that surrounded her, and wrapped her like a blanket. Walking she seemed to glide across the floor, her movements fluid. She had to be expressive, and many made Cain smile. Which often times made her blush and slyly smile. Oh her smile! When she smiled, her teeth more perfect than pearls, deep dimples formed on each cheek and her eyes gleamed. They seemed to always gleam, as if she was just told an exciting, forbidden secret. There was no denying the fact that whenever he touched her, their body parts fitting with the other, that there was a current that shot through him. It was like nothing he had ever felt before, and something he wanted to feel until the day his existence ended.

Turning a corner, Cain paused. He pondered upon his feelings, realizing that the only woman who had ever captivated him in such a way was his wife. Those feelings, though, did not form quickly. The two had known each other for a few hundred years before entering into courtship. Thinking about his wife, Cain tried to conjure up the emotions. He got nothing. Even though it never would, Cain felt as if his heart should be speeding up. He should have been worried, been nervous for his lacking feelings for his wife. He wasn't. He couldn't remember the last time his wife had captivated him in such a way—if she ever had. The thought should have bothered him, should have encouraged him to reach out to Dolra; but it didn't.

Coming up to the library, Cain slowed and stopped at the cracked door. Peaking in, Scarlet stood over the chess table, picking up one of the knights. He opened the door slowly, to keep it from making any sounds and silently moved towards her. "Do you play?" The human jumped, shaking the whole table. Cain smiled and laughed to himself, dropping the smile when she turned to face him. She looked to the black knight in her hand, and then back at him. She shook her head no. "I can teach you, if you want to learn."

You teach me?

"Yes. May I?" She nodded her head, watching him as he took a seat. Following his lead, she sat down and begun to place the pieces back on the board. After placing all the pieces back into their proper square, Cain begun to slowly explain the game to Scarlet. She seemed confused by the rules at first, but she soon caught on. They began a simple game. "You're catching on quite well." She thanked him, making her second move.

It's not checkers, but enjoyable.

Cain smiled, laughing as he made his next move. Scarlet bit the corner of her lips, pondering her next move. "Are you prepared for Pals' wedding on Sunday?" Scarlet moved a piece, her face whiting as she did. She shrugged, leaning back in her chair. "You don't know? Why not?" She casted her eyes down, and moved her hands quickly.

There will be dancing. I don't know how to dance.

"You don't know how to dance?" She shook her head no, her hands moving slower than before.

No. I never went out. I was never invited out. I worked and helped my mother.

"So you've never been to a ball or even a barn circle?" She shook her head no once more, still refusing to look up to him.

I learned a few folk dances from Renee, but nothing fancy that is performed at balls or weddings.

He face flushed with colors of embarrassment. "Then allow me to teach you." Her head shot up, and she shook her head in a refusal. Scarlet looked absolutely appalled by the idea. "Why not? I may not be the best dancer but I'm sure I could teach you a thing or two."

I couldn't.

"Please? Pals tells me you're training is going wonderfully and you deserve to have some fun."

I do not consider stepping on toes and tripping on skirts fun.

Cain stood, and reached for her hand. "Come with me." It was more of a request rather than a demand. She rose from her seat. The two left the library, their hands still intertwined. Glancing around, and seeing there was not one guard in site, they began walking. He led her through the halls, stopping in front of double doors. Opening one, he ushered her into the small ball room and followed after. Closing the door, and locking it, Cain then walked over to the corner of the room. Resting on it's own small pedestal, was the most impressive gramophone. Scarlet followed after him, leaning over his hunched back to see the machine. Picking up a record, Cain stood and Scarlet stumbled back. "This is a gramophone, it plays music. Watch." Flicking the machine on, Cain placed the record down. There was no sound for the first few seconds the needle rode on the spinning disk, and then suddenly a whole symphony filled the room. Grabbing Scarlet, Cain led her to the middle of the room. "I'm going to teach you the simple box-waltz." He placed one of her hands on his shoulder and kept the other in his own grip. They came close, closer than they had ever been. He could feel her blood, it flowed quickly through her racing heart. "Follow my lead." He stepped to the right, then back, to the left and lastly forward. Scarlet stumbled but followed him. "Now spin clockwise. Repeat. Side right, back, side left and forward." They repeated this process a few more times, a small smile forming from Scarlet. "We're going to change it now, instead of turning together this next time around I'm going to spin you out." Her body grew rigged as he spun her out, her feet stumbling. When she stopped, Cain pulled he back, twirling her once more. She caught herself with a tight grip on his shoulder, looking up to him as they begun to move back in rhythm. He met her gaze, and found himself falling deep into the glorious wonders that were her onyx eyes. Scarlet seemed to be feeling the same, because her body relaxed more; allowing Cain to full lead her. His gaze on her eyes was broken when she moved her eyes down towards his lips, her own parting. Scarlet looked at their hands, and the little space between them. Looking back to him, it was if she was almost to say something.

There was a sudden knock at the door, and the moment between them ended. Scarlet leapt as far as she could get, breaking their hold on the other. As if she had just been burned. Cain looked to the door, realizing that the gramophone had stopped playing. "Your majesty." Glancing over to Scarlet, who looked as if she was trying to shrink, Cain moved towards the door. "What is it?" Unlocking the door, he opened it just enough to stick his head out. "Sire," Isos bowed to him, "this telegram message just came from the coast. It's from Admiral Wiles, sire." Cain looked at the out stretched folded paper. With a small noise of disgust, he took the paper from his guard. Opening it, he scanned over the note, rolling his eyes once finished. Crumbling the paper, he stuffed it into the pocket of his tailored pants. "Get in contact with my cousins, have them meet me in my office in ten minutes." Isos gave a nod, a bow and then left. Closing the door, Cain looked back to Scarlet. She had remained where he had last left her. "I'm sorry." He returned to her, resisting the urge to reach out and bring her eyes back to his. "A matter has risen, I must go. Our dance lesson must be cut short." She gave a small wave to tell him it was okay. "Do not worry, Pals' wedding is still four days away." Grabbing her hand, he brought it to his lips. At the contact of their skin, Cain felt as if a bolt of lightning had been shot through him. "We have time yet." Releasing her hand, he gave a small smile. Unable to help himself. Scarlet had felt something as well, the color in her cheeks and the wideness of her eyes told him so. And that thought, that she was feeling something as well, thrilled him.

CHAPTER 18

Uncurling from the ball she had formed while sleeping, Scarlet stretched herself out like a cat. Yawning, her hands fell to her pillow. Today is the day. She thought to herself. There wasn't a moment up until that moment in her life that she felt so excited. Pals was getting married, and not only was Scarlet invited to the wedding-she was to be in it. A childhood lived out casted from any real social events had all built up to a near sleepless night from the under lying multitude of feelings. Within her bubble of bliss, the thought of what was to come after the wedding made the smile from Scarlet's face vanish. The King had informed her just two days prior, as they ended their two hours of dance practice that he was to be headed to the coast on Monday. The thought that she would be alone in the castle did not startle Scarlet, the request he made for her to come within was what made her trip over her own toes. He made the argument that his cousin Claudia would be there also, and that the trip was purely business. Having her there, he claimed, would at least make his time there slightly less dull.

Rolling from her bed, Scarlet stripped her night gown off. Tossing it to her bed, she moved through the cool morning air in the nude; going to the bathroom. She filled the bath, using all of her favorite products. The sweet smells swirled through the air, almost to a suffocating point. She didn't mind. After she was satisfied with how deep the perfume seeped into her skin, Scarlet drained the water and wrapped herself in a towel. She strolled from the bathroom to her closet, picking one of the first dresses her hands fell on. It didn't matter, she wouldn't be in it for long. Changing into the frock, Scarlet shifted her focus to her hair. Patting it dry with the towel, she then braided it. Once more, it didn't matter all too much. Her hair would only be kept in the style for a short time.

She realized as her bare feet hit the cool marble of the foyer, that she had forgotten her shoes in her room. After returning to her room and finding a pair that matched the dress, she finally entered the dining room. Renee was already seated, her plate piled with a small mount of food on it. Taking her own seat, Scarlet started to place food onto her plate from the mid-middle setting bowls. "So you are leaving straight after breakfast?" Slowly lowering her fork, her mouth chewing on her eggs, Scarlet nodded.

Pals wants us there by nine-thirty.

"Do you really think it's going to take you two and half hours to get ready?" Scarlet shrugged, taking another bite of eggs. She didn't know, and she didn't care to know. This was all but her first party. The table, as well as the room, fell silent. There would be a scrapping of forks, the movement of food. Finishing her small meal, Scarlet stood. Renee watched her, "I'll see you at the wedding." Scarlet gave a small wave, leaving the room. Coming into the foyer, she smiled as she spotted Vern. "Good morning Miss Scarlet, are you ready to go?" Nodding, Scarlet stepped out the open door. Climbing into the waiting car, she was slightly surprised when Vern followed in after her. Closing the door, he glanced over to Scarlet and smiled- showing off a sharpen pair of fangs. "I am to just see you to the Museum, by request of the King." She nodded, giving him a tiny smile of her own. She could understand why the King would place her under a guard's care.

If Scarlet had ever been to an upper class wedding, or any wedding truly, she would have realized what a strange venue a Museum was for such an event. Never the less, as she was lead to a small worker's area, her breath was taken away- as it was the first time she had seen it all. The white washed walls were so tall, they seemed to reach up and touch the sky. Under carefully placed lights were paintings along the wall, each framed in golden beauty. Behind velvet ropes, scattered throughout the floors were a multitude of different statues and sculptors of all sizes. They passed by the area where the ceremony would be held, in the largest glass room Scarlet had ever seen in her life. She had been in the green house only one other time, the day prior during the practice ceremony. She could already image the long flower canopy over her head, the soft cobble stone under her feet that made up the center aisle. The sound of Vern's goodbye pulled Scarlet from her day dream, and she waved to him.

Entering a rather small, and bland hall way, a worker showed Scarlet to the room that she was meant to get ready in. Giving the worker a nod, she jumped at the loud voice on the other side of the door. The worker rolled their eyes, spinning on their heels as they did. Left alone, Scarlet opened the door and was greeted with utter chaos. "I cannot find it-it's not here!" From behind a large pile of stacked crates, Theo popped up and frantically turned to her sister. "Theo relax, if they're not here, then they're at my shop. Go call mother or father, have them stop there real fast." Groaning Theo rushed past Scarlet and out the door. Pals took a deep breath, her eyes setting on Scarlet through the mirror. "Oh wonderful, you're here. I would hug you, but Luca would claw my eyes out if I messed his work up." The worker who stood over Pals turned, and smiled. He was a werewolf, his eyes glowing despite being near black. He held her hair in his hands. "Aye, please come 'ave a seat next ta Palsea. I'll 'ave my assistant start work on you." Scarlet noted, as she took the stool besides Pals, that he had lightened her hair, and removed the braids. He was working on flattening it, defining the sharp downward angle it held from her jaw. The werewolf working on her hair had taken it out from it's braid and was now brushing it. "Palsea, whatta you wanna give this one?" Pals glanced over to Scarlet's hair, thinking for a moment. "Curls. Lots and lots of beautiful, loose curls. Make the part deep to the left, then, take what's left and pin it to the right back half in a bun. I have a beautiful hat I wish to display." The worker nodded her head, "A'ight you got it."

By the time Scarlet's hair was finished, Pals had turned away from the mirror. A vampire with very blue hair and bright yellow eye shadow was now carefully coloring her face. It was not a normal routine, it was like nothing Scarlet had ever seen. The vampire carefully laid a fine, straight line of tan dust straight across Pals' face. "Open, let's check." Opening her eyes, Pals turned to look in the mirror. "Yes, this is turning out well. Theo, look." Theo sat on the other side of Pals, her red hair being carefully curled and pinned in a bun. Upon seeing her sister, Theo smiled. "It's wonderful." Pals nodded, and turned back to the artist. Theo glanced over to Scarlet, where the small pale green hat was being pinned to her head. She was confused by the plain line. "It's a tradition that for any life altering ceremony, in today's case Pals' wedding, that we return to the nature around us. As a reminded and a thank you. Since Pals' and Rony are getting married, it's their duties to try to connect to the planet around us." Scarlet gave a small nod, still not completely understanding the concept. So she sat silently, watching the paint be applied to Pals's lip. "So what do you want me to the human?" The vampire had moved from Pals, who was standing and moving to a corner of the room, and now was bent face to face with Scarlet. "Something simple. Natural colors. Enhance the beauty she was born with. The same for Theo, Claudia- if she ever shows up- and Maxmia." The vampire nodded, shuffling through her bag until she found the brush she had been seeking.

Claudia showed up just as the vampire was painting Scarlet's lips a soft peach. She apologized profusely to Pals, who was behind a dressing screen, and took a seat so Luca could do her hair. When the vampire deemed Scarlet finished, she took a step back to admire her work. With a single nod she moved on to Theo, who had just re-turned to her stool. Everything stood still, though, when Pals stepped out from behind the dressing screen. Scarlet felt the breath leave her lungs and not return. The gown was the palest of lavenders, hugging her body perfectly but pooling around her feet. The sleeves hugged her arms, and the sweetheart neckline framed her breast perfectly. Each shoulder had a cover, and attached was sheer white, billowing sleeves in the front. The back was a matching cape that had a train at least six feet long. Sliver rings, stacked upon each other ran from her chin to her shoulders. Connecting with the metal shoulder covers seamlessly. She stood among them, a goddess among mortals.

"Oh Pals."

"Wow."

"Look at you big sister."

Pals remained stone face throughout the wave of compliments. At the end, she gave a small head nod, and a "Thank you." She adjusted the metal belt at her hips, her eyes falling for a moment. Moving towards the crates, she pulled out a large white bundle. "It is time for you all now, Scarlet. You first, you are the only one fully ready." The other three bridesmaids casted a look towards Pals, but she ignored them and handed the bundle to Scarlet. "You shouldn't need help." Standing, Scarlet took the rather heavy bundle into her arms and went to hide behind the dressing screen. Seeing the dress fully finished, she took a moment to hold the gown to the soft steam-lamp. The plain mint-green was there, but there was now a graceful layer of green lace- the coloring matching the hat on her head. The skirt, now fully finished, expanded out slight around her knees. It was so beautiful. Not only was it the most beautiful gown she had ever worn, it was the most beautiful gown she had ever seen. Changing into it was simple as baking a pie. What she noticed, where there had once been a zipper, was now a row of fabric covered buttons. Each was no bigger than her pinky nail, the line going from her mid hip, up her side until her armpit. There, right before it would rest in a rather uncomfortable spot, the buttons then moved to the side, framing her arm, and shoulder. When it finally centered at her necks hallow, they continued upward to fully cover her neck. Once the last button was pulled through, she lifted the soft skirt and stepped out from behind the screen. Theo stood next to Pals, a pair of brown heels in her hands. Claudia was getting the final touches on her hair, and the last bridesmaid Maxmia, a cousin of the twin sisters, sat still as her face got worked on. Dropping the skirt, Scarlet looked about the room nervously as everyone now stared at her. She tried to hide the fact that her hands were shaking, and fought to keep her back straight. Theo was the first to smile, with Claudia following after. Pals moved closer, the ruffling of her beaded head piece being the only noise in the room. She had placed it on her head as Scarlet had changed. The carefully sewn beads rested against her forehead, and framed her face. They then expanded out to the rest of hair, cascading down in a large, beaded veil. Her eyes ran over Scarlet, running a few fingers down her arm. Brushing the tips of her fingers down Scarlet's jawline, Pals moved her face closer. "You look beautiful." Scarlet smiled, instant relief flooding her whole body. "Come, I have your shoes and mask. Theo, your turn."

~~~

"Places, places." Scarlet was shuffled into a line by the wedding coordinator, as he eagerly whispered at them. "On my cue-wait for it." He made a small motion, and suddenly the air swirled with a number of instruments. "Okay, okay, first girl. Walk, pause for the photo, and then continue on." Maxmia cradled the bouquet of flowers flat in her right arm, and turned the corner. Among the music, and because she
~~~

was so close, Scarlet heard the gentle click of the camera. Scarlet took a small step forward. When Claudia begun to move, that was when her heart rate picked up. She was next. Scarlet watched the wedding coordinator like a child seeing a new toy. When he motioned for her to move, she did. Thankful for the masquerade mask Pals had required any one at the wedding to wear. Columbia was the style of the bridesmaids, having matched their dresses by color and lace. Pausing, she glanced to the camera man, and smiled. Moving on, her eyes scanned both sides of the on lookers, her smile never wavering. The honor and beauty she felt out weighted any negative thought she could have at the moment.

Finally reaching the end of the walk, she took her place next to Claudia. Theo followed shortly after, smiling larger than Scarlet had ever seen her. When the werewolf took her place next to Scarlet, the music suddenly changed. The audience then stood, looking to the spot where Pals would be entering. Rounding the corner, the sound of her beads jingled through the air and Pals made her entrance. Coming to her side, her parents each hugged her and took a single step in front of her. Only then, together, did the trio move down the aisle. As Theo had also explained the day before, it was her parent's duty to lead Pals down the aisle. It symbolized their last journey together that would ultimately lead her into a new life. Unlike Scarlet and Theo, Pals eyes remained focused on one being- Rony. Though she did not smile nor frown, her face seemed softer as she stared at her husband to be.

Reaching the end of the aisle, Pals met her parents. Stepping between them, the music faded away.

"And who leads this werewolf into her next journey?" The Marriage Minister looked to Mr. and Mrs. Deaeque. Together they both replied with a swift 'we do'. The Minister nodded his head in thanks and dismissed them. They took their seat in the front row, both beaming in pride. "Good day to you all, and welcome. We have gathered here today as witnesses to Palsea Elizabeth Deaeque's and Ronford David Loth's journey into their new life together. You may all be seated." The crowd sat, but the wedding party remained standing to each side. "There is much to be said about love. Many believe that it is infinite, and that it's power is stronger than any being. As is known in our history, werewolves have always found their everlasting love through the fate-bound soul mate. To be willing to travel to the edges of the world and back, just for the chance to find true happiness. Luckily for Palsea and Ronford, they needed not to travel through the lands. Rather, they met by chance along the beautiful beaches of Seustad. Palsea was there on business, Ronford in hopes to forget about his ex." The crowd gave small chuckles, and laughs; clearly entertained.

"Upon spotting Palsea, Ronford would ask her out four times within the span of a few hours before Palsea tackled him from annoyance. After that failed to turn his attention from her, she agreed to go for a drink. That single drink would lead to two, which lead to a real date, and so on until we reach today nearly twenty years later to the date. Today these two say goodbye to separate lives, and begin the new journey together. As they do, we take this time to remember those of before us, and honor them. We honor the earth of which we were born and onto which we shall one day die. We honor their future together. For marriage is not something one goes into lightly. It is a lifelong commitment, a precious gift. It is created and upheld by love, and without will surly crumble." Scarlet took the chance to glance out to the crowd, searching for only one person. Upon spotting them, and they catching her eye, both smiled. He looked so handsome in his black mask.

"Now the beloved would like to each say something to each other, Palsea." Turning, Theo held out a piece of paper to her sister. Pals took it, turning back to her groom. "My darling Rony, I honestly cannot believe I am standing here today. Mostly because you successfully hid it for the past two years but could not hide the secret of my surprise birthday party last year." Everyone laughed, and Rony flushed in loving colors. "But I would not have you any other way. I never thought the annoying werewolf from Sunset beach would be the wolf I'd fall in love with. You annoy me, and know how to push me to my limits. But you also take me for all of my flaws, and have never tried to change me. Thank you, for everything. I love you. I love you with every breath I take, and will do so until the moment my heart ceases to move. I'm not sure if Fate chose us as Mates, but I know for a fact that even if it didn't our love is greater than any other force. I am honored to be becoming your wife and promise forever together." The Minister motioned to Rony. The werewolf pulled a folded paper from his jacket pocket.

"Pals, were do I even start? From the moment I spotted you along the beach, I knew you were the one. Despite the fact that your lack of facial emotions during our first few dates left me confused and slightly scared." Again the crowd laughed. For the first time that she'd known her, Scarlet witnessed Pals smiled. "But I refused to give up. I knew there had to be a way to get through those emotionless layer. What I realized is that the layers are not something I had to get through, but rather something you had allow me pass. Thank you for letting me pass it. Thank you for trusting me, and agreeing to be my wife. It is a responsibility I do not take lightly but gladly take on. You are the love of my life." Rony choked, and Pals reached across to wipe the tears falling from his eyes. "I will never be the man you truly need, but I will try my damn hardest to be him. I know that together as a team, we can defeat anything. Because today, together, we are starting on a new path, and I promise forever together." The two interlocked hands, and for the first time in front of many of the beings at the wedding Pals smiled. Her teeth sparkled, and the skin around her eyes wrinkled. "Palsea, in front of these witnesses, do you here today and forever more take Ronford to be your husband? Do you promise to love, comfort and keep him? Will you forsake all else and remain true to him until death do you part?"

The smile fell from Pals' face but the joy was still there. "I shall." The Minster nodded, and repeated the same passage to Rony. Smiling, he nodded his head. "I shall." The Minster motioned to Theo and Rony's best man. "May the rings brought forth now." Each werewolf handed their ring off to one of the soon-to-be newlyweds. "Palsea, please repeat after me: Ronford, in front of these witnesses and with this ring; today I thee wed." Pals repeated him, sliding the black band onto Rony's finger. "Ronford, please repeat after me: Palsea, in front of these witnesses and with this ring: today I thee wed you." Rony's hand shook as he slid the band onto Pals' slim hand but once it was done a loud howl came from the crowd. Rony laughed, his face tinting. "I hereby, with the power invested in me, pronounce you both man and wife. Please seal this proclamation, and start your new journey together, with a kiss." The Minster took a step back, just in time for the camera to snap a picture of the married couple kissing. The music suddenly filled the air once more, carrying along the joy already in the air.

Pulling away, Pals and Rony hugged. He whispered something in her ear, and then pulled away. They both linked an arm with the other, Pals quickly grabbing her large bouquet from Theo. As they walked down the aisle, and for what Scarlet could guess was for the photo sakes, Pals gave a small smile. Once they reached the end, and rounded the corner out of sight, Theo linked arms with Rony's best man and followed after. Scarlet was next, having been paired with a rather short male vampire, her eyes catching the King's once more. After rounding the corner, the two were lead to a small, blocked off room. There, surrounded by paintings, they were to wait for the rest of the wedding party. Pals and Rony were already off in another section of the Museum taking private photos. By the time they were to be done, the ceremony space was to be cleared of all wedding guest so that more photos could be taken there. Only the whole wedding party was to be included.

~~~

Just as the last photo was taken, a rather large rumble shook Scarlet's whole inner core. She hadn't realized how hungry she was until a worker walked by with a delicious smelling platter of chicken bites. Luckily, no one had heard her stomach's cries. Another point for her was that the whole wedding party was lead into the main reception room just as many sat down for their mid-day meal. Taking her place at the round center table, she only begun to eat once Pals and Rony took their first bites. The meal seemed to speed by them, with the cutting of their wedding cake and desert coming and going. After nearly all were finished, the whole crowd moved to an adjoined room. There in all four corners were different pieces of an orchestra, with
~~~

the further wall from the entrance being glass windows. There were a few seamless doors, which lead out to the impressive garden. Hanging from the high vaulted ceilings were three chandeliers, all equal in size and light. On the actual ceiling, though, were detailed paintings one would see in the home of a king.

Almost immediately upon entering the room Rony swept Pals out to the center of the room. Scarlet, along with the rest of guest, watched in a romance haze as the couple floated throughout the room, as the only dancers, for three solid songs. When the forth one begun, and others finally joined them, Claudia could be seen giving a sly smile to a rather tall vampire. Scarlet watched them, lost in the daze of the moment. "Excuse me." Suddenly the light feeling she had was pushed form her body and she found herself landing hard back upon the ground. Turning to the owner of the voice, she held back a smile. "May I have this next dance?" The King bowed to her, a hand out held. He glanced up, and Scarlet realized how daunting he appeared at that moment- even in a bow. His suit was full black, and perfectly tailored to his body. His hair had recently been trimmed, and was slicked back without a single hair out of place. His black mask popped against his pale skin. It fully covered his face minus a small area that looked at if it had been cut to perfectly expose everything from his left cheekbone and below.

Releasing her smile as she took his hand, they strolled into the dancing crowd as a new song begun. Around them people begun to move. Placing everything in it's proper position, the King moved. Scarlet followed after, bearing her eyes into his as to keep herself from look at her feet. Almost as if he could read her mind, the King smiled and tightened his grip along her waist. When the tempo started to speed up, so did her heart rate. They were now moving into positions that he had not taught her. She was fully at his mercy, and truly followed him. Never removing her eyes from his, was spun, dipped and even lifted into the air. Once in the air, she did glance at another woman and copied her free outstretched hand. Coming back to the ground, their hands met once more. At the feeling of it, of the King touch, Scarlet smiled and her cheeks were flamed. The tempo of the song soon begun to slow, coming nearer to the pace that it had started at. It was then Scarlet realized how little she had actually been breathing. Had it been physically possible for her, she would have stopped all together. Spinning out one last time, the song ended with Scarlet in the King's arms. Her head was turned up to face his, frozen. Looking to his lips, and then quickly back to his eyes, she realized how deeply she wished to feel his lips upon hers.

"May I have this next dance?" He looked down to her, his eyes running over her face. Without a single sing of hesitation, Scarlet nodded. The music started once more, and in a single blink she faced him right on once more. "Green looks good on you." Laughing more to herself, Scarlet was then whisked away into her blissful haze.

CHAPTER 19

S ticking her head out the open window, Scarlet smiled. Her whole body shook both from excitement and nervousness. The car she rode in turned into the field where the King's airship waited for them, another one taking off over her head as they did. Her grip on the window's seal grew tight, and she smiled as the great beast shadowed her. Her head followed it, and watched it until the car came to a stop. Unable, and not all too willing to wait, she opened her own door and hopped out. Taking a few steps, Scarlet then stopped, and took in the airship in front of her. It was so large, easily two-times the size of a real ship, and the balloon that lifted it into the air looked as if it could fit a whole town in it. Workers rushed from the cars to the lower dock ramps, like ants. "It's amazing, isn't it?" Scarlet nodded, glancing over to Renee as she pulled her small tote from the back seat.

I can't believe we're going to be on it.

Renee nodded, "I know." Renee glanced to Scarlet, before returning her gaze back to the ship. "You nervous?" Though she was, to the deepest part of her core, Scarlet shook her head no. "I am... I've never been more than three thousand yards from one, and now we are to travel in one. The King's at that." Scarlet, who had turned back to the ship, gently took Renee's hand in her own. Squeezing it, the two then begun towards the upper deck ramp. Releasing her hand as they came upon the opened door, Scarlet took the moment to pause. Turning, she looked out to Drale. The sun rose up behind it, the city slowly coming to life. "You coming?" Renee's hand on her shoulder pulled Scarlet from the city view. She nodded, and headed into the ship.

Upon entering, and going through a second set of doors, the two walked straight into a well sized opened area that looked as if it could be a living area of some sort. In the center of the room was pot-belly fire place, though Scarlet had been under the impression that anything fire-burning was strictly forbidden. One side of the pot belly was circled by a couch, a few chairs; the other side sat a chess table- clearly a favorite of the King's. Throughout the rest of the room were low bookcases all filled with a variety of entertainment. Over all, it all seemed fit for a King. "Ah, here you are." The King stepped into the room from the far left hall way, smiling at the two humans. "I was wondering when you would both board. Come, let me explain the ship to you all." Motioning for them to step closer to the pot belly, they did. "This is the common room, you can read, play board games, enjoy the view or just sit by the fire. The Great Adventure is one of the three airships in the world to have a burning fireplace. Now the hall to the left that I came out of leads to my stateroom, the captain's cabin and has a stairway to the flight deck above us. Below us, all our luggage is stored, the engine is in the back and there are a few rooms for the ship mates on board. Above us is the bridge, where the ship is steered, the Captain's office, the Kitchen and a few more sleeping quarters." The King begun to move towards the hall on their right, the two girls following after without needing to be told. "Now this hall leads into the dining area and where you both will be sleeping." Pointing into the only opened door way, both girls were able to peek in and view the small table for five. Moving on deeper into the hall, the King motioned to a set of spaced out doors to Scarlet's left. "These are the sleeping rooms here, they are not big, but they need not to be. Across from each door is a private sitting room; that you are free to use on our journey. This is Renee's room." Pulling a key from his pocket, the King handed it to Renee. She opened her door, stepping it. "Your room is down here Scarlet." Before Scarlet could be nosey, the King had moved a few doors down and now held a golden key out towards her. She took it, thanking him.

Unlocking the door, Scarlet stepped into her room. It was indeed tiny compared to her room in the mansion. To her right was a single bed, the left a small desk with a vanity mirror hanging over it. To each side was a built in wardrobe. The window sat in a small nook, a cushion creating a seat beneath it. Despite it's cozy size, the room was still grander than anything Scarlet had ever felt she deserved. "I took a guess that you would not want to be right next to Renee." Scarlet spun to face the King, confused to how he would know how rocky her relationship was with her friend. Before she could ask, the King answered her. "The maids tend to know everything, and I hear it all whether I wish to or not." She frowned, and upon seeing it the King smiled. He laughed, as her frown deepened. "Do not worry, they are harmless. Their lives are dull and they merely wish to spice it up a bit." Though Scarlet thought it was not possible, the frown grew deeper. The King, upon seeing her falling mood, frowned himself. Coming into the room he reached out and ran a cool thumb over her forehead. "You shouldn't frown, I don't like it." Scarlet's frown softened at this confession, and her heart rate picked up. Her eyes fell to his lips for just a moment, before Scarlet casted them away. The urge, the need as air is to her lung, to have their mouths together was over powering her once more. All from a simple, gentle, touch. The King fell back a step, going back into the doorway. "Please remain in one of your rooms until we lift off. I'll tell Renee this also, it's safest to be sitting." The King cleared his throat, standing silently in her door way for a few moments. "I shall see you at dinner."

Left alone, Scarlet closed and locked her bedroom door. She looked around the room, peaking in the wardrobes to see them full of her outfits. She settled lastly on the bed. There was a medium size brown-paper wrapped bundle with a white envelope on top. Opening the card, Scarlet glanced over the writing. Her eyes wandered over each curve, the thinning or thickening of each letter. It was some of the finest print she had ever seen. The message itself was simple, and to the point.

Scarlet

Thank you for everything.

Pals.

Taking a spot on the bed, she sat the card down. Pulling at the twine, the brown paper came open easily. Giving a small smile, Scarlet picked up the first pair of perfectly folded pants. The fabric was divine, easily the highest of quality and the dark olive green coloring beautiful. Setting the first pants aside, Scarlet pulled out the next pair, and the pair after that. In total she eight pairs. Unable to stop herself, a few tears fell from her eyes. She was so grateful.

Journal Entry Number Thirteen

We set off in a few minutes, free as a bird into the sky, but I just needed to express myself. I got Pals' gift today. She had it brought to the ship and left on my bed so that when I arrived I would see it. She had eight pairs made for me- eight pairs of pants all my own! But my gratefulness for her is not what plagued me to write. I believe I might be falling in love. He's the most wonderful man I've ever met- so caring and kind. Even when he is not, there is always a just reason to his behavior. His knowledge, and his thirst to learn is beyond anything of natural life. He has taught me so much; photography, chess and my personal favorite how to dance. He's very handsome too. I seem to fall into an abyss every time I see him. I did not think anything of these strange attractions to him before, it is not the first time I have found myself drawn to a man. We danced yesterday, for the first time in public. I did not know what I was truly doing but I knew in his arms I could not be led wrong. I wanted to kiss him. I wanted him to kiss me. Today, with just a simple touch to my forehead I was overwhelmed with the urge to feel his lips upon mine. I must admit that the whole thing- I must be going now. We are lifting off!

Without signing off Scarlet closed her journal and tossed it into her tote. Hopping from her bed, she fell into the window nook. Pressing her hands to the window, the gentle hum of the engine came below her. Suddenly, with a quick shift that sent her into one of the nook's walls, the airship was untied from it's port and they were lifting off. She watched as the ground below them shrunk away, and then looked up to the city. Scarlet had never realized how large and yet microscopic Drale could look. Adjusting herself, Scarlet watched the city fade away on the horizon into nothing. Even once it was out of her sight, Scarlet remained at the window. She was seeping parts of

Voirol she'd never seen before. Oh how my world is expanding. At that thought, Scarlet smiled.

Hello people*! I'm just here to drop a quick AN on this very short chapter. Yes, I admitted it's short. Chapter 20 will be longer, I promise.

ANYWAYS- I just want to ask all of you to take a few moments to go click on the 'external link' (found below under the 'sharing' opinions) and 'Like' my official author page on Facebook. I try to post on it often, but I promise you will not be getting a butt-load of spam from me. I mostly post updates about my Blog and Speak on there. This is just another way for you all to show your support. I see that you all read, and I hope that if you really enjoy it you'll share this rough draft with your friends and family.

I don't, and won't, do this type of thing often. I hate it when authors are like 'five stars and ten comments for next update'. I don't want to feel pressure to write and I don't want you all to feel pressure to vote or comment on something for no real reason. (I cannot stress this enough.)

Also, since I'm already writing, amazingly, I think that by chapter 30 this story should be finished. I don't normally label my books in such a way but I want to try to round this one off. I hope to get the edited version (this one is unedited) published one day in the near future if I see that enough people do enjoy my story.

Thank you all for reading, voting and following. It means so much. Love to you all!

Keep Reading! <3**

For the New Followers:

*People/Peoples is what the readers of AT Judge are officially called.

**Keep Reading! <3 is AT Judge's signature. It's been around for years. Even if you don't read her stories, AT never wants anyone to ever give up on reading.

CHAPTER 20

With the base of her floating king, Scarlet knocked out Theo's piece and replaced it with her own. Theo, who had been hunched over, shot up.

Checkmate.

"How- what?! No, no, you could not have beaten me, again. Best six out of eleven!" Scarlet shook her head, but set up the game board one more time. From where he sat by a window, the King chuckled. "Theo, just admit defeat and move on. She was taught by the best after all." Turning to face him, Theo rolled her eyes. "Oh sure, don't flatter yourself. If anyone on this air ship is the best at chess- it's myself. I am a six time reigning champion!"

"Which is why Scarlet has beaten you thus far?" The King didn't even lift his head from the book in his hand as he sounded off the offensive. Theo was prepared to respond, but the First mate entered into the room. Bowing, all four pairs of eyes were on him. "Your highness, Captain has asked me to inform you that we are coming up to Nereids Bay on the port side. We are set to lay back to land in twenty minutes." The King nodded, dismissing the first mate from the room. Forgetting about replacing the chess pieces to their proper places on the board, Scarlet hopped from her seat. In the process she hit the table, knocking all everything to the ground as she rushed to the window. Pressing her hands to the cool glass, Scarlet pushed herself against the surface. She couldn't hear Theo wondering what had gotten into her, the King's light chuckle, or even Renee who was now next to her. All she saw and heard was blue. Endless, beautiful, shining blue waters. "They've never seen the ocean." The King's voice floated freely around Scarlet, but she remained mesmerized to the view in front of her. She kept her eyes on the ocean, even as the ship turned, until she couldn't see it any more.

Scarlet longed to see the magnificent blue beast once more. "Oh, you had the building painted!" Theo was now next to the two humans, speaking on the rather nice sized home sitting up along a rock side. "The grass seems greener this year. Is that a new fountain? You really fixed the place up sire." The King, who still sat with his book in his lap, shrugged. "It was all Dolra. It's been at least three centuries since she's come here and yet she insist on keeping it 'updated'. Now please, everyone take their seat. Captain Pau'per is the finest woman to ever serve until the title for the Great Adventure, but it doesn't mean that landings are rocky."

"Well she's done quite nicely thus far I would say." Theo turned from the window and took a seat across from the King. "For what she has, but, if we were to expand the size of my Metal Birds then perhaps it can be used for civilian use as well as military." As Scarlet took a seat on the couch, Renee following after her, the King let out a sigh. "For the millionth time Theo, no. Not yet at least. Your current fleet of Birds has barely been tested; and didn't one of them stop working? I'm not going to risk the money, time and power needed to expand on a project that might fail. I refuse." Theo's face grew dark, and her eyes got so narrow they looked as if her golden glow was cutting through. The King must have hit one of her nerves. "Then I guess it is a good thing I am on this trip, sire. I can give you an up and close test of my finest creation to date! Minus Lil Grey- that's what I named my new smoke bomb." The King placed the book in the shelf beside him, suddenly tense at the mention of Theo's smoke bomb.

What's a smoke bomb?

Renee shrugged, not quite sure either. The sir ship begun to tip down at that moment, and Scarlet clutched the couch in her hands. So far her first air ship trip had been uneventful. The greatest surprise she got was seeing Theo come out of her personal cabin after lift-off. The werewolf then explained that she was on the trip to fix and test some of her latest inventions that the Navy hoped to use against Muis. She was also apparently quite upset with Admiral Wiles and Captain Kerns; for something they said about Pals. The subject was not brought up again, not even at dinner that night. Though the bed was small, and the whole cabin hummed slightly, Scarlet slept peacefully and woke just in time to watch the sun rise for the first time in months.

Up until the current moment, Scarlet hadn't thought about them landing. The take-off had been as shaky as the King had warned, and she was sure their landed would mirror it. Scarlet glanced to Renee, who looked relaxed but Scarlet could see the slight hint of worry in her eyes. Waving, Scarlet got her attention.

We'll be fine.

Renee nodded, giving a small smile as the ship was jolted again. Renee's face paled slightly before regaining it's normal color once more. It was then Scarlet realized that she could hear shouting, and the ship glided to it's port. No one said anything, the ship's slowing engine and the muffled voices filled the silence. It could have only been a minute or two since they had officially landed, but the first mate was before them again. Bowing, he gave them all a soft smile. "Captain has given us the orders that de-boarding is now allowed. Enjoy your trip, all." Bowing once more, the man left the same way he came. The King stood first, as the doors were unlocked and opened by an outside worker. "Very well, let us."

~~~

The moment they set foot off of the ship, the four beings were shuffled into a private car and driven away from the grand house. Cain had informed them that morning at breakfast that his first matter of business was to tour Jengu, the main port that the navy operated out of. Theo had to come, but he requested that Scarlet join him. Honored, and slightly excited at the thought of spending the whole day with him, she agreed. Renee went where ever Scarlet went, she didn't have any other choice to choose from. As they sped through the outskirts of a bustling town, Renee took the chance to really look at Scarlet. She was talking to the King, who almost didn't need Renee to translate for him anymore. Theo sat beside him, hunched over a notebook as she mumbled to herself. The werewolf was dead set on making sure all her calculations were correct. Renee looked back to Scarlet. She gave a small smile, responding to the King. They spoke about her hair, she wished to cut it and he believed she looked fine now. Renee frowned slightly at the thought. Scarlet had never had hair shorter than at her lower back- any shorter was against the Code. Now she wished to have it above her shoulders? Renee was not fond of changes- and her hair was not the only thing Scarlet was changing. She strolled out that morning in a pair of beautifully
~~~

tailored pants, claiming they were a gift from Pals. Luckily for Renee, the King wasn't welcoming towards Scarlet's wardrobe change either. He believed her to look more regal in gowns over pants. Theo adored it, giving Scarlet her full support. To Renee's demise, the King did not force Scarlet to change. He sub came to the human and werewolf, claiming that if Scarlet was pleased- then he was as well. So she sat now next to Renee, in the olive green pants tucked snuggly into a pair of boots. Scarlet paired the pants well, with a white button down shirt and a relaxed leather vest. Renee stared at the sheer sleeves, watching their flowing movement as Scarlet spoke. Suddenly they stopped, and Scarlet was looking right at her. She asked Renee if she was okay. Renee nodded, and Scarlet gave a hesitant nod back.

The rest of ride Renee kept her gaze out the window, wishing her and Scarlet were alone. So the only person Scarlet could talk to was her. It was a selfish thought, but Renee was a selfish person. Just like Scarlet, she had her secrets kept from others. When they neared the base, the car slowed down just long enough to be cleared past security and allowed in. From there they drove through the self-sufficient town to the largest building around. Theo climbed out first, not waiting for the driver. She closed her note book and strolled straight into the building; not waiting for anyone else. The King followed after her, and offered a hand to Scarlet once he was standing. She accepted it, and thanked him. Renee was not offered a hand, not that she truly wanted to be in all truthfulness. Following after the King and Scarlet, who in returned followed after Theo, the group entered into the building and straight into a reception area.

"Your highness." A tall man, with a thick bushy mustache who was thin in every part of his body but his belly, was waiting for them and bowed at the sight of the King. "Admiral. I trust you remember Dr. Deaeque?" Admiral Wiles rose back up, smiling. His white teeth contrasted nicely against his dark skin. "Of course sire! One does not forget the hurricane that is Theodora Deaeque." Theo let out a small growl. "That's Dr. Hurricane Deaeque to you!" The Admiral's face got tense, but the smile remained. "Of course, forgive me Doctor." He then turned his attention to Scarlet and Renee. "I do not believe I have had the pleasure." Admiral Wiles looked to the King, who looked to the two human girls. Renee took a step forward and placed her hands on her hips. "Renee, last name's not important. I'm a translator for Scarlet here." Grabbing Scarlet, Renee pulled her forward and she felt her friend stumbling over her feet. "Her last name is also not important."

"So what importance do you serve being here on my base?" Renee wanted to punch the man in the jaw- to whip out the sword on her hip and cut him into a million pieces. "Besides being my honored guest," the King stepped in the space between the three humans, forcing the Admiral to move back, "Scarlet is the Blessed human. I'm sure Captain Kerns informed you being she was at the meeting last week despite me demanding your presence." The Admiral studied Scarlet, his eyes wide yet they moved like a predator. Once, not so long ago, Scarlet would have hunched her shoulders in an attempt to shrink herself. She would move back and try to free herself from the gaze. Perhaps it was her training, or the fact she was wearing pants- it could have even be her new boots that elevated her just so off from the ground. She didn't know what had overcome her, but instead of backing down she found herself raising up. "If you're done studying her," Theo stepped up to them, breaking their stare down, "which I'm the only one on this planet granted permission to do so, I would like to be taken to my Birds. The one that stopped working preferably." The Admiral looked between Scarlet, Theo, and lastly the King. Nodding, he motioned for his Captain to step forward. "Kerns, show Theo to the Hanger."

~~~

The tour of the overall base of Jengu was interesting to Scarlet, but also extremely boring. The Admiral, and King often spoke words that she did not know or did not understand. Most of the tour she followed quietly behind, eyeing everything. The small group ended the tour within one of the smaller hangers, but with ceilings still so high. Lined at first were several war vehicles, all standard for any fighting base. Beyond that, were creations of metal that Scarlet had never seen anything of the sorts. If she could, she could call them a
~~~

metal gilder but with more. "Last but not least," The Admiral held a hand out towards the beasts, "Dr. Deaeque's Metal Birds." Looking to the line of Metal Birds, Scarlet noticed Theo up on ladder. Her back was towards them, and she hunched over the front of the first Bird in the line. As the came closer, positioning themselves to see her face, the fire torch in her hand went dead. Straightening her back, Theo popped her goggles from her eyes to her forehead. They left a clean ring around her eyes, the rest of her face being darken with soot and oil. "I take it that your tour went well Admiral?" She lowered the metal lid over the engine, the sound echoing around them.

"Of course Doctor, I trust that you have my Bird ready to fly once more?" Theo hooked the fire torch onto the ladder and grabbed onto the side rails. Releasing her feet from the rungs, Theo slid down; landing softly on the ground. "If you're speaking on the subject of my Bird, then yes. I believe it is. A simple test flight should tell us." Theo grabbed a rag that stuck out from her back pocket and rubbed her hands on it. "When will you test it?" Theo shoved her dirty rag against the Admiral's crisp uniform, "Give me five minutes." Theo begun to walk off, but stopped and turned. "And don't touch my Bird."

Theo returned in six minutes, and Scarlet assumed it was just to annoy the Admiral. One thing Scarlet had learned in their short time together that he was a stickler for punctuality. Theo returned to them cleaned face, her goggles resting in their normal spot on her head. Climbing into the back seat of the two-seater Bird, Theo locked herself into the seat. Placing a set of radio transmitter over her ears, she motioned for the doors to be opened. The Admiral made the call, and the hanger's two large doors were open. The Bird's engine roared to life, and propeller on the nose the Bird sprung to life. Theo adjusted her goggles back over her eyes, and then the Bird begun to move. It was slow, but smooth and moved by them with a gentle breeze. The group followed the Bird outside, joining it as Theo turned it onto a patch of dirt. "I'm all set, am I clear to go?" Theo's voice crackled in the radio resting on the hip of Captain Kerns. Another voice, a male one, gave her the all clear and the Bird begun to move. Scarlet watched in awe as the Bird sped down the dirt patch, taking off just moments before it would go straight into a sand dune. The Bird continued to rise, and at one point seemed to get higher than any air ship Scarlet had seen. The Bird flew high, but not too far from the base; always circling back. "It's a beautiful day today, isn't it Captain?" Theo voice crackled once more, and with the Admiral's permission, Captain Kerns responded. "Yes it is, care to join us back on the ground?" A growl came over the radio, "Very well. I'm bringing her in."

The Bird flew over them a few more times, before returning back on the dirt path. Stopping it a few feet from them, Theo killed the engine and pulled the radio transmitter from her head. Pulling her goggles up, she leaned over the side of the Bird. "See? Running like new. It was a simple wiring issue. Now, who wants to come up with me?" The Admiral stepped forward at that moment. "No, you are not allowed to fly it again. I refuse!" The glint that Scarlet was use to seeing flashed through Theo's eyes. "Hmm, let's see," She leaned against her arms, "I invited the Metal Bird, I built the Metal Birds and now I fixed this Metal Bird. I'm taking it up again. Your highness, care to join me?" The King shook his head, refusing. "Thank you Theo, but not today. Perhaps tomorrow." Theo shrugged, not at all offended. "Scarlet?" Suddenly, all eyes were on her. Theo's mischievous look told her to say yes, but everyone else's told her to say no. Looking to Theo, Scarlet nodded; her heart all but bursting from her chest. "Wonderful! Someone get her a ladder!" Both the King and Admiral looked ready to protest, but Scarlet only ran towards the Bird. Reaching it, there was lean-to ladder that she quickly climbed to the front seat. "Here, put these on and strap in." Theo handed her a leather cap, goggles and radio transmitter built in. Scarlet strapped it to her head, and then closed the harness over her chest. "You ready?" Lifting a shanking hand, she gave Theo a thumbs up. "Okay! Hold on, cause here we go!" The Bird roared to life once more, and before Scarlet could blink was moving down the dirt pathway.

The whole situation suddenly became very real to Scarlet. She hyperventilated, her hands turning white from their grip on her harness. "Okay Scarlet, see all those buttons and switches? Don't touch anything, those are all controls to the weapons of the Bird. We're not trying to kill anything. At the moment. So just, sit back and enjoy!" The nose of the bird tipped up, shaking slightly. It continued to shake and then the ground was no longer below them. The bird climbed higher, the shaking slowly fading away. The Bird leveled out, and smoothed itself. The wind whipped around Scarlet, and she opened her eyes- not realizing she had closed them. In awe, she looked around and dared to stretch a hand out to touch a cloud. "It's amazing, I know." Theo's voice cracked into Scarlet's ears, laughing. "I'll show you something great, hold on." The Bird begun to tip towards the right and Scarlet turned her head. Looking to the ground, they flew over a quaint looking town. The people below all stopped, and turned their eyes to the sky. A child waved, and Scarlet had to wave back. The Bird tipped back, and they flew through a set of clouds.

Theo landed the Bird back on the dirt path, the whole thing bouncing a few times before remaining on the ground as she slowed. By the time they reach the group of being once more the Bird was crawling and stopped perfectly. Pulling the goggles from her face, Scarlet released her body from the harness as a ladder was brought over. Reaching the ground once more, Scarlet turned to face the group.

It was amazing. I loved it.

Renee smiled, and the King commented that he was glad she enjoyed it. The Admiral and Captain both stood dumb founded, and confused. "Sire, I insist that you take a spin with me. Please, this'll be my last trip of the day. I promise!" Theo used her finger to make an X over her heart, her large eyes growing wider. She took the term 'puppy eyes' to a new level. "Please sire, let me show you what she can do!" Her trick worked upon the King, and he agreed to go up in the Bird once. He placed the same helmet on that Scarlet wore prior and strapped himself in. As she begun to move the Bird towards the pathway, Theo gave a large wicked looking grin towards Scarlet. Then the Bird was off, flying through the sky as it had moments before with Scarlet.

"You were right Theo, it's amazing." The King's voice crackled over the radio. "I know, want to see something that will truly take your breath away?" Theo laughed slightly, and the engine revving came from the radio. "Theo- what are you doing? THEODORA!" Theo's laugh grew louder and Scarlet took a step back. The Bird went from a simple glide into a ninety degree angle before flipping. "THEODO-RA!" The King's scream could be heard without the aid of the radio, and a few milling workers stopped and turned to the sky. The Bird did two more flips before leveling out and then returning to the ground. When the engine finally came to a rest, the King pulled his helmet off and hopped from the Bird. He landed gracefully, and didn't seem in any pain despite the easily ten foot drop. His eyes were so glassed over, a simple glance seemed to kill. Theo landed beside him, hunched over before standing straight. "I ought to kill you! What the hell was that?" The King looked up to Theo, his hands fisted at his sides. "Payback sire. For yesterday. You challenged my chess skill." The King took a deep breath, stepping back. "You infuriate me." His response was much calmer, and his face relaxed once more. Theo gave a small smile and pulled her goggles up. "I could still have you killed you know." Theo's smile grew wider, "But you won't." The King frown slightly, and walked away.

~~~

Scarlet strolled the beach, the wind blowing both her skirt and hair around. She stayed close enough to the tide to feel the mist but not to get wet. She had dared to wet her feet earlier, and the water all but froze her toes. So she was happy to stay along the slightly risen dune. Coming to a stop, she turned and faced the water. The sun was near to setting perfectly along it, and she didn't wish to miss it. "It's beautiful, I know." The King came up Scarlet's right side, stopping beside her. She noticed that like herself, he had removed and now held his shoes. Her heart beat picked up slightly and she turned back to the view.

I've never seen the sun so close to us before.
~~~

"I have many times, but I'm in awe every time as if I hadn't ever before."

You weren't at dinner. Were you ill?

"No, no." The King gave a small smile at her concern for him. "I got pulled into a meeting. A group of 'terrorist' attacked one of our ambassadors during a trip to Kuko. He was there to talk about an update in our alliance agreement. There is very good evidence that Muis was behind the attack." Scarlet nodded, glancing down to the sand. They stood far enough just to keep from brushing shoulders, and she looked at their contrasting feet. His were so naturally pale compared to hers.

I thought you might be mad. At Theo or me.

The King frowned slightly. "Theo is a stickler for what she believes is payback. I'm used to it and honestly should see it coming but I never do. I cannot stay angry at her for long, if I even am. I care too much for her." Scarlet nodded again, glancing to him. "I'm not sure what gave you the impression that I was mad at you. I never have been angry with you and quite honestly I don't think I ever could be."

I'm not quite so sure. I'm sure I'll do something sometime.

"You won't." He shook his head, looking away. The two watched the sun set on the water, and slowly sink down into it.

I'll never see anything more beautiful.

"I agree." Turning he reached out, pushing back a strand of hair that was pressed against her forehead. As he did, he ran his hand down the side of her face. She could feel her heart beat bouncing within her chest, and the air suddenly getting thin. Resting in his palm, her face fit perfectly in his hand. "I'm drawn to you Scarlet." He slowly moved nearer. She mouthed out 'why' and he shook his head. "I'm not sure, but I am." He turned to fully face him, and she copied him without thinking upon it. "I am sure, though, that I don't care. I like it. I care for you, like you."

It's impossible for me to not like you.

He shook his head once more, lowing his hand. "No, it's not liking." Her heart suddenly stopped and shattered within her heart. "I cannot say that, it would be a lie. What I feel for you, the way that I see you, is nothing I have never felt before. Not even for Dolra. I care for her deeply, but I do not believe I've ever loved her... And Scarlet," He took her face in his hand once more, their eyes meeting, "I love you. Crazily, and in a way that is too impossible to try to ever understand. I love you." Scarlet's heart was once again whole and suddenly flying free from her body.

I cannot say if I love you.

"You don't have to." Fully taking her face into his hands, the space between them closed in a kiss. Scarlet had never been kissed before, she had no idea what so ever of what she was to do. But, almost as if it was meant to be, she felt her body responding. It was the sweetest, breath taking, heart stopping moment of her life up until that point. Twice, in one day, had her world been blown to a new level. The kiss ended a few seconds after beginning, Scarlet pulling away.

You're married. We're wrong.

"I know." Pulling her back in, Scarlet was lost to the moment. She had now been kissed twice in her life, and both times were amazing. The feelings felt as if the others hadn't happened, and she was starting all over. Not to forget that they were given by a King. Not just any King, a vampire King. A beautiful man of whom Scarlet was falling in love with.

CHAPTER 21

I t's wrong, and I know I shouldn't have taken pleasure in it. But kneeling there in the sand, his arms wrapped around me as we watched the last few rays of the day slowly slipped away, I knew I would never care. I should care, maybe once I would have, but I currently don't. He's the first man to ever look beyond and see more for than just what I'm not. All my life I was taught I would never be loved- I could never be loved. Because I was defected, broken, incomplete. No man would ever want that, but he does. And he is a King. Perhaps I am not as broken as I have been led to believe.

-S

Finishing her entry, Scarlet blew on the ink to dry it before closing her journal. Hopping from her bed, she hid it back in her bag and left her room to meet for breakfast. The Beach house was rather tiny compared to the King's grand mansion. Consisting of three, rather than four, floors the home sat soundly on a grassy rock side. The first floor was dedicated to the basic; a Kitchen, a dining room, a den and a meeting room. The second floor held a total of ten bedrooms, three of which were solely dedicated to housing the workers and the third floor was the Royal's private area. Scarlet could assume that there was a bedroom for each the King and Queen, along with a tea room, and an office for the King. Perhaps he even had some storage stashed away. What the home lacked in size, it made up for in quality. The home was fit for royalty, each floorboard was carefully placed and every piece of wallpaper was gracefully laid. Only the finest of craftsmanship was used for the furniture, the highest quality of fabrics. It was all so grand.

Entering into the dining room, Scarlet slowed but did not stop. Sitting at the table already, talking civically about the engine used in the Metal Birds, was Theo and Renee. They both looked up and greeted her; she responded and took her seat. "Theo was telling me about her new, advance engine that uses a mixture of steam, oil and coal to run. It's quite fascinating." Theo nodded, taking a sip from her tea cup as she leaned back. "It's true, Renee and I have found a common ground."

That's great, but when did you get into engines Renee?

Renee's face slightly colored and she slowly chewed the food in her mouth. "Um, Vern has been teaching me actually. He saw how I took interest in the subject and begun to teach me a while ago."

Why didn't you ever tell me?

Renee shrugged. "Guess I never saw the point to. I'm sorry if it hurt you, that I didn't I mean." Scarlet shook her head no, and filled her glass with some juice. As she begun to fill her plate the King entered in. The three females stood, bowed, and returned to their seats. She dared to glance at him, as if it was any other morning. He sensed it, and met her gaze. Both said nothing, each of them keeping a plain face. Scarlet was not expecting anything more, she feared anything more. But the thought of the night before, of the secret held between the Kind and herself, sent reviving thrills through her.

"So, sire, what is on our itinerary today? More flight test?" The gleam was in Theo's eyes, and a smirk on her lips. The King, whose glass and plate were brought to him already filled, took a sip of red from his glass. "Testing, yes, but not of your Birds. The Admiral shows the most interest in your steam boots." Theo made a face, as if the orange she was eating was sour. "My boots? But why? I've only got the prototype. It's barely been tested on land, let alone risked over water. I don't even think they'll work over water." Theo shoved another piece of orange into her mouth. The King gave a tip of his head. "Well, during the last war meeting I had with my high ranks we discussed some of your projects. Captain Kerns must have been impressed with the idea and passed it on to the Admiral." Theo rolled her eyes, groaning like a child. Then a thought came to her and she stopped. The King frowned at this, as if he knew what she was thinking but said nothing.

~~~

"So like a plant, these little plates will gather the sun's rays and convert it into energy! More accessible, readily available and more powerful energy." Theo lowered the blue pints to the ground, and smoothed them out. It was a motion she had done a number of times over the past few minutes as she explained her Sun Plates to the group. Scarlet didn't fully understand, Renee looked excited beyond words, the King seemed impressed and the two navy members appeared bored. Theo's smile fell as she casted her eyes on the last two. Folding up her map, she moved towards the table. Motioning for them to follow, only three did. Placing the map on the table, Theo tipped her head to face the two unmoving humans.

"This next one, I'm very proud of." Theo picked up a round, metal ball from the table of her inventions, "I call it Lil' Grey." and tossed it in her hand. "Yes, yes, but when are you going to demonstrate your boots. That is what I want to see, not these little knick-knacks." Scarlet took a step back, as Theo's face grew dark. "I'll get to it when I get to it. First I'm going to show you Lil' Grey." The Admiral rolled
~~~

his eyes under his goggles as Theo turned. "Fine." She faced Scarlet and Renee, her voice low. "When you hear the third beep, put on a mask." Twisting the metal ball, Lil' Grey, she pressed her thumb to a small button. Turning, she smiled at the Admiral. "So what does this, thing, do?" Theo picked up a mask slyly from the table with her free hand. Scarlet and Renee copied her, safely watching her experiments from the opposite side of the table. Theo tossed the ball down towards the Admiral and Captain, they both stood on the opposite side of the 'testing circle'. "You'll see." As she said that three high pitch beeps filled the air, hurting even the human's ears. Lil' Grey suddenly expanded, sending a cloud of menacing smoke suddenly into the air. Scarlet fumbled with the mask in her hands, getting it on just as the blast hit her. With the mask held to cover her mouth and nose Scarlet glanced over to Renee who looked back. The smoke was thick, and Scarlet couldn't see the King- who had been two or three feet from her. As quickly as the smoke filled the room, it was pushed out. With full visibly returned to the room Scarlet could see that the King was looking at only one things- two bodies on the ground. Unstrapping the mask from her face, Theo's grin was brighter than the sun. The King removed his mask, making his way over to the Admiral and Captain. Theo let out a satisfied laugh as the King bent over the two humans. "Are they dead?" Three pairs of eyes turned to Renee, who held her mask nervously in her hands. Theo let out a scoff, "No, just knocked out. That's all Lil' Grey does, knock out any and all species. Vampire, Werewolf, the rare witch, humans-

he does it all. It's not like they didn't have it coming." She kicked

the Captain's foot with her boot. "It was just pay back." tossing the

smoke bomb in her hand, Theo reset it. "How long will they be out?"

The King rose as he asked his question, no concern laced on his face

at all. "Eh, I'd say three, maybe four..."

"Minutes?" Theo laughed at the King. "Hours." The King's jaw

dropped, and Scarlet sat her mask on the table. She made mental

note to herself to never get on Theo's bad side. "Theo!" The werewolf

jumped slightly at the King's tone, dropping the bomb as she did.

The room stopped moving. After a few seconds, and no eat piercing

beeps, the werewolf picked the bomb back up. "I barely gave them

anything. Lil' Grey's full force could kill if I wanted it to! Not that

I've tested it, yet." The King sighed, and rested his forehead in his

hand for a moment. "Well, there goes four hours. Renee, go alert

someone to get the unit doctor." Renee nodded, dropping her mask

on the table and scurrying from the room. "What are we to do now?"

Theo grinned once more, "The summer solstice festival is taking

place today in town." Renee returned a few moments later, a Doctor

following closely after her. He looked between the King, the two

females standing by him, and the bodies on the ground. "They were

knocked out by a simple chemical reaction." The King stepped up,

daring anyone in the room to challenge him. "I shall be leaving now but please have me alerted when they come to. Until then, we'll be in town."

~~~

If there was one thing Scarlet quickly came to understand, was that to many of his subjects the King was a name and nothing more. Unlike the High Lord of Tobus, whose picture was hung clearly everywhere, The King barely had more than two portraits of himself in his castle. And that was to include the one in the Grand Hall of Rulers. The small group was able to walk freely through the crowd, the occasional town folk smiling and wishing them a happy summer. It was near midday, the sun almost reaching it's peak. Happy, joyful movements and sounds surrounded them. Roads were blocked off, different booths- of both food and goods, and games set up in place of cars. In the center of the town, where normally was a simple cross roads, was a dancing square. A small band was set up along one corner, and a merry group danced around in sets of pre-determined motions. Unlike the dancing at Pals wedding, Scarlet recognized some of the music and knew what moves the dancers were performing. There was so much going on, and Scarlet was so caught up in everything that she didn't notice Theo and Renee slip away as they passed the street filled with outfitted Steam vehicles. Something colorful caught the corner of Scarlet's eye. With eyes like a child, she reached for the scarf and wrapped it over her hair as she sometimes saw Pals do. Clutching it,
~~~

she turned and rested her hands under her chin. Smiling at the King, he nodded in approval. "She looks lovely, no, no?" The King nodded to the salesman behind the display table. "She does, how much for the item?" The salesman's smile grew bigger. "For this one? Well it is made of the finest silk made by the rarest of worms from the peaks of the Endless Mountains." The King made a face that told the salesman to get to the point or risk losing his business. The salesman cleared his throat, "Uh-hm, yes, twenty-five gold, two silver." Scarlet paled at the amount, quickly removing the scarf from her head. That was easily a third of what her mother was able to make in a yet, let alone have enough to splurge on a simple scarf. With a simple blink the King removed his wallet from his pants pocket and begun to write a Note out. Dropping the scarf carelessly to the table, Scarlet reached out to physically stop him. Meeting her gaze, he pulled away gently. "Allow me." Finishing the Note, the King pulled the paper free from its booklet and handed it to the merchant. The salesman smiled, handing the scarf over to Scarlet in almost a full on toss. She caught it, holding it carefully in her hands. As the two begun to move away the King held a hand out, "Allow me." Taking it, he wrapped it loosely around her neck, smiling. "Green is your color." She blushed, but unlike those of the past Scarlet didn't mind if he saw. Suddenly the band begun to play a well-known partner dance, and Scarlet found herself nudging her way to the front of the gathered circle. The King followed her, reaching her by the time her body was already bouncing to the beat.

Renee taught me this one. It's my favorite.

The name of the dance was quite fitting, and truly explained the idea behind it. During Caught, each pair of partners is given a ribbon that is held on each end by the other. Moving in a preset arrangement of steps the goal of each person is to wrap their partner in the ribbon. The only rules were to never let go of your ribbon or touch your dance partner. The music always started out fairly slow, but gradually it would built itself up into an allegro. The audience, normally rooting for a particular person on each team, would normally join in by clapping to the tempo of the song and encouraging whoever they sought to win. It was a simple idea, turned into a simple dance that almost the whole world seemed to know. Typically played three times in a row, it allowed couples to try to beat each other out fairly or allow new ones to join in. "I don't believe I ever learned it." Scarlet looked at the King as if he had grown a third eye. He leaned in close to her, his breath hot. "Royal dance teachers do not teach barn room dancing I'm afraid." Scarlet smiled, for no particular reason but unable not to.

Watch their feet, learn it. We can join in next time.

The King appeared to want to say something but instead he did as Scarlet suggested. By the time of the third round, the two found themselves square in the middle of the make shift dance floor. Scarlet wrapped the silky ribbon around her wrist once, to keep a good grip. The music begun, and they moved. Simple at first, they simply stepped in a large circle before spinning themselves and starting in the opposite direction. Turning they moved near, and then far from each other- their bodies never touching. Coming back in, they spun, and walked away from each other. During this time they were still moving around the floor, other couples copying them. Filling the ribbon grow tense, they moved in one last circle. There was a sudden shift in the music, Scarlet grabbed her skirt- grateful she chose to save her pants for another time. A quick spin on her toes, a bounce of her hip, and Scarlet was rushing towards the King. They met in a middle ground, skipping along the dance floor. The rest of the dance Scarlet spent on her toes, avidly avoiding the King's attempts to catch her. The crowd clapped and cheered; Scarlet felt herself get lost in the moment of the dance. She found herself going in every direction, and getting so dizzy she felt as if she would fall over at any moment. Stopping suddenly with the last note, she smiled through the pounding in her head. The King was tightly wrapped in the blue silk, laughing at his defeat. Still lost within the moment, she leaned forward to wrap her arms around, and then kissed, the King. Realizing what she was doing, Scarlet quickly pulled back. The King said nothing, but most likely noting how red her face was. She had kissed him, and in front of all the people who weren't even paying attention. Smiling at her, he kissed her burning cheek.

After freeing the King from the ribbon, the two left the dance circle. They strolled the streets together, looking at everything and trying so many different foods that Scarlet lost count. As they passed by an open store front, a voice calling out them stopped them. "Please, please, stop." They turned to the merchant, who beckoned them to enter into his shop. "A lovely couple as yourself should have this moment in time captured forever, should you not?" He motioned to his shop's hanging sign, that adversities photographs. "Allow me the pleasure to capture it for you." The King begun to shake his head, most likely remembering how Scarlet had taken to getting her photograph before, but stopped when Scarlet nodded yes. "You wish to do this?" She nodded again, pleading with her eyes. He smiled, and that made her inside core melt, "Very well." The photographer smiled as the two, linked at the elbows, entered into his shop. He quickly ushered them to an area behind a black curtain where the camera and background were set up. Setting their half eating food on a table to the side, the photographer then instructed them on where they should go.

The first pose was stiff. Scarlet sat on a stool, the King behind her with his body angled. They did not touch, nor smile. The second one was slightly less stiff than the first, but as painfully awkward. Standing side-by-side they held hands and each gave a small smile. The third was Scarlet's favorite. With both her arms wrapped around one of the King's elbows, she rested her head on his shoulder with a wide grin. The last one, as the King would later admit to be his personal favorite. They stood like the second, only instead of looking into the camera the two looked at each other. Scarlet had never seen quite a pose for a photo, but when she looked at the King she couldn't help but smile. Because he was staring right back, with a grin as equally as large as her own. When she looked at him, Scarlet felt truly happy. The photographer went to develop the photos, leaving the King and Scarlet alone. He brushed a hand over her cheek, staring at her. Smiling and feeling like she was in some strange dream. Scarlet moved away from his hand and went to the bathroom. Splashing cold water on her burning cheeks, she stared at herself in the mirror.

How had it only been last night that the King admitted his feelings for her? Scarlet felt that deep down, she always held something more for the King than just admiration. They had barely admitted to anything and yet it felt as to her that they had always been together. As if it had always been meant to be. The point of his marriage meant nothing. Clearly he was willing to defy his vows, and she was willing to accept that betrayal to the Queen. The Queen. It sent a spike of ice through Scarlet's soul to think what the Queen would do if she was to ever find out. Queen Dolra did not like to begin with, she would most likely want Scarlet dead for kissing and lusting after her husband. Scarlet wished that she could come clean to the Queen, and tell her she had nothing to fear. The thought of being a Queen herself was never what Scarlet desired. She only wanted the King. Not his title, his status or money; merely the vampire man. It was then that Scarlet felt the cold weight of reality settle over her. She had thought she had already dealt with it- but she was wrong. Oh so very wrong. She was becoming someone she always sought to be, but never in such a way. The woman who looked at her- wasn't Scarlet. She wanted desperately to break the mirror.

Exiting the bathroom, the photographer was handing the King an envelope, which held their fresh photos. The King paid and thanked the man, and Scarlet started for the door. Reaching her easily, the King called for Scarlet but she only stopped moving when his hand wrapped around her upper arm. "What's wrong? Are you okay?" Scarlet sought to move her head up and down but instead she shook it 'no'. "What happened?" Looking at the concern on the King's face, she realized then that he had always cared for her. She had seen that look directed at her so many times but she had been so blind.

We did. We're wrong. You're married, and I cannot. I don't want to do this. I can't.

She cared, she loved him. He could see it in her face, in her eyes- and she knew it. Scarlet removed her scarf, and handed it back to the

King. Unable to help herself, and overcome by the guilt, she broke down in a wave of tears. She didn't wish to seek his comfort, but when the King took her into his arms Scarlet did not pull away. Instead, she pushed herself deeper into his chest. His smell was intoxicating.

~~~

If looks could kill, then Theo would have been struck down a few times over from the glares of the Admiral and Captain Kerns. Theo, who was zipping up her boots, glanced over to them. "Oh quite your hissy fitting. I don't like either of you but I only knocked you out because you both deserve it. I'm fair like that." Standing up straight, the two humans shuffled back a step, on edge. Theo rolled her eyes, plopping her goggles over her eyes. Scarlet, who stood a few feet away with the rest of the group, copied her. "Okay, so with a quick snap of my heels the boots should power up. No one freak out over the smoke and steam, that's normal- for now. I'm working on it." The Admiral and Captain took another step back, just as Theo bashed one heel against the other. Nothing happened. She repeated the process a few times, mumbling under breath as she did. The more she repeated, the more upset she was clearly getting. "I knew it, I knew it was too good to be true. Another failed invention by Dr. Deaeque. At least we figured it was a flop before giving out to the mass population. Saved a lot more lives this way." Theo growled at the Admiral, her eyes flashing. "I told you good and well that those
~~~

water tanks weren't ready to go out. I told you they needed more controlled water bound testing before going out. You chose not to listen to me. If those deaths- including the one of my boyfriend who was the main creator those underwater metal tanks- are to be blamed upon someone then it shall be you!" With those final words Theo bashed her heels together. Suddenly, and rather loudly, the boots came to life. Steam shot from the soles of her boots, pushing and, lifting Theo from the ground. "We both lost someone that day, Wiles. Don't ever forget it." She remained in the air, easily two feet from the ground, thanks to the near constant stream of air. Crossing her arms over her chest in an empowering moment, she looked down to the two humans. "Doubt me again, or ever speak of Jim like that again and I will personally claw your eyes out. Then gladly deal with the consequences." Spinning to face the others, her arms dropped and she smiled. "I present to you, the Steam Streams." Theo's voice was loud and echoed. Moving her feet, she glided over to them. "Working purely on steam power they can lift you as little and five inches from the group up to three and half feet." Turning, she showed them the sides of the boots. Which were covered in tiny nobs on the outer sides. "Just calibrate how much steam you wish to exhaust and that determines your height."

"How long do they last?" The King had almost yell in order for his voice to be heard over the boots. "Depends on how much steam you use. The lower the lift, the longer float time. I'm trying to figure out a way to get height with long life but it's proven difficult." Theo bent down, pressing a few buttons on the boots. The steam lessen, and she sank closer to the ground, remaining hovering. "Can they go higher?" Theo looked at the Admiral, not needing to physically say anything. Readjusting the nobs, she went back higher in the air, but no more than what she was at before. "No, higher. You said up to three and a half feet. Can they go higher?"

"Of course, I just haven't had any real test yet beyond-"

"Then let's test them now!" The muscles in Theo's neck grew tense. The Admiral did not back down. Scarlet found herself scooting back a few inches, memories of the last fight she had seen Theo in resurfacing. The only difference now was that Pals was not here to stop her sister. Not that she even would in this situation.

Adjusting the nobs Theo rose higher, much higher than three feet. Admiral Wiles nodded his head slightly, clearly pleased with the boots. Easily up by five feet, Theo glided around the room. She bounced, losing a few inches, every time she switched lead foot. The smudge smile on her face was only a short lived one. With one last shoot of steam, the boots gave out. Theo sensed it, her face changing as the boots coughed out the last stream of steam. She cursed, Renee gasped, the King called out, the two navy officers scattered out from under her. Her body, falling, never fell to the ground.

Opening her eyes, Theo looked around before stopping on Scarlet. With a hand held out, Scarlet kept the werewolf suspended in the air. "By fate." Captain Kerns was the first to speak, the Admiral nodding his head. Speechless. The Captain looked pallid, prepared to pass out. The Admiral's tight kept on her forearm kept her up. Scarlet slowly lowered Theo to the ground, releasing her grip only once the werewolf sat on the concert. Taking the hand offered by the King, Theo stood back up. No one said anything as she walked to Scarlet, or when the werewolf wrapped her arms around the human. "Thank you." Theo released her. "You not only saved my bones, but also my boots."

"I had my doubts, but she truly is the Blessed one. What else can she do? How powerful is she exactly? Can she lift a car? A whole loaded ship?" Scarlet nodded, slightly proud of herself.

I've never tried but I know I could. Renee translated to the two navy officers, both getting flushed with excitement. "Show us. I must see it with my own eyes." Scarlet was prepared to accept, but the King's voice stopped everything. "No. You've pushed enough limits today Wiles, no more. Scarlet needs to prove herself to only one person and that is me." Their faces all went grim.

I want to. I know I can. Let me.

The King shook his head. In that moment, as the wave of disappointment begun to rush through her, something in Scarlet snapped. With her lips pressed tight, she rushed passed the group to the nearest door. They all called after her, chasing her. Entering into the cool afternoon, Scarlet set her eyes on the closest docked ships. Crates and wooden boxes were currently being loaded and unloaded from the ramps of the three beast. Taking a stance, she focused and closed her eyes. The world around her begun to slip away, as she became one with the power from within.

~~~

Reaching Scarlet first, Renee held her arms out. Acting as a physical barrier, she stopped the other three from moving any closer. "Don't. We're too late. Breaking her concentration now would not end good for those three ships." Shouts and cries of confusions came from the ships, as Scarlet lifted them from the water. The Admiral called orders for everyone to remain calm and in their current spot until the ships were back in the water. Rising, one blocked the sun from them and they were in it's shadow. Water dripped and poured off of the metal hulls, gleaming. They easily went fifty feet into the air. "I need to sit." The Captain crumbled to the ground, her neck still craned up at the floating navy ships.

A total of thirty seconds passed before Scarlet begun to lower the ships once more. Renee could see the beads of sweat rolling down
~~~

her temple as she did. Clearly having strained herself greatly to prove her point of power. Renee could see her body relax the moment she released the ships and turned to them. Smiling, Scarlet brushed back the hair that stuck to her forehead. Her chest moved as if she had just run a marathon. "That was absolutely amazing! You are beyond physics itself!" For the first time Scarlet smiled at the Admiral, perhaps more proud with herself than from his praise. She thanked him, her face suddenly going neutral as her eyes rolled into her head. It happened within a second, seeing the whites of Scarlet's eyes before her body crumbled. "Scar!" Renee moved to try to reach her but was beaten out. As he had done once many months prior, the King was quick enough to catch her before she could fully reach the ground. "Scarlet." The King ran his hand across her forehead, cupping her cheek. "Get the medic!" Looking up, all the nearby seamen and women- who had stopped to watch the display- were now rushing to find the unit doctor.

~~~

"I've never worked with a Blessed before, but from all my years in the service I'm going to say that she just over exerted herself. So no more ship lifting Ms. S. Got it?" Scarlet nodded at the doctor, thanking him once more. She hadn't planned on passing out- or even knew that she would. "I give you a clean bill of health then, have a wonderful day." The King offered a hand to help her from the bed.
~~~

She took it, and released it just as quickly. Now alone for the first time since that afternoon, the King stopped her from opening the door. "The others are waiting in a nearby room and the car is waiting." She nodded, unsure to why he would stop her for that. "Everything I've said over the last two days; I've meant it. I know I'm married, and I know that it's unfair to either of us to pursue something. But I feel that if I don't, if I allow you to slip away to someone else, I'd die. I don't know why but I do. So I won't let you go, but I won't ask anything of you either."

They're waiting.

Scarlet left the room, saying nothing more. The car ride back was filled with awkward conversation meant to try to vaporize the silence that would otherwise reign. Arriving back at the beach home, each being went their own separate direction. The King went to his office, Theo rushed to the back where her make-shift lab was set up in a shed, Renee went to her room and Scarlet to hers.

Journal,

I'm so conflicted. If only he was not married, then we would be able to truly be together. But I don't care that he's married and that's what scares me.

Closing her journal, Scarlet brushed at the few tears on her cheeks. As she stuffed it back into her bag, her eyes caught something in her bathroom. Going into it, she reached for the green scarf on the counter. It was folded perfectly, and needed no note. Bringing it to her chest, Scarlet took a breath. Leaving the bathroom, she opened her small carry on and dug out her journal. Wrapping it in the scarf, she made sure both were hidden at the bottom of the bag. Looking around her room, Scarlet felt utterly bored. Leaving her room, she went across the hall to Renee's room.

Entering without knocking, Renee jumped when Scarlet opened the door. Upon seeing her, she scrambled to get the papers spread out on her desk. "Scar, what are you doing here, no don't." One of the papers Renee rushed to get together fell to the ground, and Scarlet reached it before she could. Renee ended up stumbling from her chair, the rest of the papers flying everywhere. Scarlet, upon picking up the paper, read it and frowned. Dropping it she picked up another one, and repeated the process one more time. Renee, who had been scrambling to gather the papers to her chest, looked at the one in her hand. "Scar, let me explain." Scarlet threw the paper at her, standing. "Scar!" Renee dropped the papers, and reached for her friend. "Scar, wait!"

Wait for what? For you to say sorry again? You've been on me about changing and making my own choices and yet you've been writing letters to Tobus! Your family knows you're alive and well.

"Scar, I can explain, please."

No! I'm over you. You keep saying I've changed, well I guess it takes one to know one. Because you've changed even more.

Scarlet shook Renee from her arm, leaving the room. As she did, Scarlet nearly ran into a maid. The small girl announced that dinner was ready and the King was already waiting for them. Brushing the maid off, Scarlet just went into her room.

Renee stood in her door way, looking at the small maid. "Thanks, she'll be out soon." Closing her bedroom door, and locking it, Renee headed to the dining room. Entering, she was greeted by the King and Theo. Bowing to the first one, Renee then took her seat and a plate was brought out to her. "Where's Scarlet?" Theo tore into her steak with her teeth. "Oh, um, she just need a few minutes. She'll be done soon."

Scarlet wouldn't come down for dinner at all. When she finally came into the dining room doorway, the small group was on after-desert drinks. The King had just taken an envelope from a maid, as Theo and Renee discussed the engine behind the steam power boots. The two sensed Scarlet first, but Theo was the only one to greet her. Scarlet waved back, stepping into the room but not sitting down. Renee stood, moving towards Scarlet. Scarlet stared at her, daring her to move closer. Renee remained where she was. "Oh my." The three women looked to the King, who held an open letter in his hand. "What is it sire?" The King shook his head, clearly not able to form words at the moment. He sat the letter down on the table, and Theo leaned over. "My Love," she read out loud, "before I give you anything on my current trip I have the most wonderful news to share with you. I'm pregnant!" Theo's jaw dropped and she patted the King's shoulder. "Congratulations sire." Pregnant. The word echoed through Scarlet's mind and the last thing she felt was her whole inwards exploding.

"Scarlet!" Renee was within an arm's length of her friend and held her arms to catch her. Scarlet's body went limp, and despite being caught in Renee's arms, still went down. Scarlet's body pulled Renee down, and with a yelp landed on Renee.

~~~

"When we return to Drale tomorrow you're going to be checked out by Dr. Cartson." Scarlet sniffled, trying to slyly wipe away the tears falling. The King had walked silently on the sand, and she was too focused on the setting sun, her own thoughts, to realize he was approaching.

I'm fine.

"I don't care, she's still going to check you out." He lowered himself beside her, leaving distance. She refused to look at him, she couldn't. Instead she drew her knees closer to her chest, resting her head on her knees. "I know how it looks, but everything I've ever said to you,
~~~

I've meant. I do love you Scarlet. Dolra might be pregnant but it doesn't mean my feelings for you change. It just means life gets more complicated. I'm sorry, for everything." Scarlet took a deep breath in an attempt to control her tears, and hugged her legs tighter. "I'll just leave these here. I kept the last one. It was my personal favorite." Standing he left her alone. Scarlet glance to the folder resting beside her. Reaching out, she opened it. Sighing, she stared at the photos-taken just hours before. Something twisted in her chest and she closed the folder. Standing she turned to find the King still walking away. Clapping her hands, she begun to run towards him. He stopped, turning just in time to catch her in his arms. Her fingers dug into his cheeks, she wanted to rip them out and kiss them all at the same time. Pulling his head to hers, she kissed him. It was a desperate kiss, sloppy and needy.

I don't know what I'm doing. They pulled away from each other just enough for Scarlet to sign. "Neither do I."

I have these feelings and I don't know what to do with them.

"Give in."

You have a wife, who's pregnant. The ping of pain shot through her innards once more. "I know, but she doesn't love me. She never has. But I have never truly loved her, so we are equals. Scarlet, I love you. I want you. I will live every day of my existence proving that to you if you wish it. But you have to be okay, you have to be happy. That's all I want. Is for you to be happy." A single tear fell from her eye, and he gently wiped it away. She did not cry at the softness, the realness, of the King's words. She did not cry for the fact that she had followed in her mother's footsteps. She did not cry for the Queen. She cried for herself, because she knew what a mess she was choosing to enter into.

CHAPTER 22

The summer seemed to pass in a series of a few days rather than months. Every day was filled with something new. Some days Dolra found herself doing absolutely nothing, which was utterly relaxing but others were filled. Events starting from the rising of the sun to the early morning of the next day. It only made sense that she didn't notice the first signs of pregnancy. Upon first finding out, and having a doctor confirm it, she was utterly shocked. She hadn't realized it was a fertile time for her, she hadn't gone through a fertile spell for nearly four decades. After the shock wore away, Dolra wasn't quite sure what to think. She had realizes early on in her marriage that at some point she was expected to produce heirs. It came with the title of Queen. Yet she never favored the idea of children, and often avoid the subject with anyone who dare ask her upon it. She had realized that coming home to Drale after her three month trip would have her coming with more than she left- she just hadn't realize that some of it would be the form of a small, pudged stomach. The only thing she could take comfort in during the cursed time was that her pregnancy would last for almost a full year, so her gowns were only gently let out by this point.

~~~

There was a chill in the midmorning air, signaling the change of seasons. Dolra pushed on the back brim of her hat as she glanced around to her city, her home. The moment only lasted a few seconds, ending when she got into her car. The car ride was filled with the news from the radio. The newsman spoke of advance number of men and woman who had signed up over the past few months for the King's service. Dolra ran her finger tips over her stomach, rolling her eyes. The newsman made it seem as if the stupid saps were doing a noble deed. All they were doing, besides the fact that they're signing up to risk their lives, was lining up to train in a field. Roll around in the man-made mud and sleep in the cold. Dolra snorted to herself, thinking of an actual battle taking place.

Upon entering through the open gates, Dolra frowned at the site. There was a whole lot worth of cars lining both sides of the drive way, and people seemed to be rushing about. Her car stopped short of it's normal spot, another set of cars blocking the path. She hadn't seen such chaos since the news of her in-laws tragic accident- which led to their sudden departure from the world. Dolra didn't wait for her
~~~

driver to open her door, or to even fully stop the car. For some odd reason, a feeling of fear rushed through her body and she needed to know that her husband was safe. Moving up the steps, her hat falling away, Dolra pushed open her front door. Grabbing the first person she could, Dolra shook the poor maid as she demanded to know where her husband was. "The second floor war room." Knowing he was okay, Dolra was able to regain her composure and climbed the stairs in the most dignified way. Upon entering into the war room, Dolra was met with a greater mess.

"How many-"

"What exact time-"

"Civilians?"

"Military?"

"We don't know."

"I need-"

"Is that confirmed?"

Voices came from every direction, from all the different military personal. Cain was hunched over a map at the far end of the table, two other high ranking officers with him. "Cain. Cain." Dolra said her husband's name a total of five times, getting louder until the room grew silent from her voice. With the room still, Cain looked up. Before he could say anything, Dolra spoke. "What in hell's name is going on?"

"Port Del Ray was attacked this morning. The island section of the base there is gone. As are any living." Dolra frowned, and bowed her head. Those looking on would see it as a sign of respect, she truly only did it automatically; an action bred into her. Dolra felt pity, for the loss of innocent souls, and she felt anger for now her country truly had to go to war. A pair of hands around her shoulders had her eyes open, her head up. "I am glad to see you return home safely, and early. Go, rest. I shall join you for dinner. I have much to do." Dolra nodded, and her husband's hands fell from her. She gave him a small smile. "I came as soon as I heard, oh, well. I'm clearly late." Standing in the door way, Pals looked around the room. There was much about her that shocked Dolra. The large diamond that graced her wedding finger, the hand of which it belong to resting upon her enlarged stomach, and her hair a near pale blonde and a large portion shaved off on her upper left side. "You're pregnant." Half of Pals' mouth twisted in a grin as she stepped into the room. "And not only have you returned, but as are you; your majesty." Pals bowed her head. "I would bow to you but my physical state prevents me, now I must excuse myself for I have business with your husband." Dolra nodded, and Pals stepped around her greeting Cain. Dolra was in a state of shock. Pals had never once smiled at her before. Yes the queen had seen photos of the werewolf where a small twist graced her lips but to get one in person was unlike Pals. Perhaps it was the onset of newly wed bliss mixed with the hormones of pregnancy. Whatever the reason, Dolra didn't care. She regained herself. Realizing the room had begun to move again, Dolra no longer felt fitting and removed herself.

Strolling the halls, servants stopped their busy work to bow to her before quickly moving on. Without even thinking upon the action, Dolra's hands rested over her stomach. A quick glance out a window as she passed had Dolra stopping short. Returning to the window, she watched what had caught her eyes. Pals, as Dolra was discovering, was not the only one to change over the summer. Sitting hunched over, legs crossed on a stone bench, was the Blessed human. A blade in her hand caught the sun's light, and she carved at her hand- or an object within it. But it was her physical body that changes Dolra had taken notice of. Under the near skin tight clothing were defined muscles. Her hair, which was once longer than the sun's rays, was nothing more than a short stump pulled back on her head. Finally finishing her work, the Blessed human stood and strolled to the lake. She was tiny to Dolra at that point, but the Queen was able to see the human lift her arm and toss something into the water. Reaching down, the Blessed human picked something up and returned to the bench. Repeating herself.

~~~
~~~

A frustrated groan, near mirroring a growl from a wolf, rumbled Dolra's throat. In angry huffs she pulled and tugged her body out of the gown that the maid had been attempting to dress her in. With a single kick of her leg the fabric went flying from her body to the air. Landing in a heap, another maid quickly rushed to get the garb and place it back into her closet. "None of these gowns fit! How is that even possible?" Like a toddler Dolra stomped her foot. Unlike all the gowns she had over her summer trip, the gown left behind had never been altered. Not made for her current shape, Dolra made sure that every maid in her room knew of her frustration. Another gown was brought to her, and with some tugging, she was able to fit within it. Glancing at the clock on her mantle, she let out another groan. She was late for the dinner party- her welcome back dinner party. Pushing past the maids, she quickly slipped on her shoes and left the room.

Upon entering the dining room, Dolra was wrapped within the life of the room. Cain sat at the head of the table, the empty seat to his right left for Dolra. To his left was Klaus, his cousin and Claudia across from him. Along with the Blessed human, who was seated to Klaus's free side, the four held a solid conversation. Next to her was Renee, and then Theo. Across from them, and the ones they currently spoke with, was Rony and Pals. All conversation paused when she entered though, and the room greeted her. Cain held her chair out for her, giving her shoulders a gentle squeeze before returning to his own seat. "May I ask what the topic of the night is? If it is war, please do lie to me."

"Actually, Dolra, we were speaking on the topic of the Slave Trade. It just came through town the other day and was met with protest." Dolra nodded a thanks to Claudia, taking a sip from her glass as she did. "Well I personally see no wrong doing in it. Those people had unsettled debts. At least with their sacrifice their families are free from the harassment that the debt caused." The Blessed human made a sour face, just slightly, and her hands moved. "She has to disagree with you my dear. And I think I might have to agree with her." Dolra looked at her husband, studying his face. The Blessed human went on, and he translated. "Scarlet has never owned a debt to anyone. She was kidnapped from her land and unwillingly forced to Traded." Dolra casted her eyes to the Blessed human. The human who blushed, and ducked her face away from everyone was the girl she had last seen before her summer trip. The girl in front of her, was no longer the same girl. Her face was ablaze in the passion of her feelings and she kept a steady, silent gaze on her. It was true, more than just the human's clothing and hair had changed. She had changed just as much, if not more so, inwardly. "Well, you are just one case." Scarlet shook her head. "During her time in the Trade, Renee and Scarlet came across quite a few others who had been kidnapped. It's more common than we might wish to believe." Dolra glanced to Klaus, who had his eyes casted at the table and deep in thought.

Claudia frowned slightly, taking a sip from her drink. Dolra knew of her dislike for the Slave Trade, and that her cousin in law held a pitifully deep sorrow for anyone in pain. "Though off the subject, why, darling, are you translating for Scarlet? Why is not Renee doing it? It is the reason you bought her in the Trade. Is it not?" Dolra took another sip from her glass, inwardly proud of herself. "It is, but you know as well as I that I own no slaves. They are freed, and work for income within our household. I give them food, shelter and work. Many here I know send most back to their own families rather than keep it for themselves. So being that Renee is free, she is allowed to have other conversations without Scarlet in them. As is the same for Scarlet. Clearly, Renee is caught up with Theo and Pals. Why force her out of her own conversation when nearly everyone at this table can understand the basics of Scarlet's language? I know you cannot, and thus wished only to make it easier on you until you catch on."

About to fire back with her own venom, Dolra was stopped by the line of waiters bringing out the dinner meal. Klaus used that moment to switch the conversation, moving on to the topic of some new music he had just heard on the radio.

The dinner was divine, and the conversation kept light after the brief spat between the husband and wife. It was during the second round of after dinner drinks that Dolra finally excused herself for bed. Knowing that Theo was a sucker for a good cup, Dolra knew that Cain would be kept busy for at least a few more hours. Standing, Cain kissed her hand, but did not stand from his seat. Accepting the small gesture, Dolra quietly left the dining room.

~~~

Opening the door to her husband's bedroom, Dolra slipped in and quietly locked the knob. She had spent a good portion of the last hour within Cain's office trying to find the stupid folder of his notes from his lesson with the Blessed human. She refused to allow him to ever put her in such a humiliating spot ever again. She refused to allow herself to just catch on to the Blessed mute's little hand signs. No, she was going to jump head in first. Dolra was going to learn the whole damn language without her husband's, or mute's, aid. Repeating such things to herself as she dug, Dolra smiled when she spotted a stack of folders in the bottom draw of her husband's night stand. Pulling out the box that the stack rested in, Dolra opened up the first one. She was met with her husband's graceful hand writing, and somewhat questionable drawings. She quickly flipped through the pages, once more filled with pride. Closing the folder, she sat it on the ground. Opening the second folder, she frowned. There were no notes, only photos. The one that struck her the most, mainly for the fact that it was the first photo of the pile, was of the Blessed human. She held a small group of ducklings in her hands and was beaming at the camera. Picking the photo up, Dolra quickly scanned
~~~

through the rest, but they were all simple shots of the estate's lake and land. Keeping the photo of the human out, Dolra placed the closed folder back into the draw. She kept the photo, and the first folder, out though. Taking both into her bedroom.

So, we've skipped forward a few months and a lot has changed. Thoughts, opinions? I would love to get some feedback. Keep Reading! <3

CHAPTER 23

Scarlet glanced behind her, lifting her head from her book as the doors to the library opened. Seeing that it was merely the King, she sighed and relaxed once more. He entered, closing and locking the door behind him. Scarlet silently closed her book, and watched him. "An extremely drunken, admittedly also very happy, Theo has been sent home safely. Peron has seen to it." Scarlet sighed, resting her book in her lap.

'At least someone had fun tonight.'

The King came up to her seat, resting his hands on her shoulders. "Come now, it wasn't that horrible." Scarlet looked up to him, his adoring gaze reassuring her. If there was one way the King hadn't look at the Queen tonight, it was as he was doing to her.

'I shouldn't have come tonight. The Queen has never liked me.'

The King squeeze her shoulders, lowering his face until his lips the curve of her neck. "Yes, but my wife doesn't truly like anyone. Not even her so called friends- all of whom I didn't invite tonight and she never said a word of." He kissed her then, in a sweet spot. "Don't take it to heart." Looking at him, Scarlet smiled when he kissed her cheek. She wasn't going to allow it to reach her heart. It barely penetrated through her leather corset. Because the facts at the end of the day, the King was with her and not his wife.

'You're not going to join her tonight?'

"Why would I be here if I was?" The King kissed her, softly. Moving back, he kept the distance between them small. Just enough to allow him space to move to fully face her. He kissed her again when he could, the second and third one each rougher and deeper than the last. The fourth one, the King frowned. "What's bothering you?" Scarlet shook her head, running her fingers down the sides of his face. "No, tell me. Something is bothering you. Are you still thinking about dinner tonight? Was it about our discussion of the Slave Trade?" Scarlet looked away, and shook her head. Standing, she sunk next to the fire place.

'It's about this morning. Those poor people. I'm angry about it all.'

The King followed her, taking her hands within his. "I know, we all are. I made the official announcement this afternoon and shortly after launched a counter-raid against a few of their mountain bases. Tomorrow I have phone meetings all day. I'm hoping that my agreements of allies with Kuko and Irn might gain me more public support. They are our closest neighbors." Scarlet nodded, feeling comforted by his words. The King had come to trust and confine to her on many matters, and she found her once little bit of knowledge on politics more expanded than it had ever been. "Atios and Seustad are my next concern. The Endless Mountains block everyone else from us. They'll have no reason to join any treaty just yet." Scarlet squeezed his hands.

'I have faith in you.'

"I know, it's why I love you." Scarlet tensed at the words as they came from the King's mouth. They flowed so smoothly from his lips- as water would. He said them to her so many time, those three simple words. Three simple words she had never said back.

~~~

Scarlet struggled to her robe on over her nightgown, one sleeve slid- ing off of her shoulder. Opening her door, Vern stood there with a package in his hands. "Good morning miss Scarlet. This came just right now, I believe it's from the seamstress." Releasing the hold on her robe, Scarlet clapped and grabbed the package. Thanking him, she closed her door once more. Tossing the box to her bed, she
~~~

pulled her curtains open and was over taken with the morning light. Rushing back to the box, she gleefully tore away the brown paper. Dropping the lid of the box to the ground, she pulled out the top of her new two-piece sleeping set. Though pants had become a staple piece in her everyday wear, this was the first pair she had made meant to be slept in. Holding the top to her chest, she spun around once. Dropping the top back in its box, she slid out of her night grown and robe. Walking into her closet she drug through a draw and slipped into a pair of under garments. Grabbing one of her training outfits, Scarlet carried it to the bathroom.

During the passing of the summer, Scarlet's lessons with the King slowly trickled away to a point that they were no more. There was no point. He understood her nearly as well as Renee, and the tension between Drale and Voirol needed his attention. The Silent War could only build up so much. With her days now fully free, and the memory of fainting after her trip to the Navy base still fresh in her brain, Scarlet devoted herself to training. Throwing knives, swords, spears, the bow, hand to hand combat, the dagger and even her own power. If she could learn and practice it; she did. Claudia and Pals, until her pregnancy physically stopped her, were both willing to teach her whatever she asked of them on one condition. They preferred her to focus on only one or two, to perfect the methods and learn the basics of anything else. Scarlet chose the throwing knives and her own power. The only way she ever truly live to what she was meant to be, was to expand her personal powers to their max. Renee, being she had no powers nor desire to learn more, focused her power solely to the sword. That was another thing Scarlet seemed to have lost during the hot season. While she and Renee had agreed to be friends once more, the friendship was different. It lacked the comfort of faith and total trust that it once held. Thus, the two were less likely to go to each other's room at night, staying up late talking; and more likely to exchange polite conversation before going off in separate directions.

After a quick stop by the kitchen, where Ariana already had a piece of toast and an apple waiting for her, Scarlet went down into the belly of the house. Upon entering into the room, she was met by the small hustle of a few workers. Standing in the far corner, also Scarlet's favorite spot, Pals held a bow and arrow; aiming at the foam target. Claudia stood a few feet beside her, knives tucked between each finger. "My mother is hoping for at least three, my father doesn't really care, and Theo thinks it's five!" Pals lowered her bow, shaking her head. "Well, you are rather large Pals. I can see how your sister sees five. Though I have my money on three. What does Rony think?" Claudia threw a set of knives, each one hitting a piece of the bullseye. Scarlet headed to the center mat to stretch and Pals lifted her reloaded bow once more. "To be truthful, Rony just want whatever comes out of me to be healthy. Personally I'm praying for twins. I can't imagine taking care of one pup, let alone five." Pals shot her arrow, and lowered to reload once more. "Well, what are the chances of you having one pup this time around?" Claudia pulled her knives from the wall, walking back to her throwing point. "Slim to none. It's unheard of a werewolf only giving birth to a single pup. Litters are so common it's painful. And by painful, I mean painful to the women who bear them all." Pals released her last arrow, and lowered her bow. "I already told Rony I wasn't going to willingly bear anything more than five pups total. We just have to be careful during my heats. I refuse to allow my body to become a factory." Pals pulled her arrows from the wall. "I feel ya Pals. I feel you. It's why I'm happily single. Klaus started to see someone seriously recently and she drove straight into the subject. The woman's a total lunatic. Not to mention roughly 2,000 year younger than him." Claudia threw another round of knives. Pals gave small smile, though her voice seemed even flatter than normal. "Rony is 80 years old than myself, you know. And I trained with the girl years ago, during a trip to Lubas. She seems fair and is strong in her combat skills. Plus I believe your brother brought her to my wedding. Isn't she coming today?" Claudia nodded her head, "Yes, I invited her to come around ten. She should be here soon. She just got back from a trip to Lubas, had some family matters to take care of there." Pals lifted an eyebrow. "Like what?" Claudia rolled her eyes. "Family drama, which I can understand but all I hear from my brother is how much he misses her and blah-blah." Pals gave another small, quick smile.

It was so strange to see Pals express herself. It was nothing compared to a normal being, or Theo, but it was emotions. Before she always remained stone faced in front of Scarlet. She was sure that the werewolf smiled- she had others who cared for her and she cared for others. She had friends. But she never expressed herself in front of Scarlet. Not until her wedding. Even after then, when she returned from her two week long honeymoon, she remained cool. It was only around the time of announcing her pregnancy that her hard exterior begun to crack. A low side comment from Theo blamed the hormones coursing through Pals' body. Newly mated and expecting pups tended to turn even the hardest piece of stone to a piles of pebbles. Or so Scarlet was told. She didn't quite believe it. Having sat in a few minor meetings with the King and his high officials, Scarlet had seen the stone mask come back. Whatever cracks were there, nor whatever put them there, Pals had no issue hiding. Her cracks were only shown to those who she seemed truly comfortable around. Scarlet was grateful she was one of those few.

"Good morning Scarlet." The two finally took notice of her, but it was Pals who greeted her first. The smile was gone from her face, but the mood of the room did not change. "My gibbon! Good morning, didn't even hear you come in!" From where she was stretched out on the ground Scarlet waved. Scarlet watched Claudia stick her knives back in their holders along her belt as she moved towards her. "So, whatta we going to do today?" Moving into her next stretch, Scarlet found her balance before responding.

'Powers today. I going to start focusing more on them.'

Claudia nodded, not questioning her. "Very well, I'll go get the weights. I expect you to pick me plus three sets up today." Claudia stood, signaling for her men to move three racks of different sized and shaped weights to the center of the room. Once there she helped them spread them out among the mat. "Set yourself." Scarlet took her stance, and a few of the aids took their places. "On your mark Pals." Pals, who had gone back to her bow, didn't turn to watch. "Go!" The men charged first. The one on Scarlet's left wielded a sword, the right had his wrapped fist up in the air. Focusing on the sword man, because of his larger weapon, she quickly flicked out two knives. They landed in the man's protected vest but he fell back as if he was injured. Turning just in time to duck from a swing from the second attacker, Scarlet jabbed a knife into his shoe. Careful to miss his actual body, the man was stuck in place. Rising back up, she took a quick swing at him. Her fist hit his jaw bone, and with a very real crack; the man fell to the ground. Knowing she had at least a few moments before the next attack, Scarlet extended her powers, the invisible tentacles quickly sliding to the ground from her body. Wrapping around Claudia and the weights she barely had them off a ground before they bounced. She had been hit from behind in her side. Keeping one hand out, she shot the other to her side. Blindly reaching the man with her powers, she forced him into the air. He flipped over her, landing in a huff. He was quick to recover and was now charging full force at her; a knife in hand. A dagger shot from her boot into her hand, and was up in time to block his attack. She pushed the knife away, but he was back on her once more. This time he applied so much pressure that her wrist released the weapon as it went flying back. From the clanging it made, she knew it was far from her grasp and now a lost cause. Unarmed, out of knives and with the man coming back for the final shot, she did the only thing that came to her mind. Run. She ran towards the attacker, swinging out a leg as she did. Her hands caught his arm as her foot made contact with his knee. The man let out a small cry, falling to the ground. Seeing her chance, she twisted back his arm. Forcing him to the ground, she sat on his back. Grabbing his head, she pushed it into the mat, once and hard. The man went limp but his chest was still heaving.

Claudia clapped from where she was floating in the air. "Good, good! And look- you didn't drop anything when you focused your hands elsewhere! That's a first!" Scarlet smiled, climbing off of the man. He stood as soon as she was off, as did the other two men. Reaching a hand out, she lowered everything, including Claudia, back to the ground. Claudia looked ready to say something, but a voice behind them had the two girls turning. "You were just floating!" Standing in the doorway was a ghost. Or, the vampire's pallid appearance gave her the illusion of death. Not even a little vein was visible, her slightly tipped eyes lacked any pupil. "Kay, right on time. Wonderful, please join us." Claudia greeted the vampire- Kay. As she came closer, Scarlet could see that Kay did indeed have pupils- but they were as white as the rest of her eyes. "So if you were just floating, this must be the Blessed human. Hello, I'm Kay Hu." Clasping her hands together, Kay gave Scarlet a small bow of her head. "Kay, this is Scarlet Solomon." Scarlet looked to Claudia, who encouraged her to copy. She did. "It's a pleasure to meet you." Scarlet nodded, smiling. "So you truly can't speak?" Scarlet shook her head. "That's okay," Scarlet noticed that despite having a rather musical voice, Kay always spoke as if she was out of breath, "who needs words when we have swords?" Looking fully at the new vampire, Scarlet took notice of the thin handle poking out over her right shoulder.

"Kay, it's been much too long." Kay looked past the two, to Pals. She was doing her best to not wobble as she walked towards them- bow still in hand. "Palsea, as I can see. Another congratulations are in order. The last time I saw you was at your lovely wedding, and now you appear ready for labor!" The two bowed heads to each other. "I'm still two months away, actually." Kay gasped. "I could not even image. I'm going to guess we won't be fighting today?" Pals shook her head, holding up her bow. "No, today I'm on the bow. I- wait," Pals stuck her nose into the air, "do you all smell that?" Scarlet took a sniff, but only got the sour mixture of body sweat, plastic mats and metal. She wrinkled her nose, regretting the deep breath. The two vampires also seemed to miss whatever it was Pals was smelling. Pals took another deep sniff, "bacon. Ariana is making bacon wrapped chicken. I think I'm going to go take a break now. I shall return." Tossing her bow to Claudia, Pals rushed from the room.

Slipping the bow over her back, Claudia chuckled. "Back to business, Kay, I asked you here because Scarlet has been expanding her fighting styles. I figure who better to teach her the ways of the North than you?" Kay's black painted lips parted, revealing teeth as white as the rest of her body. "I'm getting to teach the Blessed human?" She squealed, and Scarlet cringed at the sound. "Oh this is amazing! I'm not even nineteen hundred years old and I'm teaching a Blessed human! This is so cool!" Claudia held a hand out to Kay, as if she was a wild animal she wished to tame. "Kay, calm down. Take away the powers and Scarlet is no different than any other human. Before you two start though, I want her to see what the North is all about."

Calling over an aid, Claudia led them to a corner mat where they typically practiced their hand-on-hand. The vampire, who was easily larger than a bull and called such, pulled his shirt over his head as he headed towards his corner. Tossing it to the ground, he picked up a metal stick. With a simple swing it extended out into a staff. In her opposite corner, Kay removed her sword just long enough to remove her neck-sleeve piece, corset and over-layer. She remained left in a simple sleeveless top tucked into high waist leggings. Tossing her two side pony tails over her shoulders, Kay check the bun on top of her head. Her hair was as black as coal, yet there was a solid white strip that ran through the near-center of her hair. It was rather beautiful. Satisfied that it wouldn't fall during her demonstration, Kay nodded once. Removing her shoes, she took a spot in the center mat. Bull followed, his staff in hand. "On my mark... Go!"

All Scarlet caught was Bull's first attempt to side-sweep Kay. She sensed it, and was able to stop it- with her bare hands. After that point, it all so happened so quickly Scarlet could barely register it all. Kay pulled her sword out, and the sound of metal against metal mixed with the grunts and groans of the fighters. What Scarlet could notice, that unlike her rough hand on hand combat that had been taught to her; Kay and Bull were much more fluid. They aimed, and attacked in ways that Scarlet had never seen. At one point both lost their weapons- the flying things sent Scarlet and Claudia dashing for cover. The fight went on. Each move was precise, meant to hit an exact spot. Scarlet was shocked, to see such a sweet seeming and bubbly woman turn into such a monster. She held no mercy for Bull, nor did he offer her any. Though he towered over her, and was easily three times her size; she used it to her advantage. Turning, twisting and even flying through the air during- she used it all.

It was when Kay's scream filled the air that the battle finally ended. Having grabbed Bull's forearm, Kay twisted herself and threw
the large vampire over her shoulder. He landed with a groan, and
surrendered. Kay, who not only looked furious but held a flat hand
straight at Bull's neck, relaxed. Standing straight, the bubbly vampire
had returned once more, no longer over shadowed by the monster.
Smiling, she looked around. "Where'd my miao dao go?" Claudia
held the sword out, hilt first to her. Kay thanked her, and placed it
back in it's scabbard. As Kay did that, Claudia looked to Scarlet. "So,
you still think you want to learn the fighting of the North?" Scarlet
looked between the two a few times, and quickly nodded her head
yes.

~~~

"I would say dinner was divine tonight, would you not agree?" Scarlet
nodded her head, gracefully becoming drunk from the buzz that
came every time Cain's lips met her skin. They were hidden away
in her sitting room, the door locked. Together the two occupied a
corner of the largest couch, a burning fire warming the room. Scarlet
laid willingly in his embrace, his arms locking her to his chest. His
lips brushed their favorite spot on her neck. Though her through
were hazy, she could still remember the pure excitement on Kay's
face as she bowed to the King. Scarlet also learned that Kay was no
average vampire, she was the only daughter of a long line of high
~~~

ranking warriors. It didn't surprise Scarlet too much, she had witness the little vampire take down Bull- one of Claudia's best fighters. Until recently, though, Kay rarely left her home country of Lubas. Deciding to take some time to travel and see the land; was how she met Klaus. And then King of Voirol himself.

"Your thoughts on Kay?" The King's hot breath hit Scarlet's ear, and his lips kissed it.

'She wild, but very skillful.'

The King nodded. "So I've been told. The only person who doesn't really prefer her is Claudia. But she is the elder sibling, and I highly doubt any being will ever meet her expectations for her family."

'She likes me. Does she like the Queen?'

The King's lips curled, "She doesn't. She has enough in her to tolerate and produce kindness towards my wife." Scarlet smiled at the thought, her whole body warming. Looking up to the King, she reached a hand out to his cheek. Pulling him in, their lips met. Unlike most of the sessions they had held together, the kisses didn't start off soft or sweet. There was a bit of force behind it, right from the start. Turning her body, the King nipped at her bottom lip. She could feel his extended canines scraping at the flesh. She opened her lips, allowing him entrance. His hands moved from her waist to her hair. His fingers tangled through her short locks, the slight tugging made her body tingle from the pain. Wrapping her arms around his neck, she could feel the blood starting to rush through her body. His moved from her head, sliding down her sides. Feeling every curve. She dug her nails into his shoulders, bunching the fabric.

They stayed like that for an unknown time, exploring the other though never truly doing more. Scarlet lost all sense when she was with the King. When she finally pulled away, the mantle clock read eleven.

'We should get to bed.'

The king nodded, agreeing with her. "I don't want to leave you though." Leaning forward, she pecked him with her lips.

'Don't.'

The King said nothing, silent seconds ticked by. He suddenly sat up, sending Scarlet falling back. Catching her, he crushed his lips back to hers. Butterflies filled her from her toes to her head as the King stood. She wrapped her legs around him, grateful for her new sleeping pants. If not, then her night gown would have been up to her waist by this point. Breaking the kiss, Scarlet moved her lips across his face, trailing kisses. Her eyes were closed, but she heard a door open and felt the change in temperature as they entered her cool room. She wasn't sure what to fully expect, but one moment there was nothing behind her back and the next she was on her bed.

His hands found their way under her shirt, moving to slip the garment off rather than unbutton it. The feeling of his nails gave her goosebumps. Her nipped at the area behind her ear, but not enough to draw blood. She still gasped, which was cut short by his lips. The kiss was stopped to pulled the fabric past her head. Throwing it behind him, the King looked down at Scarlet. Scarlet, her rising chest fully exposed to him, watched him. Shaking his head, the King begun to lean forward. "You're beautiful." He mumbled against her collar bone, slowly moving lower. She kept her hands on his shoulders, unsure of what to fully do. Closing her eyes when he met the valley between her breasts, her toes curled. His fingers curled around the band of her pants, easily undoing the two buttons holding it close. Allowing them to be pulled away, Scarlet opened her eyes, meeting his heated gaze. Feeling his hands on her outward thighs, they never broke eye contact. He moved back up, trailing his mouth from her navel. Locking lips once more, she dug her fingers into his hair. Feeling his hands move inward, she moved her legs outward to give him full access to her most private area. She gasped at his touch, the invasion of her body. The feeling strange and unknown to her. At the same time, it was welcomed and she craved more. Breaking their kiss once more, the King moved to her breast. Scarlet found her fingers clawing at the sheets, the kisses going to her navel, and then lower. Her body tensed, yet floated freely at the same time as the King sent her mind to places it had never been before. There was also a something in her lower belly, a new feeling which sparked and fizzled. Building up, there was an explosion so strong it sent her back and toes curling. Over her rising chest, she watched the King rise once more. He used a clean finger to wipe his lips, and then ran that finger over her own lips. Taking his finger into her mouth, she cleaned it. Freeing him, Scarlet brought her hands up and begun to tug at his clothes. Unlike the King, she pulled forcefully at his shirt. It popped open, and she even saw a button go flying over her head in the dim light of the room. With his chest fully exposed to her, she carefully ran his fingers over his lean chest. He was perfect. It was fitting that he was near immortal, because his body deserved to be seen by many. He placed his own hand over hers and moved them. Reaching the waist band of his pants, she undid his belt. The King, at the same time, unhooked the button. Once they were removed, Scarlet ran her fingers inward along his pelvic line. Stopping short, she looked up to him. He nodded. "It's okay." Nodding in response, and moved her hands once more; she closed her eyes.

~~~

Scarlet's eyes flung open as she took a deep inhale. She sat up, black dots dancing throughout her vision. She was so confused. Looking to her left, she was met with the perfectly made, unslept half of her bed. Tossing her covers aside, she flung herself from the bed. She was fully dressed, not a button out of place. Running her hands over her head
~~~

she rushed to her sitting room, but the fire place was cold. There was a single tea cup and pot on the table, along with her book, but no sign that if the King had been there last night. Was it only just a dream? She asked herself. If it was, why does it feel so real? Her body was still humming, as if the ecstasy she had experienced in her dream was real. Turning to face a mirror hanging on the wall, she examined her neck. It was bare, not a single bruise nor bite mark upon it. Rubbing her hands over her neck, she ran one until it reached the collar of her shirt. Scarlet crushed the collar in her grip, sliding down the wall. Coming to the ground, she brought her knees up. She had never had such a dream, never been so captivated that it was real. It scared her. The only thing that scared her more about her life-like dream was the urge deep within her, wishing that it had been true.

Chapter 24

"I'm sorry." With those words, Scarlet sighed. Hanging her head, she forcefully wiped at her eyes with the heel of her palm. Theo threw the folder to the table, slowly moving away. "It doesn't make sense." Leaning against the seal of an open window, Theo looked to the street below. Shaking her head she pushed off, and kicked a small waste basket. It tumbled to its side with a clang, and trash went across the floor. "It just doesn't make sense! I've run every test I could on you- hell I even created some test in the process and I got nothing!" With a growl she grabbed two glass beakers, one filled half way with a blue liquid and flung it across the room. They both impacted the wall with a shatter, and where the blue liquid hit came smoke. Nothing caught fire, but there was a small sizzling sound as if meat was being cooked. Theo returned to the charts, looked at the spread out papers. "Everything is normal, your body is that of a normal human woman. There is no reason for you to have these powers." Theo then screamed at the table, clutching a few papers in her hands as she did. Taking a moment her eyes closed before she glanced back to Scarlet. "I'm sorry," she glanced up to Scarlet, "I tried and I'm just so frustrated at that I failed."

'You didn't.'

"I did. I promised you answers and all I got was that you're human. No different than Renee or some strange off the street."

'It's okay. I've accepted that I am me. One of a kind.'

Theo gave a small smile and begun to shuffle the papers back into the folder. Scarlet sighed quietly to herself. Though deep within her soul she knew Theo wouldn't find anything, it hadn't stopped her hopes from rising. She got lost in her thoughts. The thoughts that she might have true answers, and the disappointment she felt. She was thankful for Theo though. "Enough moping. How would you like to see some new prototypes I'm working on?"

'You won't use them on me?'

Theo laughed, "Of course not. So is that a yes?" Scarlet nodded her head, and Theo picked up the folder. She motion for her to stay sitting. Opening a small closet, she set the folder down. Before closing it, she pulled out a rather large box and carried it to the table. Scarlet stood, curious to what was in the wooden crate. Theo sat the top to the side, and reach into the box. Holding it out to Scarlet, she was slightly confused. It was a metal hand, thin and wiry. "This is, well, I haven't thought of a name for it but, watch." Theo took the hand a slipped her hand into almost like a glove. Locking the wrist guard, she then attached each finger to her own. Taking a step back, she swung her arm into the air but then paused. Grabbing a pair of goggles from a nearby table she tossed them to Scarlet. Scarlet caught them without fumbling, and slipped them on. Theo then slipped on her own, and repeated the motion with her arm. Bringing her hand back down, there was a slice that filled the air. "How cool is this?" Theo held up her metal covered hand, where extended, knife sharp claws had come out of the metal hand. "They're titanium! I got the idea a while ago. Since Pals been pregnant, she can't fully shift during the full moon- because you know, the babies and body changing stuff. It wouldn't be pretty. Back to the point, since she can't her body turns into this weird hybrid thing. It's super gross and yet amazing at the same time, and one of the things that changes is her nails. They extended out five inches and are like bone. If bone was sharpen to a point. It took me a few weeks but I finally figured it all out." Theo clicked a small button at her wrist, and the blades fell back in. She removed the device and handed it to Scarlet. It was rather heavy, but not as heavy as it appeared. "I haven't gotten around to making any more than the one, most because it has to be able to find an arrangement of hands. Different sizes." Scarlet nodded and handed it back to her. Theo placed it back in the box and took out a small glass container. Unscrewing the top, Theo poured the peach colored liquid into a pan. "This, isn't mine. I found the blue prints for it about a year ago, when I was cleaning. They were drawn up by my boyfriend, Jim. Didn't do anything until recently only because of the war. It's supposed to be a water resistant rub-like putty. Bouncy so that enough of it could act like a bumper." Theo picked up the slim, stretching it out. "I got the stretch and it repeals water. I can't get it to stick to anything. Clothing, skin, or even itself." Theo dropped the slim, and shook her head. "That's why it was Jim's. He was always good at chemicals. Me, I went for the mechanical. It's what made us such a great team." Theo poured the slim back into the jar, not allowing Scarlet a touch.

'Do you miss him?'

"All the time. It's been about five years, but for me it feels like it was only last week. The down side to living hundreds of years. I mean, we didn't have that much time anyways. He was a human and into his thirties when we met. If we were lucky, we would have another twenty years before the accident. And we wouldn't be able to have children. Fate's a bitch like that. Vampires just turn someone and boom- life is good. Werewolves got the short end, long lives and no way to change or create a future with those they love." Theo shook her head, "Look at me babbling on as if you didn't know this already."

'What happened? No one talks about it.'

"Admiral Erik Wiles happened. Jim had been working on this un-der-water ship that could be used to sneak up on the enemy and sink them from the bottom up. He called it a water tank. Neither of us were ever good at names." Theo chuckled at the thought, she tipped a little sealed container. The brown liquid moving with the motion. "Everything was going very well, the test and prototypes. When Wiles caught wind, he demanded to see them in action out in the open ocean. I wasn't sure about it, but Jim, damn Jim. He was willing to risk himself to prove a point. He had so much faith for the both of us. It was never enough." Theo finished packing her crate back up, clearly not willing to show anything else off. When she took a seat, Scarlet could see she was far off, somewhere else.

"The test day came around, as we all waited near the edge of a large navy ship. It was fine for the first twenty minutes and then a storm started to move in from the sea. Jim was having them bring it back up when something went wrong. Wires crossed, some gas caught a spark or something, I don't really know. There was screaming from the radio, distress calls, alarms in the background and then nothing. It went from being noise every where, to not even a single being breathing. We sat in silence for three full seconds before learning the fate of the five souls on board. The water tank ended up exploding. Shook a thirty story naval ship to nearly fifty degrees starboard tip.

The project was canceled after that. The other four water tanks we had made are sitting in one of my family's warehouse in Seustad, collecting dust. Wiles lost his twenty year old daughter, I lost my boyfriend, a family lost their brother, and two children lost both parents." Scarlet reached her hand out, wrapping it around Theo's. And in a move that was less than called for, the werewolf pulled the human to her. The two embraced, as true friends would.

~~~

Scarlet climbed out of the car, her stomach rumbling. "If you stop by the kitchen, I'm sure Ariana will have some of the lunch still left." Vern gave a small smile at Scarlet, climbing the steps with him. Her mind was already lost on the thought of warm potatoes with gravy, and some freshly cook veal. Scarlet's daydream was interrupted by a voice calling her as she entered into foyer. Renee came into the room from one of the back halls. "Scarlet, I was hoping to catch you. I need to speak with you. I have tea and cookies in my room." Scarlet followed after Renee, waving a good bye to Vern. The two walked silently to Renee's room, taking seat in the corner by a window-where her seating area was set up. Scarlet took a seat, sitting as she had done so many times before but none so recent. With a hand of fresh cookies, Scarlet watched Renee grab something from her desk. Taking a seat across from her, Renee unfolded the paper in her hands, and then refolded it; words up. "I um, I don't think I can say
~~~

it out loud." Renee kept her gaze down, her voice growing thick with emotions. "So, um, I'm just going to, you know, let you read it." She held the letter out to Scarlet and pointed where to start.

To answer your question on how Ms. Solomon is doing, I am sad to inform you that due to both her illness and weaken state she has died. I saw to her burial, it was small. Her home is now in the hands of the local Appointers of the High Lord, I barely had time to get her things before they were rushing to rent it out to another family. I kept a few items, the most important, but most I had to sale. We have no extra room to store her things.

Scarlet looked to Renee, both numb and unable to say anything. A small sob escaped her friend's lips. "I'm so sorry Scar. She got a cold and it ended up turning into pneumonia and, she wasn't strong enough. I'm sorry Scarlet. I wanted to tell you sooner, but I didn't know how." Scarlet frowned. What had her friend meant by sooner? Unfolding the letter, Scarlet looked at the dating. It was dated a few weeks after Pals' wedding; early summer. Hot tears, from both anger and pain, filled Scarlet's eyes. She threw the paper at Renee.

'Don't ever speak to me again.'

"Scarlet." Renee grabbed her, and held on. "I wanted to tell you sooner, I just didn't know how." Scarlet pulled her wrist free.

'So why now? What's changed?'

"We're going to the battle front." The two girls turned, looking to the King. He stood in the doorway, the handle in his hand. "I specifically told Renee to not say or do anything to upset you. Clearly this is yet another order she chose to ignore from me." He turned his gaze on her. She held her chest out, not backing down. "She deserved to know." The King frowned. "Scarlet," he kept his eyes on Renee, "you should go pack. We leave in a day." Taking the hint, Scarlet nodded to his order. The King moved into the room, giving Scarlet room. Leaving the room, wiping the tears as she did. Closing the door, his eyes grew cold towards Renee. "You really should learn how to hold your tongue, Renee. Scarlet no longer needs a translator in this house, your being here is now by my good grace and not necessity." Renee rolled her lips, turning back to her sitting area. Taking a seat, she motioned for the King to follow. He remained standing in the middle of her room and she wished that she had made her bed that morning nicer than she had. "So you don't agree with me, so you don't like me. It's not as if I'll be in this home for much longer." The King moved forward slightly, clearly interested. "And why do you say that?" Renee snorted, picking up a cup of tea.

"I'm no fool, I have had much free time on my hands lately. I have taken advantage of your great library and it is recorded that no Blessed human has ever out lived their 30's if lucky. They all step up to save the world and then they die."

"That is why I trained her. Scarlet is unlike any other Blessed human."
The King took a seat across from her, folding one leg over the other.
"That's a lie. She's no different than the others. So I thought she
deserved to know the truth before she died. I did it out of love." She
took a sip of tea, hiding her shaking hands.

"That's shit Renee and you know it." Her blood ran cold as he went
on. "You were feeling guilty." Renee had never heard the King curse
directly to her ever. She was taken back. "You've been hiding the fact
that her mother died almost three months ago, and when I told you
we were going to the front this afternoon you got worried. You told
Scarlet so that if she dies then you live on with a guilt free conscious.
That's not love." The King stood so fast that Renee jumped and spilt
her tea. "Now I suggest you pack warmly, the base of the mountain is
always colder than the rest of the country this time of year." Leaving
her alone, the tea cup fell from her hands as the door slammed shut.
Renee slid from the chair, her shaking, curling fingers running along
her face. Unable to breathe, she hyperventilated until everything
went dark.

~~~

Mindlessly, numb, Scarlet stared out of the window to her left. The
country passed below her, a rainbow of greens for the plants and an
arrangements of browns and greys for towns. It was all so beautiful
and yet she couldn't find any part of her inner being to come ap-
~~~

preciate it. She had not even glanced at Renee in almost twenty four hours. At her request meals were brought to her room. They traveled in a separate car to the air ship, and once aboard Scarlet locked herself away in her small sitting room. Alone, as she had been for the last day, she allowed herself to get lost within her thoughts.

Though she knew the day would come, and she had come to the terms of never seeing her mother once more- it still hurt. Perhaps she had been lying to herself. As anyone, Scarlet held a small hope that one day she would escape the hell that had become her life. To return to her mother once more, to their home.

Her mother would be one break from sewing, hunched over their small garden. Stopping on the edge of their property, Scarlet would let out a small, silent, sob. At the sound of the gate opening, her mother would pause, and look to who had entered her land. Upon seeing her daughter, she would let out a cry. Standing, her head would shake because she wouldn't believe it. Her daughter, the one she thought she had lost, had returned to her. Rushing towards her the two would meet half way, and embrace. They would clutch at each other, neither one willing to let go. Mumbling her disbeliefs, Scarlet would reassure her mother with kisses to her cheeks. Together, still in each other's arms the two would head inside to catch up for lost time.

Of course, that hope was now crushed. For even if Scarlet could get out of the war alive, her mother was gone. Her house was the High Lord's and what little belongings they had were sold away. She could return to Tobus, but she would be returning to nothing. That was not the thought that made her weep. Her tears did not fall for the fact that her mother was gone, Scarlet had never stop truly missing her and now she knew she'd never would. Her cheeks were stained because she never got to say goodbye. Her mother had the left the world, and Scarlet was burdened with regrets. None were too great, but just large enough to cause her pain at their thought. They were scores she would never get to settle, and thus forced to live with their pain.

There was hand upon her own, embracing it. She glanced over to the King. Lifting her hand, he kissed it. Keeping it to his face, the King's eyes closed as he drunk in her scent. She moved her thumb along his cheek, his skin cool to the touch. He glanced up to her. "Tell me your thoughts." It wasn't a demand nor a question, it was a simple request of a lover. Scarlet shook her head, glancing back out the window. "We'll be landing soon." The King leaned closer to her, looking with her.

'We've reached the base so soon?'

The King shook his head. "No, we're landing in a town a four hours' drive from the nearest base. I can't risk anyone spotting my ship so close to the front. The cover story is that we have come to visit a local vineyard for Theo's and Pals' birthday. The vineyard is about an hour from the particular base we're heading to." Scarlet nodded her head. More secrets, more lies. It's all her life had ever been, and she realized that it was all it ever was. Hide your powers, pretend to be normal. Control your powers, save the world. Love, but only in secret and behind locked doors. Surround yourself with people you think you can trust, but know they can never be trusted. Always remember that those we love, leave us in the end. Turning her body towards him, she held his face in her hands. Leaning in, Scarlet kissed the King. Advancing it, the King wrapped his arms around her. She moved, her legs wrapped around his waist and her arms around neck. They held onto each other, her grip on his shoulders so tight it was as if she feared him floating away.

~~~

"All I'm saying is I don't get why you're here." Theo chased after Pals down the ramp as they deboarded the air ship. "I'm one of the top ranking warriors. That's why I'm here." Pals, annoyed at Theo and wobbling from her protruding stomach, did not turn to look at her sister. "That's not what I meant- we all know you're one of the best. I just don't see why you have to be so close to the front! You're almost full term!" Pals sighed, leaning against a car with one had as she looked to her sister. "Because I want to be here, that's why. Rony is here and
~~~

my due date is just under a month away. I have time. I'll be here for a weeks' time now for the last time, get off my back on the subject. You aren't my mother." Pals climbed into the car, Claudia already waiting inside, just as Rony placed the last bag in the back. Climbing in, Pals cracked her window and yelled to the King. "I shall meet you there." As the car started to drive off Theo chased after it for a few feet, screaming foe her sister. Finally giving up, Theo kicked the ground and started her return to the others. As she did another car pulled up. Climbing out from the back, Klaus looked back at Theo. "What's the fuss all about?" Klaus bowed to the King, and then embraced him in a hug. "Theo is still upset with Pals coming." Klaus nodded his head, understanding. "I see, well, Pals is grown. She is free to do what she wants." The King nodded. "Not to mention," Klaus went on, "she's a pregnant wolf and you don't piss off any being that's pregnant. Let alone a werewolf." Klaus cracked a smile, and a laugh. The King said nothing.

The car ride to the vineyard was long, boring and quite. Along with the King, there were two guards in the back with her and thus she had to refrain from straying from a status of 'follower' to her 'leader'. Upon arriving at the vineyard, they were escorted through a secret passage in the wall filled with stairs. The stairs led to a series of tunnels, and from there they were in some sort of warehouse like room. Lead to a large, cargo truck the whole group entered. A bench lined each side, and their bags were stored in the space between. They all found a spot, slipping an arm into the straps that lined the walls. Scarlet kept her eyes casted down, still refusing to meet Renee's- who looked at her from across the bags. The ride in the truck, unlike the car and airship, was bumpy to say the least. If Scarlet hadn't kept a grip on the bench, she would have surely flown from the seat. Once it ended, and the drawn out journey couldn't end any sooner than it did, the back doors opened. Muffled voices were now clear, as the group got their first look at the military base. They were inside a large warehouse, not has high as the navy one off the coast but the length was equal. Multiple types of all kinds of vehicles were lined throughout, with large packs of ammunition scattered throughout.

They all begun climbed out, Pals with the aid of Rony. She let out a long breath, closing her eyes. When it came Scarlet's turn she graciously accepted the King's hand. Once firmly on the ground she held onto his grip for just a second too long, forcing herself to let go. "Your highness, I'm glad to see you all make it here safety." The General, and three lackeys behind him, bowed. "Yes, thank you General. I trust everything is going according to plan here as well?" The werewolf, who was clearly in his later years, gave a small frown. "Not exactly, but we will discuss the matter over dinner." The General cleared his throat, though it sounded almost as if he had water in his lungs. He went on, "I am sure you are all hungry. My men will see that your bags are brought to your barracks." With a snap of his finger and a hand signal the lackeys behind the General were moving past them, each step perfectly precise. "Please, follow me." The General begun to move, glancing back to make sure they were following. Moving across the warehouse, the General led them through a set of double doors. They entered into a hall, white and crisp. After a few turns, and a passing of many doors, they stopped in front of another set of double doors. The General opened the door, and they were ushered into yet another room.

The mess hall was like the hallways, white, crisp and clean. Though it could easily seat three hundred, the room was empty. "The last set of men just finished their meal prior to your arrival. But the Cook was prepared for you all." As he said this, the General led them to a pre-set table. The meals were all on sliver trays and their utensils were plastic, but the steam rising told them it was fresh. "Please, sit." They all took a stool, though Pals was forced to sit on the end. Her stomach prevented her from fully facing them while also sitting at the table. Everyone begun to eat, though the food didn't stand close to Arianna's cooking. Everyone that was minus Pals and the King. "Rey, what's gone wrong with the plan? What are you not telling me?" The General took a sip from his water. "Though his men have not advanced, King Minus is sending more. We might not be over powered, but we will be outnumbered and that's an issue." The King nodded and General Rey went on. "I also got a message from our main camp on the other side of the mountain this morning. A mole we deployed a few months ago has finally sent us some information."

"And what is it?"

"King Minus sets out for the mountain base tomorrow, heading a marching brigade of five thousand men." As the General said this, the reactions around the table differed. Theo and Rony let out profanities. Pals' hands went straight to her stomach, her eyes casting away. Claudia hit her brother, demanding to know if he knew about this. Klaus admitted that he did. Scarlet could image Renee's color going pallid; because her own had. The King's face changed shading, going from pale to red in a matter of seconds. "What?" The General nodded. "He's heading to the battle front?" General Rey nodded once more and the King slammed his fist onto the table. "Damn it! We head out in the morning." The King stood, his food still untouched. He looked as if he was about to say more but a high pitch squeal suddenly filled the air. Alarm lights along the walls flashed red, changing the atmosphere. "Attention, attention. We are in code black, everyone to their stations. I repeat, everyone to their stations." The voice spoke over the alarm, giving clear orders. "What's going on?" The King looked to the General. The General looked to the solider rushing through the double doors. "General, we're surrounded. There's a fleet of airship from the North and the East and West both have men marching in." General Rey nodded once and the solider left them. "Your highness, I must insist that-"

"No. I'm coming with you. Klaus, Claudia; see to it that everyone gets to a bunker below." They nodded, having clearly been to this base before. The King and General Rey then rushed from the room. "Come we must hurry." The two vampires motioned for everyone to follow them out a single door. "Like hell. If you think I'm going to sit on my ass while shit gets blown up around us you got another problem." Theo remained by the table, arms crossed. "And just how are you going to fight, sister, when you have no weapons or armor?" Pals held on to Rony with one hand wrapped around his arm, the other around her stomach. "I'm not unarmed though, sister. I have a metal bird here. Klaus, where it is?"

"Klaus, do not dare tell her where that death trap of a flying machine is." Pals glared, a real glare, at the Vampire. Theo pushed him. "Klaus tell me."

"Do not."

"Klaus."

"Theo you can't go out there."

"I'm going not just because they need me but I'm one of the best damn flyers."

"No!"

"Yes!"

"It's in warehouse C, right next to us." Theo nodded, avoiding her sister's deadly natural face. "Good, can you take me there?" Klaus shook his head. "I can't. I need to get the others to a safe bunker."

"Claudia will do it, plus I need a second person in the plane. One to fly, one to shoot." Just as Klaus shook his head, Claudia stepped up beside him. "I'll go." Everyone ignored Pals calling out the Claudia, clearly upset. "Klaus can take them to the bunker. I've flown in it before and I know it can't be much different then shooting a normal gun." Claudia glanced to Pals. "I'm sorry, but its what needs to be done. Keep my godchildren safe." Claudia rushed to Theo, grabbing her. Together they ran from the room. Pals let out a stream of profanities and curses, only stopping when Klaus motioned for them to follow him. They did.

~~~

With a small slam, the metal door to the bunker closed and locked. The bunker was simple, two hanging lights, four sets of bunk beds built into the walls, and a small washroom separated by a curtain. With a great sigh Pals was lowered onto one of the bottom bunks by Rony. Her eyes were closed, and in the dim, swinging light, Scarlet could see light beads of sweat on her forehead. Rony sat close to her, their hands intertwined. The whole room shook as something above them impacted it. The shaking was less violent then when they were rushing through the base, but it shook enough to still make
~~~

your head hurt. Scarlet took the bottom bunk across from Pals and Rony. It was only the three of them. Renee insisted on going out and helping, and not allowing anyone to stop her. With her sword drawn she parted from the group. Once reaching the bunker, Klaus claimed he needed to help in the control room. Remaining on the other side of the door, he closed them into the bunker. Scarlet peaked under the bunk, opening the drawers. Next to some basic leather guards, and clothing, there was food, a first aid kit, a communication radio and a knife. Scarlet stuck the blade into her pants, her own packed away in her bags. With nothing else to do, Scarlet laid down and closed her eyes.

Pals whimpered, in such a way that Scarlet sat up almost at once. She avoided nearly bumping her head, and swung her legs over the side of the bed. The room shook. The light was questionable but Pals' condition was not. There was a shining layer of sweat coating her face, which color had turned much too pale. A wet cloth had been put on her forehead, but whatever its use was not being met. She laid on the bed, one hand on her stomach. "What is it?" Rony, who sat on the ground beside the bed, looked up to his wife. "Rony." He nodded, though her eyes were closed. "Yes?"

"Rony." Pals repeated herself once more, taking a deep breath before speaking more. "It's time." Rony looked as if he were near passing out. Scarlet felt her heart stop in her chest. "It's time? How?" Pals' head barely moved as she shook it. "Don't know."

"How long have you been in labor?"

"Since the truck ride, guess the bumpy road did it." Rony shook his head, running his free hand over his face. "I don't know what to do."

"Hospital. We need to get there."

Rony wanted to protest, but his eyes agreed with his wife. He was lost. Scarlet bent over, remembering the radio under her bed. With it in her hands she fell to her knees and handed it to Rony. He thanked her and begun to call out to each station. When he finally caught one, the voice on the other end was cut off and replaced by the King.

"Rony, what's wrong?"

"Palsea's in labor, we have to get her back to the town."

"She can't be in labor, that's impossible!"

"It's not!" Rony's face twisted in pain, and a glance at his discolored fingers told Scarlet Pals was in much more pain than she was allowing to show. "I'm going to carry her back up, I need a truck to be ready!"

"What? No! You need-"

"You don't get it! SHE'S DYING!" As Rony screamed into the radio he crushed the box in his hand. Cleaning his hands, he stood. "Love, we're going to get you back to town. I promise." Rony slipped his arms under her. "I'm going to pull to you to my chest." Like a rag she fell against him, the rag on her forehead falling to the ground. "Scarlet, I'm-I'm." Rony turned, facing her. As he had spoken to the King, she had slipped the leather chest and arm pieces onto her frame. They were clearly made for someone more filling, hanging from her body. The knife was in one hand, the other was turning the large wheel on the door. "You shouldn't come." The door opened with a release of pressure. With determination on her face, she motioned to Pals and him. Then herself. Up to the ceiling, and lastly a motion of driving a car. Flipping the blade to point outwards in her hand, she led the way from the room. Rony followed.

~~~

The warehouse was still standing, but all of the vehicles that had once filled it were gone. Scarlet scanned for anything, or anyone. "Scarlet, Rony!" Standing in the bed of what looked like a farm truck was Renee. She waved to them until they were almost at the truck. "Come on." Renee jumped from the bed, and Scarlet noticed multiple cuts along her shirt into her shoulders. Clearly ignoring her own pain, Renee helped Rony get Pals into the bed of the truck. Scarlet climbed in after them, as she did Renee leaned through the small back window of the cab. The truck begun to move towards the open doors, and it was then Scarlet saw her first taste of a real battle.
~~~

The dark sky was lit up by explosions, and gun fire. Above them propellers roared, lines of gunshots flew across the sky like lightning bolts. Small fires on the ground gave the light to soldiers fight. Any type of combat that was imaginable was taking place as they rushed by. The driver was going near blind, any light on the truck turned off. Soon enough Scarlet found herself bent over, the threat of getting hit too real. The truck suddenly swerved and she shot her head up just as a blast went off not far from them. Somehow, despite all the noise, Scarlet could hear Pals whimper and whisper to her husband. "I'm sorry I lied." The truck swerved again, but this time Scarlet spotted the bomb before it hit the ground. Catching it, she set it back at the enemy's air ship. "Don't be, you're fine. You'll be fine" Pals shook her head, her lips dry. "I'm not, I'm not strong enough." Rony wiped her forehead. "Don't say that." Scarlet begun to block more attacks at their speeding truck, and even found herself breaking a sweat as they cleared the inner ring of the base. In the light of an explosion above their head, Scarlet glanced at Pals. She looked worse. "Don't give into the darkness when I'm gone, our pups will need you."

"Don't say that, we're going to get you to the doctors. You're going to be just fine."

"I'm so sorry, I love you." She sounded so tired, so frail. "I love you too, keep talking to me." Pals said nothing.

"We're coming up to the gate- Scarlet you and I will need to jump!" Renee, who had been silent for the most part, screamed over the noise. Scarlet nodded, look to the road ahead. The dirt path led into a rather dense looking forest, and she knew that once they made it to the trees the werewolves would be fine. "Ah shit." Scarlet looked to Renee, who was looking behind her. Turning, Scarlet cursed to herself. A rather determined group was chasing after them on tag-team motor bikes. One drove, the other shot from behind. "Pals keep talking to me." Scarlet focused on each arrow, bullet and even knife thrown; catching each one and tossing it to the side. "Scarlet, we need to jump!" Glancing back, the trees were just feet from them. Turning back, Scarlet held one hand out to Renee. Lifting them both from the truck, they remained in the air as she used her other hand to pull down trees. Blocking the road from the motor cycles. The bokes stopped short, and the soldiers looked up to the two floating girls. They wondered out loud, in shock. Scarlet lowered them, and glanced to Renee. "She'll be okay, I know she will." Scarlet nodded to her friend, looking at the soldiers as they climbed from their bikes. Taking a stance with her sword Renee met eyes with Scarlet and nodded once. Scarlet returned the nod, and flung her arms out once more. Releasing her powers out, racing towards the enemy.

CHAPTER 25

Scarlet closed her eyes, forcing them to close as much as possible. "It hurts, I know." She nodded, focusing on her breathing in an attempt to take her mind away from the bone crushing pain she felt in her arm. "The bastard got you pretty good, deep into the muscle." Opening her eyes, Scarlet glanced to the cut on her upper left arm. In the weird brown antibacterial liquid, her cut remained open and angry. When the doctor grabbed the rather large needle from the metal tray to his side, she looked away again. The pinch of the needle was nothing compared to the pain in her arm, but Scarlet had never been a fan of sharp objects piercing into her body. Soon after the needle was pulled back, her whole upper arm begun to go numb. The doctor pinched her in a few places, none of which she felt. He deemed her ready for stitches, and a nurse brought over another metal tray.

"At least you're better off than me." Scarlet glanced to Renee. She laid on a bed a few down from Scarlet. Another doctor worked on a rather nasty cut on her ribcage, as a nurse wrapped her cut shoulders. Scarlet rolled her eyes, and motioned that she was crazy. "Crazy? I'm not crazy!" The soldiers in the beds between them watched the two as if they were both crazy.

'You. Fought. Cuts. Death.'

"Yeah I fought, it's what was right. And yeah, I got hurt. It's a risk worth taking, and am I not here right now?"

'Why?'

"Why? Why have you been training? Why are either of us in this infirmary? Because we are meant to fight." Renee cringed in pain, but made no noise.

'I only helped Pals. All I wanted.'

"Well, I wasn't there to help Pals. I was fighting. For the first time in my life, I was actually doing something that could change the world! When I was in the middle of it all, hectic and unknowing my next move, I felt... alive." Scarlet frowned at her.

'Who are you?'

"Who am I? Who are you? You said it yourself, we're changing. You know your path and now I've finally found mine. That's something I'm never going to give up." Scarlet looked away from Renee, just as the doctor finished the last stitch. He wrapped her arm in gaze, taping it off. Grabbing a cloth, he tied it around her neck; slinging her arm into it. "There, Private Hancock will take you to the King." The low ranking officer offered Scarlet a hand. She willingly took it with her good hand, and hopped from the bed. Releasing her, Scarlet followed after the man. He led her to a single door, opening it without knocking. "Your highness, General Rey. Special Force's Flower is delivered to you sirs." Stepping in behind the man as he saluted his commanding officers, Scarlet left the door open. "At ease, good job. Now return to your commanded post."

"Sir, yes sir!" Doing an about face, the man left. "I trust my men took care of you?" Scarlet looked to the General, who sat at the head of a table. His hat was removed, revealing his bald head. She nodded to him, meeting eyes with the King for a moment. They showed relief, and annoyance. "Wonderful, please have a seat." Scarlet took the seat that the General motioned to. "You're just in time for our update. For you." A solider from behind offered her a note pad, along with a stylus and ink. She took it, and nodded a thanks to the girl. Flipping to a random page, she tossed the lid to the ink a side.

Is Pals okay? Her pups? She slid it to the middle of the table, for everyone to read. Her eyes, though, looked directly at Theo. Sighing, Theo glanced away. "She gave birth to four heathy puppies; three boys and a girl. They ended up having to cut into her, because her cervix hadn't stretched but her water broke. But all four came out okay." Scarlet took the notepad back. And Pals? "She lost a lot of blood, but with rest and time she's expected to make a full recovery." Relief flooded Scarlet, and she lowered her head into arms. She cried, for the fact that Pals was okay, and that she had four perfect puppies. Scarlet had been so scared for Pals. So scared for herself, for Renee.

After knocking the trees to block the road, Scarlet and Renee took on a total of twelve soldiers from the enemy line. It had been a battle worth seeing, considering it was her first real battle. Everything Claudia and Pals had taught her had been tested and put to use. It was towards the end of the battle, when only three men remained, that they both got injured. Two came after Scarlet, and the third aimed for Renee. For a majority, Scarlet had the upper hand against the two-taking one out with a solid punch to his nose. The satisfaction was short lived, because behind her Renee cried out. Scarlet turned just in time to see her friend land on the ground, bleeding. Realizing her attacker was advancing, Scarlet used her powers to grab the man and fling roughly into a tree. His body impacted the truck like a rag doll. Knowing Renee was safe, Scarlet turned her attention back to her own final attacker. Once more, she turned just at the right time. The man aimed for her heart with the blade in his hands but Scarlet was able to move fast enough to avoid a hit to her heart. Instead the blade sliced the soft, exposed skin of her upper arm. Letting out a silent cry, she stumbled away. Holding her upper arm, she moved her left hand up. The man, who had turned to attack once more, was frozen in the air. Like a child with ball, she forced his body high into the air before slamming it into the ground. Seeing him neither move nor breathe, she fell to her knees. The pain was over coming. Suddenly she remembered Renee. Looking to her fallen body, Scarlet stumbled over to her. Scarlet moved Renee to her back. She was still breathing, but bleeding greatly from the wound in her side. Though Scarlet had voiced a hatred for Renee, in that moment she could only feel fear. They had been anything but on equal eye level the past few months, but Renee was the only family Scarlet had left in the world. Her father was unknown. Her mother was dead. Renee was all she had left. So with all her strength, and mostly her good arm, Scarlet picked up her friend right under her armpits. She dragged her back up the road, the military base visible as a shadow in the first few rays of day light. Making it to the first gate, Scarlet stumbled in. As she did, Scarlet lost her grip on Renee and fell to the ground. Looking to her friend, she cried, and held her hand. Left to hope that someone would find them before it was too late. Reaching out, she held onto Renee's limp hand, her eyes closing as she did.

Scarlet only had small snips of what happened after she blacked out. She remembered hearing voices, at one point she was in someone's arms and the next she was lying in a moving truck. There were more voices. She went from being outside, to in; the titled ceiling racing above her head. When she finally regained consciousness, she was in the infirmary surrounded by other wounded men and woman.

"What's the official number?" Scarlet was brought back from her inner thoughts to the room by the King's voice. "Roughly 600." General Rey slid a paper towards the King. "Just us? What are their numbers?" The General shook his head, "We don't know exactly." The King looked at the paper. "Well we have quite a few of their bodies. That's something." Theo rolled her eyes, standing. "Not that I care about the numbers, I really don't, so I'm going to go. My metal bird needs a few repairs before this afternoon's flight."

"Theo, are you honestly leaving? Now of all times? Can't your invention wait?" Theo gripped the back of her chair in her hands, looking down to the King. "No, sire it can't. We got attacked last night, were unprepared, and good soldiers died. In order to keep their deaths from being in vain, I'm getting my ass back to my bird so I can get it to the other side of the mountains. To the real battle." Pushing her chair in, Theo left the room without another word. Scarlet watched her until the door shut, and then looked back to the King.

'When do we leave?'

"Within the next two hours. Is Renee almost ready?" Scarlet hesitated, but nodded her head yes. Renee had attempted to control her life, Scarlet was not about to do the same thing. She may not have liked that her best friend wanted to go into the heart of the battle, but Scarlet could not stop her either. "Very good, how are you. How's your arm?" Scarlet could hear it in his voice. Though barely there, she could hear the pain. She wished he could comfort her, to wrap his arms around her and kiss her until she forgot the pain. But he couldn't.

'Sewn up, and in pain.'

"I'm sorry."

'It was worth it.'

She gave him a smile, thinking about Pals and her heathy pups. The General cleared his throat. "If we may get back onto the more dire matters at hand?" The King nodded. "Of course Rey, go on." The General tugged at his top, his chest puffed out slightly. "Yes, as we speak a small elite group of my men are preparing our transportation through the mountains. In order to more protect you all, rather than keep an element of surprise, we shall be traveling through a series of old mines. It's not the cleanest but it's quick and secluded." The King nodded, both agreeing and telling them that that was the plan they were to follow.

~~~

Scarlet's arm throbbed, despite being bound by the sling. She rubbed it slightly, the pain easing for those few moments. Standing to the side, Scarlet watched as their small bags were loaded into one of the further mine carts. It had taken them roughly twenty minutes
~~~

through twisting tunnels to finally come to their send off point. Though their numbers were small. Besides the King's party, there was the General and four of his men. The last bags had been packed away when the General suggested that they all climbed in. Scarlet, Renee, and the King got into the most center cart. Both humans needed the help of others to get over the sides, but were able to do so none the less. Claudia and Klaus took the cart in front of them, along with the General. Their two carts had been outfitted with wooden benches on each side. The four soldiers took spots on each end cart, both of which were handcars. Clearly they were to be the main power of their journey. Scarlet wasn't quite sure how, General Rey said it would be a few hours to get through the mountain. There was no way four men- three of whom were werewolves and the other a vampire- could pump the three heavy carts. "Onward men, onward."

Following General Rey's order, the men made no noise as they begun to pump. And after a few moments, and some jolting, the carts begun to move. Besides the lamp in each cart, and hanging from each end of the handcars, the tunnels were absorbed in black. What lied a head and what they left behind was unseen. The men pumping the hand cars stopped as the small train entered into a large cavern. They each took to their knees as the train dipped, and gained speed. That was all the train needed to move on it's own inertia. Looking up and around, whenever they entered into a cavern, Scarlet saw faint tracks surrounding them. Higher, lower and sometimes even parallel to their own. When the carts would slow, typically during a span in a flat tunnel, the men on the ends rose and carried them through. Having lost count of how many caverns and turns they had taken, Scarlet's eyes fell heavy. Glancing at the King, who was across from her, her eyes closed.

A jolt shook her body, and she felt her head hit something rather hard. Opening her eyes, Scarlet looked to see where she was at. A quick glance up at Renee, who was holding back a curse through her clenched teeth, told Scarlet her head had been in her lap. Looking to the cart wall, which her head should have hit, it was blocked by the King's hand. "Would it have killed if you made the stop a bit smoother?" Rising, Scarlet noticed Renee holding her bad side. General Rey looked to her hand. "I warned you that the stop would be rather rough. That last dip always increases our speeds greatly." Scarlet sat up, rubbing her eyes with her good arm. The small cavern they were in was near identical to the one they had started in, dark and empty. "Never the less, what done is done. We must be going, our contact ride is waiting for us." General Rey and the two vampires in his cart stood. Beside her, Renee grumbled as she stood and hopped out of the cart. Scarlet copied her, using both her good arm and the bench as an aid. The King was last, but was handed a lantern by one of the guards. Going up to General Rey, the two men fell into an equal step and led the group. Once more they were led through a series of darken tunnels, yet the General and guards all knew their way. The group remained silent, their shuffling feet echoing almost too loudly.

Rounding yet another corner, the group was met with guards and the entrance of the mine. Upon seeing them the guards snapped to attention, and the General dismissed them. Nodding, they clearly had pregiven orders as they begun to move about. One took a bag or two from our men, another updated the General. The last two gathered and handed out cloaks, dried meat pieces and water canteens. A guard unfolded the cloak, wrapping it around Scarlet's shoulders. There was a single metal clasp at her left shoulder that held the fabric together. Scarlet stuck her hands out of the two small slits in the fabric and graciously took the canteen and meet. "You all will want to put your hoods on, it's quite cold and rainy out today." The head guard clasped his hands, putting on his own brown cloak. Turning to leave, and lead them, he pulled his hood over his head. Scarlet stuffed the dried meat into her mouth, forcefully chewing the stringy, tough and desperately under seasoned meat. Pulling the hood onto her head, she took a swing of water. In the hopes that the liquid would help the poor excuse for food down to her empty belly. If she never had to eat that again, she would not be upset by the fact at all.

The guard hadn't been lying to them. Though the entrance of the mine was at the base of a mountain, the wispy gray haze of fog hung in the air. The sky matched in color, and a faint mist fell from it.

Scarlet still blinked, her eyes adjusting. Gravel crunched under their feet as they walked up the path to yet another truck. Scarlet wondered to herself why the military seemed so set to only drive around trucks. Unlike the pervious trucks, this one had a metal frame over it's cab. A canvas had been stretched across it, and tied down. The flaps over the back of the truck had been pulled back to allow them access. Claudia and Klaus climbed in first, followed by Scarlet and Renee- who let out a string of curses from the pain put on her side. General Rey followed after her, clearly not impressed with her language. The King was the last one to climb in, and as he took a seat next to Scarlet the group was covered by darkness. The flaps had been closed, and tied. The group left to sit in the dark. Scarlet, for the first time, didn't mind the dark. Because as the truck hummed to life below them, she felt a hand tracing up her leg. As they begun to move, cool fingers found her own. Trying to hide it, Scarlet smiled and tightened her grip on the hand.

~~~

Though Scarlet stomped through the mud, the edge of her cloak still got dirty as they were lead through the camp. Unlike the base, the camp was literally a city of tents. Line in perfect formations, all the tents centered on a group of three tents that were larger than the rest. The group was led to the second largest of the round tents. Inside, surrounding a simple rectangle table was a group of high ranking
~~~

officers. The one in the center glanced up, and took a second look. Standing, the other men stopped their talking and glanced up. Upon seeing both the King and the General, they copied the center woman. "Your highness, General Rey." They all saluted him. General Rey nodded. "At ease men." They all went into a more relaxed, but just as stiff looking pose. "Your highness, may I introduce Lieutenant General Shannon Evans. To her right is Major General Aron Louise and Brigadier General Edwards Hop. Brigadier General Barrel and Major General Nimitz are each at their own camps with orders from General Evans." The King nodded, and General Rey went on. "To General Evans left is Colonel Green and Pritle." Upon hearing Klaus and Claudia's last name, Scarlet took a second look at Colonel Pritle. He indeed share similarities to the other two vampires, mostly in body and face shapes. His physical features differed from them. The King nodded once more. "It is good to see you all in fair health. Now General Evans, I must request that you, Rey and I have a private meeting at once." General Evans nodded her head. "Of course, men you're dismissed." The men around the table nodded and left the tent. The three then looked to the two humans and remaining vampires. "The guards outside will lead you all to your tents. Dinner will be soon." General Evans smiled. She wasn't a vampire, nor was she a werewolf yet there was something off about her. Scarlet couldn't name it in that moment. Claudia and Klaus left without a word or bow. Renee bowed her head, and Scarlet copied her. Exiting the tent, Scarlet joined the remaining members of the group.

Their tents were all next to each other, lined perfectly like the others. And like the others their fabric was the shade of a muddy brown, blending in with the ground. Though they were meant to sleep six men or woman at a time, Scarlets only held four. Claudia, Renee, herself and once she arrived, Theo. The King had a private tent and Klaus was sharing with a few high ranking males. The way the men greeted him told Scarlet that they all knew each other prior and were fine sharing such small quarters. Entering into their tent, their packs were already waiting for them. Each was placed at the end of a perfectly made sleeping mat. Looking at the padding on the ground, Scarlet grew home sick for her bed back in the King's home. With a sigh she removed her cloak, though her body ached for the warmth it brought. Scarlet was just about to lay down, when a distant, but great, roar filled the air. Hoping up, she struggled to get her coat and cloak back on. Running from her tent, her fingers fumbling with the metal anchor on the cloak as she did. Not realizing it at the time, but others joined her as she looked up into the far sky. There was no way for them to see what approached with the fog in the air. Scarlet wasn't scared though. A few soldiers around Scarlet wondered what it was, some voiced fear of an attack. All went silent as one scream, "I got 'em on the radio! Listen!" The crowd hushed, in an attempt to hear the crackling voice.

"Tent City this is T-Bird coming in from your south, requesting permission to land." Scarlet glanced towards the group of huddle soldiers. Their radio was clearly not for communications but hooked up with those along the camp. An efficient, and smart way to get news out to a makeshift base. "T-Bird this is Tent City, permission granted. Wind is low as is ground visibility. Please use the ground light indicators to land East of the base." Scarlet waited, her heart pounding to hear Theo's voice once more. "Roger that Tent City, warnings noted and are being taken into account. Landing time t-minus three." Scarlet jumped up from where she had hunched over the radio. As she did, Scarlet looked up just in time to see the faint outline of Theo's metal bird. Scarlet jumped up and down, running to Claudia who caught her from falling. She quickly apologized to the vampire, who only smiled. "It's fine, I'm excited to see her too. Let's go." Wrapping her arm around Scarlet's, Claudia then pulled her off towards what Scarlet assumed was the landing strip.

They reached the strip just as Theo was hopping from her Bird. "Theo!" Claudia screamed out, while Scarlet waved. Theo popped her goggles from her face, and met the two. "Guys!" They hugged. "Glad to see you make it over the mountains."

"Same to you, the mines weren't too rough were they?" Groups of soldiers begun to crowd along the outskirts of the landing strip. Most having never seen a Metal Bird in their lives. A few dared to step forward, but they were clearly there to help the werewolf. "The only thing rough about it was being stuck in the same cart as my brother and General Rey. We argued the whole way." Theo laughed, clasping them both on the back. "Well I'm going to unload the Bird and put it somewhere safe." They nodded, each understanding. "Oh Scarlet, before you go." Theo jogged over to them. She pulled an envelope from the inside of her vest. "Got this right before I left, it's from Pals." Scarlet took it, thanking her as she did. Licking her lips, she held the envelope close to her chest. Falling in step behind Claudia, she carefully opened it. There was a folded letter, and a picture.

Scarlet,

We couldn't have made it without you.

Thank you,

Pals, Rony, Ford, Eli, Shi and Lettie Loth.

Scarlet looked at the beaming group in the photo. The two parents looked exhausted but the new born pups in their arms rested peacefully. Flipping the photo over, Pals' graceful cursive covered it. In bed: Palsea. In arms, left to right: Ronford David the fourth, Elias Matthan and Shiloh Nahor Loth. Standing: Ronford (the third). In arms: Scarlet Elizabeth Grace Loth. Scarlet flipped the photo back over, leaning in to look at the pup in Rony's arms. She had an upsloping nose, and cheeks that were plump and full. Peeking out from under cap were dark, wispy curls. Scarlet couldn't believe it. Pals had named her daughter, her only daughter, after her. She had never felt more honored, or lucky in her life than she did walking through the cold and mud that day. Holding both items to her chest, she quickly returned them to the envelope and hid her hands back under her cloak.

She stopped, looking around. Scarlet realized, having been distracted by the letter; that she had lost Claudia. Now alone, and surrounded by endless tents, Scarlet had no idea where her own was. Finding the large center tents, Scarlet made her way back to them. As she came into the clearing, she nearly ran into General Evans. Though the General had been turned away, she was able to move out of the way in time. Scarlet begun to fall forward, but before she could release her powers out, hands caught her waist. "Careful." General Evans let her go, and Scarlet resisted the urge to rub her hips. The spots that the General had just been holding her were tingling in a way that Scarlet didn't like. Nodding a thanks, Scarlet looked away from the General's stare. To just even feel the General's dark orbs on her made Scarlet's skin crawl. "You seemed a bit preoccupied, have you lost your way through the camp?" Scarlet looked up, meeting the General's eyes. The world around her blurred out, as she felt herself glued to the woman. Scarlet stared into the General's eyes; her pupils expanding until there was no white left. Unable to look away. Scarlet's mouth opened, as if she could actually say something.

She wanted to, the urge bubbled under her skin. "Scarlet!" The trance broke, Scarlet blinking her eyes hard. Looking up to the General, her eyes had returned back to normal. Both women turned to the jogging Claudia. "There you are! Thought I lost you." Claudia wrapped her arms around one of Scarlet's. "If you'll excuse us General, we've been invited to a camp fire side meal." The General's lips curled slightly. "Of course, enjoy yourselves. I will see you both later." Claudia pulled Scarlet off, not saying anything for a few moments. Once they were clear of the General's earshot, Claudia glanced to Scarlet. "You okay?" Scarlet nodded. "Okay, cause it's okay if you're not. Even I get risen skin around witches." Scarlet wanted to stop walking right then, but Claudia kept her moving. General Evans was a witch! No wonder she gave Scarlet such uneasy feelings. Glancing back, Scarlet bit her lip. The General had remained where they had left her, and her eyes were focused solely on Scarlet.

~~~

That night, after the wonderful meal and the chatting with the soldiers; Scarlet laid on her mat. Her side hurt her greatly, and she was still focused on the fact that General Evans was a witch. Scarlet had never met a witch before. They were a rare breed, almost fully died out. Like the elves of times before, the witches were hunted down. For either the manipulation of their powers or their deaths. Unlike the elves, who had been a peaceful race, and both vampires
~~~

and werewolves, who had the ability to easily overcome an opponent; witches were not scarred to fight but lacked the ability to overcome the greater beings. Their powers were great, but short lived.

Yet there was one in this camp. Sleeping just a bit over. Alive. Fighting for them.

Scarlet slowly sat up, looking to her companions. They were all peacefully sleeping, Theo snoring lightly. Licking her lips, she slid from her covers. Remaining on the ground, she crawled to the tent's closed flap. Opening the corner she peeked out, the fire they had once sat around was nothing but black soot now. There was barely any moon, and she saw no patrolling men. Leaving the tent, she stood as the flap gently closed. Her bare feet sunk slightly into the still damp ground, and she silently slipped into the tent next to her own. Though it was nearly impossible to see, her eyes made out the soul sleeping mat. And the one body on it. She went to it, slowly lowering herself next to the sleeping figure. As she rested her head, he stirred. "Scarlet?" The King's voice was heavy in sleep, rough. Scarlet had never heard it as such before. "What?" He sounded more awake now. Turning to her side, her heart threatened to jump through her skin. She scooted back, molding her body into his. The King said nothing, he did nothing. His body did not stiffen and he didn't push her away. Instead he wrapped an arm around her waist and dug his face into the top of her head. She could feel his deep intakes and it intoxicated her.

Though her heart still race and her body buzzed; she found herself relaxing. Enough so that she was finally able to find sleep.